RIDES THE LONE STAR

THE WESTERN ADVENTURES

TIMBER U.S. MARSHAL

ROBERT HANLON

**FOR MORE BOOKS BY
ROBERT HANLON
SEARCH AMAZON OR VISIT
www.roberthanlonauthor.com**

Copyright © 2025 by Robert Hanlon

Published by DS Productions

All rights reserved.

This book may not be duplicated in any way without the express written consent of the publisher, except in the form of brief excerpts or quotations for the purposes of review.

The information contained herein is for the personal use of the reader and may not be incorporated in any commercial programs or other books, databases, or any kind of software without written consent of the publisher or author. Making copies of this book or any portion of it, for any purpose is a violation of United States copyright laws.

This is a work of fiction. Names, characters, places, and incidents either are the product of the author's imagination or are used fictitiously. Any resemblance to actual persons, living or dead, events, or locales is entirely coincidental.

ISBN: 9798310891807

❦ Created with Vellum

VOLUME ONE

JUSTICE IN THE LONE STAR

1

Jake Timber rode along with no idea of where he was heading. He had just come out of a town where he had helped a young man secure the fortune left to him by a dying uncle. He had checked out the sheriff's office before leaving for wanted notices of any men in the area he could go looking for and he had two of them stuffed in a pocket. Both men were only wanted for minor crimes and although Timber would check them out he was really looking for bigger game.

Timber had been a sheriff and was now a U.S. Marshal. It wasn't something he had aspired to; it had been thrust upon him. There had been a time when he was happily married with a daughter but that had been taken away from him when they were both brutally murdered by a man Timber had stopped from raping a woman. The man had been so angry at being stopped which was something that never happened to him that he found Timber's family and killed them both in a horrible way. That had so inflamed Timber that he went out and found the man and subjected him to a really dreadful death as well.

The result of that was Timber going to jail. He spent time in there in the depths of despair, his whole world gone. It was only when the Territorial Governor, the Honorable Robert Pierce Fullerton came along and offered Timber his freedom in return for working as an independent law enforcement officer that he got out of there. He now worked as a man who is above the law and reports directly to the Governor. The Governor gave Timber the power to arrest, detain, or execute criminal individuals as he sees fit. This included any local law enforcement, or locally elected or appointed official who attempts, in any way, to interfere with his official duties. He was given the job as the Governor wanted the territory cleaned up before they applied to join the Union.

Since that day Timber had worked hard and had taken out a lot of outlaws, murderers and villains. Sometimes by getting them locked up but most often from the barrel of his gun. He wore two Colt .44 revolvers in his holster. He found he enjoyed the work given him. He had seen enough of bad men and he was as keen as the Governor to take out as many of them as possible. He wondered if he would meet any in the next town he arrived at?

He had been riding for three days heading east from the Davis Mountains in Texas. He found the weather here better for him as he wasn't used to being cold as he had been in the mountains at times. Here on the plain it was warm, very warm. There wasn't much around to provide any shade either. He was out in cattle country. As he rode along he saw herds of cows and cowboys tending them so it was no surprise that the next town he arrived at was a cattle town. He passed a sign for it telling him it was called Spring Point.

The town was bigger than a lot he had been to with a wide main street that had other streets leading off it. Timber rode down the street on his big bay horse called Scout. He'd had the horse since it was a foal and he had come to love it as the horse did him. He had taught it some tricks, tricks that could be useful and already had been instrumental in saving his life at least twice. He kept on going looking at the buildings.

They were packed in along the street all made of wood, mostly with fascias on declaring the wares they sold or what they were. He passed by two saloons before deciding to stop at one. He chose the one that looked a little better and bigger than the others figuring he could always check those out later. He looped scouts reins around the hitch rail outside and climbed up onto the sidewalk and then on to the door. There he stopped as was his custom to get his eyes adjusted to the gloom inside and to see who was in there before going in.

He had upset a lot of people in the past by killing their friends or family, only if they needed it but it still meant that now and then someone would come looking for him to get revenge. Timber scanned his eyes around the saloon room and seeing nothing there to threaten him he walked in.

His long black boots thudded out on the boards as he approached the bar. He waited while the bartender served a man before he turned to him.

"A beer, and what food you got?" Timber asked.

"Beer you can have now, food takes a while," the bartender answered opening a bottle for him, then he carried on, "We got beans, biscuits and potatoes."

"That's fine, give me all that," Timber paid the man then looked for a table. He found there were plenty available so he picked one with a view of the door and sat down to wait for the food. While he waited he pulled his pack of cards from a pocket and started to play solitaire.

The food arrived and he began to eat it leaving his cards spread out on the table. As he ate he began to listen to the conversations going on around him. There were two men at a table close to him and they were complaining about someone.

"Yeah he took all the best food there was and left me and the wife with virtually nothin',"

His friend had a moan too, "Like always, he just has to have everything going."

At a table to the other side of him there was a man sitting alone and he grumbled and groaned at the words the men were saying. Looking around Timber didn't see any smiling faces at all. He carried on and finished his food then went to get himself another beer. He needed one, as the food was very salty.

As the bartender poured his beer Timber asked, "What's with all the glum faces around here, they all look like they got hold of the wrong end of a skunk?"

"You wouldn't know I guess if you've just arrived in town but we got ourselves a heck of a problem here."

"Which is?"

"Which is mister you'd be better off not knowing and just ride straight out of here."

"That's not my way, so tell me, just what is your problem?" Timber's interest was piqued now.

The bartender looked around then spoke quietly, "We got us a land baron here who thinks he owns the whole damn place and all the people living in it and that ain't all. He owns cattle ranches and farms around here too and he keeps on grabbing land to add to it."

"Sounds like an interesting man, he got a name?"

"Sure he got a name, he goes by Ezekiel Ramsey."

"He about town?"

"How the heck should I know?" The bartender then carried on, "If he is I doubt he'll be alone. He usually has some of his boys with him."

This sounded like just the kind of man Timber should find out more about, "So where does he live?"

"He has more than one place," the bartender was going to say more but he got called away by a customer so Timber went back to his table intending to talk to him again later. He heard the two men talking again at the table close by and what they were a saying didn't sound good so Timber walked over to them.

"You fella's got a beef with Ramsey?"

The both shut up and stared up at him. They saw a big man with black hair under a wide brown hat. He had stubble and green eyes that burned into them. He was wearing deerskins, which looked oddly out of place in there.

"You work for him?" one of them asked.

"No but I'd like to know more about him."

They both turned away from him, as the man said, "Not from us you won't."

Timber shrugged and went back to his table. The man at the next table moaned and groaned again. Timber turned to him.

"You got something to say?"

"You wanna know about Ramsey?" the man was swarthy and in need of a bath. Timber could smell him from where he was.

"Sure, you gonna tell me?"

The man left his chair and sat opposite Timber at his table, "Depends mister on who you are?"

Timber showed him his Marshal's badge, "I'm passing through but maybe I'll stay if what I hear is interesting enough."

"Okay, well the names Duke Hamblin and I'll tell you what I know not that many folk around here will. What we have here Marshal is a power struggle between that dirty rotten polecat Ramsey and the law abiding citizens of Spring Point."

"How can that be, don't you have a town council or a sheriff?"

"Town council," Duke scoffed, "All friends of his and as for that sheriff?" Duke looked for a spittoon and spit at it, "He ain't worth the tin star pinned to his chest."

"That sounds bad."

"Sounds bad, it is bad and no one here to help us," Duke looked at Timber, "Say, you think that's interesting enough to stick around?"

"Could be, I need more information though before I do anything."

"You go looking for it Marshal its all there but as I say most folk won't talk for fear of reprisals, that Ramsey has some pretty mean men working for him and he's pretty mean himself."

"I'll take that into account thanks."

Duke got up, "Well I've said enough for now, I'll see you around," he then made an unsteady walk to the door.

Timber sat a while longer thinking and listening. He didn't get much more information so he went back to the bartender.

"He don't come in here often," he replied to Timber's question, try the Silver Dollar Saloon that's more to his liking, can't miss it, just around the first corner down the street."

Timber thanked him and walked out.

2

Timber walked around the town for a while and spoke to some people along the way. He asked them if they knew of Ezekiel Ramsey and all of them said they did but none of them would talk to him about the man or what was going on. They all hurried away from him just as fast as they could. Timber knew he had stumbled into something that he was just going have to straighten out if he could but he needed to know more first. He visited the Silver Dollar saloon without finding Ramsey or anyone who would talk about him. So far only Duke Hamblin had been man enough to talk to him, he needed to find the man again so he went back to the same saloon he had found Duke in, he wasn't there but he reckoned the bartender would know him.

"I'm looking for Duke Hamblin, you know where I might find him?"

"You stay here for a while he'll be back, he just can't keep away for long."

Timber thanked him and walked out to the sidewalk. Most of the day had gone and he could see that he was going have to stick around for a spell yet. Scout needed feed and water so Timber rode him down to the end of the street where he found a livery stable. He found the hostler in the entrance as he got there.

"You looking for board for the horse?" the hostler called to him.

"Yeah, could be a few nights too."

"Okay, well I got a spare stall right here," he said pointing to one.

"Thanks," Timber led Scout in and began to unsaddle him, "What we got a night here?"

"A dollar a night, and that includes feed."

Timber went to him and gave him a dollar, "We'll work it out day by day, I don't know how long I'll be here."

"That's fine, I got room. Just help yourself to feed and see me tomorrow if you wanna stay on."

Timber thanked the man as he moved off then he finished seeing to Scout's needs. Once that was done he walked out again looking for Duke.

He found him back in the same saloon again. He knew the man drank whiskey so he bought a bottle, got a beer for himself and walked over to where Duke was sitting alone at a table.

"You again," Duke said as Timber sat down, "You found out more about Ramsey yet?"

"Not a lot, that's why I'm here," Timber filled the man's glass then sat back, "So tell me all you know."

Duke drained the glass then refilled it himself, "Well now let me see, where to begin with that dirty rascal? I guess from when I first met him. I was new in town looking for work and I met him in a saloon around the corner. He was with a group of men that I found out later were his bodyguards. I never thought anyone would need them until I got to know Ramsey."

"There are men who do need them, cowards mostly," Timber interrupted.

"Yeah well you can count Ramsey in with them. Things started off pretty good with him. I had drifted in to town and needed work. He overheard me in the saloon asking the bartender if he knew of anyone needing a hand and he came over to me and offered me a job just like that."

Timber cocked his head at him, "Just like that?"

"Yeah, well almost like that. He asked me what I did, what was I good at. I told him I'd been working over at the Double D ranch over in the valley, a couple of days ride away as a linesman and discouraging anyone coming onto the Double D land. He seemed to think that was good enough to offer me a job, working with his men helping them complete his business deals. That was a laugh, business deals. What he wanted were more men to continue his tyranny of the town. He is into everything and he owns a lot of the town and places around here as well as two ranches, what he doesn't own he uses tactics like protection and gives loans at high rates of interest that go up so high that folk can't afford them so they then have to sell out to him. My job was to help enforce his tyranny. Well I got sick of it. I hung back as much as I could and I helped folks out where possible but he discovered what I was doing and he wasn't happy about it."

Timber could imagine that a man like that wouldn't be happy to have a paid hand going against him, "So what happened?" he asked.

He had me beaten up first by the men I was working with. They took what money I had and ridiculed me to everyone as being a no good loser. They threw me out with nothing after all the work I'd done for him, at first anyway. Then he got wind of where I was staying. It was with a widow just on the outskirts of town. She had put me up and I paid my way and did odd jobs about the place. Anyway he sent men around there and smashed the place up, hurt the lady as well. Just to show people not to go up against him is what he said. I hate him for that; there was no need to hurt her. I did what I could to do the place up then I kept away so they wouldn't go there again."

"Quite a story, so what do you do now?"

"Whatever I can, odd jobs here and there."

"And spend it all on whiskey."

"What else is there for me to do?"

"Well you can help me to put this situation right."

"What, you're going up against Ramsey and his men, you must be mad, he has at least twenty hard men working for him and no doubt he could bring more in from the ranches if he needed them."

"Then I won't be going up against him alone I'll have you for a start and maybe we can rustle up some other help in town?"

"A tall order Marshal, but for what its worth I'm with you, I guess whatever happens it will be better than getting drunk in here every night."

"Okay, it's getting late, tomorrow morning I'll meet you here and we'll see who we can get. I also want to see some of these men of Ramsey's."

"You'll have no bother recognizing any of them. They are about the only ones in town who wear guns."

"Okay, tomorrow morning then," Timber got up to say the meeting was over.

3

Timber wasn't worried about the amount of men Ramsey had, he knew it was usually just a case of taking out the main man and maybe one other then the rest would crumble up. He just had to discover who that man was. Maybe there would be more than one in separate groups, well bring it on he was ready for them whoever they were.

He walked on down the street looking for a hotel to spend the night at but before he went to book a room he went to see Scout and made sure he was okay and had all he needed. The horse was pleased to see him and whickered as Timber entered his stall. Timber stroked his muzzle and neck and talked softly to him before he gave him some more feed and water. Then he went off along the street. As he walked along he became aware of two men on the opposite sidewalk keeping pace with him, he glanced across quickly taking the two of them in then looking forward again - they were wearing guns.

Timber carried on walking. The hotel wasn't far off; it stood on the next street corner, big and brash with a fancy veranda around the first floor. He could hear the two men talking but he didn't catch what the words were until they suddenly left that sidewalk and came across the street to stop just a few yards in front of him.

"We've not seen you before, you new in town?" the biggest one of them asked.

Timber stopped and took a better look at them. They were both burly men obviously very confident and they both had their guns tied down to their legs.

The smaller man looked at him, "My, I guess you can't shoot too well to need two guns mister," he laughed at his friend who joined in with him.

"No Jasper, I'm guessing he can't, he can't afford any clothes either," his friend said enjoying the banter.

Timber looked at their smiling faces, "You boys want to die today or are you just joshing?"

Jasper lost his smile, "What do you say Earl, has this fella got some guts or is he just plain stupid?"

That got them both laughing again. Timber stood his ground his hands hear the butts of his guns.

"You know boys having two guns can be real handy as it means I don't have to aim twice with one gun." Timber's words and his expression stopped the laughter, "anytime you wanna try it," Timber said.

He saw in their eyes they were going to draw on him so he drew first and fast. He had his guns aimed at both of them before their guns had even cleared leather.

"I'd just leave those irons where they are boys. The fun is over for tonight, now get back to whatever hole you both crawled out of."

"You ain't seen the last of us," Jasper said as he moved off with Earl following him.

"Oh goody, more entertainment to come then," Timber called out after them, then he went on to the hotel.

He got a room there and had a bath before he turned in. He kept his guns close to him and as he always slept very lightly he was sure he would hear if anyone came looking for him. The two men he had met in the street may come looking but he considered that unlikely. Maybe he would meet them again tomorrow; if he did he wouldn't hold back on shooting them if they became hostile.

The next day dawned bright and hot as Timber stepped out from the hotel. He'd eaten in the restaurant so he was now all set up to start his day. The next thing he did was go to meet Duke who was exactly where he said he'd be.

"You ready for a busy day? Timber asked him.

Duke had been leaning against the livery stable wall, now he was pleased to see Timber.

"You bet, what do you wanna do first?"

"Introduce me to any townsfolk you know, I wanna hear their stories and find out more about what's happening here."

Duke nodded, "Okay, let's take a little walk," he moved off so Timber tagged along with him.

Within a short while Duke stopped a couple walking towards them, "Hi Tom, Nancy, I'd like to introduce you to a friend of mine, Jake Timber here, he's a U.S. Marshal."

"Of all the friends I thought you might have Duke, a U.S. Marshal sure ain't one of them, good to meet you," Tom said holding out his hand to Timber.

"You too, Duke's been telling me that you got some bother around here?"

"You mean from Ezekiel Ramsey?"

"That no good piece of work," Nancy said.

"Yeah, he is a real pain in the backside, he thinks he owns everything and everyone," Tom said.

"So you've had bother with him?" Timber asked.

"Not so much with him but some with his men. He sends them out to do his dirty work for him and they ain't friendly, that's for damn sure."

"We're only trying to live a peaceful life here Marshal," Nancy said, "Most folks in town and outside town are the same but most if not all of us have been subjected to Ramsey's tyranny at some time or other."

"He runs a tight ship Timber, he keeps everyone here under his rule. What he says goes. If anyone wants to build anything they have to go through him and he charges high prices for everything. He decides what prices saloons and other establishments should charge and he creams off some of the profits too." Tom told him.

"He sounds like he has it all under control."

"He sure does," Tom gave Timber a long look, "Say are you thinking of going up against him?"

"Could be, I'll need to see what criminal acts he is doing though, if any."

"If any!" Nancy spoke up again, "He makes our lives a misery around here. He just controls everything. I'm sure you'll find lots of criminal acts if you look deep enough."

"Well thanks for that ma'am I sure will take a look into his dealings but it's some proof I will need."

As they spoke other people walked up and joined them as they realized what the talk was about. Timber was pleased to see them and soon there was quite a group all of which had a complaint of some kind about Ramsey.

"He had a man flogged once just for trying to keep Ramsey's cattle of his land," one man said.

"I heard he has folk beaten if they don't go along with what he wants," said another.

Gradually Timber got the picture of Ezekiel Ramsey and he didn't like what he saw, he knew he was going to have to meet the man and probably soon.

The group of townsfolk hadn't gone unnoticed by Jasper and Earl. They were still in town working as spies to keep an eye on the comings and goings, reporting back to Ramsey every day.

"Something going on over there Earl, we'd better check it out," Jasper said watching the group of people standing around Timber.

Earl nodded hoping for some action. There hadn't been much to do for a couple of days now and he was getting bored. Together they crossed the street and came up behind Timber who still had men around him wanting to tell him the experiences they'd had with Ramsey. Timber was pleased to hear it all even though he was surprised at the change of heart, he didn't think anyone wanted to risk saying anything to him.

"I've been telling folk you're all right Timber and as a U.S. Marshal you've come to straighten Ramsey and his men out," Duke explained. Timber was about to answer him when he heard Jasper behind him.

"Well now lookee here, if it ain't the mountain man again."

Timber turned around to face the two men, "What makes you think I'm a mountain man?"

"Why those deerskins you're wearing of course."

"These deerskins serve me well enough. You got a need to be here?"

"Yeah, Mister Ramsey don't like groups of people meeting up like this, you'll all need to break up now."

Some of the people began to move until Timber waved an arm saying, "The only people moving away is going to be you two."

At the sound of his words the people stopped but edged away behind Timber leaving a gap between him and Ramsey's men. Jasper grinned at Earl but stayed where he was facing Timber.

"You were lucky on the draw last time my friend but you wont be so lucky this time."

The words were hardly out of Jasper's mouth before Timber drew both of his guns. He never let anyone draw first if he could help it. He guessed they would talk first then wait to draw after, well now he had them at a disadvantage. Jasper went for his gun fast and cleared leather just as Timber aimed at him. Seeing that Jasper wasn't going to stop Timber fired taking the gun from Jasper's hand and two of his fingers. He screamed like a baby and hopped around shaking his bleeding hand. Earl almost cleared his gun but let it slide back in again seeing he was facing Timber's gun for the second time.

"I done told you boys last night to behave yourselves, now maybe you'll listen this time. I want you two out of town because if I see either of you two again, it will go much worse for you."

Earl stepped back with Jasper shocked at what had happened. No one had ever stood up to them before.

"Just who are you mister?" Earl asked.

"Jake Timber, U.S. Marshal, now you two go back to your hole like I told you last time."

Once the two men had left heading for the doctor's place Timber got slaps on his back and words of praise for his action.

"That is just what we need around here Timber, a man to stand up to Ramsey's men, but be careful mind there's plenty of them," Tom said.

4

The people around Timber began to disperse, some of them were keen to get away from Ramsey's men while others stood watching them smiling at the way Timber had taken them down.

Timber watched the men walk off thinking he'd probably not seen the last of them, then he turned to the people still with him.

"If anyone here has more information for me especially of any wrong doing of Ramsey or his men than I'd be obliged if you would speak up," looking around he added, "We can go someplace quiet if you prefer."

A man did step forward and two women behind him, "Maybe if we could talk somewhere else?" one of the women said.

Timber guided them along to a cafe and found a table inside well away from the window. He ordered coffee for all of them then he sat down to listen.

The women were eager to talk first and the man let them carry on with one of them saying, "I'm Emily and this is my sister Dorothy, mister...?"

Timber pulled his Marshal badge to show them, "Jake Timber U.S. Marshal pleased to make your acquaintance."

"And us yours I'm sure," Emily said, "Now you say you want to hear about unlawful things Ramsey has done?"

"I sure do yeah."

"Okay well then, a couple of weeks back now we were working in our shop, we own a haberdashery place just down the street here when two men came in, not the two you just kindly shooed off for us. Anyway these men told us that Ramsey wanted to buy our business. We told them no of course. It does well for us and we have no intention of selling out to anyone."

"Do get to the point Emily," her sister said taking over, "the thing is Timber that one of them said we had to sell up to them or they would be repercussions."

"What kind of repercussions?" Timber asked.

"They didn't say and it didn't get to that because the man with him said we could pay them to protect the place for us."

"We asked who from?" Emily said.

Dorothy gave her a glare and carried on, "We have been paying protection money to them every week and it has about ruined us, the cost is so high."

"Okay so they are operating a protection racket, anything else?" Timber was pleased to get something more concrete to go on.

Emily looked at Dorothy who then spoke again, "We have a friend Timber, a good friend who visits us every week and he was telling us that he was robbed by Ramsey's men. Apparently they visited his place, which is just outside of town asking for water but when our friend gave them some they walked into his house and took what they wanted. When our friend challenged them they told him to let it go or it would be worse for him."

"I have a similar tale to tell," the man started, "I have a small holding a couple of miles north of here and I have visits too. In fact the last time Ramsey himself showed up with some of his men. He wanted to know just how well I was doing and I told him I was doing okay but only just. He didn't believe me and he came and looked around the cabin I have then the barn and my outbuildings. I tried to argue with him but his bullyboys kept on pushing me away. After a time he decided I was doing better than I said I was and he took with him all the good stuff I had. So I had nothing to sell and it was hard Timber, very hard to keep on going."

"So if these things are happening here where is your sheriff?"

"Huh, sheriff, he's well into their pockets, a puppet for Ramsey to order around, he's no use to us"

"Really? I guess I'll need to call on him, do you have a town council?"

"We do, well we used to have until Ramsey decided he was gonna run it."

"I think you ought to ask around a little more Marshal," Dorothy said, "I know land has been stolen from farms and small ranches in the area from talk around town and I wouldn't be surprised to discover there has been some worse things happen."

"Worse things?"

"Yes. Go visit Missus Haynes at her small ranch, its called Pine Hill, you can't miss it, it's a few miles due south of town. She lost her husband recently in suspicious circumstances."

"Okay, yeah, I'll do that. Thanks very much for talking to me. I guess I'd better run along and check all that out," he stood up as they all did. They said their farewells and left him there.

Timber walked out thinking Pine Hill might be a good place to go and visit next, so he walked on down the street to the livery stable.

Scout was pleased to see him and nuzzled at the hand he offered. He was all saddled up and ready to go before he saw the hostler who came walking up to him.

"Just the one night then?" he asked.

"For now but I might well be back," Timber was about to go when he turned and asked, "You ever had any trouble with a man called Ramsey?"

"Ezekiel Ramsey. Huh yeah. He lives out in his plush ranch while everyone else has to pay homage to him and live like paupers."

"What can you tell me about him?"

"Now why should I tell you?"

Timber showed his badge, "Because I might be the only man who can help you folks out, that's why."

The hostler nodded, "Okay, it's about time we had a law officer here. Ramsey keeps himself very much to himself. I never see him without he has some paid goons with him usually carrying guns. He's been here a few times. Never left any horses overnight. He takes a look over any stock I have here. Why he knocked me down real low on a filly he fancied."

"Thanks, I'll bear that in mind."

"You here to arrest him?"

"Now why should I do that?"

"Why? Because he's a lousy scoundrel who's just plucking at what he can get and he don't care how he does it or who he steps on."

"I might need more than that but I thank you anyway," Timber mounted up and rode out heading due south.

He got to the Pine Hill ranch easily enough and saw that it was only a small place but then everyone had to start out somewhere. He rode up to the main building, which was a log cabin and called out but there was no answer. He rode around and found a barn where he could hear some sounds coming from it. Leaving Scout outside he walked into the gloom of the building to where he saw a woman in dark trousers and a blouse cussing as she tried to settle a wheel on an old cart.

"You wanna hand with that?" Timber called to her.

The woman spun around her face all red, her long blond hair tousled, her blouse dirty and her hands covered in grease, "Who are you mister?" she called back.

"Jake Timber, I'm a Marshal and it seems to me you have a problem there."

"Yes. The damn wheel fell off this old thing, I've been trying to mend it."

Timber strode over to the cart and lifted the axle up then placed it on a wooden beam she had been trying to put it on then he fitted the wheel for her, talking all the time.

"As I say I'm a U.S. Marshal ma'am and I'm out here investigating Ezekiel Ramsey. I was wondering if you know of him at all?"

"Ramsey, yes I know of him, who hasn't around these parts? By the way the name's Lucy Haynes."

"I've heard some people have had problems with him."

"Oh yes I've heard."

Timber stopped to take a look at her, "But you haven't?"

Lucy wrapped her arms around her and looked away before looking back at him, "Problems, no not really no until now anyway. He's ridden through here. He came with his men when my husband was alive, they talked some and then he left. It was just a few days later my husband died."

Timber finished securing the wheel and accepted a pitcher of water and cloth to wash his hands with, "That's really too bad. How did he die if you don't mind my asking?"

"He was found out on the range just on the border of our land, he had a broken neck. He must have fallen from his horse."

Timber cocked his head, "Really?"

"How else could it have happened?"

Timber had an idea but he didn't say it, "How do you manage out here without him?"

"Its difficult. A neighbor stops by quite often to help but I've been under pressure to sell up and before you ask, yes by Ramsey."

"Has he been forceful?"

"In words yes. In fact he has given me just a month to sell out to him or..."

"Or what?"

"He didn't say. Didn't have to, he'll find a way to make it impossible here for me to stay here I know. That's why I'm repairing the cart to take my things away in. Thanks for helping me out with that."

"And where will you go?"

"I have family back east, I guess I'll go there."

"You may not have to."

Lucy looked hard at him.

"I have to see the man yet but I won't let things lie as they are you can be sure of that. I'll be back when It's all straightened out with him and let you know the situation."

Lucy smiled at him, "That sounds hard to do and I wish you luck with it. I'll be waiting on your next visit."

Timber smiled back at her as he went off for Scout.

5

Timber rode back to town with enough information to go and see the sheriff. According to what he had been told that would probably be a waste of time but time he had to spend anyway. He found the office fairly easily way down the main street. Looping Scout's reins around the hitch rail he went to the door.

He stopped as he got there as he could see through the window next to it and what he saw made him sigh and shake his head. Then he opened the door and walked in. He then stood in front of the desk and looked down at the man sitting on the other side.

Sheriff John Oakes looked up at Timber as though he was in a daze. Timber looked at the nearly empty whiskey bottle on the desk and at the man who was hardly awake. His eyes were bloodshot, his clothes dirty and disheveled and it looked like hadn't had a shave or a haircut in some time. Timber looked around the office to see it was untidy and dirty just like the sheriff.

"Who are you?" Oakes asked in a croaky voice.

Timber got to it and pulled his badge, which he held before the sheriff's eyes, "This tells you I'm a U.S. Marshal, the name's Timber."

Oakes pulled himself up and made to look as though he was sober which he definitely wasn't, "So what do you want?"

"I was going to ask for your help but I can see that ain't gonna happen."

Oakes shook his head to clear it, "Help with what?"

Timber pulled a chair up and sat down, "Help with getting this town rid of Ramsey."

"Ramsey, you must be joking, you'd need an army, he has one," he reached for the bottle to finish it but Timber grabbed his hand and relieved him of it.

"You've had enough of that. So tell me why aren't you out there straightening Ramsey out?"

"There's no chance of me doing that or you doing it, you'd do well just to leave town now while you can."

"I have to believe that you were a good sheriff once, so what happened?" Timber said ignoring his comment.

"What happened here was Ramsey. He's always had money and he got bigger and bigger and just took everything over. He threatened me, him and his bullyboys and yes okay, he pays me not to do anything against him or his men."

"Is this how you want it to be?"

"How else can it be?"

"You could fight him, get some townsmen to help you."

"Yeah sure, traders and farmers against hired guns, how long do you think we would last?"

"Just how many men are we talking about here?"

"He has around twenty at his main ranch, another ten at the smaller ranch and other men he can call on who work for him, far too many for us to fight."

"So why haven't you called on the army to help out?"

"Ramsey gets any whiff of that, and he would, then I'm dead."

"So what you gonna do, sit here and drink yourself to death?"

"Look Timber, I'm one man, you get an army together and maybe I'll join you, until then leave me alone."

Timber stood up, "Get yourself sober and cleaned up, I'll be back," he then walked out and closed the door.

6

As Timber got out on the sidewalk a familiar figure walked up to him.

"So you've called in on the sheriff then?" Duke asked with a grin.

Timber grinned back at him, "Yeah and as you say he's as much use as a two legged donkey."

"I did tell you, so what now?"

"I need to go and see Ramsey myself."

"Oh I wouldn't do that..." Duke started to say.

Timber held up a hand, "Yeah I know. I will but not until I have tried to get some of the townsmen here to back me up."

"Well that sounds more like it, and a whole lot safer, although I don't know what good they will be against Ramsey's men."

"It would be safer. They won't have to do anything much, just be there to show some numbers as a threat, so we just need some men to join us, any ideas?"

"I'm with you for one and not just to make up numbers. I have a Colt .44 and I know how to use it."

"Okay that's great, we need more though."

As they stood there a man walked up to them. Timber looked at him, "Hey Tom," he said as he recognized him.

"Timber. I overheard that you are looking for men to join up with you to tackle Ramsey?"

"That's right. So Duke here has been busy," Timber grinned at him.

Tom continued, "Well I'm volunteering. The wife ain't that happy but shucks we gotta stick together on this."

"Okay, you got a gun?"

"I got me a rifle. A Winchester. I shoot game a good deal and I'm a pretty good shot if I say so myself."

"Shooting game ain't the same as shooting men Tom," Timber watched Tom's face as he talked.

"I knows that but heck, these men are just varmints aren't they that need putting down?"

"Could be yeah. Get your rifle and be ready to come when I call."

Tom grinned back at him, "Sure thing, will do. You just holler when you need me," he backed away then strode off.

Timber cocked his head to one side at Duke.

"I reckon there's another man we can try," he walked off so Timber joined him.

They walked down to a store and went inside and up to the counter where a portly man stood behind it.

"Hi there Eunice, I have a Marshal with me here who is looking for men," Duke said.

"I kinda heard something of the kind, you still looking?"

"Yeah, I am," Timber replied.

"Well now so long as there's enough of us to go straighten Ramsey out I got a sawn off shotgun behind this counter. I can sure do a lot of harm with that."

"I'm sure you can, just make sure I'm behind it when you pull the trigger," Timber said, "You figure on joining me then?"

"Yeah, as I said. I don't want to be the only man though."

"You won't be. I'll be back. Make sure that shotgun is loaded."

"Oh it will be loaded all right and my pockets full of shells."

Timber nodded and walked out with Duke.

"There is another man we gotta go see," Duke said.

"Yeah, who?"

"You'll see," Duke ran a finger beside his nose and set off with Timber down the street. He stopped at a gunsmith's shop, "Now this man knows a thing or two about guns and shooting," he said before leading the way inside.

Inside they found a tall thin man busy arranging a rack of rifles, he turned as they walked in.

"Hi Duke, who's this you got with you?" he asked looking Timber up and down.

"I'm Jake Timber. I'm a U.S. Marshal and I'm looking for men that might help me bring down Ezekiel Ramsay's tyranny."

"Are you now? And you reckon on adding me to that list?"

"If you're up for it?"

"'Cause I'm up for it. Why the number of times his men come in here and just take what they want. I need to get some of it back and teach them a lesson."

"That sounds good. I hear you're pretty good with a gun."

"Pretty good. Why I won enough championships around here in marksmanship."

"You ever killed a man"

"No can't say I have but I have wounded a couple in my time who tried to rob me."

Timber nodded, "So you are prepared to help out."

"Yeah, just say where and when. I'm called Bernie."

"I'll do that and thanks."

Timber went with Duke to visit three other men who also agreed to join them and they had guns, which they said they knew how to use.

Coming away from the last one Timber said, "That means there are now seven of us, that should be enough."

"You sure, we could be meeting up with more than that," Duke sounded concerned.

"Maybe yeah."

"Then we should get more help."

"Naw I don't figure it that way."

"Oh, then..."

"We only need to take out one or two to stop any others."

"How do you figure that?"

"Every group has a leader and that leader will usually have a right hand man. Take those two out and the rest will crumble."

Duke shook his head, "If you say so, but I doubt it."

"Ah, you wait and see. Now here's what we do. When I say, you round up those townsmen and get them down to the livery stable and any more you can get, again just to look good when we ride out. We will then go over to Ramsey's smaller ranch and check it out."

"Shouldn't we go straight to Ramsey?"

"No, I need to test the water first, we take the smaller one and clear out the men there. Get Ramsey worried and stirred up, then we go to see him when I'm ready."

"Sounds dumb to me but if you say so."

"I do say so, you just have the men at the stable when I give you the word."

Duke agreed to do that and went off leaving Timber alone, but he wasn't quite alone. Over the street a man had been watching him carefully and he had followed him around. He had also been in to talk to the people Timber had visited. Now that Timber was alone he pulled himself away from the porch post he had been leaning on and he walked out into the street. As he saw Timber stop to look at him he called over.

"I hear your building an army Marshal Timber?"

Timber stopped and took a good look at the man. He saw he was of average size wearing trousers, black shirt, a leather waistcoat and a Stetson. At his waist was a tied down gun.

"I wouldn't call it an army," Timber called back. He walked off the sidewalk and took a few steps closer to the man where he stopped facing him.

"Neither would I. It won't take much for me to get them to leave you."

"Really? Now why would you wanna do that?"

"Because I work for Mister Ramsey and I'm sure he wouldn't be happy to learn of what you're doing."

"I don't give a rat tailed backside whether he's happy or not. In fact he should be worried."

"What because of one Marshal and a few amateur townsfolk? Ramsey has plenty of real hard men, all good with a gun."

"Well thanks for telling me that, and where are all these men?"

"They're around."

Timber nodded, "You one of them?"

"What do you think?"

"I think you're as stupid as you look. An amateur yourself approaching me like this."

The man bristled with hurt pride; no one ever spoke to him like that, "So you wanna make something of it?"

"Do you?" Timber answered as his hand gripped the butt of his right hand gun."

The man wasn't expecting Timber to draw so soon and so he was a split second behind Timber, which was all the time Timber needed. He drew fast took a quick aim and fired.

The man just wasn't fast enough. He had his gun clear of its holster and cocked, almost aimed too but almost didn't cut it. Timber's bullet took him in his heart dropping him like a sack of flour.

Timber kept his gun aimed at the man as he walked over to him and kicked his gun away then he turned him over to check he was dead, which he was.

The shot had alerted Duke and a group of townsmen to go and see what had happened. They were surprised to see the dead man, especially the gunsmith who had come out to take a look.

"That man came in my shop only a short time ago, he was asking about you Timber," Bernie told him.

"Well he can't ask any questions now or go telling stories to Ramsey. Get the undertaker will you."

Timber checked the man's pockets and took what there was apart from his gun. When the undertaker arrived Timber told him to keep the gun to pay for the funeral, which he was happy to do.

7

Timber was a little surprised when the sheriff never showed up although he must have heard the gunshot. It told him a little more of what the man was like. He was more interested in the comments and smiles from the townsfolk who appeared from nowhere to congratulate him for removing one of Ramsey's men. It also made them all warm to him a lot more. Some of them had harbored doubts about him, which had now all disappeared.

Timber talked a little with them trying to get more support for what he figured could possibly be an all out war. A lot were sympathetic but didn't consider themselves the kind of people to get involved in gunfights or any other kind of fights. Timber respected that but it was good to get to know more people and hear their views and experiences.

He moved off but didn't get very far before a woman walked right up to him. He had seen her approach from a little way off. She was the kind of woman any man would notice. She was tall, not as tall as him but taller than most of the women around town. She had long brown hair hanging down to her shoulders and she was wearing close fitting trousers and a white shirt. It was her face that Timber looked at most, as she got closer to him. It was long with smooth skin, a generous smile and bright green eyes, the same color and intensity as his own. She walked right up to him then stopped.

"Marshal Timber, right?" she asked.

"Yeah I'm Timber."

"Sarah Thompson," she held out a hand like a man would do so Timber took it in his big bony hand.

"What can I do for you ma'am?"

"It's Sarah. Maybe something but maybe I can do something for you."

Timber was getting intrigued, "Like what?"

"Like I've heard you are going up against Ramsey and need some help?"

Timber had to grin at her serious expression, "Gunmen maybe..."

"I can use a gun Marshal but maybe I can just help in other ways. Look can we talk somewhere less obvious?"

"Sure."

Sarah beckoned at him to follow her and walked off down the street a little way where she went into a small shop selling womens clothes.

"This is my place, we can talk here without anyone hearing us or seeing us together."

"Does that matter?"

"It could do yes, to me anyway. You've already found one man here who was trouble, there are others."

Sarah went to the counter and then behind it to a door which she opened and beckoned Timber through into a back room. Timber took great care in following her in case it was some kind of trap but he didn't see any threat. He walked into a small room arranged with a table and two chairs. There was a sofa, a fireplace and a couple of cupboards.

"I have a room upstairs too and there's a kitchen out back," Sarah said as she saw Timber looking around.

"Nice and cozy."

"It suits me very well. Won't you sit down?"

Timber sat at a chair beside the table and Sarah took the other chair.

"So what do you want to talk about?" Timber asked.

"Ezekiel Ramsey of course. I know a lot about him and I thought the information would be of use to you."

"I'm sure it will," Timber waited for her to carry on.

"I've lived here all my life Timber. My folks got ill and died a few years back and I've been running my shop on my own, which ain't been too bad but then a few months back two men came walking in telling me I had to pay them to protect me. I asked who from and it turned out to be from Ramsey's men. They made threats to my place and to me if I didn't pay up so I had to do that. It made it harder to make a living from the place."

"I can imagine. Do the same two men come to collect it?"

"Mostly yes. I think they must do the same thing to a lot of businesses in town. Anyway, about a month ago Ramsey himself came to town, which I know he does from time to time but on this occasion he came in my shop. I was surprised to see him. He said he had heard about me and had come to take a look at me himself."

Timber could see why men would notice her, she was a good-looking woman, and single, "So you can describe him to me?"

"Yes I can. He is a little shorter than you and quite broad, maybe he used to be fit and strong at one time but a lot of that has gone to fat now. He has white hair, lots of it. A rather distinguished face I suppose with a neat mustache. The thing is he asked me out."

Timber raised his eyebrows at her, "Did you go?"

"You know that first time I did. I wanted to know more about him. Find out what he was like and try to get him to call his men off only it didn't work out. He took me out to dinner here in town. He had men with him who sat close by in the restaurant where we ate but when he got me back here he sent them off. I could tell what he wanted but I wasn't having any of it so I sent him packing."

"I guess that didn't go down too well."

"No it didn't. He went off in a huff and he didn't call his men off either although he had said earlier that he would do."

Timber nodded, "So what did you find out about him?"

"That he is a conceited, arrogant bully who likes to get his own way and sulks when he can't get it. He talked all about himself and how he has two ranches, a big one and a smaller one but he's going to enlarge the small one by buying or taking the land he needs for it. He has money, lots of it and he has men to help him do those things."

"How many men do you reckon?"

"I can give you an idea but that's all. I did see some of them when he took me to his ranch."

"I thought you said you only saw him the once?"

"That's right I did. We rode out there first, so he could show off no doubt, then we came back to town later to eat, and so he could try it on with me when he brought me back here."

"So what's his place like?"

"Big, very big. I don't know how much land there is but the ranch house is a long single story brick and timber building. There are outhouses, barns, bunk houses, you name it, all big and all looking good.

"Did you get to go inside the ranch house?"

"Yes for a little while, again he wanted to show it off to me. He has a housekeeper who asked about how many for dinner. He got angry with her and said he was eating out. I guess if we'd have stayed that would have cramped his style somewhat."

"So what's it like inside. I might need to go in there so anything you can tell me would be useful?"

"There is an entrance hall behind the front doors which leads to a corridor. That goes right along the building with rooms leading off. The first one is a big sitting room, laid out with expensive furniture and decorated to a high standard. The corridor obviously goes along to other rooms but I didn't get to see any of them."

"Okay, that's something anyway. What about his men?"

"He always seems to have two with him, sometimes more. At the house there were men walking around the paddocks outside, most of them with guns or rifles. I counted six outside, plus the two he had with him who he told to wait outside when we went in. The two who come for my money are different so that makes ten at least and I suspect there are more of them as well."

"Okay thanks."

"You intending to go over there then?"

"At some time I will yeah."

"Alone?"

Timber shook his head "Hmm maybe, maybe not."

"Okay well I thought I'd tell you what I know," Sarah kept eye contact until Timber looked away. Then he got up, "I should be going."

"Where to?"

"Oh a saloon I guess for a spell while I think of my move," he walked off for the door and went out.

8

The saloon Timber chose was the same one he had used before, it was good enough for him. He walked to it, ordered a beer and sat at a table to think. There was a definite need for him to go over to visit Ramsey but he didn't want to show his hand too soon. He had already shot dead one of Ramsey's men and he expected some kind of reprisal for that, not that it worried him. He had a few men who would ride with him if he went out there but even that was a risk to them that Timber wasn't happy in doing. They would just be as a threat, nothing more.

He sat for a while in thought as the saloon began to fill up. He was so much in thought that for once he didn't notice a figure walk in the door and circle around to him. Then he looked up as someone got up to his table.

"Sarah, what are you doing here, how'd you know where I'd be?" Timber was surprised to see her.

"I thought I'd join you, this is only the second saloon I had to try. I remembered something else."

"That's good to hear, you want a drink?"

Sarah looked towards the bar and caught the bartender's eye. She put a finger up and he nodded back to her then she sat down opposite Timber.

Timber had to grin as he watched the bartender bring her a glass over with clear liquid in.

"Gin, that's what I always have," Sarah said taking the glass.

"So what have you remembered? Timber asked, re appraising his opinion of her.

"There is a man at Ramsey's ranch you ought to know about. I should have told you earlier but it just slipped my mind."

"Okay, who is he?"

"Jonas Summerfield. He's the foreman at the main ranch. Now he is a good guy strangely enough. He works hard to keep a lid on things and he does what he can to keep the peace."

"Now how the heck did you find that out?"

"I've not been especially straight with you Timber. I wanted to check you out first. I've been looking at Ramsey ever since he arrived in these parts. My husband was a lawman. Oh not a very good one I have to admit but he did his best. He got into an argument with Ramsey and he killed him."

"You witnessed that?"

Sarah paused, "I was on the scene just after. I saw Ramsey ride off. Arnold was still alive, he told me what had happened before he died in my arms."

"What did you do about that?"

"I went to the town council and asked for help but no one would do anything, they're all scared to death of Ramsey. They said there was no proof and it all fizzled out. I buried him and that was that. I've been keeping an eye on Ramsey ever since to find a way to get to him. The date I had with him was useful but I just couldn't risk another with him. He's shrewd and clever, he'd spot something was wrong very quickly. Besides I just couldn't stand the thought of him touching me."

"I can imagine."

"That's why when I heard about you and saw you shoot one of his men I just had to see you and talk to you."

"I'm very glad that you did."

"The sheriff in town now is a good man too but he has been taken over by Ramsey."

"I've already learned that."

Sarah looked away to a nearby table, "Those men there are on Ramsey's payroll, nasty sons of bitches all of them."

Timber slightly turned to get a glimpse of them and he saw three men sat huddled around a table talking.

Sarah held a finger to her lips and cocked her head towards them. Timber strained his ears to listen in to them.

The three men didn't realize they were being overheard as there was a fair amount of noise in the saloon and with people standing around talking and drinking they thought no one would be listening to them.

"So what did Ramsey say exactly?" one of the men asked.

"Jesse he done told me we got a lot of straightening out to do with the townsfolk here." This came from the biggest of the three men.

"In what way Nash?" asked the third man.

"Hank, he ain't bothered much way how we do it. We just gotta get rid of all the people here who oppose him and those who ain't about to sell out to him."

"That sounds like a lot of fun for us and a lot of bother for them."

"Yeah it sure does?"

"When do we start? Jesse asked.

"Just as soon as I get the word and we may bring in some help from the Spring Water ranch too."

As he finished speaking a group of men got close to them so they changed the subject. Sarah leaned over towards Timber.

"Did you get all of that?"

"Enough. You know where this Spring Water ranch is?"

"Yeah, it's Ramsey's smaller ranch, I could take you there."

"We'll see about that I might just be happy enough with directions."

"You staying here tonight?"

"I was figuring on going back to the hotel."

"You could use my sofa, its big and comfy," Sarah sat smiling watching Timber for his reply.

"That actually sounds good and I could keep an eye on you too, make sure you're safe. After all you have been seen with me in here by quite a few men now."

Sarah nodded, "Well that's right. So you'll come?"

"I don't see any reason not to."

They both got up and walked out the saloon then along the sidewalk towards her place. All the time Timber kept a sharp lookout for any threats from anyone they saw. They got to the shop uneventfully and went inside. Sarah locked the door and they went through to the back room.

"I'll get you some blankets," Sarah said as she went upstairs.

Timber followed her up wanting to see the layout of the place. She went to a cupboard in the bedroom and turned around to see Timber standing there. She kept on holding the blankets and gave him smile.

"You always walk uninvited into lady's bedrooms?"

"Not usually no, I just need to be sure."

"Sure of what, that I haven't got some of Ramsey's men up here?"

"That did come to mind but I can see it's unwarranted."

"You bet it is. Come on I'll help you get settled."

Sarah arranged blankets for Timber as he removed his hat and gun belt, which he put near the sofa.

"You're not a very trusting man are you Timber?"

"I got me caught out a couple of times before. It don't hurt to be prepared."

Sarah walked right up to him and laid her hands on his arms, "I bet you're always prepared for anything," she gave him a kiss on his cheek then backed off, "I'll see you in the morning."

Timber watched her leave; he shook his head and gave a sigh then turned in. Staying in town to straighten out Ramsey was going to be interesting.

9

Timber was awake very early the next day. He hadn't slept well as the nightmares had come back to haunt him about the murder of his wife and daughter. He got up off the sofa and folded the blankets then went into the kitchen to make some coffee. He was on his second cup when Sarah came downstairs.

"Did you sleep well?" she asked him.

Timber found it easier just to say yes then he went to pour her a coffee. Sarah sat on the sofa and accepted the cup he handed her. He had a cup for himself and Sarah patted the sofa inviting him to sit next to her. He wasn't sure about doing that but he did.

"I'll make us some breakfast soon. Oh you will stay for some won't you?" she asked turning to face him.

Timber wasn't one to turn down things offered to him especially if they were free, "Yeah sure, I'd be glad to."

"Fine, it's good to have someone in the place again, especially a man," Sarah said as she smiled at him.

Timber smiled back, "It was good to be here and know you are safe. I still wonder who may have seen us in the saloon last night."

"There were a few in there and it is a wonder that Ramsey's men didn't notice us, but then why should they? They can't all know you, not yet anyway."

Timber had to agree with that. It was good for him to sit with Sarah; it had been so long since he had sat with a woman to talk to. The fact that she was so good looking and that she seemed to like him only made that all the better. Sarah went and cooked them some breakfast, which went down very well for both of them as they sat at her table.

They chatted while they ate then after Sarah asked, "So what are your plans for today?"

"I figure one more visit to the sheriff, give him a chance to redeem himself. Then depending on that I need to find Duke and get the townsmen together."

"What, to take them all to Ramsey?"

"Not directly no. Oh I'll get around to visiting him but first I need some evidence of his crimes. This smaller ranch he has, now that might be a good place to start at and see what I can find there if anything. Having some townsfolk with me will be good as witnesses to what I do find. At this point I'm not looking at all out war."

"Glad to hear it, although I figure it may come to something like that to stop Ramsey."

"Maybe but that's my plan for today."

"Okay well let me know when you are leaving, "I'll ride along with you."

"That might not be a good idea if it turns into trouble."

"If it does or not I'm going with you," she paused for a moment, "Timber, I can handle a gun and aim straight just as good as any of the townsmen you are taking with you."

Timber was finding out something new about this girl all the time.

"You can tell me how you learned that later, right now I'd better get going."

Sarah went to the shop door with him and opened up, "Good luck with the sheriff, although I doubt you will get anywhere and don't forget to take me with you when you go."

Timber promised to do that even though he had doubts about taking her along then he walked off to the sheriff's office. When he walked in he found the man sitting behind his desk filling in some paperwork.

"So you do get some work done then?" Timber said to him.

As Oakes looked up at him Timber could tell the man wasn't entirely sober, "Sure I do, more than you think."

"I should hope so. You ought to know I had to shoot a man yesterday."

Oakes went back to his writing and answered with his head down, "I heard."

"Aren't you interested?"

"You're a Marshal ain't ya?" Oakes looked up at him, "then I guess you can do that."

Timber shook his head, "Just how much is Ramsey paying you to play possum like this?"

Oakes fumbled around then threw his pen down and scowled up at Timber, "You don't know what it's like, you don't have a goddamn idea. I was a good sheriff here in town until Ramsey started taking over. It was either go on his payroll and help him out or get killed and he would have killed my family as well."

"Then come and help me bring him down."

Oakes scoffed at him, "What you and a couple of tame townsmen? No sir, you ain't got a chance against Ramsey and his men."

Timber walked up to the desk and slammed his fist down on it, "I'll bring Ramsey down one way or another. If it comes to a war I can't handle I can bring the army in. Either way he is going to be straightened out. Now it would look a lot better for you if you were involved in that."

Oakes shook his head, "It's not just me Timber, it's my wife and kids. I just can't risk it."

"Okay, then here's what you do. You keep me informed of any information you get about Ramsey and his men, their movements, numbers anything you can find out then when it comes to it I'll stick up for you. Maybe you can even lend a hand at the end."

"Okay Timber, yeah sure I can do that."

Timber nodded and walked out.

He was surprised to find Sarah right outside, "I told you he wouldn't be of any use."

"You listened in?"

Sarah blushed, "Yeah, wouldn't you?"

"Come on we need to talk some more," Timber led her away down the street to the livery stable where there were quiet places to the side of the building among trees where they could talk in private. He got her up against the boards of an outhouse and stood in front of her.

"I get the impression you aren't being exactly honest with me."

Sarah sighed, "Oh Timber, this is just so important to me. That man Ramsey is responsible for my husband's death. He takes money from me as well as most folk in town. He imposes his will everywhere and then he wants to have me as well. I just have to help you get him."

Timber cocked his head at her and she carried on.

"Yes okay I'm not just a simple girl running a dress shop. My husband taught me how to shoot with a rifle and a handgun, and he taught me good. He taught me other things too. How to look after myself," Sarah stopped and took hold of Timbers arms, "Look I really do want to help and I am sure that I can if you'll let me."

"Okay, you got it." Sarah reached forward and planted a kiss on his cheek. The second time she had done that. Timber wasn't sure how to take it but she sure looked genuine to him.

"Thanks Timber. I'm guessing now you want to round up the men you need to take out with you."

"That's about it."

"Okay then I'll come and help you. You want Duke first yes?"

"I do and I know where to find him."

They walked off together side by side and the whole time Timber was aware of her beside him. They chatted as they walked as they got to know each other a little better. They found Duke in the saloon where he usually was. He was pleased to see Timber but surprised to see Sarah.

"Sarah, what you doing here?" he asked her.

Timber was surprised again, "You know each other?

"Yeah 'cause we do. Sarah here is a bit of a loose canon. She knows her way around and who's who and if there is any bother in town you'll find her not far away."

"Is that right?"

"Don't take any notice of Duke Timber he likes to josh around."

Duke turned to Timber, "Is this it then, is it time to go?"

"Yeah it is. Round up the men will you Duke and bring them all down to the livery."

"You got it, some action at last," he smiled and hurried off.

Timber turned and followed him out with Sarah right beside him.

10

At the livery stable Timber went in to get Scout saddled up. As he worked he asked Sarah if she had a horse.

"Of course I do. He's out back, I'll go get him."

Minutes later Timber led Scout out to find Sarah out there on her horse, a black gelding a little smaller than Scout.

"I'll need to call in the shop on our way out to get my gun," Sarah said.

Timber nodded looking up the street at the gaggle of men making their way down towards them. Some were on horses while others walked along with them. Those walking disappeared inside to get their horses.

Duke pulled up in front of Timber and Sarah, "They are all here Timber, just like they said."

Timber took a look at the men gathered around. He saw Bernie the gunsmith, Tom, Eunice and several other townsmen, some he'd seen before, some he hadn't.

"Duke, do you know where the Spring Water ranch is?"

Duke looked confused, "Yeah, but we're going to Ramsey's main ranch, the High Basin ain't we?"

Timber shook his head, "Not today. Today we're going to the

Spring Water ranch and see what we can find. Gently gently on this one Duke."

Duke shrugged, "Whatever you say. Okay let's go," he turned his horse and headed off up the street. Timber rode beside him with Sarah next to Timber. The rest of the men formed a group behind them. Several townsfolk stopped to watch them ride past and some of them waved their hats at them. Timber wondered if any of Ramsey's men were in town and it was those men he kept a lookout for. If any were in town they didn't show themselves and soon they were out in open country. Sarah kept close to Timber all the time, she wanted to talk which Timber was happy to do although his thoughts were on where they were going and what he may have to do when he got there.

They rode on in a group all of them excited and anxious at the same time as to how it would all pan out. Just over an hour later they arrived at a point where from a slight rise they could see the ranch laid out before them. Timber stopped them all to take a look before advancing. It all looked quiet enough. There were some men out in a corral who appeared to be breaking in horses but apart from that Timber couldn't see anyone else there so he rode on with the men around him.

As they got closer the men in the corral stopped work and looked at them then they came out of the corral and while two of them waited for Timber to arrive, two others ran off behind the ranch house to the side of the corral. Timber rode on up to the two men waiting for him and pulled up just a few yards from them. They were jittery and kept on looking behind them.

"How many more men are there here?" Timber called to them.

"Er none mister just us, what do you want?" one of them asked as they both cast a nervous look at the men with Timber.

"I want you two to drop your guns and go stand over by that there corral fence and I want the other two to do the same," Timber looked around at the men with him saying, "Keep them here," then he rode off behind the house. He got behind it to see the two men who had run off in a close talk with two others. He drew a gun and rode on towards them.

"You men there put your hands up and come where I can see you."

They spread out but they didn't raise their hands, instead they went for their guns. Timber shot the nearest one in his arm making him drop his gun. Another man decided to shoot it out and raised his gun but before he could take aim Timber shot him. That was enough for the other two and they dropped their guns and raised their hands.

"Okay now get back to the corral all three of you."

"I'm bleeding Mister. I need help," the man said as he held his arm.

"You'll get help at the corral, now move it."

They all walked back with Timber riding behind them.

"Some of you stay here and look after this man will you and make sure they all stay where they are," Timber said to his men, "Sarah you and Tom come with me and bring one of Ramsey's men with you. Bernie you take Eunice and check the out buildings."

"What are we looking for Timber? Bernie asked.

"Anything out of place, things that don't belong there. You'll see if there is anything," Timber turned and rode around to the front of the ranch house with Sarah and Tom. At the door he dismounted and stood to side of the door. He got hold of the man Tom had forced to walk there and pushed him towards the door.

"You're going in first," he said and swung him around by his arm so he had to run into the doorway. Two shots rang out and the man fell dead.

"That's one way to kill your own men, whoever you are come on out or I'll burn you out," Timber winked at Sarah who was right beside him and waited. He didn't have to wait long before a man threw his gun and walked out with his hands up.

"Don't shoot mister," he said.

"Who else is in there?"

"No one, there was just me."

"Come here."

Timber checked he had no other weapons then he said, "You're going back inside in front of me. Tom, Sarah wait outside until I holler then come in," Timber then took hold of the man and pushed him back to the doorway. Then making sure he was covering his front he pushed him inside. No shots came and Timber went further into the hallway keeping behind the man. He checked a couple of rooms before he called for Tom and Sarah to join them.

"Check each room out, look for any paperwork that might incriminate Ramsey or any other evidence of wrongdoing you can find. I'll check out the rest of the rooms." Timber shoved the man along and checked all of the rooms, only when he was happy that there was no one else there did he march him back out again and then got Bernie to take him to the others who had returned from the outhouses and told Timber there was nothing there. Then Timber went back in to find Tom and Sarah busy searching the rooms. There was one room in particular he wanted to search. He had thought of asking the man he had taken around but then what would he have told him? He walked on to the room then called for Sarah who hurried to him.

She walked into a room set up as an office. Here was a desk, cabinets and shelving. There was also a lot of paperwork there.

"Start going through this will you, I'll be back," Timber left her and went back to Tom.

"You found anything?" Timber asked him.

"Nothing of interest Timber no."

"Okay, leave it and come and help Sarah," he led him to the office.

"Well now, this is more like it," he said and began going through piles of paperwork.

Timber was keen to find something that would give him positive proof and it was Sarah who found something. She had been going through the drawers of the desk when she came across a book listing businesses in town and who was paying what in protection money. It was a clearly laid out. Once she was in the right place Timber helped her and they found more evidence in the way of forms, letters and accounts, which proved that criminal acts were being committed.

Timber looked through everything that was found then shook his head, "All of this good but it isn't going to help us."

Tom and Sarah stopped work and looked at him.

Timber looked back at them, "This proves criminal actions yes but it doesn't prove it was done by Ramsey."

"But these documents are specific Timber..." Tom began.

Sarah waved a hand, "No Tom, Timber's right they don't implicate Ramsey at all, he's been very clever."

"He's kept all the incriminating stuff right here in his second smaller ranch which is what I suspected he would do and that is why I came here first hoping to find something really solid against him."

"I see, and we don't have that," Tom said.

"Not yet no, unless there is something else," Timber said looking around.

"If there is I can't find it," Sarah said.

"Then there probably isn't any. Of course the fact the men here tried to kill me when we arrived will help our case but it's not definitive. They would say they thought they were being attacked which in a way is true."

"So what do we do?" Tom was confused.

"We take what we have back to town and continue to build our case and facts."

"Then what?"

"Then Tom, I go see Ramsey."

Tom grinned while Sarah frowned, "That would be dangerous and could be foolish," she said.

"Maybe both of those things but visit him I will," he kept on looking at Sarah.

She nodded, "Okay, then I'll go with you."

Timber turned aside to have a smile then he turned back, "Okay wrap up what we have, we're leaving."

11

Riding back to town it became obvious that the men he had taken with him were all very pleased no real conflict had happened, not for them anyway. Timber had been the only man to use his gun, which seemed fitting to them seeing as he was a Marshal. Some of them voiced fears that the men there may recognize them and that there could be repercussions but the others reassured them that as they had been wearing bandanas over their faces and of the places they'd been to that it was extremely unlikely. They all hoped that would be the case.

Timber was thankful that they had found something to take back with them although it wasn't what he had hoped for; still it was a lot of proof, which would be useful for him. Back in town the men dispersed back to their places of work or home. Timber was going to get a room at the hotel to go through all they had but again Sarah convinced him to stay with her. She argued that he would be safer there and he figured she would be safer if he stayed with her so after taking their horses back to the livery stable they walked back to her shop.

Once inside Timber laid the paperwork out on her table and sat down to examine it more closely.

"Take your time Timber, I'll get us some coffee," Sarah went off leaving him to it but she was soon back, almost before Timber had made a start. She sat down next to him to help out.

"Did you kill a man back there?" she asked while looking through a notebook.

"Only the one, oh and wounded another I guess," Timber didn't look up from his work.

"Won't that get Ramsey all angry and want revenge?"

"Could be yeah."

"You don't seem concerned."

"I'm not. This thing is gonna blow wide open one day and it may as well be sooner rather than later, " he stopped and looked at her, "when it does you are going somewhere safe until it's over."

"Are you going to make me," she grinned at him.

Timber grinned back, "Maybe yeah. You were seen as being a woman out there, those men won't forget that."

"But they don't know who I am."

"How much working out will that take?" Timber kept his gaze on her.

Sarah squirmed around a bit then played with the book she was holding, "I don't know. There are other women in town."

"Sure there are, but none that I've seen like you. This shop of yours, I've yet to see a customer. How can you leave it all day anyway?"

"Oh it works okay. I get by. One day won't make any difference."

"And if you do come to Ramsey with me?"

"Okay then two days. Look Timber it's my place, I can do what I like with it."

"Sure you can. Just be careful what you're doing."

After that the conversation turned to the information they had spread out on the table. They took a long time going through it and got it all organized. They realized there was more there than they had first thought and there were pieces of evidence that would lead straight back to Ramsey, which pleased Timber. Those items he put to one side.

"I'm getting hungry, what say we eat now?" Timber said.

"Well I can make us something I guess..." Sarah started.

"No we go out. There's a restaurant I saw just a little way from here we could go there."

"But I thought you wanted to keep me hidden?"

"That was before, now I say we go eat."

"Okay, give me a minute there's something I need then," Sarah went upstairs leaving Timber thinking.

When Sarah came down she looked just the same only now she had a long jacket on. Timber got up and they went out. The restaurant wasn't far away and they got there without seeing anyone that could have been a threat. Timber kept their time there light and friendly. They chatted in general before Timber asked her to tell him more about herself. She was reticent at first but then she began to talk.

"I was made an orphan at an early age. An aunt and uncle looked after me but as soon as I could I left and made my own way in life. I got a job working in a store, then different stores. I saved up and got my own shop. I met my husband who was a sheriff. He worked here for a spell but he got killed in what looked like an accident but I know Ramsey murdered him. My husband taught me well Timber and I will get my revenge on that man. That's really all you need to know."

They got to know each other a whole lot better over dinner then they walked back to the shop, as Sarah was insistent that he stayed there another night, which he was pleased to do. There was something about Sarah, something more he had to find out about her. The other thing was that he was getting to like her, more than he knew he should do and more than he really wanted to but being with her seemed right somehow so when she was about to leave him that night to go to her room he let her kiss him. It was when she was up against him that he noticed something hard and cold against him. She hadn't told him she had taken a gun out with her.

That night the nightmares came back to him of how his wife and daughter had been murdered and what he had done to their killer.

When he woke up from the dreams he then had thoughts about the other women in his life. His second wife who had left him and gone back to Chicago who hadn't been a true love, she had just been convenient. The child they had was better off not knowing him, for he had become a violent man. A man who no longer cared what reason a person might have for their behavior, just that they had crossed the line and now they were to be killed, no questions asked.

Then there was Miss Laura, the next woman in his life, a woman he had fallen in love with when she had nursed him back to health after a violent episode. She had been killed by her ex husband and then something had changed in Timber, he lost all mercy and tolerance. He became eager to fight. He became short-tempered and unfit company for man or beast. Maybe it was a death wish, because he felt he'd never find love a fourth time, and he felt life wasn't worth living if he had to live alone.

Now here was another woman showing an interest in him. A woman he was getting to like very much although there was something he couldn't quite put his finger on about her, he was just going to have to keep on digging until he found out what it was and for now he would stay with her and see what happened, although he didn't think it was right for a man like him to fall in love again.

The next day Timber said he had things to do and that he would go off and see to them and let Sarah run her shop. Sarah was obviously not keen on that idea and wanted to go with him but Timber insisted he needed to go alone. He went out leaving her there. Minutes later he was sending a telegram to the territory Governor informing him of the situation there with a couple of questions thrown in.

12

Ezekiel Ramsey sat back in his black leather chair behind the fancy wooden desk he'd had imported from the east. In front of him were two men from the Spring Water ranch. They weren't happy to be there and they had tossed a coin with the other men there to see who would go to give the bad news.

Ramsey took his time; he liked to see men squirm even over the smallest thing.

"Now let me get this straight, you're telling me that a group of men visited the Spring Water ranch, one of them a Marshal who shot Edward dead and wounded another and there was a woman with them as well."

"That about sums it up yeah," the bravest of them replied.

"Sums it up?" Ramsey said in a calm quiet voice. Then he suddenly thumped the desk hard and shouted out, "What the heck were you boys doing? You were there to prevent anything like that happening, what are you men or mice?"

"I'm sorry Mister Ramsey," the man answered, "It happened so quickly. They were around us before we had a chance to do anything."

"Why weren't there guards posted outside the ranch like I said there always should be?"

The man spread his arms, "It's been days, weeks, with no one coming anywhere near."

"And then men did and a woman. Who is she?"

The man shrugged and looked at his friend before turning back to Ramsey, "We don't know, she was just a woman."

"Just a woman. Blond or brunette, tall or short. Come on man you saw her."

"Heck, I only got a glimpse but yeah, she had long brown hair, she was slim but she had her face covered."

Ramsey nodded, "So this Marshal, what's he look like?"

"He's big, he wears deerskins and he has a wide brown hat, rides a bay."

"Okay. So tell me again what was taken?"

"A lot of paperwork from the office. I don't know exactly what, but I saw them leave with an armful.'

"And who took it?"

"As we were saying there was a U.S. Marshal there by the name of Timber. It was him that did the shooting and he carried the paperwork out, so he has it now whatever it is."

Ramsey shook his head, "Some guards you are, I should fire the lot of you."

The man shook his head and pursed his lips, "We did our best,"

"Your best! Why it ain't worth two bits. Get yourselves back over there and keep a proper look out this time like I told you."

The two men were happy to get out the house with nothing worse being said or done to them.

Once they were gone Ramsey turned to the man who came in after them, "Now Casey, I got a job for you."

Casey had been standing outside listening so he guessed what the job would be.

Ramsey carried on, "There is a Marshal in town, poking his damn nose into my business and I want him stopped. I also want whatever he has of mine, there's paperwork at least. Go and arrange it."

Casey didn't have to open his mouth he just walked out again. He didn't figure it a big enough job for him to do but he thought of a couple of men who would do it for him. He went off to find them which wasn't hard. They were both supporting the corral fence up laughing at the man inside trying to break in a horse.

"Eddie, Charlie, I got work for you," Casey said as he got closer to them.

The both turned around to face him.

"Anything interesting?" Eddie asked.

"Oh yeah, you're both gonna love this. I want you to go to town and find a U.S. Marshal by the name of Timber. He's a big guy, wears deerskins and a brown hat. He has some paperwork of Mister Ramsey that he wants back. Make him give it to you then make sure he won't be able to steal any more, any time."

"Yeah that does sound like fun, "Charlie said, "What about the sheriff if we get seen?"

"Never mind about him, if you're lucky he might even help you, now git."

Both men walked off for their horses smiling broadly. They hadn't had anything to do for days, now they could go and enjoy themselves in town for a while. Within a couple of hours they were there looking out for Timber. They had the description Casey had overheard being said but they still thought they were going to have to ask around to find him.

Timber came out the Telegraph office and stood taking a look up and down the street. He knew Ramsey's men visited mainly to get the protection money from the businesses but he didn't see anyone who looked like suitable candidates. He was pleased to be free of Sarah for a while and decided to take a walk to the saloon he had been visiting, maybe he would learn more about Ramsey in there.

Even at that time of day there were a few men in the place, most of which Timber had already talked to. The few that he hadn't weren't very productive, not that it mattered so Timber went to the bar and ordered a coffee.

The bartender gave him a look, "Coffee?"

"Yeah, you do know what it is?"

"Yeah, but we don't serve coffee. Beer, whiskey, gin yeah but not coffee."

"Well that's what I want," Timber stood staring at him.

The bartended mumbled under his breath and went off to get Timber a coffee. Once he had it Timber found his usual table was vacant so he sat and relaxed. It gave him some time to think. Sarah had come onto him pretty strong and he had to wonder if it was just his good looks that had caused that or something else? There was still something about her that he couldn't figure out, maybe he would find out before he left town. She was a pretty gal that was true and he was attracted to her but with his history of women he was going to play it cool.

He was determined to go and visit Ramsey sometime but again he didn't want to do that alone, he figured it would be better if he had some men with him to back him up if only from a distance. Besides if he did visit it would either be early morning or in the evening, for now he could relax.

Eddie and Charlie rode into town figuring it would be easy to find their man and even easier to dispose of him once he had been forced to hand over the stolen paperwork. They rode through stopping now and then to ask people if they knew of him and where to find him. No one wanted to talk to them especially those who knew about Timber. One man they asked denied knowledge of him and then hurried along trying to find him to warn him. He had seen Timber in a saloon earlier so that was where he went. He was pleased to see him at a table with a pack of cards laid out. As he walked over to him Timber looked up and waited for him.

"Timber, I had to come to warn you. Two of Ramsey's men are in town asking about you. I'm sure they mean trouble."

Timber grinned at him, "Thanks for the heads up. What do they look like?"

"Both are young, early twenties I'd say, both of them are wearing white shirts and dark trousers. There's a tall one and one a lot shorter."

It wasn't much to go on but Timber figured it would be enough, "Okay thanks, you get off now and if you see them again tell them where I am."

The man looked at Timber as though he'd lost his head but he just nodded and walked out again. Timber went back to his cards taking a frequent look at the door.

Eddie and Charlie got frustrated at asking around so they abandoned that and went from saloon to saloon looking and asking in each one. Timber saw the two of them enter and weighed them up as they went over to the bar. The bartender there didn't want to say anything but his eyes betrayed him. As he told them he didn't know Timber his eyes involuntarily flashed over to where Timber was sitting. They both noticed that and turned to take a look into the room. Timber sat waiting for them to make their minds up about going over to him then he solved their question for them.

He stood up saying, "You boys looking for me?"

They both looked at him while Eddie asked, "Your name Timber?"

"U.S. Marshal Timber yeah, what do you want?"

"Well now we want the papers you stole from Mister Ramsey, that's what," Eddie answered.

"You can want things but sometimes you don't get them," as Timber spoke he noticed the customers moving away leaving a good space around the three of them.

"We always get what we want Mister. Now you just come along with us so we can go get them then we'll be on our way," Eddie was playing it cool to get that part done first, recovering the paperwork was going to be the hard bit.

"The only place I'll go with you is down to the undertakers with your dead bodies. You'd do well to just leave right now."

Eddie turned to Charlie smiling, "Quite the joker ain't he?"

Timber was ready for his next move. As Eddie turned again reaching fast for his gun Charlie did the same but Timber was already ahead of them. In a blur he had both of his Colt .44 guns in his hands and they were spitting lead at the two men. Both of them went down without either of them firing a shot.

Timber then went over to them and searched them both. He took their guns and what they had in their pockets as men began to gather around.

"Someone fetch the undertaker will you, don't bother about telling the sheriff," Timber said. He checked their faces against the wanted notices he had but neither of them fitted them. He then walked out to check the street. Seeing no other threats he walked off back to Sarah's shop.

13

As Timber walked along be became conscious of a figure walking up behind him. He stopped in a shop doorway to try and see who it was in the reflection from the windows. The man kept on walking towards him and stopped when he got close.

"Marshal Timber?" he asked.

Timber turned to face him, "Who wants to know?"

"You won't know me. My name is Jonas Summerfield. I work as foreman for Mister Ramsey at the High Basin Ranch."

"So?"

"So I wanted to search you out to explain to you my situation, can we talk, somewhere private?"

"Sure we can," Timber led the way down a gap between two buildings to the rear of them where there was a stand of trees, "We won't be disturbed in here."

Jonas gratefully went in among the trees with Timber, "I have to be careful that none of Ramsey's men see me talking to you."

"So what do you want to talk about?"

"I want you to know my situation in all this Timber."

"In all what?'

"Why the situation Ramsey has put this town into, surely you know about it."

"Yeah I know about it. I was just testing you."

"I have worked at the High Basin ranch for a good few years Timber and all was well until Ramsey appeared on the scene and bought the previous owners out. Then things changed, a lot. Ramsey brought men in, gunmen some of them, some just strong-arm types. Then he began to take over everything everywhere buying up businesses and property he liked the look of. If the owners didn't want to sell he would arrange for some men to go and see them, then they did. The man is a tyrant and he needs stopping."

"You'd say he was a criminal?"

"You bet. I heard him arrange to have folk beaten up and killed on occasion."

"And you'd testify in court?"

"I reckon so, that is if his men are straightened out first."

"Now why would you do that?"

"I done told you. The man is a tyrant, he needs locking up."

"I can see that. What I can't figure out is why you want that to happen?"

"He's been bad to me Timber. Reduced my pay and he allows his gunmen do whatever they want to. They roam all over the place laying the law down when they have no rights to and pushing me around."

"So why not look for work elsewhere?"

"I got family close by here. The next ranch ain't for miles. I need to stay here."

"Okay, so are you saying you will help me bring him down."

"Yes I will."

"Then tell me now all you know about him and the layout of the ranch."

It was nearly an hour later before Jonas slipped back into town.

The death of Eddie and Charlie hadn't gone unnoticed. Ramsey's men going into town soon discovered what had happened and word then got back to Ramsey.

Ramsey was surprised to hear that the Marshal had shot both of his men so he called for Casey to go see him.

Casey walked in to Ramsay's office having heard the news, "You wanna see me boss?" he asked.

"Why did you send Eddie and Charlie for that Marshal fella?"

"They had nothing to do and they should have been able to take that one guy out easily."

"Yeah right, but they didn't did they. Now I'm two men down," Ramsey leaned forward, "Now I want you to arrange it so that I get back what he has stolen from me and then kill him, you got that?"

"Yes sir," Casey answered rather theatrically.

"Put better men on it this time and oversee it yourself," Ramsey said as Casey walked out.

Ramsey was angry and upset. He thought two of his men would have been enough for one Marshal as Casey had done. This Marshal must be of a strong breed. He had met men like him before so it was going to be interesting to see how this next attempt faired.

His thoughts then went back to when he had arrived at the ranch and before that. He had aways been a man to make things happen. He had been brought up by a very strict father to always get his way and to push forward all the time, which is what he had done all his life. It had got him where he was now, rich, a landowner with two ranches. He had men working for him to control things as well as the town he had taken over. He had done very well for himself. The one thing he had failed at was with women. There was a time when he thought he had mastered that too with a woman he had found in Dallas. She was a red haired beauty and she knew it. He found it easy to woo her and get to know her very well but then that was only after she had discovered just how wealthy he was. She became too demanding and a real pain to him so she had to go. He arranged for one of his men to take her to town one day and she never came back.

Here in town he had seen Sarah and felt an immediate attraction to her. He had wined and dined her but he got nowhere, she just wasn't interested in him. The only woman in his life was the woman who served as housekeeper for him. She was getting on in years but she did the job really well for him. He had tried to get close to other women at times but it was always the same, they only got friendly with him for his money. The reason was that he wasn't a nice person at all, not to anyone, even the women he fancied. So he lived alone with his own thoughts and with no one to influence him.

Casey left the ranch house wondering who to send next. He had things to do around the ranch and there were two businesses that needed his attention to go and straighten out. He figured that if he put enough men on the job it would get done and there were plenty of men around the ranch to send, so which ones was the only question. He walked over to the bunkhouse where he knew a few men would be. There he found just the men he wanted.

Jack Houston was a broad hulk of a man and because of his strength and bloody mindedness he took control of any situation he was put in. Most of the men just fell in with his views and ideas so he was a good candidate to lead a group of men to go and kill the Marshal. He was sitting outside a bunkhouse together with three other men who were often with him, which was just perfect for Casey.

Jack saw him coming up to them so he knew something was afoot, "You got something on your mind Casey?" he asked.

Casey stopped and took a look at the four men. There wasn't any four as bad as these anywhere. All of them had committed crimes of some kind or other including murder in Jack's case.

"Yeah I got a little job for you four to go do."

"What do you call little?"

"In town there is a Marshal by the name of Timber. This man has taken private paperwork from the Spring Water ranch and Ramsey wants it back then he wants Timber dead. Do you think you can manage that?"

"What's the bonus?"

"Aw you'll get a good one don't you worry."

"Okay, consider it done. Come on you let's go," Jack said the last words to the other three who dutifully got up to go with him. All three of them had done jobs with Jack before and they knew he did most of the work so they were glad to tag along for an easy bonus. Casey gave them the brief description he had of Timber.

The three men were Davy Douglas, a man nearly as big as Jack and just as heartless. Jim Booth was a thin man but with no empathy he played is part. Jerry Lane was younger than the others and not as big, his skills came in the form of being a fast gunslinger. Together they made a formidable foe that Casey was sure would get the job done. He left them to it and went about his own business.

14

Jack led the men to where there horses were and then asked around for anyone who had been down at the Spring Water ranch at the time Timber had taken the paperwork. He was lucky in that one of them was there. Jack questioned him on what Timber looked like hoping for more information than Casey had given him.

"He sat tall in the saddle. He's a big man; he wears deerskins and a wide brown hat. He rides a big bay, that's about all I can tell you," the man said.

Jack had to accept that and reckoned that would be enough and he could always ask in town about the man. Plus having the sheriff in their pocket they could ask him about Timber as well. Once mounted up they all set off for town.

They were all happy at the thought of having some fun and getting a bonus for it. All of them were very confident men having grown up the hard way and they all had lots of experience in bringing pain and suffering to others.

When they arrived in town Jack thought it would be an idea to drop in on the sheriff first and see what he knew about Timber. They pulled up outside his office and went in. Jack had been pretty sure that Oakes would be in there and he wasn't disappointed.

"Howdy Oakes," Jack said as he walked in to find the sheriff cleaning out a cell. He was looking the worse for wear in a vest and dirty trousers. There was an empty whiskey bottle on the cell floor and the bunk had a pile of untidy blankets on it, "I can see you're looking after yourself well," he said grinning at him.

Oakes wasn't happy to see him. Of all Ramsey's men he disliked Jack the most. He was an uncouth horrible man. He tried to make light of Jack's comment.

"Just keeping the place tidy," was all he could think of as a reply apart from asking what Jack wanted.

"Be an idea to make yourself tidy," Jack gave Oakes a look of disgust which made Oakes squirm.

Jack then carried on, "We've come for a Marshal who I'm told is here in town, a man called Timber. What can you tell me about him?" Jack perched himself on the edge of Oakes desk to await an answer while the other three moseyed around the office picking things up and looking around.

"Timber, yeah he's been here."

"I gather he's been causing trouble."

"He has killed three men here in town, all of Ramsey's yes," Oakes said it almost as a warning to Jack.

"I gather he has, so he considers himself a gunslinger then?"

"I doubt that he does, he just does his job I guess."

"Like you do," Jack cast an eye about the office.

Oakes leaned on the brush he had been using, "Like I used to until you boys arrived with Ramsey."

"Now don't you get yourself all worked up, you get paid well enough to do nothing. So where will I find this Marshal?"

"Hard to say, he ain't at the hotel anyway I checked on that. You could try some saloons. He killed a man in 'Grady's Palace', that might be a place to start looking."

"Sounds good to me. Okay we'll leave you to your work as I can see you're a busy man," Jack got off the desk laughing at him which the other men joined in with then they were gone much to Oakes relief.

Timber had watched the ranch foreman walk off wondering what help he might be then he had carried on back to Sarah's shop. He found her at the counter with a customer, the first he had seen there. He waited until the transaction was complete and the lady had left before he walked up to Sarah who looked at him.

"Did you get all your jobs done?" She asked expecting an answer.

"Yeah, thanks," is all Timber told her then he looked around the shop, "You doing well here?"

"Well enough," Sarah walked around the counter to get closer to him, "You want some coffee, I got me some heating up out back?"

"That would be welcome," Timber followed her into the sitting room and then through to the kitchen where Sarah poured two cups for them then they carried them back into the sitting room and sat together on the sofa.

"What if a customer comes in?" Timber asked.

"There's a bell on the door as you know, it'll ring to warn me, to warn us."

Timber got the message. Sarah was sitting close beside him and she had put her coffee down on a table next to the sofa. He caught the scent of her hair and sighed, she smelled just like... He pulled his mind away from the vision of his wife and took a big sip of his coffee. Sarah edged closer to him and laid a hand on his knee.

"Good to see you back, I wondered..."

"I had to come back, you have the paperwork here," Timber turned to her with a grin.

Sarah smiled back at him then leaned in closer to him as she answered, "Its all safe. I have it tucked away, you can have it when you want it."

"That's fine, I'll need it later."

"So when are you going to have it out with Ramsey?"

"That can wait until later too."

Sarah gazed up at him as he put his cup down.

It was an hour later when Timber got up off the sofa and the shop bell hadn't rang once. Sarah got up and adjusted her hair.

"So tell me Timber what are your plans now?"

Timber wasn't sure of her meaning but he answered, "I guess I need to find Duke again and plan out a visit to Ramsey."

Sarah slowly nodded her head, "I see, yeah well okay I guess. I'll come with you."

"What about the shop?"

"No one's been in the last hour so I guess I can spare another hour. I'll just be a minute," she went back upstairs leaving Timber alone. In a few minutes she was back wearing the long jacket again. She then locked the shop up when they left and started to walk up the street.

Jack knew where Grady's Palace was. The name didn't exactly fit the place as no one could actually describe it as a palace. He walked straight in with the three other men beside him and stopped to take a good look around. There was no one there who matched Timber's description.

There was one man there they would know if they had seen him. Duke was sitting way back in the saloon out of the way but he saw them come in. He turned his back on them to avoid being seen. He'd had trouble with Jack before and he sure didn't want any more today.

Jack called out if anyone there had seen Timber to which he got either no reply or negative replies.

Duke downed the rest of his whiskey then went to the far wall where there was a back door. He let himself out and went off looking for Timber.

He was surprised and pleased to see him walking up the street towards him with Sarah. He hurried on to get to them.

"Timber, Timber, wait up," he called as he got close.

Timber and Sarah stopped as he carried on towards them.

"Jack Houston and three other Ramsey men are in the saloon looking for you. They are bad men Timber you need to get away."

Timber raised his hands to calm Duke down, "Whoa there, steady on, which saloon?"

"Grady's. Timber those men mean business."

"Then I should go and do business with them."

"Really, you would be mad to do that."

"Maybe I am mad Duke, but I'm still going."

Duke shuffled around before saying, "Okay, I'll keep your back but that's all, I ain't going up against any of them."

"I wouldn't want it any other way," Timber started off and Sarah went with him until Duke spoke again.

"Hey wait a minute, you ain't going surely are you?" he said to Sarah.

She shook her head at him swirling her long hair around, "Sure, why not?"

"Why not? I done just told you why not."

Sarah looked up for a moment then back at Duke, "Four men right."

"Yeah, four bad men."

"That's only two each unless you join us then its less than that."

Timber was enjoying the conversation. He figured on taking on all four by himself so he was interested in Sarah's comments.

"As I said I'll stay and watch your backs but that's it," Duke scowled and lowered his head.

"Then its two each," Sarah said looking at Timber.

"The way I see it it's four men for me to tackle. No need for either of you to get involved, although I appreciate you keeping my back Duke."

"Now listen here Timber. I told you I can handle a gun and I ain't afraid to use it," Sarah pulled her coat open to reveal a Colt .44 in a holster tied down to her leg.

"Well now, you never fail to amaze me," Timber said then he got serious," Now just listen up. When we get in there It will be me going in front and it will be me tackling them. If you two want to stay behind me and help out then I can't stop you but keep out of my way when the action starts," he got no answers but he could see his words had struck home then he walked on towards the saloon.

15

Jack continued to ask the men in the saloon if they knew of Timber and if they had seen him. Getting no answers he went to the bartender and harassed him about Timber. The bartender tried to keep busy so he wouldn't have to answer him but eventually Jack cornered him.

"Yes okay he's been in here but he ain't here now," he said still trying to get away from him. Looking over Jack's shoulder he saw Timber enter and his eyes gave him away. Jack turned to take a look.

"Are you Marshal Timber?" Jack called across the room.

Timber stopped to get a good look at who had spoken as well as a look around the room to see who else was in there.

"I'm guessing you're Jack Houston."

"That's right I am," Jack said as he edged away from the bar.

"I hear you've been looking for me?"

"Yeah, and now we've found you."

"You sure have, so state your business."

"My business is to stop you poking your big fat nose into other people's business."

"So what if I continue to do just that, especially Ramsey's business?"

"Then we have to take action."

"Oh goodie, so I get more entertainment."

Jack had to laugh at Timber's directness. He glanced across to the three men he had with him, "Is this man for real, he can sure make jokes?"

Davy grinned back at him then looked across to Timber, "He won't be joshing with us soon."

"Are you fella's gonna keep on chatting 'cause I ain't got all day," Timber called to them.

Jim and Jerry were closer to Timber than Davy and Jack. They were both very confident, even more so now that they could see Timber. Sure he was a big man but that just meant he made a bigger target to shoot at. Standing there wearing deerskins and a big floppy hat he didn't look like any threat to them at all.

Timber had walked a good way into the saloon leaving space behind him for Duke to slide in to cover his back as he had said. Sarah also slid in to the other side of Timber and she carried on sliding further along the wall.

Jim moved in front of Jack with Jerry beside him, "We'll see to this man," he said.

As Timber heard the words he pulled both of his guns and as he saw Jim and Jerry pulling theirs he fired taking them both down at the same time.

The sound of the shots made the customers move away from them as fast as they could. Gun-smoke drifted up from Timber's guns as he looked for the other two men.

Jack and Davy quickly moved from where they were, reaching for their irons. Jack dived down at the end of the bar while Davy dashed across the room and then down behind a table he turned on its side.

Timber moved as well, down to the floor below the tables where he looked for either man. Davy took a shot at where he thought Timber to be. The bullet passed through the table just as Timber moved. Timber then fired a shot in the direction of Davy to keep his head down while he changed position.

Jack felt quite safe where he was so he also fired at where he thought Timber was then as Timber fired he changed his aim hoping to hit him. Timber moved fast around the room from table to table keeping low down all the time to where Davy was. He got close to him and then Davy moved trying to get to where he could hear Timber moving. Timber got sight of him from under the table where he was. He then fired at him hitting Davy in his right leg. Davy screamed in pain as the .44 slug took a big chunk of his leg away. He fired his gun involuntarily emptying the chambers and clicked the hammer on an empty one telling Timber he was out of bullets. Timber then made a dash over to where he was and crashed his gun down on Davy's head knocking him out and stopping his screams.

Jack heard the noises and fired a couple of shots towards Timber with no effect. Timber now knew he only had the one adversary to see to. Knowing where he was he began to circle around to get to where he would be able to shoot him. Jack realized what he was doing and kept looking for him.

Duke had stayed exactly where he was until he heard Davy's screams. Knowing there was only Jack left he felt more confident to go further into the room to help out if need be. He went past frightened men who were cowering where they could. There weren't many of them as those that could had already gone out.

Sarah had stayed where she was but now she edged away nearer the corner of the saloon where she could get a view of the back of the bar knowing that Jack was behind there. Taking a look she saw the bartender down there on his knees with his hands over his head. Behind him she could see a glimpse of Jack and then he was gone so she started back to see around the front of the bar.

Jack had been surprised at just how good Timber was and to have taken out the three men with him without a scratch was very good. Now he was on his own to find him and kill him and he knew he had to do it quickly before Timber was on him. He had a good idea where Timber was so he decided to run out and fire as soon as he saw him. He got up and dashed off across the saloon. Timber heard him coming as he was creeping around to get close to him. There was no time now for any of that. He stood up and saw Jack approaching. As

Jack saw Timber he let out a yell and brought his gun up to shoot him. Timber stood his ground then stepped to one side as he brought his gun to bear on Jack. They both fired at the same time.

Jack was sure he was going to kill Timber and fired as soon as his gun was aimed at him. With Timber stepping to one side at that moment the bullet whizzed past him. Timber aimed straight as he fired and caught Jack in his throat taking a part of his head away behind him. Timber then stood and looked around. All four men were down. Duke got up from where he was and Timber was relieved to see Sarah over at the wall by the door. He went over to Jack and as he often did he took his gun and searched his pockets. He found a few dollars which he took. As he did he heard a warning shout come from Sarah. As he turned to see what was happening Sarah fired her gun at Davy who had raised himself up and was aiming his gun at him. Davy fell with a bullet in his chest. Timber looked over to Sarah and saw the smoking gun in her hand. He nodded a thanks and then checked on Jerry and Jim taking what they had on them as well. Then he walked over to Sarah.

"Thanks you did well."

"Saved your life you mean," she said, her face somber and serious.

The men in the saloon gradually got up from where they had taken cover and a few came in from outside then one went off to get the undertaker. Timber took a good look at all of the faces and then compared them to some wanted notices he had in a pocket.

"Well what do you know," he said as Duke came up to him, "Two of these men are wanted."

Sarah took a look at the notices, "So they are."

"I reckon it's about time we paid a call on Ramsey. Duke can you round up the men again and be ready to move out tomorrow morning like last time only tomorrow we will be going to Ramsey's ranch."

"Sure thing Timber."

"Time to call on the sheriff again, I need me a couple of bounty tickets," Timber walked out and Sarah not wanting to be left behind hurried after him.

They got to the sheriff's office and went in. Oakes didn't look as bad this time and he greeted them as they entered.

"I heard shooting, I guess this is about that?"

"Sure is, I need bounty tickets on these two," Timber handed the wanted notices over, "I was attacked in Grady's Palace and there are now another four men of Ramsey's dead in there."

Oakes looked at the posters then back at Timber, "These are two of Ramsey's main men. Jack Houston and Davy Douglas."

Timber nodded, "Good, write the tickets out will you?"

Oakes sat at his desk then handed the filled out forms for Timber to present for the bounty money.

"I intend to go and see Ramsey tomorrow morning will you be coming along?" Timber asked.

"Who else is going?" Oakes answered after pausing a second.

"I am," Sarah said, "and Duke Hamblin and a few other honest men from town."

Oakes bowed his head in thought then looked up, "I'll come but I don't know how much help I'll be, it all depends..."

"On how successful we are. I know Oakes but I'd still like you along for the ride."

"Okay, I'll go with you."

"Good. First light tomorrow, meet us at the livery."

"Okay. Where will I find you if I need you tonight?"

"I'll be at Sarah's shop," Timber answered then walked out with Sarah right behind him.

16

Ezekiel Ramsey was listening to a man who had ridden hard from town to see him.

"This Marshal killed all four of them!" Ramsey was amazed.

"Yes sir, shot 'em all dead. He had help from a shop owner too Sarah Thompson."

Ramsey looked hard at the man, "You sure of that?"

"Yes sir, why it was her that finished Davy off."

Ramsey had some difficulty taking that in but he then let the man go and sighed. So it had come to this, she would have to go as well as that Marshal, he thought. Seeing as the men already sent to do the job hadn't managed it he called for Casey. When he arrived Ramsey slammed him for not sending men good enough to do the job. Then he calmed down.

"You are going out with me tonight and together we will finish this. Both the Marshal and the woman must die tonight."

Casey had known it would come to this when he had heard from the man from town what had happened. Well that was fair enough he would go and kill this pesky Marshal himself and show Ramsey how it's done.

"You get yourself back here at dusk ready to go," Ramsey said.

Casey grinned and touched his hat, "Okay sure, I'll be here, this time the man will die," Casey left. His mind full of how he was going show just how good he was to the boss.

He returned later to find Ramsey's horse outside the house and then Ramsey himself come out. He was dressed in a dark long jacket over black trousers with his hat pulled low.

"We take it easy into town Casey, I don't want folk to know we are there, not until this is over anyway," Ramsey told him as he mounted up.

As they rode along together Casey was interested to know how they would find Timber.

"He's with that bitch who turned me down, me Ezekiel Ramsey," he said turning to Casey to show his disgust, "So we're going to her place, a clothes shop she has. We'll find both of them there I'm sure."

Once they arrived in town Ramsey had them leave their horses at a hitching rail some way down the street then led the way on foot towards the shop. Ramsey wanted to creep up on Timber and he thought that was the best way to do it.

"How do you want to handle this?" Casey asked.

"I don't care, I just want both of them dead. Shoot the Marshal in the back if you can, that way there will be no danger to us, just get the job done."

Casey grinned at Ramsey showing his true colors.

Timber had gone back to Sarah's shop but they hadn't stopped there long before Timber had taken her out again to eat. They went back to the same restaurant they had used before and enjoyed a leisurely meal together. They spent time there talking and enjoying each others company until they decided it was time to leave. It was late when they came out and it was getting dark not that it mattered as they only had to walk along the sidewalk down the street a ways to get back to the shop.

Ramsey stopped walking and grabbed hold of Casey's arm, "Wait, look that's Sarah, that man with her must be the Marshal."

Casey stopped and looked ahead. It was difficult to make out exactly who they were in the dark under the porches along the sidewalk but Casey had to agree that the man matched what they knew about him and he knew that Ramsey would be able to recognize the woman.

Just to be sure he asked, "You are sure that's him?"

Ramsey wasn't sure, not completely although he couldn't think of who else it could be.

"We'll follow them a little further, be ready to shoot him anyway."

They carried on keeping a little distance but getting closer all the time.

Timber talked to Sarah as they walked along oblivious as to what was behind them. They got to the shop door and Sarah went forward to unlock it. As she did so she glanced up the street and noticed someone there. Her eyes opened wide as she struggled to speak. Timber saw her and wheeled around to see what she was looking at.

Ramsey had seen enough of Timber now to be sure enough that he was the Marshal. If he wasn't he didn't really care anyway as he was happy for Casey to shoot whoever it was and Sarah then take a look at him afterwards. Once they were close enough Ramsey slowed his steps to fall behind Casey as he told him to shoot them.

Casey drew his gun and brought it up to aim at Timber as he was very happy to shoot him in the back if he could but he didn't get a chance. Sarah had the door open and she dived inside pulling Timber with her just as Casey fired. His shot whistled past them as his targets disappeared into the shop.

Timber told Sarah to hide out of the way as he turned back to the door. Casey was wary now that he didn't have anyone to shoot at. He figured storming the door would be a foolish thing to do so he ran across the street to where he could see into the open doorway. He looked to see if Timber or Sarah was there but in the poor light he couldn't tell so he fired two shots into the doorway in the hope of catching either of them. Nothing came back at him, no shouts, nothing. He stood there wondering what to do. In the meantime Ramsey had crossed over to be close to him.

"Did you get them?" he asked expectantly.

Casey shook is head, "Damned if I know," he kept on looking at the shop with Ramsey. This wasn't working out the way Ramsey had thought it would. He was annoyed with Casey who he thought had been too slow in firing when Timber and Sarah were on the street. They were easy targets, now they were aware of Casey being there and they were in cover while Casey and him were out in the open. He also didn't like the fact that they were there after firing shots that would alert the townsfolk to come looking at what was happening.

"Get in there Casey and kill both of them."

Casey looked at him, "Maybe I didn't hit either of them, they could be waiting for me."

"Either way get your butt over there and check and fast."

Casey wasn't sure of doing that but he couldn't look to be a coward, even so he only walked a couple of yards away from Ramsey before he called out.

"Hey Marshal, come on out, we have a score to settle."

Sarah had dragged Timber right into the shop much against his wishes. He'd have preferred to stay there and have it out with the man trying to shoot him.

"That's Ramsey with Casey his main gunman Timber," she told him.

"Okay, it looks like they have come to me, save me going to them," Timber had a gun in his hand ready to fire.

Sarah gripped his arm, "Be careful Timber Casey is dangerous."

"So am I. Keep away from the door," Timber edged closer to the door but kept well to one side as Sarah moved off further back to her rooms behind the shop. Once Timber reached the door he peered around it and saw where Casey was across the street. He was now hunkered down behind a water trough.

"Who's with you?" Timber called to Casey.

"No one Timber, Ramsey has gone so it's just you and me."

Timber knew he wouldn't be able to hit Casey where he was and he also knew he had to work fast. Ramsey might have gone but he might not have. He took a chance and firing a couple of shots in Casey's direction he ran out and down the sidewalk to the end of the shop where he could take cover beside the building. He then looked over the street again. He saw Ramsey talking to Casey and he heard the words said.

"I'm going back Casey. I can't be seen here doing this, you finish it and then come back to the ranch."

Timber watched as Ramsey ran off back up the street. So now it was just Casey he had to straighten out.

Casey had seen Timber come out but he'd had to keep his head down from Timber's bullets. Now he had to move again to get an angle on him but then he had an idea. Instead of advancing he began to move off to bring Timber out to him.

Timber saw him move and when he felt it was safe enough he ran across the street to the opposite sidewalk. Then he advanced on Casey seeing the man was walking away from him. Casey got to the end of the building he was at and stopped to look back around the corner as he hid behind the building. Seeing Timber still coming on towards him he hurried on down the side of the building and he kept on running fast back around to where he came out opposite Sarah's shop again. Checking carefully he then ran over to the shop and glanced into it through the open door. It looked empty so he went inside. He thought it would be fun to shoot Sarah first which would bring Timber running back so he could shoot him as he approached the shop.

Going in the shop it was dark and he had difficulty seeing where he was going so he tripped over a low counter. He cussed himself for making a noise and then carried on to the door that led to the private rooms beyond.

When Timber had left Sarah had ran into her rooms and upstairs to where she kept her gun. She found it and not bothering with the holster she checked it over then began to go back down again but as she came out the bedroom she heard a noise from the shop and froze. Who was down there? She almost called out but then she stopped herself realizing that it might not be Timber but either Ramsey or even Casey. She stayed right where she was hardly daring to breath as she waited for another sound.

Casey got into the room behind the shop without any more

mishaps and strained his eyes to try and make out if the room was empty or not. Going in further he figured it was empty. He had his gun at the ready and he stepped around as quietly as he could. He carefully checked the kitchen before going back into the room. So where was Sarah? He wondered if she had slipped out of the shop or whether she was hiding somewhere. He also didn't know if she had a gun with her if she was still here so he had to exert all caution. He got to the stairs and looked up. There was a small amount of moonlight filtering down which he figured must be from a room with an open door. Very slowly he started up the stairs.

Sarah heard small sounds and she crept back into her bedroom figuring that would give her the best chance if it was someone coming to kill her. She then reasoned that it must be as Timber would have called to her by now if it was him. She got into the bedroom and across behind the bed to wait. As the seconds slipped by she got nervous and she felt her hand holding her gun getting wet with sweat.

Casey continued up the stairs until he got to the top. There was only one room here which he could see by the moonlight coming in through the window. He moved on to the door and very carefully and slowly he peered around. He grinned as he saw Sarah standing at the far wall behind the bed. He didn't see the gun she held by her side so he went in.

"Sarah it's been a while since I last saw you," he said.

"That's right. You were in the ranch when Ramsey took me there."

"And now I'm here."

Sarah was shaking; this was a situation she hadn't been in before. She gripped the gun tightly and then began to bring it up. Casey saw the motion and he didn't hesitate, he aimed at Sarah carefully in the dim light. The sound of the gunshot reverberated around the room as they both stood there. Then slowly Casey slid to the floor. As he did so Sarah saw Timber standing behind him holding a smoking gun.

She nearly collapsed with relief before running around into Timber's arms.

"Oh Timber, I just couldn't get the gun up fast enough."

"Good thing I got back then."

Sarah looked into his face, "What happened."

Casey was crafty and lured me out. I only realized what he was up to when I got around the building he had run to and I came straight back here."

"I'm so glad you did, thank you."

"You're welcome."

"Timber there is something you ought to know and I should have been able to take him myself."

"Oh, and what is that?"

"I'm not just a shopkeeper, I'm a deputy law agent."

17

Timber held Sarah back and stared at her, "Say that again?"

"I know I should have told you earlier but I had to wait until I really got to know you and then well it just didn't seem right to say it but now I have."

"What kind of law agent, to whom?"

"I am employed by the Territory Governor, a little like you. He employed me when I wrote to him about my husband when the town council wouldn't help me. He figured a woman like me would never be suspected of being such a thing so he employed me to keep my eyes and ears open and report back to him, which is what I do. I've been working under cover on Ramsey for a spell now, but I also know how to look after myself," she hurried on with before she blushed and looked down, "Except tonight I guess."

"Don't beat yourself up about it, it happens. I knew something was odd about you but I never figured on you saying that."

"Well now you know. Does it make any difference to us?"

Timber shook his head, "Not to me it doesn't."

"Good, I'm glad."

Timber looked down at where Casey was lying, "I'd better get him out of here before he begins to smell," he slung him over a shoulder and with some difficulty he got him downstairs where he deposited him to the side of the shop. Sarah followed him down opening doors for him.

"I'll get the undertaker for him in the morning," Timber said as he dropped him.

Sarah looked up the street, "I wonder where Ramsey is now?"

"If he has any sense he will have hightailed it back home and surrounded himself with his men."

Sarah shrugged and looked back at Timber, "I guess. You figure we are safe tonight then?"

"I guess so yeah, maybe we should go back inside."

Sarah smiled and led the way.

Timber woke up early the next morning and listened to Sarah's breathing as she lay beside him. He wondered if he should have stayed. He knew he would be leaving soon, there was no point in getting involved with a woman again, especially one in his line of business. He had to smile as he thought of the Territory Governor knowing they were both here going after Ramsey. He thought he'd be rather pleased at him having back up here in case it went wrong.

Sarah woke up then they both got up and got dressed. While Sarah made some breakfast for them Timber went off and brought the undertaker for Casey then he went back into the shop. Breakfast was ready so he sat down to eat with her.

After they had eaten Timber said, "There's only one thing left to do now I guess."

"Let me guess. Go and get Ramsey?"

"You got it. Not alone though. We take the men with us who will go as back up just to show we have some numbers not necessarily to do more than that. I'll get Duke to round them up."

"You do that and you know now why I must go with you."

"I do and you know why you must always be at least one step behind me."

Ramsey was seething with rage. He had run off out of the way leaving Casey to do his work. He had found a place to hide and wait. He got anxious as time went on. He heard a gunshot then he was amazed as he saw Timber carry Casey out with Sarah and dump his body in the street. If Casey couldn't kill Timber then there was no point in him trying to, he went back to his horse and headed back to his ranch.

All the way home he thought of how he was now going to end this. It had to be done, now more than ever. There had to be a way. As he rode he thought it through and by the time he got back to the ranch he had it all figured out. He stormed into the ranch house and got himself a large whiskey and sat in his favorite armchair, his mind still reeling over what had happened and what he was going to do. He was still there as the sun came up and as his housekeeper came into the room surprised to see him there he told her to go get his foreman.

When Jonas came in Ramsey ranted at him, "Where the heck have you been, I've been waiting on you?"

Jonas was surprised at the outburst, "I was over at the far corral, it takes time to get here," he answered.

Ramsey calmed down a little, "Okay, now who we got over at Broken Creek?"

Jonas thought for a moment, "Er well a whole bunch of boys, looking after the cattle there."

"Get more over there and get Wyatt and Arnold in here."

Jonas was confused, "But those two guys aren't any good with cattle."

"I'm aware of that just do it and I want to see them now. I'm going over to Broken Creek. I want you to stay here and keep things running smooth until I get back."

Jonas said that he would then backed out wondering why he wanted those two men. He never got on with them; they were useless with cattle and always very belligerent. He didn't like the fact that they always carried guns either whatever they were doing, still if Ramsey wanted them he would get them.

The two men walked into Ramsey's room a half hour later. Ramsey had calmed down some more helped by the breakfast the housekeeper had prepared for him.

"You want to see us Mister Ramsey?" Wyatt asked.

"Yeah, I have a little job for you two, nice and easy, so easy even you two can't mess it up."

Wyatt wasn't sure if that was an insult or a compliment, "Okay... what is it?"

"You two boys are going into town pronto and spread the word around town that I'm going over to Broken Creek and that I might be there for a while."

Both men stared back at Ramsey, "And what else?" Arnold asked.

"You just make damn sure that the Marshal Timber hears about it."

The two men grinned at each other, "That sounds real easy."

"As I said, so easy even you two can't fail, now get going. Once you are sure he knows about it get over to Broken Creek."

Later that morning found Wyatt and Arnold riding around the town telling the story Ramsey wanted everyone to know. They called in at every saloon to spread the word at each one and took the opportunity for a drink at Ramsey's expense.

Timber went up to the saloon where he knew he would find Duke. As Duke saw him enter he went over to him.

"Say Timber, two of Ramsey's men have been in here. They are talking about him going over to Broken Creek for a spell."

"Really. Now that's funny as I've come to ask you to get the men together, it's time to go see him."

"It will be harder now."

"How come?"

"Broken creek is where the most of Ramsey's men are usually at. There is a way station there where he keeps cattle and cabins for the men. There will be too many of them for us to get anywhere near him."

Timber took that in then said, round up the men as soon as you can anyway, we'll meet at the livery stable like usual."

Timber walked back to the shop to tell Sarah what he had heard.

"But Timber that does sound dangerous. Ramsey is on to you, he is getting prepared and he will have plenty of men there."

"Then we have to take care, either way I'm going."

Sarah took on a serious face, "Then I am too."

Wayne and Arnold had been everywhere they thought they needed to then they leaned against a building over the street from the last saloon they had been in. They had only been there for a few minutes when Arnold nudged Wyatt's arm, "Say that man sure looks like the description we have of the Marshal."

Wyatt looked across at Timber, "Yeah he sure does."

"You reckon he'll get the message?"

"Let's mosey over there and find out."

The two men walked over the street to the saloon and stopped beside the door. Arnold leaned in to take a look and saw Timber talking to Duke and from the way Duke's arms were flying around and the expressions on the men's faces he was sure the message had been delivered. He turned back to Wyatt.

"Time to go, he knows all right."

They went to their horses and rode off pleased to have completed what had turned out to be an easy job.

18

A little while later found Timber and Sarah at the livery stable with their horses saddled up and ready to move out. They only had to wait a few minutes longer for Duke and some of the men to arrive.

"So we can finally go and straighten out old Ramsey" Bernie said to Timber.

"He will be straightened out yeah but your role is in support not in any action, well hopefully not."

Duke had to break into the conversation, "Timber there will be a lot of men there how do you figure on doing this if these men aren't doing anything?"

"I'm not figuring on taking out all the men Duke. I take out the leader, arrest Ramsey and the rest will fall apart."

Duke wasn't convinced, "Doesn't sound like much of a plan to me."

"It's the only one I have and it's the one we are going to use. Who else is coming along?"

"There's just two more and here they come now," Duke pointed to two men riding down towards them.

Timber was pleased to count ten men with him now, more than enough for what he wanted them to do, or at least he hoped so.

Now they were all together Timber stood in front of them, "Okay now listen up. We are going off to Broken Creek because that is where Ramsey is. I hear he has a good amount of men with him but don't let that worry you none because all I want you boys to do is make a show of me having men behind me if I need you," Timber paused, "Of course it could come to some shooting so bear that in mind and if any of you don't think you're up to any of that then back out now. I will need to rely on the men I have with me."

There were a few words between them but no one dropped out so Timber carried on, "Once we get to Broken Creek we will stop and assess the situation before we move in," Timber then mounted up and with Duke as a guide they rode off.

As they rode up the street Timber was surprised to see sheriff Oakes riding towards them, what's more the man looked to be sober.

"I hear this is it Timber, you're going to have it out with Ramsey?"

"Yeah we are."

"Then I'm going with you, if nothing else it will make it more legal."

"Be good to have you along," Timber started the men off again with the sheriff and Duke on his right and Sarah on his left.

Ramsey walked out of his ranch house after Wyatt and Arnold had left and called one of his men to go get his horse. He checked his gun over while he waited then once his horse arrived he mounted up. He felt lost and alone without Casey and as he never went anywhere alone he rode around to the corrals where men were working. He took a look at who was there and called two of them over to him.

"You boys get your horses you're riding with me today."

This was unusual for the two of them so one man asked where to?

"Brady we're going over to Broken Creek, now come on I ain't got all day to hang around waiting on you."

The men hurried up so that within a few minutes Ramsey was riding off with some support in case he needed it. He figured he'd been quite clever with his choice of ranch hands. He knew some of them were outlaws working as a way to hide from the law for a spell. Others he chose were hard men that would be useful in keeping others in order and some of them were just gunmen he had hired anyway in case he lost some which he recently had. Together they rode at a lope for Broken Creek as Ramsey was keen to get there, to see who there was at the ranch and to prepare for Timber to arrive with whoever he brought with him.

When he arrived Ramsey quickly found who was in charge there. Usually he left such things to Jonas but now he was taking control. The leader there turned out to be a hulk of a man by the name of Brandon. He was a confident man who seemed to know everyone and everything when Ramsey questioned him.

"Yeah Mister Ramsey we have fifteen men here, some are just cowboys who keep the cattle where they should be but others as you know are here to keep people away and carry out the work we give them," he winked at Ramsey as if that was necessary. Ramsey knew all too well what the men were there for.

"Okay Brandon now we might have a little problem cropping up sometime soon. There has been some trouble in town and now a bunch of guys are coming out here to try and give us trouble. I want everyone here to be prepared for them coming."

"Sure thing, man we ain't had any entertainment here for quite a spell now."

"You should have some pretty soon. Now I want you to arrange the men so that when our visitors arrive they don't see the half of them but have them handy okay. Then the ones we have out in view have them doing some casual work or other but ready to tackle our visitors when we need them to."

"I'm going to enjoy doing that," Brandon gave a smile that showed a few gaps in his teeth and made Ramsey reel back from the smell.

"I'll be in the cabin and I want the two men I brought with me and Arnold and Wyatt to join me, now go and arrange all that. When you've done it come back to me."

Brandon went off very pleased to have work to do and the chance to show off his skills to his boss. Ramsey went in the cabin. It was a large building as it was going to be the ranch house for his third ranch when he got around setting it up. He was pleased to see it was a strong well-made cabin with windows on all four sides. It was set apart from anything else and so would be easy to defend. He took a good look around it before his men arrived. There was a stone fireplace at the far end and some furniture in there; a table with a bench on one side and three chairs on the other. A bed sat along one wall and there were cupboards against another. He greeted the men as they came in and got the four of them to take a window each to keep guard at then he sat on the bed to wait.

Timber rode on with Duke and told him to stop when they were just out of sight of Broken Creek. To achieve that Duke took them on a round about route to go up a rise that then gave them a view of the whole place from a good distance. From there they could see the layout of what was there. Timber could see a cabin set by itself and then one corral just in front of it and two more behind it, one of which held a bunch of horses. To the left of the cabin and a little way from it was a barn. What he was most interested in was the men there. He could see three working with cows in the front corral while at the back there were two more with the horses. Duke alerted his attention to where a herd of cattle was being tended by five more men some distance away.

"I make it ten men Timber," Duke said.

Timber looked across at him. They were sitting on their horses side by side just below the skyline with their men gathered around them.

"I don't know much about Ramsey but I reckon he'll have more than that someplace."

Duke nodded, "Could be, so what do you want us to do?"

"We need to draw the men out away from the place. That's something you can do."

"You got an idea how?"

"Oh yes, give me your shirt."

Duke looked at Timber surprised, "My shirt?"

"Yeah I'm gonna give you mine and we change hats then you take half of these men here and ride up towards the cabin. The men there should come out to greet you. Fire a couple of shots over their heads and then ride off across the bottom of this rise. They should hopefully come out and follow you. I noticed there is a hollow about half a mile from here, go there. I will send the other half of these men to the hollow. Then when Ramsey's men get there turn and hold them up with the help of these men and just hold them there. I figure you should go with the second half of the men sheriff, make that part legal while I work here."

"Okay, yeah I guess I oughta do that," Oakes replied happy to be away from where Ramsey was just in case.

Duke took it all in then he said, "Hold them for how long?"

"Until I come to you now give me your shirt."

19

Sarah was sitting on her horse close by and she turned around as Duke and Timber exchanged clothes. Duke's shirt was tight on Timber and some of the buttons didn't meet whereas Timber's deerskin shirt hung from Duke. Timber figured it wouldn't matter as Duke would be riding along and it was just his clothes and hat he wanted Ramsey's men to focus on. He just hoped they would take the bait.

Timber waved at five men to go with Duke leaving another five with him. Duke rode off anxious to make this subterfuge work, he was pleased to have men with him, this was dangerous.

As soon as Duke had left Timber told the other five where to go, then he said to Oakes, "When Duke arrives make sure you get around behind Ramsey's men and hold them up. Don't let any of them escape."

Oakes said he would make sure none of them would get away which Timber hoped he would be able to do as he rode off with the men. Now Timber had his part to play.

"It's just us two now Sarah, are you up for this?"

"You bet I am. A chance at last to go and get Ramsey. What are we waiting for?"

"Duke to do his part, then we go."

They both watched as Duke led the men down the rise in a cloud of dust. Then as the men approached the cabin they heard some gunshots, which were answered by men at the corral.

Ramsey heard shouts from his men that riders were approaching and then the shots before he could get outside to take a look. He was pleased to see the person he took as being Timber riding towards them with a bunch of men. That was perfect. He called over to where Brandon was at the corral.

"Go get them, kill all of them."

Brandon was on it. He shouted out for men he had hidden to get out after them. Before they could do that Duke turned the men for the hollow. Brandon saw it as an act of cowardice having seen his men so he sent ten of his men riding off after them, leaving just nine with him and Ramsey.

Duke was a little worried. He didn't know exactly what kind of men were chasing him but he knew what men he had with him and he doubted their ability to go up against them. The other men had just better be at the hollow when he got there and then together with them he hoped to be able to hold all of Ramsey's men up. He hoped the sheriff would be useful as well. He looked behind him a few times trying to count how many there were. He got it to ten, which meant he would have them outnumbered if only by two. Surprise was the key to doing this which he reckoned he had, time would tell if it would work.

The hollow came up and he rode into it fast. Looking around he saw a couple of the other men so he just hoped they were all there. Then he was in the hollow. He circled his horse around, as did the five men with him waiting for Ramsey's men to arrive. He didn't have to wait long as they came galloping in only to have to pull up quickly seeing the wall of men in front of them. The remaining five then came in behind them. As soon as Duke saw them he relaxed a little as he heard Oakes shout out to Ramsey's men.

"Hold up there and drop your guns we have you surrounded."

The men looked around them to see guns and rifles aimed at

them from all sides. They only thought for a minute before they could see they had no choice but to do as Oakes had said.

Timber watched just long enough to be sure that Ramsey's men had taken the bait before he nodded to Sarah and began to ride down to the buildings. He took a route that would bring them to the side of the barn so as not to be seen by whoever was still there. Sarah kept just a little way behind him as he had asked her to do. She wasn't at all sure that his plan was going to work but not having any better idea she was happy to go along with what Timber was doing.

Brandon was the only man now left outside. He felt very vulnerable and alone which was something new to him. He looked around as he assessed his situation then he looked back to the cabin. Ramsey was at the door and he shouted out to him.

"Go check if there is anyone else about."

Brandon shook his head; trust him to get the short straw. He wasn't that concerned as he had seen Timber and his men ride off being chased by his men so there really shouldn't be any chance of anyone being around. He waved a hand to acknowledge he had heard Ramsey then set off walking around checking up on everywhere. He scanned the land around at the same time just in case though.

The corral areas were all deserted so he walked around the buildings and poked his head in the bunkhouse just so he could tell Ramsey he had been thorough as he was sure there would be no one in there. That just left the barn to check out.

Timber signed to Sarah to dismount and leave their horses to the side of the barn furthest from the cabin then he led the way to the corner closest to the cabin to take a better look at it. He quickly moved back and signed to Sarah to back off as he saw Brandon walking towards them.

Brandon kept on walking. He figured he would take a look inside as he was pretty sure Ramsey would be watching him then go back to the safety of the cabin. He got to the barn door and opened it to take a quick look inside. As he suspected it was empty. He began to close the door then froze. What had he just heard? Some sounds had come to him, sounds of someone on the outside wall of the barn. What was he to do? He was now on his own and he cussed wishing he'd kept at least one man back with him but it was too late for that now, he would just have to go and investigate, but carefully.

Timber had whispered to Sarah as to what he wanted her to do and then he had gone back to the front corner to wait for Brandon. He hoped the man would come around to him so he could deal with him without anyone in the cabin seeing him.

Brandon decided to go through the barn and go out the door at the back to surprise whoever was there. He hoped it was one or more of his men come back for some reason. He hurried through the barn then silently opened the back door and stepped out with his gun in his hand.

There was no one there at the back so he crept along to the corner to where he'd heard the noise and looked around. Unfortunately for him his boot scraped on the ground so he alerted Sarah who was standing way back from Timber, now she was closer to the danger than she would have been if Timber had just let her be. She whirled around to see Brandon peering around the corner. Brandon was surprised to see her and reached out for her but Sarah was too quick for him and she stepped away out of his reach. She called out as she moved making Timber turn around. Brandon now had a bigger threat facing him. Timber was holding a gun and it was pointing straight at him. Brandon pulled back around the corner as Sarah drew her gun. She started back for the barn when Timber called for her to stop then in seconds he was there with her and he waved her back as he took a look. He saw Brandon going back into the barn.

"Go back to the front corner and watch for him coming out, I'm going in," Timber didn't wait to hear her reply but dashed to the door and with a look inside he jumped in and rolled to the ground and up again behind a hay bale. He then looked for Brandon.

Brandon had been shocked to see the man there. Who was he and he was with a woman of all people too? He had ran in and would have gone straight out the front doors but as he approached them he heard Timber come in and he knew he would be highlighted at the door making him a perfect target so he dropped down behind a pile of bales and looked for the man.

Timber gave him a chance by calling out, "I'm U.S. Marshal Jake Timber. Now you just throw your gun out and stand up with your hands held high, you don't need to die today."

Brandon could hardly believe his ears, "We saw you ride out," he called back.

"Naw, what you saw was a decoy, so what's it gonna be?"

Brandon didn't know what to do but his mind was made up for him when he heard a sound by the front doors and saw the shadow of someone there for a moment on the ground. That panicked him so he got up and ran back for Timber shooting as he went. He figured he would keep his head down and get to him in time to kill him.

Timber saw him coming. He rolled over away from the bale into an open area and as Brandon got closer showing himself against the bales and items in there Timber fired at him. Brandon was bowled over and he fell to the ground still shooting in a jumble of arms and legs then lay still.

It seemed very quiet in the barn as the shooting stopped. Timber looked at where Brandon was lying for a few seconds before he got up and advanced on him, keeping him covered all the time.

Sarah looked in the barn again and seeing Brandon she walked over, "He's all there is Timber, there aren't any more out there."

"Good, so it's just the men in the cabin we have to deal with now to get to Ramsey."

"Yeah," Sarah stood away from the dead man, "They will have heard the shooting let's hope those men gone after the decoy haven't heard it."

Timber nodded and went with Sarah to the front doors. He looked out to where he could see part of the cabin. As Sarah had said there was no one out there that he could see.

Ramsey had heard the shooting. He wasn't concerned too much as he figured it would be Brandon taking care of any more of Timber's men who had arrived so it came as a shock when Arnold said, "Hey I can see a man over by the barn and he has a woman with him."

Ramsey pulled him away from the window to take a look for himself, "Well I'll be a son of a gun. Arnold you and Wyatt go out there and get them."

Arnold looked at Wyatt then they both looked at Ramsey, "There could be more of them boss," Arnold argued.

Ramsey turned to them, "I doubt that very much. That Marshal won't have had time to get many men out here. I can see what he's done. All you have out there is the Marshal and a woman now get to it."

Figuring it was just the one man and a woman they got up and went to the door. Arnold opened it carefully and looked out before dashing out to the corral out front to hide down by the fence posts. Seeing that he made it there okay Wyatt then followed him.

Both men hunkered down with their eyes on where they had seen Timber and Sarah. The thing was there was no sign of them now.

"What do you say Arnold, do we rush 'em?" Wyatt asked.

"No way, that Marshal is one clever dude, we take this careful like," Arnold thought of what to do. The cabin was set in a clear area, which was great for defending the cabin but out here they had nowhere to go, "You need to cover me, I'm going for the side of the barn. Once there I'll cover you over to me."

Wyatt nodded; his mouth was too dry to talk. Arnold took off like a cat on a hot tin roof and hightailed it to the barn wall where he stopped pressed up against it breathing hard. He then looked at Wyatt and seeing there had been no threats he beckoned him across.

Timber had seen the cabin door open and the two men run out so he had pushed Sarah back around the barn and got himself to where he could just see around the building. He then watched as Arnold came dashing across weaving from side to side. He was so fast that Timber didn't get the chance to get a bead on him. He was ready for Wyatt however. As the man dashed across Timber took aimed and fired. Wyatt ran on a few steps after the slug hit him before he fell to the ground in a cloud of dust.

Arnold was shocked and he knew now that Timber was close, very close, just around the barn. He crept towards the corner ready to spring around it.

Sarah was frustrated; so far she hadn't done very much apart from get in Timber's way, now she was set to put the record straight. She walked down the barn wall and round the back to the far wall where she looked around very carefully. She could see Arnold and she watched as Timber shot Wyatt. As she looked back at Arnold she saw him heading for the corner. To stop him and to warn Timber she called out to him.

"Hold it right there," she said aiming her gun at him.

Arnold took a hurried look at her unsure of who to go for first. He didn't have time to decide as Timber came out from around the barn and seeing Arnold bring his gun around to him he shot him dead.

20

Sarah hurried up the barn wall to join Timber, "I would have shot him," she said defiantly.

"No need to worry about that now, your chance could still come, we still have to get Ramsey out of that cabin."

They both turned to where they could just see it from the barn corner. It was too far away for a handgun which was why there hadn't been any shots from it but Timber knew the men inside would have seen the death of the two men.

Ramsey had watched Arnold and Wyatt get themselves killed and now he was getting worried. He looked at the only two men he had left and wondered if they would be able to protect him until his men came back from going off after the decoy. He pulled his gun and checked it over for the third time wondering if it would come down to him having to kill Timber himself and maybe Sarah as well? Whatever, he was in a hard place now. He considered getting away on his horse back to High Basin where he still had men. Once away from here maybe he could bluff his way out of any trouble that came to him, after all what did the Marshal have on him anyway? The more he thought about that the more he realized that wouldn't wash, there was plenty of evidence of his crimes. He looked out the window for Timber but he had gone out of sight around the barn.

The one thing Ramsey couldn't do now was to stay where he was. He knew Timber was out there somewhere. Sure he had his men but they had all gone off after the men Timber sent as a decoy. He had no idea where they were now or what had happened to them. He hadn't heard any shots and the men hadn't come back and they should have done by now.

"What do you want to do Mister Ramsey?" Brady asked.

Ramsey wasn't sure. From being the biggest man around and having plenty of men to protect him he was suddenly down to just these two men in between him and Timber. He knew if Timber got to him it would either be one of them dying or him going to jail, maybe for a long time. He felt he had to get out of the cabin as he could easily be trapped here.

"Okay, here's what we do, we burst out of here, get to the horses and ride off to find the rest of my men."

The men weren't sure that was a good idea, "You sure of that, we are pretty safe in here,"

"Maybe we are Clint but I'm telling you we are going."

Clint looked at the other man, "We're gonna have to move fast Brady and cover each other."

Brady nodded, "Ready when you are."

Ramsey checked the window facing the barn one last time then he went to the door and opened it, "You two cover me first then each other," Ramsey ran out heading away from the barn to a corral where the horses were. Brady went next followed by Clint who tried to cover for each other although there was no sign of anyone to threaten them.

Timber had gone around the barn out of sight of the cabin with Sarah. He took her to the far corner where they could see the cabin clearly then stopped.

"My guess is the rest of the men in the cabin will come out and Ramsey with them, we have to be ready for them," he told her.

"There's a lot of open ground between us Timber."

Timber nodded, "Yeah there is. As soon as they show we follow them."

"You reckon they'll go for their horses? Ours are here we could mount up ready."

Timber thought of doing that but he considered it to be too risky for Scout. He wouldn't want to get him shot, "No we stay on foot, the horses are safe here."

There was no time to discuss it any more as Timber suddenly saw Ramsey running for the corral.

"Come on they're on the move," Timber ran out after Ramsey as he saw the other two come out. He kept the cabin in between him and them as he ran on. Sarah took off behind him drawing her gun.

Ramsey ran on with the two men close behind him. There had been no shouts, nothing to alert them so they felt they were going to make it to the horses okay. Timber came up fast behind the cabin not that far behind them. As often as he could in such circumstances he gave the men a chance to give up.

"Just stay where you are or I'll start shooting," he called out.

His voice alerted them and Clint turned to take a look with Brady while Ramsey carried on running. The two men panicked seeing Timber running towards them with Sarah some way behind. The both had their guns in their hands so now they stopped to take aim at Timber who dropped to the ground to make a small target. Sarah carried on at a tangent out of the line of fire.

Clint dropped to one knee and held his gun in both hands to steady it. The thing was it took too long as Timber already had him in his sights. Timber fired in a steady even pull of the trigger. The shot flew true and plucked Clint off his feet ploughing a hole in his chest.

Brady had turned as well but he panicked more and just started shooting at Timber without really taking aim. Timber aimed carefully to fire but didn't need to as he saw the man fall and the sound of a gunshot. Sarah came running up to him.

"Come on we can't let Ramsey get away," she said as she ran past him.

Timber got to his feet; shaking his head again at the surprises Sarah sprang on him.

Together they ran on to the corral where they saw Ramsey trying to mount his horse. Timber ran in front and fired a warning shot over Ramsey's head that served to spook the horse, which danced around preventing Ramsey from mounting it. Ramsey gave up and turned to face his adversaries who were now in the corral with him.

"So Timber we come face to face at last."

"In not so good circumstances."

"Indeed not. I guess you have evidence from Spring Water ranch?"

"Yeah we have. Time for us to go to town and straighten this all out."

Ramsey nodded and looked across at Sarah who was now close to Timber, "Its a pity we didn't get on Sarah, we could have been great together."

"I don't think so. Not after you murdered my husband."

Ramsey knew it was over so he carried on, "Yeah well the man wasn't going to be in my payroll, he just refused so he had to go."

Sarah nodded, rage seething up inside her, "Then you put that puppet in as sheriff."

"He was paid well enough."

Sarah couldn't take any more she raised her gun to kill him but then changed her mind; she wanted to beat him to death with her fists so she launched herself at him. Timber saw her start and shouted out to her to stop but she was too far gone and she carried on up to him. Ramsey saw her coming fast, so fast that he didn't have a chance to draw his gun before she was on him, her fists beating on his chest as she screamed at him for killing her husband. Ramsey shoved her away and slapped her to the ground as he fumbled for his gun.

Timber didn't see him try to draw until the last second as Sarah was in the way as he advanced to pull her off. As he saw Ramsey drawing his gun he drew his and without pausing he shot him. Ramsey fell but he still tried to shoot Sarah. He pulled the trigger but the shot just missed her, then he collapsed into the dirt.

Sarah got up crying with frustration and pain and walked closer to Ramsey. Timber took her in his arms, "Its over Sarah, he's dead."

Sarah sobbed in his arms while he held her then she pulled away and wiped the tears from her face, "Thanks Timber. I'm so glad you came to town."

A shout came from behind them so they turned to see Oakes riding in with the townsmen surrounding Ramsey's men all of whom were now unarmed having had their guns taken from them.

"Is that Ramsey I see on the ground there?" Oakes asked.

Timber shouted back that it was. He looked at Ramsey's men all surrounded by townsmen. Then he addressed them.

"Your boss is dead there's no wages for you now. Things are gonna change around here. I'm gonna check each one of you against wanted notices, any of you that aren't wanted can leave or get a job with Jonas, if he wants you. We all go back to town now and straighten this out."

Timber got a couple of men to help him get the dead men across their horses to take back with them then rode into town with them all while Sarah rode beside him.

In town Timber did check out the wanted notices Oakes had but found no one matched up. That wasn't to say there weren't any wanted men there but that was for another day. He sent them all off to either go elsewhere or go and see Jonas about keeping their jobs. He reckoned only a few would be going back to the ranch.

It soon became common knowledge about town as to what had happened and Timber found himself the hero of the day although he told them about the help Sarah and the sheriff had given him. He told them of Duke as well, who he couldn't have done it so well without. Duke found himself a popular man about town which suited him very well.

That night Grady's Palace saloon was packed out with everyone celebrating the demise of Ramsey's tyranny. Timber was given a lot of free drinks as was Sarah and Duke. There was a happy atmosphere in town that it hadn't had for a long time. It was very late that night when Timber and Sarah went back to her shop. They were also late up the next morning, late for Timber who was normally up before first light. Once they were ready they went together to see the sheriff who they found to be in a much better frame of mind. He was also in clean clothes although he did smell of liquor but then they all did.

"Hi there Timber, Sarah," Oakes said with a smile as they entered.

"Just checking everything is as it should be," Timber said, "But it looks like it is."

"You bet it is, now I got control of this town back everything will be as it should be. I'm riding out this morning to see Jonas, the opinion of everyone seems to be that he runs the ranches while all the formalities are straightened out about Ramsey."

"That sounds good, did he have any kin?" Timber asked.

"Doesn't seem so. If none come forward then the ranch will go to auction."

"I hope they will keep Jonas on, he's a good man."

"Oh I'm sure of that, there'd be a riot here if he didn't stay on as foreman. So what are your plans now?"

"First off I want to take another look through your wanted notices to see if there are any men of interest for me. After that I guess I'll be moseying along."

Sarah scowled at that but kept quiet, there would be time to talk later. Timber checked the posters and put two in a pocket then he said his farewell and walked out with Sarah.

"Are you really moving on Timber?" Sarah asked as she looped an arm through his while they walked out and along the sidewalk.

"I guess I will be yeah, I have work to do. Talking of which we need to make a call," Timber took her to the Telegraph office so they could both report in to the Governor. There were some interesting messages that passed between them. Timber then went back to the shop with Sarah. They stopped just inside and Sarah put her arms around Timber's neck.

"You know you could stay right here."

Timber sighed and allowed one kiss before he gently pulled away, "I'm sorry Sarah, but it's time for me to go. I'm really not the man for you."

"Are you sure about that?"

"I've been close to women before Sarah and it always turned out bad. You really will be better off without me. The right man will come along for you I'm sure."

Sarah stood back and wiped an eye, "Okay Timber but anytime you're passing by..."

"Oh I'll be sure to call in," Timber doffed his hat and walked out. Then he went to the livery stable where he began to saddle Scout up. The hostler came up to him and refused the coins Timber offered him.

"You did a fine job here Marshal we all appreciate it."

"All in the line of work," Timber said as he finished getting Scout ready to go."

"So where you off to now?"

"Wherever I'm needed I guess," Timber mounted up and rode off without a backward glance.

It was just an hour later when he pulled up at Pine Hill ranch. He hollered at the cabin but got no reply so he rode around and then saw Lucy out back feeding some hens. She looked up as he approached and waited for him.

"I just rode out Lucy to tell you Ramsey is dead so you have no need to leave now. What you have is yours."

Lucy stared for a moment then walked over to him, "Thanks Timber its good of you to come way out here to tell me that."

"Its a pleasure."

"Won't you stay a while, have a coffee with me?"

Timber thought about that then seeing her face he agreed. They talked about the ranch over coffee and Lucy was much happier now.

"Did Ramsey kill my husband Timber?" she asked quietly.

"I reckon so yeah, but he can't do you no harm now."

Timber stayed a while until Lucy smiled again and then he left, for where he had no idea.

THE END

VOLUME TWO

BLOODSHED IN THE LONE STAR

1

The town of Little Bend in Texas stood in a semi arid area of land nestling in the shadow of the Davis Mountains. Normally it was a peaceful friendly place but not today, today it was anything but. Jack Keller was in town with his men.

The peace was shattered as Jack rode into town. He had the nickname of Crazy Jack, which suited him well, his mind just didn't work in the way that most folks did.

Jack had always been a bit crazy even as a boy. He never had many friends because of the way he treated them and those that he had soon disappeared when they found out just how crazy he was. His parents despaired of him and his antics. His father was always on at him about the things he had done. He left home when he was sixteen years old and that was only because his father threw him out. He didn't care about anything or anyone only what he wanted to do or thought was fun at the time. He got involved with bad people and into committing crimes with them. As time went on he gradually got higher up the chain of command as he learnt how to fight and shoot and with his mentality he soon gained a reputation for doing bad and crazy things hence his nickname of Crazy Jack.

To make things worse the men with him were all nearly as crazy as he was which was hard to do, especially his right hand man, Douglas Hamilton.

Jack had led his men across the open plain in search of some excitement. They hadn't had any for a quite a while and Jack reckoned they deserved some. He came across the town of Little Bend quite by chance and rode hard into it surrounded by the twelve men he had with him. The first place he saw that looked to be of interest was a saloon, he yelled out to his men as he saw it and rode his horse straight in through the bat wing doors whooping and shouting as he did. He rode into the room with his horse crashing into tables and sending glasses flying all over the place together with men as they scattered out of his way. Other horses met them as the men closest to Jack also rode into the place. The saloon was in total uproar especially as some of the men fired their guns into the ceiling letting off their high spirits.

The bartender was outraged and upset at their actions so he reached under the bar for a shotgun, which he brought up to menace the men with. Jack saw him and gleefully shot him down before he could even take aim with it. That led to other men in the saloon getting shot as they either tried to get out of the way or drew their guns in defense.

Jack thought it to be great fun and carried on shooting as more of his men entered, some on horses some on foot as the room began to fill up. The screams of the dying men and the blood spattering all around spurred Jack and his men on to finish the job they had started. They found it to be great fun and they didn't stop shooting until every man in there was dead.

The shooting stopped leaving a cloud of gun smoke drifting over the saloon room. Jack got down from his horse and left him to wander around while he went behind the bar. Other men came to join him with one in particular.

Douglas Hamilton was a hulk of a man; he was bigger than any of them and almost as crazy as Jack although in a different way. He had no care for anyone and only responded to Jack who he had formed a friendship with.

"That was fun Jack, and free drinks as well," he said. His face had a broad smile on it which looked incongruous among the heavy stubble he had and the dead men in the room.

"Help yourself Doug, they won't be wanting it any more," Jack said as he lifted a whiskey bottle off the shelf behind the bar.

Soon Jack's band of outlaws were laughing, joking and drinking all they wanted and for more entertainment they smashed glasses and bottles against the walls and floor and shot holes in the pictures around the walls.

Out in the street the noise and shooting had alerted all the townsfolk who came out to see what was going on.

The general store owner was more worried than the rest of them knowing that his place was a prime target for men like these. He tried to gather support from those around him.

"Go get your guns folks we need to settle this and get the sheriff," Stan shouted at them.

"Yeah where is he anyway, he should be here?" the man from the small bank in town added, he was as concerned as the store man was.

Stan looked at him, "You know Frank, he's not the best sheriff we've ever had here."

Frank nodded trying to get the men organized, That's for sure but he should still be here."

Some men hurried off for their guns while others stood around not wanting to get that involved but happy for those that were to get on with it.

Sheriff Nathaniel Baxter had been busy, his desk was piled high with paperwork when he heard the commotion. It was rare that such a thing happened. The only other time he could remember was when a bunch of cowboys rode into town, got drunk and started larking around firing their guns into the air and at anything they took a fancy to. He imagined such a thing was happening again and knew he would have to go over there and calm things down, no doubt the noise would guide him to it.

He started off down the street to be met by a band of townsmen all brandishing some kind of weapon from handguns to rifles and shotguns. Nathanial held his hand up as they approached him.

"Whoa there boys, there can't be a need for all of you, I'll go and straighten out whoever's having fun."

"It ain't no fun sheriff," Frank said, "We got big trouble at Casey's Saloon."

"If we got cowboys shaking off their energy again I can handle it Frank no problem."

Frank stood in front of him, "Sheriff, these aren't just a bunch of cowboys letting of steam. These are hardened men and they are killing folk."

Nathanial stood shocked for a moment at the news, "Killing folk?"

"You bet," Stan was keen to get a word in, "From what a couple of men told us who got out of there they killed the bartender and what men were left in the saloon, 'cause I can't say how many as I ain't been to see but they told us it's hell in there."

Nathanial wasn't sure now what to do. He thought of himself as being a good lawman but months of nothing happening around town apart from his basic jobs that always meant paperwork meant he hadn't had to do anything, certainly not go in a saloon against a bunch of outlaw cutthroats."

"'How many men are in there Stan?"

"A lot, maybe nine or ten so I'm told and there are a couple of men standing outside as well."

Nathanial knew that whatever else he was going to have to go to the saloon and try to straighten out whoever was in there.

"Okay, I'm glad to see so many of you are with me so let's go," he said marching off up the street sounding a lot more confident than he felt.

As they approached the saloon the two men leaning against porch posts took an interest in them. They had been changing over from time to time so that all of the outlaws had a chance to go in the saloon and enjoy the whiskey, beer and other drinks in there. Now they lifted the rifles they were holding as a threat. The one nearest to the saloon doors leaned across and called a warning in to Jack.

Stan was out in front of the men being bold in front of his friends who were all behind him. Nathanial was having trouble keeping up with him. Stan called out as they got close to the saloon.

"You men had better just stop what you're doing, we got the sheriff here."

The outlaws outside the saloon were Gregg and Thomas who looked at each other and smiled, "Looks like the fun will never end here," Thomas said.

Gregg had to agree, he raised his rifle and without a care he shot Stan down. That caused a panic with all the townsmen who ran every which way looking for cover. Nathanial found himself suddenly on his own with Thomas aiming his rifle at him. He quickly chased after a couple of men out of the way and to stay with them and got down below the sidewalk boards opposite the saloon with them. Some of the townsmen decided they could take the two of them out and began to shoot at them. In their panic the first couple of shots missed which gave the outlaws time to take aim and kill two of the men. Thomas and Gregg had taken cover on the sidewalk behind a pile of barrels. At the sound of the shooting Jack and the men inside came to the doors and the saloon windows to look for targets to shoot at.

Jack was giggling with joy and spittle was dripping down his face as he drew his guns and fired at every man he could see. The street turned into a bloodbath with only one of the outlaws being hit as he came out the saloon doors and that was just a flesh wound. Clouds of gun smoke drifted across the street and Nathanial was forced to call the townsmen off and tell them to move away. As they did so and it became quieter he shouted over to the saloon where Jack was standing in the doorway.

"Who the heck are you?"

"Us boys? Why we're called The Crazy Jack's on account of me I guess."

"There's been enough killin' here, don't shoot any more."

"You keep these townsfolk well behaved and we won't have to," Jack shouted back.

"Okay you get your way this time but you need to get out of here and fast. Hold your fire, drink your fill and go."

Jack laughed at him, "Some sheriff you are. We are leaving soon anyway, you just keep people, away from here or more will get killed," still laughing he walked back into the saloon along with his men leaving Gregg and Thomas outside.

Nathanial took the chance to stand up in the open and call for the dead men to be collected and taken away. He daren't go in the saloon to collect any dead bodies from there; they will have to wait until later when the outlaws had left.

2

Jack walked over to the bar in the saloon laughing at the memory of seeing the townsmen all scrambling for cover before they shot some of them. Then to see the sheriff helpless to do anything was even funnier. He went behind the bar and grabbed another bottle of whiskey then turned around and leaned against the bar as he watched his men come back in and get themselves whatever they wanted.

"How long d'you figure on hanging around here Jack?" Doug asked.

"Aw we'll move on soon and take a look at what else this one horse flea bit town can offer us."

Doug was happy with that, "There could well be a lot of takings here for us."

"Could be," Jack thought for a moment then pulled himself away from the bar, "Okay come on let's go see what there is," he said leading the way out of the saloon.

Those that still had horses in the saloon mounted up in there and rode them out to join the others outside then Jack led the way around the town. They came to the general store and stopped to go inside. With the owner dead there was no one there to stop them from taking what they wanted. Several townsmen stopped to look at what they were doing but none of them dared do anything about it.

Frank was getting very upset and tried to persuade some of them to make another stand of it.

"We need to stop these men," he said to them.

"How are we gonna do that Frank, we already tried once and look where that got us?" one of them said.

As they talked the sheriff walked up to them, "A bad business this," he said.

"You should be arresting those men," Frank told him.

Nathanial gave him a look, "And get myself killed? I don't get paid enough to take chances like that."

They all watched as the outlaws came out the store and loaded up their saddlebags. Then they watched as they rode off further down the street. They were then more upset to see them stop at the bank. Nathanial stepped forward determined now to stop them as Frank urged him on.

"You can't just let them rob the bank man, do something."

Nathanial walked on with four brave townsmen with him leaving Frank behind watching them. They got up to a few yards from the bank when six outlaws came riding up to meet them and stopped them.

"Just where do you think you're going?" Thomas asked them.

"Just stand out of my way, or I'll arrest you," Nathanial said.

Thomas laughed at him as the others did. At the same time Jack and a few other men came out of the bank carrying two bags. Jack waved towards Nathanial as he fastened the bags to his horse.

"We've got all we want sheriff, you can have your town back now."

"You said it Jack," Doug called out taking a bag off him.

Thomas and the others backed off keeping their eyes on Nathanial and the men with him then they all mounted up and rode out of town whooping and yelling while firing their guns in the air.

Nathanial watched them go, he was thankful they had left but upset and angry that he hadn't been able to stop them. Frank came running up shouting his contempt for the sheriff as he carried on to the bank.

Nathanial turned to the men with him, "Thanks for backing me up, its a pity we couldn't have done more."

They all nodded their heads and moved off. Nathanial went back to the saloon to find people there carrying out the dead men while stepping over broken bottles and damaged furniture.

"This place is a mess," he said to the people there trying to clear up.

"We never had a situation like this before Nathanial," one of them said.

Nathanial shook his head and helped out for a while. Then he went out and visited the store. Stan's son had family members in their counting the cost while he was out taking his father's body to the undertaker who was overwhelmed by the sudden amount of business.

The day was spent counting the bodies and the cost of what had been taken and destroyed. Later that evening the sheriff and a good amount of townsfolk gathered in the cleared saloon to discuss the day.

"You reckon on them returning Nat?" a man asked him.

"I doubt that, what would they come back for?"

It was a good question as the outlaws had taken everything they could possibly need already.

"What about forming a posse and going after them?" another man called out.

"I can't see the good of that. They have twelve men that we know about and we tried to stop them here and look what happened. No, I guess we won't be doing that. Just be thankful they have gone."

The talk went on for some time before they all left and went back to their homes. Nathanial went back to his office and looked through the wanted notices he had, looking for any faces he could recognize.

3

Jake Timber had ridden west for two days on the trail of an outlaw he had a wanted notice for. As a U.S. Marshal he was authorized to take out any outlaw he could find as part of his paid job for the territory governor, the bounty money he got on their heads was all bonus money for him. He had tracked the man so far and figured he would catch up with him at the next town or so.

It was mid morning on a fine hot day that saw him ride into Little Bend. It wasn't that big a place but big enough to have a long street with wooden buildings to both sides and it looked like some buildings went off behind them too. As he rode along he noticed that people took a good look at him then moved out of his way. A couple of women stopped and pointed at him then hurried inside a shop. Timber wondered why they did that, hadn't they seen a man wearing deerskins before? He carried on looking for a sheriff's office so he could ask him about the man he was had been tracking.

He found the office easily enough so leaving Scout at the hitch rail he walked up onto the sidewalk to the office where he entered without knocking. Inside he found Nathanial looking through a pile of papers. Nathanial stopped and looked up. He studied Timber for a few moments until Timber spoke to him.

"Will no one in this town give me a welcome?"

Nathanial came to his senses, "Er yes, sure Mister. I'm sorry I thought..."

Timber cocked his head at him, "You thought what?"

"We've just had a lot of bother in town from a group of really bad outlaws and I thought you might be one of them."

"Sounds like we need to talk. I'm Jake Timber a U.S. Marshal," Timber showed him his badge and his letters of authorization.

Nathanial read them and relaxed. He gave his name then he looked back up at Timber, "Well now, a Marshal huh? We could have used you four days ago when they were here."

Nathanial walked around and sat on his chair behind the desk. Timber pulled a chair up to sit opposite him.

"Now, tell me just what happened here?" Timber asked.

Nathanial narrated the story of the outlaws coming to town then he said, "I heard the name Jack Keller being called out, Crazy Jack he's called. In fact the men he is with are called 'The Crazy Jack's'. They were pleased to tell me that.

"And you say there were twelve of them?"

"That's what we counted yes plus Jack. They left ten dead men behind them Marshal," Nathanial emphasized the word ten.

"That's pretty bad."

"Pretty bad? I'll say it's bad. The townsfolk here have it in for me for not stopping them."

"So why didn't you?"

Nathanial gave a scowl, "You ever been up against thirteen hardened criminals all looking to shoot you down."

"Not for quite a spell now."

"Are you joshing with me?" Nathanial pulled a face at Timber.

"No why should I? It sounds like a serious situation."

"The most serious I've ever seen in this here town. Several townsfolk joined in with me but they are all too scared to go out in a posse for them now," Nathanial stopped then asked, "Have you come to straighten those men out?"

"I came looking for an outlaw but I guess I could help you out, seeing as I'm here."

As he talked Timber took a look around the office. It was untidy, far more so than it should have been and it didn't look like the sheriff owned a broom.

"You could help out by going and arresting them if you think it's so darned easy," Nathanial carried on.

"You know, sarcasm isn't gonna help here. Sure I'll go looking for them and no I won't need your help, at least not until I've properly investigated all this."

Nathanial calmed down at that then gave Timber a stare, "What, you will go looking for them on your own?"

"I've always found that to be a good way, apart from on the odd occasion. Why, do you want to come with me?"

"No sir, I'll let you go and see for yourself what an evil band of men they are."

"Okay. You got anything else to help me out with here."

Nathanial turned to look at the papers on his desk, "Yeah as a matter of fact I do I have some wanted notices here that match some of the men including Crazy Jack."

Timber took the papers from him and looked through them, "Just six of them here."

"That's all I've got but I'm sure they are all wanted men."

"I guess so," Timber stood up taking the notices, "Okay well I guess that about does it," he turned to go then turned back and pulled a wanted notice from a shirt pocket, "You ever seen this fella?"

Nathanial looked at it, "No sorry, I don't know him.

"No bother, I'll catch up with him one day" Timber added the notice to the others and stuffed them in a pocket, "Well, I'll Be seeing you," he said and then walked out leaving Nathanial watching him open mouthed.

Timber got back to Scout and looked around at the people who were giving him strange long looks. He shook his head at that and decided he would take a trip to a saloon, get a drink and see what else he could find out.

As it happened the saloon he chose was the same one that the outlaws had wrecked. Timber walked in to find it had been cleaned up somewhat although there weren't many tables or chairs and there were stains on the wooden boards. The men in there looked at him as he entered as all the conversations stopped.

Timber walked across to the bar, his black boots resounding on the wooden floor. At the bar he stopped and looked straight at the barman who looked nervously back at him. He was new and not sure of himself. Timber then turned around to face the room. He pulled his U.S. Marshal badge out and held it up for all to see.

"For your information I am not one of the outlaws you've had bother with, I am Jake Timber, U.S. Marshal who will be going looking for them once I have had a drink."

The atmosphere changed immediately as Timber was now met with smiling faces. He turned to the bartender who now asked him what he wanted. Timber ordered a beer and was told it was on the house. Men came over to him and asked him if he really was going to go after the outlaws and who he was going to take with him?

"I'll be going alone," Timber answered amid looks of disbelief and shock.

"There's no way you will be able to arrest all of them there's at least twelve of them," a man told him. Others took this up.

"I'm still going alone, they won't be expecting just one man to go after them."

"You got that right," the man said, "you gotta be out of your head to do that."

"Or very good," another man said.

Timber smiled at both of them, "Whatever, I am I'm going after them."

"Well good luck," the first man said.

After that the drinks kept on coming for him and he spoke to all the men in there to get as much information as he could.

"The same two men were always out on guard wherever they were," one man told him.

"Jack Keller has a right hand man. A big fella who was always at his side," another said.

"Did you get a name?" Timber asked.

"Yeah I did, it was Doug."

Timber thanked him and got as much other information as he could. He had seen a small hotel down the street so once he was happy he had learned all he could he went out and rode down to it. He booked in for the night then took Scout to the livery stable just a little further down the street. It was going to be good for him to have a night in a bed, it had been a while since he had done that and it sounded like he ought to get a good nights sleep before tomorrow.

4

Timber slept well and had a good breakfast at a cafe just down the street. He came out of there ready to start a new day. The sun was just coming up over the buildings throwing a red then pink glow over the town as he walked down the street to get Scout

With the information he had he figured on riding out northwest seeing as that was the direction the townsfolk had said the outlaws had ridden off in and see if he could come across them. The fact that he was heavily outnumbered didn't faze him, he'd been up against insurmountable odds before. He was going to find them first then figure out what he could do about them after.

He rode out looking for sign knowing it would be old now but then twelve or thirteen riders all together should leave something for him although they were now a few days old. In fact he found what he thought would be their tracks fairly quickly. There were a lot of tracks just outside of town but as he rode further away he saw tracks that fitted the bill going off the trail leading towards the mountains. It was as good as anything he had and they were heading northwest so he took off following them along.

The tracks he could see traveled pretty much in a straight line just going around areas of trees and rocks so after a while Timber didn't need to check so often as he was sure they would just keep on heading the same way. After a couple of hours he came up on a farm. He could see the buildings from a little way off. As this was on the route he was taking he wanted to stop and ask the people there if they had seen the outlaws so he rode on up to the wooden house to ask. It was very quiet as he got closer with no one about which seemed odd to him then it all became clear as he closed in on the house.

A man came partway out of the door keeping most of his body out of view and he was holding a shotgun, "Just stay right where you are Mister, I ain't afraid to use this thing," he called out to Timber.

"Just take it easy fella, I mean you know harm. I'm guessing you've had a visit from some men?"

"You're darned right we have, and what's to say you ain't one of them come back for more?"

Timber held his badge up high, "The name's Jake Timber, I'm a U.S. Marshal on the trail of a group of outlaws."

The man lowered the shotgun, "Well why didn't you say?"

"I just have."

The man came out to take a better look at Timber, "I have to say you don't look like any Marshal?"

"Oh, what does a Marshal look like?"

In spite of everything that made the man smile, "I had to be careful, Don Edwards, won't you step down."

Timber dismounted as a woman's voice came to them, "Who is it Don?" Timber looked over to the house and saw a woman standing there, she was slim wearing a long green dress and a white blouse and she had her hair tied up in a bun.

"It's all right Maggie, he's a friend, a Marshal and his name's Timber," Don called back.

Maggie came right out to get a good look at Timber and she wasn't impressed. She saw a big man wearing deerskins and a wide brown hat. He had long black boots with silver toes and heels. The fact he was wearing two guns, both tied down didn't miss her attention either but it was his face that struck her the most. It seemed to lack any kind of emotion. His green eyes seemed to burn right through her as he smiled at her through the stubble. She wasn't sure about him and they didn't get many visitors but if Don said he was a friend then that was good enough for her.

"Would you like some coffee Mister Timber?" she asked him.

Timber smiled again, "It's just Timber, and yes please that would be right neighborly of you."

Timber waited until Maggie and Don had gone in before he followed them. The room he went into wasn't that big but it had everything Maggie and Don needed. He sat on a stool at a small table while Maggie brought him a cup of coffee.

Once they were all holding a cup Timber asked, "So tell me about your visitors?"

Don cocked his head to one side, "You said you were chasing them?"

"That's right I am, but I would like to hear about what happened here."

"Sure, right, okay. Well we were working out in the fields when I saw the riders approaching; it was the first time I'd seen so many at once. Not knowing their motives I sent Maggie off to hide around the hen coups."

"That sounds like a good idea."

"Yeah well I figure it was, those boys rode straight up to me and demanded to know who lived here and what I had. I figured that was a bad start especially the way their leader said it, he had a way with him."

"Oh yeah, what kind of way?"

"It was like he wasn't all there or as though he was very young which he wasn't. He was kinda crazy and there was a strange look in his eyes."

"Okay, did you get a name?"

"Oh yeah, the others called him Jack."

Timber nodded, and waited for Don to carry on.

"They were all hard looking men, and I reckon they'd been riding for some time by their appearance. I took an instant dislike to them. They came riding in here like a bat out of hell. I wondered what was happening. I was pleased I had Maggie hidden away. As I say they wanted to know what I'd got, which isn't a lot but that Jack he looked all round the house and everywhere else but he didn't find Maggie."

"Did they take anything?"

"No thank goodness but they took a good look. They were larking around having fun just like a bunch of boys would. They worried me as they looked like they would be capable of doing anything. I was glad when they left."

"I guess so."

"So what can you tell me about them?"

Maggie interrupted them seeing Timber's empty cup, "Don, would our visitor like some more coffee?"

Don smiled at Timber, "I guess he would."

Maggie went for the coffee and they waited for her to return with a full coffee pot and had filled their cups before Don began to talk again.

"They were all heavily armed which you need to know if you have any thoughts of going after them although I don't know why you would do that seeing as you're on your own."

"Sometimes that works, sometimes I get help. The first thing is for me to catch up with them and see just who they are and what the situation is."

"Good luck with that. I sure wouldn't want to come across them again."

"We don't get that many visitors Timber," Maggie said, "Those were the kind we don't like, but I'm mighty glad to see you here and to know that a lawman is on their trail."

"I do my best. Can you give me any descriptions or other information that might be useful for me?"

"They all looked pretty similar, all in dark clothes with most of them wearing long coats. The horses were all bay's or black, nothing to really distinguish them. Sorry I can't be of more help."

"It all helps Don, which way did they leave here?"

"Why they headed northwest."

"Okay thanks," Timber finished his coffee, "I guess I'd better be running along now, thanks for the coffee," he got up and walked out followed by Maggie and Don.

"Good luck," Maggie called out as he rode away.

5

Timber rode away from the ranch only a little bit wiser about the men he was following. Sheriff Nathanial Baxter had called them 'The Crazy Jack's', he wondered just how crazy they were.

Traveling northwest Timber knew he was a good way behind them but that didn't worry him as he was sure he would catch up with them before too long. In fact he didn't have to wait long at all before something happened.

Riding ahead and at a tangent to Timber were three men. Two of them were unarmed riding in front of one who had a gun and a rifle. They were riding slowly enough so that the man at the rear could keep a good eye on the other two.

Timber saw them from a distance and noticed that they were heading northwest and would cut across his trail if they kept on their current route. There was something about the look of them that didn't seem right. The two in front seemed detached from the man behind, Timber could see that they looked ill at ease. He had to go and take a closer look. He changed course to come across them from behind which he figured was going to be the safest way.

Brody was the man at the rear. He had been in town that day, checking things out there and on the look out for two men, men that he had been sent by Crazy Jack to find. It hadn't been that hard either, the two of them had stood out from everyone else being as dirty as they were. Brody saw them after just a short while in town as they walked down towards the sheriff's office. He rode to where they had secured their horses to a hitch rail just up from the sheriff's office and left his with them then he hurried on after them. He caught up with them just as they passed from one sidewalk to another then drawing a gun he forced them into the shadows between the buildings.

"Now just where the heck do you think you're going?" he asked them.

The two men exchanged nervous glances and one of them stammered back, "Brody, we weren't doing nothin' we just needed to come to town that's all."

"And go straight to visit the sheriff huh?" Brody kept a couple of feet from them with his gun aimed between them.

"What? No Brody, we wouldn't do that."

"No well you ain't gonna get the chance to try, now you two are coming back with me, you try to escape and I'll shoot you down."

The two men had no doubt that Brody would carry out his threat, they had seen him do it before so they just agreed and walked out in front of him.

Brody was pleased the hitch rail was full at the sheriff's office so they'd had to stop a little way from it. Now he was in control of them. He urged them along back to their horses and got them to mount up as he did so himself then he had made them ride back out of town keeping in front of him where he could see them and shoot them if they tried anything.

Timber urged Scout, his big bay horse to a lope so he could catch up with the riders from behind and to the side of them. As Timber got closer Brody heard his horse approaching and looked around at him. He stopped and ordered the two men to stop with him. He then waited for Timber to catch them up.

Timber rode up a little closer but kept a short distance between them as he reined up.

"You want something Mister?" Brody asked once Timber was within range.

"Maybe," Timber glanced at the two men with him and saw the look in their eyes, "I'm on the trail of some men, maybe you've seen them?"

"I ain't seen anyone. Now if you don't mind..." Brody turned his head around to ride on.

"Maybe I do mind. These two men with you aren't very talkative," Timber glanced over to them again and saw them both about to speak up but Brody interrupted them.

"These are just two workers I'm taking in today."

"Now where would that be?"

"It's none of your concern..." Brody started only to be interrupted by one of the men saying it was to a silver mine.

"Really," Timber cocked his head at them, "You wanna go?"

"Now you look here Mister," Brody carried on, "I don't take kindly to folk messing in my business now you just ride on and we'll be on our way."

"I don't take kindly to people messing in my business either. Why don't we just ask these two men here what they think?" Timber was square on to Brody now watching for his every move.

Brody raised a hand to stop them from talking but one of them was a little braver than the other, "This man is forcing us to work Mister," he said, his eyes watching Timber beseechingly.

Brody swore and scowled but kept on looking at Timber, "They're just joshing, they are on their way to work now."

"It sure don't sound or look like they wanna go to me."

Brody pulled his horse around a little to get square on to Timber, "You looking to make something of it?"

"That all depends on how much you wanna keep those two men with you," Timber sat still waiting for a reaction.

The two men began to fidget on their horses. Brody knew he wasn't just going to be able to ride away from this. He had to do something to get rid of the man harassing him and there was only one way of making sure that happened. He thought Timber looked like a mountain man who probably didn't know one end of a gun from the other. He went for his gun.

Timber had been watching closely for such a move. In fact he didn't wait for the move. That quiet couple of seconds before he went for his gun was enough. Timber had his gun cleared of leather before Brody made a move. Timber leveled his gun at Brody intending to disarm him but he could see the time for that was passed. Brody's expression and his actions told him that. Timber fired just before Brody got to aim his gun. The bullet took Brody in his throat taking him out of his saddle to land in a heap in the dirt.

The two mens horses skittered around a little while Brody's horse took off a few yards. The men then stopped and waited for Timber to speak, not being fully aware of his motives.

Timber holstered his gun while he said, "Why don't you two come closer and tell me what the heck is going on here?"

"Thanks Mister whoever you are," the braver man said.

"I'm Jake Timber and I'm a U.S. Marshal on the trail of some outlaws called The Crazy Jack's."

"Well ain't that a gift from above. Fella you came to us just in time. My name is William, folks call me Bill and this here's my good friend, Isaac. We are sure glad you came along."

"That I can see, so what's this work you were being forced to do?"

"This last week us and a few other men were rounded up, mostly out of town and taken to a silver mine just in the mountains here," Bill pointed in the direction.

"They make us work there Mister to speed up the work of the regular miners," Isaac said.

"Why so?"

"The way I figure it is this Crazy Jack means to get more silver out of the mine in record time."

"You telling me Crazy Jack and his men are at a silver mine?"

"Sure, that's what I'm tellin' ya," Isaac carried on with.

"Then I'm on the right route."

"You sure are. Last night me and Isaac here snuck out of there and got back to town," Bill said.

"It was scary Timber, we were afraid we'd get caught. We were lucky to get our horses and ride out of there," Isaac said.

"But you still got caught."

"Yeah we did, that dirty coyote Brody there," Bill pointed to the man lying in the dirt, "He was sent to town to find us and take us back and he would have too if it hadn't have been for you. There is often one of the gang in town, sometimes more of them. They go for entertainment and to look for free labor."

"So what are you two intending to do now?"

"Why get back to town of course and keep our heads down," Bill told him, "Work at the mine is hard and we don't get fed much either or paid anything."

"They keep you there as prisoners."

"Yeah that's right. There are two cabins they keep us in at night and there are guards all around the place."

"I need to go take a look at it, where is it exactly?"

"If you're going there go get some help first because those men mean business," as Issac got no reaction to that he pointed out, "Go through that gap you see in the foothills of the Davis Mountains there," he said pointing, "and keep on heading west. You'll go over a high rise and then down into a valley, the mine is at the bottom, can't miss it."

Timber nodded his thanks as the two men swung their horses around. They both wished Timber good luck and then they were gone, galloping off back towards town. Timber got down from his horse and checked Brody's pockets. There wasn't much but he took what there was and his gun. Brody's horse wasn't hard to catch and he checked his saddlebags to find just the usual stuff, none of it any use to him but he took the rifle. He checked the man against his wanted notices and found he hadn't got one for the man not that it said he wasn't wanted. He figured it would be too difficult now to take his body back with him so he left it where it was then he unsaddled the horse and set it free before he mounted Scout again and set off for the mountains.

6

Jack Keller was standing in the office of the silver mine raised up as it was against the cliff face. He looked across the desk to the current mine owner, Jeff Collins. In front of him a man was lying on the floor, a bullet in his chest.

"That kinda solves our problem Jeff," Jack said, "Pity James didn't want to go along with my little plan."

"No he didn't and now he's dead," Jeff was a square shouldered man slightly overweight with slicked back black hair.

"Ain't that the truth?" Jack said, "Now we keep the men working here and get what silver out of the mine that we can for a while longer," Jack then sat down opposite Jeff across the desk.

"Just how long are you figuring on?" Jeff asked scowling at Jack.

"Well you know I'm staying right here until we have the amount of money that I want from this mine. I reckon we should have one thousand dollars each, that will set us up for a spell and shouldn't keep us around here for too long, so you can then go back to whatever it was you were doing."

"You say there are twelve men plus you so that means you want thirteen thousand dollars in total?"

"My my, you are good at doing sums ain't ya? Yeah that's right thirteen thousand dollars. Now how long do you reckon it will take to get that amount of ore out and purified enough for us to sell it?"

"A while, just getting it out will take time, all the good seams have already been worked out. Then the purifying process, well that takes time too depending on what comes out of the mine but I guess to give you an idea you are gonna be here for a few weeks."

"I ain't got a few weeks to hang about here, I want it done faster than that."

"Jack, Jack," Jeff said waving a hand to slow him down, "It just can't be done that quickly, not for that amount anyway."

"Okay now listen to me, you pull out all the stops, all of them okay and you get that silver ready for sale just as fast as possible, no slacking now, work through day and night if you have to. If you need more labor I'll get it."

Jeff looked up at Jack as though he was crazy, which he was, "I'll do my best but you have to understand..."

"You understand this," Jack pulled his gun and waved it around, his eyes went back and spittle began to run down his chin.

Jeff recoiled from him not knowing what the crazy man might do.

Jack had another man in there with him, Douglas Hamilton had been propping up the wall listening in. He was never far from Jack; the two men were virtually inseparable.

"You want me to convince him Jack?" he asked

"Oh I think he gets the message all right, don't you Jeff?"

Jeff just gave him a scowl as an answer, "What about James, we can't just leave him there?" Jeff changed the subject.

"Jack looked down at the body, "No you're right. Doug, get a couple of men up here will you and take him away?"

Doug nodded, spit out a match he was chewing and went out.

"So then Jack you do intend to sit it out for the amount of money you want?"

Jack didn't answer straight away, he was thinking, then he looked across at Jeff, "I'll stay for as long as I want to and you can be sure I will be checking the silver every day."

"You do that Jack, then you'll find out just how hard it is to get this stuff out and refine it then sell it."

Jack looked in Jeff's red face and grinned, "But I won't be doing the work though will I? Or arranging all the paperwork or arranging the refining because you will be doing that won't you?"

Jeff became serious, "I'll do my best."

"You bet you will. Well I guess I'll be running along now, I got me some men to go see, make sure they're all working well," he ended the conversation by grinning as he went out just as Doug arrived with two men.

"What d'you want us to do with James?" Doug asked.

"What do I care, just get rid of him."

Doug shrugged and carried on into the office with the two men behind him.

Jack went outside and stood on the high platform outside the office. It was like a small veranda that then descended down a staircase to the valley floor. The office was itself situated partway up the cliffs around the valley giving views of all the working area, the entrance to the mine shaft and the ways in and out of the valley.

Jack got thinking of how he had gotten into the silver mine. He had come across it quite by chance and had thought it looked to be of interest. Not wanting to pass up on something that could be lucrative for him he went in together with his men. He saw miners there working away and figured there must be some money to be made from it. He stopped a man and found out where the owners were then he went up to the office with Doug leaving his men at the bottom.

The owners hadn't been pleased to see him, especially James who took an instant dislike to them. Jack questioned them on what was going on and discovered about the silver ore being extracted, purified and sold on. That was enough for him, he had to get involved. He questioned them some more and found Jeff to be more co-operative than James. There was also something about Jeff that told Jack he could work with him. Jack had been abrupt with them and told them he was taking over and wanted all the money they had there and the silver from the mine. That had inflamed James who had argued with Jack so much that Doug had gone in to them to help out if necessary. James was very unhappy as he knew Jeff had something up his sleeve. As Jack found out more about the mine and how it worked it became obvious to him too that Jeff wasn't being straight with James.

James finally told Jack and Doug that he wasn't going to be robbed by them so he opened a cabinet drawer and pulled out a gun. As soon as Jack saw him do that he drew his gun and killed him. Then it was more talk with Jeff to find out what was going on. Now they had an agreement and Jack was happy although Jeff wasn't as the plan he'd had was now shot to pieces.

From where he was Jack could see where men were working on purifying the silver. They had vats and presses they were working on which looked like being hard slow work. This was the part Jack had no idea about. He had hardly any idea about digging the ore out of the mine either but he could guess and imagine that a lot better than the purifying procedure. He just hoped Jeff was stringing him lies on how long it would take to get the silver ready to be taken to town to be tested by the Assay office and then sold through the man there as he didn't want to stay there any longer than he had to.

Jack had been at the mine for a few days now. It had been quite easy for his men to take over the place. When Jack found out there wasn't enough men there to do the work in the time he wanted he had gone off to town with some of his men and kidnapped whoever he thought would be useful. He had stopped at a farm on his way through but he didn't figure the farmer there would be useable so he had ridden on. He now had a total of twenty-five men working there which he was happy to increase if required by going off to find some more. For now he stood by the rail and watched the comings and goings of the miners and the men he had brought in together with his men he had as guards patrolling around the place. They had orders to kill anyone who tried to leave. Surprisingly one night two men had escaped. That had infuriated Jack and he had sent Brody to bring them back who he was now waiting to return. That had been a long time ago and he was wondering where he was.

He moved out the way to let the two men carry James down the stairs, and Doug who followed them. James had been a pain. He had refused to go along with Jack's audacious plan even though Jack had tried every means to convince him. It was lucky for Jack the mine was owned by two men and he only needed one to complete the details of the testing and sale of the silver so Jeff was now the only owner left and there wouldn't be much left for him to own once Jack had finished with the mine which he knew was on its way out anyway.

He watched as James was unceremoniously dumped by a pile of waste soil and rock from the mine soon to be covered up and lost forever. Doug then climbed back up to be with Jack.

"Brody's taking his time ain't he?" Doug said as he got to Jack.

"That lazy son of a bitch, I'll tan his hide for him if he ain't back here soon."

"He might be in some saloon someplace."

Jack scowled at that, "He'd better not be, I need those two men back here, he'd better have found them and be back here soon or else."

Doug grinned thinking of what entertainment that would be, "You want me to check the mine Jack?"

"Yeah, you ain't been there in a while, make sure they are all working just as hard as they can."

"You got it," Doug hurried down the stairs looking forward to bullying some men around.

7

Timber followed the direction the men had sent him on. It was an easy ride over the open area of scrubland with just areas of bushes and cactus until he got to the foothills then the terrain began to change. It was still rough ground but now it began to get a little greener as he advanced. He took his time not wanting to be surprised by anything or anyone.

He climbed up higher into the foothills looking for the landmarks the two men had given him while all the time looking out for any riders. If Brody had been to town and back then others may well do so and he had to take care. He didn't come across anyone else until he reached a rise from where he could look down and over towards where the mine obviously was. He was still a distance from it but that was exactly where he wanted to be. There were plenty of places where he could leave Scout out of sight and he chose a bunch of bushes that had grown up around a rocky knoll thinking he would be out of sight there from anyone. He knew Scout wouldn't make a noise if he told him not to which is what he did. Then he began to make his way over to where he could see a steep rise that should give him a clear view into the mine valley.

The first part was easy enough but as he got closer he slowed down to be sure of not making any sounds and then he bent over to do the last stretch where he got down on his belly to take a look over the top. He had chosen a place where there was greenery and a few bushes growing to hide among. Once he got right to the edge he was able to see the mining area all laid out below him.

The mine shaft entrance was over to his right just a few yards up from the flat bottom of the valley. In fact Timber could see it was in more of a gorge than a valley but it was quite extensive with two ways in and out. Timber had his spyglass to take a proper look around. The entrance to the actual mine was quite wide at about four yards and about the same height. He could only see a couple of yards inside from the angle he was at. There was a man at the entrance and he was holding a rifle.

Down in the open area were two large wooden cabins that Timber guessed were for holding the miners as the men he had rescued had told him. Around the mine entrance were a few shacks and sheds, no doubt to hold mining equipment but possibly to house men as well. Also in the area were large vats and pieces of machinery that Timber had no idea what they were used for only that men were working there doing something. More interestingly to one side were two wagons no doubt used for transporting the silver. There were horses in a corral Timber reckoned would be the outlaws and for pulling the wagon maybe even for the miners as well.

Another building of interest was situated at the far side from the mine entrance. It was a small building built partway up the cliff face and there was a staircase leading up to it. Timber reckoned this must be the office as it would give a good view over the whole area.

Looking around he was interested now in seeing just who was working and who was guarding them. It was hard to count the miners and workers, as he had no idea how many would be in the mine or any of the buildings but he counted ten men. Then it was the outlaws that he had to pay the most attention to.

There were guards all around the mine and at least one that he could see at the two cabins in the open area. Counting them up he came to eight men. He had been told there were twelve but with

Cody out of the picture that left eleven so at least three men were unaccounted for. They could be in the mine or they could be elsewhere. Timber knew he had to take care as he didn't want to show his hand just yet, not until he knew where every man was and the whole situation about what the heck was going on here.

He lay there for two hours watching the movements of the men and looking for those he hadn't yet seen. One other man had come out of the mine to talk with the man standing outside but then he had gone back inside again. Although Timber was a good way from anyone their voices did carry over to him and he picked up the odd word. Over time these added up and it seemed like the guards were talking about the men they had working there and how they had to be watched the whole time which was just what they were doing. Timber was about to leave when something new happened.

The door to the office opened and a man came out he hadn't seen before. He was tall, taller than he was and broad. He said a couple of words to the man behind him then he went down the stairs and marched over the vats to talk to the men there.

It was the man behind him that took Timber's attention. He stood at the guardrail and looked over the mine. Timber guessed he was in charge, which most likely made him to be Crazy Jack. The man stood there looking over until the door opened again and another man came out. This one was very different. Whereas all the men he had seen were dressed scruffily or just with shirts, trousers and hats this one was wearing what looked like a suit. Not the kind of attire a miner or an outlaw would wear, so who was he? Timber figured that it had to be some kind of manager or even owner of the mine, that being the case why was he allowing the Crazy Jack's to do what they were?

That was interesting and something he was going to have to find out about. The day was coming to an end and Timber needed to get back to Scout, he'd left him there long enough now. He crawled away from the edge of the cliff face and made his way back down to his horse. He was just where he left him. Timber had water with him, which he gave most of to Scout. He had seen a stream to the far side of the valley tumbling down the mountain, which he figured he would be able to get to for fresh water from later when it got dark. He had food with him, which he had to eat cold as there was no sense in risking a fire. Once he had eaten his fill and given Scout the few oats he had with him it was time to go and find the water and check out the mining area from the other side and the entrance to the valley there. He had seen one entrance from where he had been and that just went into the foothills and away, he now needed to know where the other one led.

8

Timber didn't have to wait until dark, by the time he'd ridden Scout on a round about route to get to the far side of the mine the moon was already up. He was lucky in that it was nearly a full moon to guide him which was useful but probably wouldn't be so useful when he wanted to keep hidden when he took a closer look at the mine.

He got around to the stream without any incident and filled his water canteen and let Scout drink his fill then it was a case of carrying on up the mountain to where he would be able to see the other entrance to the valley. Eventually he arrived at a point where he could leave Scout below the skyline on the opposite side to the valley and then he crept up for a look. This entrance was more interesting. For one thing there was a man on guard resting against the far wall, he obviously wasn't expecting visitors and why should he at night?

The entrance wound around a little so Timber followed it with his spyglass to find that it then led around a jumble of rocks before heading straight back to town. This looked like the main way in and out and so would most likely be the way they would transport silver from the mine. Slowly he was getting a picture of the whole operation but there were still a few things he needed to see. One of them was where did the miners and outlaws go at night?

He looked down into the main valley area and saw that there were lights in the windows of the two cabins. There were also lights shining at the tents and shacks. Someone was in them and Timber needed to know who was in where. He left Scout ground reined where he was so he could call him if he needed to then he began to make his way around to where he had seen a possible way down to the valley floor. Carefully in the light of the moon he made his way down to arrive behind a shed with no lights on that was hopefully just used for tools and suchlike. He looked around the shed knowing from above that there were no guards near where he was. Then it was a quick dash over to a piece of machinery where he got down to wait and listen. He heard a guard cough a few yards away but he couldn't see him as he was around the far side of the vats. Timber took a good look then made another quick dash to get up to the side of one of the cabins. Here he found an open window and got close up to it to listen.

He heard men inside talking and they weren't outlaws. They were talking about how they were going to break out. Timber got right up to the window and risked a quick glance inside then he got up to the window again and holding a finger to his lips he whispered to the men inside.

"Don't worry I'm a Marshal come to help. Who are you all, are you being held captive here?"

His words brought most of the men towards the window and two of them came right up to him.

"Mister we are being held here and made to work for a gang of outlaws. They have us working all hours. They intend to have us working through the night as well from tomorrow, are you really a Marshal?"

"Yes I am," Timber showed then his badge, "How many of you are there?"

"Altogether in both cabins there are twenty five of us."

"So are the outlaws here all the time?"

"Mostly, not so much at night. Some stay over, some go to town, they take it in turns. Can you get us out of here?"

"Not tonight. I need to be prepared and have a way of getting you all safely away. You are going to have to hang on knowing I will free you as soon as I can. Which one of you is in charge here?"

"We ain't really got anyone like that but I guess Casey here fits the job," a man said as he made way for a tall men to push his way to the window.

Timber was aware of how long he was taking and he didn't want to be discovered, "Okay Casey just make sure no one mentions me coming here tonight, I'll be back," Timber waited for an acknowledgment before he slipped away again.

He crept over to the other cabin and again looked for an open window. He found one easy enough and like the others they were secured so they only opened a short way. Looking in one he had the same result as at the other cabin. Men clustered around wanting to know who he was. Timber had them quieten down and told them who he was again then asked for a man in charge. This time a man came to the window.

"That will be me Timber. My name's Mike and I am, well was the foreman here." He was a big man and Timber could see from how he conducted himself how he had got the job.

"I'm going to try and get you all out but you need to be patient, I'll get back to you."

"You reckon you can do that Timber, who you got with you?"

"No one, there's just me."

MIke grimaced at him, "One man alone, you're as mad as Jack, there's no way you can get us out of here without being killed."

"I'll do my best, now you be ready the next time I come to you."

"We'll be ready, and thanks. I just hope you know what you're doing," Mike said as Timber slipped away. He dashed back to the machinery then made sure all was well before getting back to the shed. Then he climbed back up to arrive a little way from Scout. A short whistle brought the horse up to him. He needed a few hours sleep and he also needed to feel safe. The location he had been in before offered a lot more protection so he rode Scout back there to where he had left him last time.

9

Timber felt quite safe where he was. Scout was hidden away with a little amount of greenery to graze on while it was very private and out of the way among the rocks and trees. They were also a good few yards from the top of the rise so there was very little chance of any small sounds they made being overheard by any of the men in the valley, even so Timber didn't risk starting a fire so it was cold rations again.

Timber never slept for more than two hours at a time and that night was no exception. Each time he woke he checked the rise and took a look down into the valley, each time with nothing to see. He rose for the last time just before first light and took one more look over the rise to find nothing had changed. He then packed his things away ready to move out, or to go in. That would depend on what he saw as the mine began to wake up. The light was coming up fast over the foothills and a northerly wind had sprung up, that was helpful as it would mask the sounds he made and take sounds from the mine to him

As before he left Scout where he was and crawled up to the edge of the rise to watch what was happening. He saw the outlaws come out of the tents and shacks at the mine entrance and set about making breakfast for themselves over fires. He heard banter between them and then the miners and workers were let out by other outlaws so they could go over to an area obviously set aside for them where they also got fires started and prepared food given to them by the outlaws.

Time went on, food was eaten and then the miners were pushed along to the mine entrance and the other workers to the vats and machinery to start work. What interested Timber more was a group of men he watched ride in from the far entrance to the valley. They had obviously been out all night, so it was right what the miners had told him, some of them did spend the night in town. He saw the man he suspected as being Jack come out of a shack and go over to the office where he was joined by the man in a suit who was one of the men from town. It wasn't long after when Jack came out again and called over to Doug who went to him. After a short conversation Doug then gave two of the outlaws a bag that looked heavy and sent them riding off out of the mine. That was too interesting to pass up. Timber edged back from the edge and was very quickly riding Scout to follow them.

Timber found it easy enough to get behind the men and he followed them all the way into town from a safe distance. Once in town it was easier to close the gap so he could see where they went.

Gregg and Thomas were the two men and they were happy to do the errand for Jack. They had been in camp all night so it was good for them to have the chance of a ride into town. They knew there would be no rush back which would give them some time to enjoy a trip to a saloon at least while they were there after they had completed their errand.

They had chatted on the way in and had already decided on which saloon they would visit which also served good food which was served by pretty saloon girls. It was a win win situation for them. Timber rode to the opposite side of the street and kept just a short distance behind them as they rode down the street. He stopped as he watched them pull up at the Assay Office. They tied up outside and went in carrying the bag. Timber left Scout close by and walked along until he was close to the office to wait for them coming out again. As he waited he made sure he would identify their horses when he saw them again.

Gregg and Thomas came out a few minutes later and Timber watched as they rode back up the street only to pull up again at a saloon. Timber eased himself away from the wall he'd been leaning against and went in the Assay Office.

He was the only person in there apart from a thin wiry looking man behind a counter that ran across the room. He looked up at Timber and flashed an artificial smile at him showing rows of yellow teeth, "Now what can I do for you?" he asked.

Timber advanced to the counter and didn't answer until he showed the man his Marshal badge, "I'm Jake Timber, U.S. Marshal, those two men who were just in here, what did they want?"

"Well now Timber, old Jacob don't get many Marshals in here and that's for sure, why do you want to know?"

"That Jacob, is my business to know not yours, so what was it?"

Jacob's smile vanished to be replaced by an evil glare at Timber, "I get men in here all the time, usually wanting to know the value of things?"

Timber nodded, "So what did they bring?" Timber knew it had to be silver but he wanted Jacob to tell him.

"Ah, just a couple of pieces of ore that's all."

"I figured that, so just how good was it?"

"For you to ask the questions you have I guess you know what they brought in to me?"

"Silver ore purified I guess to a good enough standard to have it verified and valued."

"You should take up Assaying."

"Just you tell me, I ain't got all day to chew the fat with you."

Jacob saw a man that he didn't fancy telling lies to and he didn't see why he should. After all he knew Crazy Jack and his men so he felt safe enough to talk.

"It's good, very good and certainly worth working for. Of course I have to fully test this latest sample but I'd say it will be as good as all the rest they have brought me."

"So you'd say it was worth money?"

"Oh yes, I'd say so. Is there anything else I can help you with?" Jacob was hoping to a quick end to the conversation.

"Yeah. So once you've agreed the value, where is it sold?"

Jacob scowled at Timber and didn't answer straight away. He looked down then back up at him, "It's brought out of the mine to me here in the wagons they have then I sell it on for them. I have contacts who come and collect it."

Timber didn't doubt it, "When is the next shipment?"

"I never know, when they have enough to bring me."

"Okay, I'll be back," Timber turned and walked out. He then rode Scout up to the saloon where the outlaws horses were tied outside. He left Scout there and walked up to the door where he took a look inside before entering.

Gregg and Thomas had found a table to sit at and they were both nursing glasses of beer when Timber walked in. They didn't notice him from any other men in there and carried on with their conversation. Timber bought a beer and walked to where he could hear them but not so close as to be noticeable.

"I reckon Jack's gonna need more help soon if he's thinking of working nights as well as days," Gregg said.

"Could be and that's gonna mean more work for us I guess."

"Easy work and that would also mean more silver quicker..."

"Which also means more money for us."

They both laughed and clinked their glasses before taking great gulps from them. Gregg turned around and looked at the bar.

"I reckon it's time for some more," he got up and walked to the bar. As he did he walked past Timber without a second glance. There was no reason why either man should recognize Timber but that convinced him that he hadn't been seen by them up to now. He waited until Gregg sat down again and continued the conversation.

Timber found out that half the men working the mine were

captives and they used the regular miners to do the digging and the captives to do the purifying.

"Jeff taught them well Gregg," Thomas said, "Not that there's much to learn."

"No that Jeff Collins is a kinda quiet man though ain't he? I hardly ever see him."

"Me either. Strange fella, still Jack seems to have him under control."

"Yeah, I wonder what happened to the other owner. Not seen him for a spell now."

"Who cares, one is enough and I guess he'll have to go when we do."

They both laughed at that as they got a little tipsy on the beer.

Timber took in the information and then waited for the men to finish up and leave. He saw there were finished plates of food on their table so chances were they were leaving to go back to the mine which suited him very well. Gregg and Thomas got out to their horses before Timber stopped them.

"You boys enjoy being involved in kidnap and forced labor?" he asked.

They both turned to look at him surprised by the question. It was Gregg who replied.

"If you mean the men at the mine, they get paid for what they do, we just encourage them to work for us. What's it to you anyways?"

"What men work for isn't up to me. Who is employing them in this case is?"

"Oh yeah, why so?"

"Because as I see it you are part of a group of outlaws known as the Crazy Jack's and you are all guilty of murder, robbery and maybe a dozen other things I haven't thought of yet."

Gregg and Thomas could hardly believe their ears and were stunned for a few seconds until the full meaning of Timber's words struck home.

"You got a big mouth Mister, whoever you are," Gregg stood still, his hand close to the butt of his gun. Thomas edged away to give them both some shooting space. Neither action went noticed by Timber.

"I'm Jake Timber U.S. Marshal. Now I want you two boys to use a finger and thumb and drop your guns on the ground nice and easy like."

Timber knew that wasn't going to happen. As soon as he saw the flicker in Gregg's eyes he drew both of his guns. Gregg drew his fast and he was nearly fast enough in fact he had his gun out and almost aimed before Timber shot him down. Thomas had been crafty and had left the deed to Gregg while he stepped away sharpish out of sight around the side wall of the saloon.

Timber strode forward to go after him when a voice came from behind him.

"Hold it Timber, what's going on here?"

Timber turned to see the sheriff right behind him.

"Goddamn it Nat, can't you see I'm busy," Timber turned again and looked for Thomas but he was long gone.

10

Timber ran down the way Thomas had gone to look for him but he couldn't find him. He realized the man could have gone off in any number of directions. Nathanial had gone after Timber and he helped search around before Timber noticed him and shouted at him to go back to the saloon where Thomas had left his horse. They were both very frustrated when they found the horse was now missing. Timber was about to complain to the sheriff about leaving the horse alone but then that would just be a waste of time.

"Looks like he got away whoever he was," Nathanial said.

"And will no doubt get back to the mine before I can stop him."

"Ah that's too bad, so are you gonna tell me what's going on here?"

"I followed two of Crazy Jack's men to town. They visited the Assay office and I tackled them. Now one of them is dead and the other has gone back to Jack to tell him about it and about me being here."

"I'm sorry if that has cost you Timber, I should have stayed with the horses."

"For a minute Timber wondered if the sheriff was in on something to have done that but then he put it down to just carelessness. He was still unhappy, carelessness can cost lives.

"It looks like that's all I can do here now," Timber checked the wanted notices in his pocket and found one that matched Gregg, "Have me a ticket on this man next time I see you will you," Timber went off to Scout and mounted up leaving Nathanial to organize the undertaker for Gregg. He still wasn't sure of the sheriff.

Thomas was pleased to still be alive. He wondered how a Marshal had got on their trail and what he would be able to do, after all he was just one man unless he was able to bring more lawmen onto them. He had to get back and warn Jack. He galloped on wondering what Jack was going to say about the fact Gregg had been killed and the Marshal being in town.

Jack watched Thomas ride in from the veranda outside the office. Thomas was riding way too fast and Jack could see his horse was covered in lather, plus he was alone. Jack ran down the stairs to intercept him.

"Thomas what the heck has happened?" he shouted at him as Thomas rode up.

"We got trouble Jack. There's a U.S. Marshal in town and he just shot Gregg dead."

"Get down from that horse dangdamnit and tell me everything," Jack shouted back as he looked around for Doug. Seeing him he waved for the man to come and join them. As soon as Thomas was off his horse Jack got hold of his arm and steered him away from the workers and sat him down at a bench that was for the outlaws to use, then he stood over him.

"Now then you start again from the beginning," Jack said as Doug closed up on them.

"It's like I said Jack. Gregg and me we rode into town just like you said and took the sample to the Assay Office then we called at a saloon, just to slake our thirst," he added looking up at Jack.

"Come on man tell me what happened?"

"We had a couple of beers, that's all Jack I swear then we went out and this man came up to us. He said how he didn't like us forcing men to work. Then he carried on and Gregg went to draw on him. That's when the Marshal shot him dead. I was lucky to get out of the way and get my horse to come back here."

"Did you get followed?" Doug asked.

"What, no of course I didn't I'm better than that."

"Horses leave tracks Jack," Doug said to him.

"There's no one in that town who would dare to try and attack us, so we only have this Marshal to take care of," Jack looked down at Thomas and he had another question for him, "So why didn't you kill this Marshal?"

Thomas looked up at him wide eyed, "There was no way Jack, he's good, very good."

Doug looked down at Thomas, "You sure that Marshal is working alone?"

Thomas shrugged, "I guess. He's the only person I saw apart from sheriff Baxter who came up just as the Marshal shot Gregg. If it hadn't have been for him talking to the Marshal I'd be a goner as well."

"This comes on top of Brody being missing and the two workers who got away from here," Jack stood thinking for a few moments, "We have to get this Marshal. Thomas, you're going back to town and I'm going with you. Doug you take care of things here. Now tell me what this Marshal looks like."

Doug grinned not giving much thought for the Marshal's chances once Jack found him as Thomas gave a description of Timber.

Jack gave Thomas a fresh horse and saddled his own up then he took off with Thomas, his thoughts full of how he was going to rid them of a U.S. Marshal.

A couple of hours later found them riding into town. On the way Jack had made Thomas tell him again what Timber had said, what had happened and what he looked like so he had a good idea of him but he was still relying on Thomas to point him out. They rode down the main street looking for him but without success.

"Looks like we're gonna have to check a few places out," Jack said as he reined up outside the same saloon Thomas had been in with Gregg. They checked inside and then walked out again. Jack made Thomas walk with him up and down both sides of the street checking every saloon and every other building they came to where Timber might be. The only building they didn't check inside was the sheriff's office, Jack was leaving that till last. Once everywhere else had been checked out that was the only place left.

"Okay Thomas, we'll go see the sheriff now," Jack said as they got close to the office. They arrived at the door and Jack tried the handle. It was unlocked so he walked in to find the office empty.

"Did you see Baxter in the street Thomas?" Jack asked.

"No, I didn't and I was looking around."

Jack shook his head wondering where he was. Then he shrugged and walked out again, "Take me back to the saloon you met the Marshal at," Jack told Thomas.

Thomas was pleased to do so and it was only a few minutes later when they arrived. They went in again but they still hadn't seen Timber or Baxter.

"You reckon they've teamed up?" Thomas asked.

"What, Baxter get involved. I don't think so," even so Jack thought it odd he hadn't seen the man. Having looked everywhere and not found Timber Jack was now getting frustrated. He walked outside with Tomas following him. As a man walked past him to go in the saloon Jack grabbed hold of him and spun him around.

"Say, you live around here?"

"Yeah, what of it?" the man answered shocked at being accosted.

"You must have seen the Marshal then, a man called Timber?"

"Marshal, no I ain't seen no Marshal."

Jack pulled the man up by his shirtfront, "Now you wouldn't be holding out on me would you?"

The man looked into Jack's black eyes and saw no mercy there, "No mister I ain't. I swear I don't know any Marshal."

Jack let him go and returned to Thomas, "It looks like your man has left town already, we'll go back to the mine, after we've had a drink," Jack walked back in and pushed his way to the bar. As men saw who he was they made a space with most of them getting out of the saloon. Soon there was plenty of room at the bar much to the bartender's displeasure. He didn't say anything but he kept his eyes firmly on the two men while they drank their fill. Jack took a look around grinning at the looks he was getting.

"Y'all know me from last time huh?" he shouted out.

No one dared answer him. Those that were still in there only because they didn't want to walk past him kept their faces away from him.

Jack laughed and joked with Thomas then finished his drink and walked out without paying for it.

11

Timber rode along on his way back to the mine. He counted up in his head how many outlaws there would be. He had killed one out in the open and now one in town so there should be around ten left. It was still a lot of men for him to handle but then less than there were in the first place. He kept on riding. His path took him past the farmhouse he had visited before and as he got close he saw Don out working who waved to him. Timber changed course a little to go up to him.

"You having any luck with those men yet?" Don asked.

"Some, some to do."

Don squinted up at him into the sunlight, "You wanna get down for a spell, we got coffee?"

Timber could tell Don wanted to talk so he rode Scout the short distance to the house and ground reined him then he followed Don inside when he caught up.

Don called out to Maggie who was in the field tending some crops as he walked back. She left off and went to him.

"We got our Marshal here and I bet he's thirsty," Don said to her.

Maggie got the message and went inside while Don motioned to

Timber to follow her. Once inside he said, "I'm concerned Timber about those men that came here that day."

"You should be, have they been back here?"

Don shook his head just as Maggie came out the back room with coffee for them all. She sat next to Don having smiled at Timber and after greeting him she said, "You're onto them aren't you?"

"How'd you figure?"

"Oh you coming back here so soon after last time and being a Marshal and all," Don interrupted giving Timber a look as Maggie watched them.

"Those men who came here are a bad lot Don. They caused a lot of deaths and trouble in Little Bend and now they have taken over a silver mine just over the rise there," Timber said pointing.

"That mine was here when we started our farm Timber," Maggie said.

"Yeah the mine seemed to do well for a while then it went kinda quiet. We have only seen a few men coming past here that are obviously to do with it for quite a while," Don carried on with.

"There must be some good silver left because the Crazy Jack's have taken it over and they have employed forced labor as well to work on it."

"But we have seen the odd miner who was there before Timber," Maggie said.

Don interrupted her, "Yes but only when there are other riders with them."

"The outlaws do keep a close eye on the men yes so I guess they are not happy about being there, possibly because they're not being paid for their labor."

"Oh my Timber, and so close to us," Maggie was not happy.

"Now don't you get upset ma'am, I intend to straighten this whole thing out before I move on."

Maggie gave Timber a big smile, "That would be much appreciated."

Don gave him a smile too, "It sure would but Timber you are just one man."

"You know Don, I get told that a lot and it's not stopped me so far."

"I sure hope it won't this time," Don looked down, "I'm sorry I won't be able to help you," He nodded in Maggie's direction.

"I know that and I wouldn't want you to this isn't your trouble to get involved in."

"So what are your plans then Timber?"

"I don't have one, not exactly anyhow. I'm going back there and check it out some more then I'll work out how I'm gonna winkle them outta there."

"So long as you don't send them our way," Maggie said.

Timber had to smile, "No way, I'll keep you out of it you can bank on that."

It went quiet for a minute as Timber finished his coffee. As he was about to get up a sound came to him he wasn't happy with.

Jack rode back to the mine with Thomas wondering about the Marshal. He began to figure that he must have ridden on knowing he was up against insurmountable odds. It gave him a smile, he was invincible, he had plenty of hard men so what if he did come after them, one man didn't have a chance against him. When he arrived back he took a look around and he wasn't happy at what he saw. He found Doug and had it out with him.

"I thought I said to increase production Doug not slacken off?"

"I'm doing the best I can Jack, we need more men."

"Then get some, send Thomas out and put someone with him."

Doug shrugged and went off to find Thomas. He didn't take much finding.

"Hey Thomas," he said as he walked up to him, "Jack wants you to go and find more workers for us and take Billy with you," Billy was standing close by watching the men at the vats so he was convenient to let go for a while.

Thomas thought he was being put on but then going out was more fun than just standing around watching the workers so he readily agreed. He went over to Billy and told him what they were to do then they went to get their horses. A few minutes later they were riding out of the mine.

"You got a mind on where we're going'?" Billy asked as they rode clear of the valley.

"Not especially, we'll just see where we get to," he grinned across at Billy. He was younger than Thomas and not so experienced. Thomas was pleased as it put him in charge of what they did and where they went. He considered going to town like he always had but today he reckoned on trying other places. He knew there were farms and ranches around and he thought they might be worth a try. What he didn't reckon on was what he found at the first place they got to.

They rode on until they saw a farm of sorts coming up. At first Thomas thought that might be a good place to look for any hands working there but as they got closer his eyes fixed on the horse he could see outside. He'd seen it before, then it came to him,

"Hey Billy we struck gold here, I know that horse, it belongs to Marshal Timber," Thomas had a wide smile.

"Marshal?"

"Yeah, he's the man who killed Gregg and possibly Brody too."

"You don't say?" Billy looked over at Thomas, "I guess we're going over there."

"You bet we are. It will be good to go back with the Marshal over his horse. Jack will be pleased with that."

"I guess so," Billy was sure Jack would be pleased but he wasn't at all happy at going up against a Marshal. Thomas had no such concerns.

"We gotta do this crafty like Billy. We can't just go riding in there," Thomas looked at the farmhouse wandering if Timber was inside and if so who with. He also wondered who else was around the place. He had to find out before going in the house, "Go around the back from this side Billy see who's there will ya. I'll mosey around the other side."

Billy was happy with that and took off at an angle away from the buildings. Thomas watched him go then he took a long loop around to come up on the house from the opposite side. He got in close and looked around the hencoops and into the land around which satisfied him there was no one there. He just needed Billy to show himself now then he could go and check out the house.

Billy rode around the back of the house and the sheds he found out there without seeing anyone so he continued around until he got to where he could see Thomas who then waved him back. Billy got the idea, he was to go to the far side of the house so that they could be on either side of the door when they decided to go in. He hurried back and left his horse close by then he drew a gun and approached the door. Thomas left his horse where it was and approached from the other side until they met up at either side of the door.

Timber had distinctly heard someone coming up close outside. He put a finger to his lips as he stood up. Then he quietly made for the door as Don wisely kept on talking to give whoever was out there a false sense of not being discovered. Timber got close to the door and then stood well to one side, a gun in his hand.

Thomas wanted to be the one to take Timber out but he was worried. He didn't even know for sure if Timber was in there and if he was who else might be in there with him. He was going to have to find out but he was going to prefer it if Billy went in first. He signed to him to go in and that he would cover him. That put Billy into a predicament. He didn't want to be the first one in especially as he knew Tomas would be hard pressed to cover him at the narrow doorway but on the other hand he couldn't look a coward. It was a small farm, so thinking about it he reckoned there couldn't be more than two men in there and Timber would most likely be the only man with a gun, he had to try it. He tensed himself up then lunged for the door, his gun held out in front of him.

As he came through the door the first person he saw was Don. Billy didn't know Don from Timber as Thomas had neglected to tell him what Timber looked like so seeing Don he fired his gun at him. Maggie screamed as Timber's gun burst flame and smoke at the same time. The bullet flew into Billy knocking him down. Thomas was already partway into the house behind Billy when Timber had shot him making Thomas withdraw back outside fast. Timber wasn't going to let him get away. He had seen him enter and then back out to the left so he went to the right of the door and peered around the doorframe. Thomas was just a few feet away anxiously waiting for Timber to appear. He fired as he saw Timber begin to come out but too soon, Timber dived back in and aimed around the doorframe firing then he looked around and fired another shot. Both bullets struck Thomas, the first one in his belly then the second in his heart. Thomas collapsed on the porch like a sack of flour.

Timber then looked back in the farmhouse, Maggie was supporting Don's head as his face creased up in pain. Timber went to him and checked him over.

"My you're a lucky man. It must hurt but it's only a flesh wound, you'll be just fine."

"It don't feel fine," Don croaked.

Timber helped Maggie get Don on the bed and ripped open his shirt to see the wound better then he helped her to clean it up and bandage it.

"I'm sorry to have brought them here Don, you can be sure I'll make sure none of the others pay you a call."

"I guess they would have come again at some point and you have taken those two out so thanks for that."

"Are you going after the rest of them?" Maggie asked.

"I guess so, you look after him now, he's going to need some time to recover."

"You can be sure of that and Timber, take care won't you?"

Timber nodded and went to check over the two men dead. He emptied their pockets and took their guns, which he gave to Maggie.

"Hang onto these just in case and get the men's horses hidden away, I'll be back for them and the bodies to take to town, they may have bounties on them. Is there someplace I can leave them until I get back?"

"There's a shed out back, we keep a few tools in there, I'm sure there will be space for them."

Timber moved both of the bodies, checked again on Don then he mounted up on Scout and set off for the mine.

12

Timber rode on for the mine happy now that there were two less outlaws to worry about when he got there. He kept a good lookout for any others along the way but none showed up. He went off up the rise to where he had gone the first time in order to keep away from the main entrance to the valley to see what the situation was now.

He left Scout in the trees like last time and made his way to the top so he could look down on the mine. It was midday and the sun was shining down as hot as it got in the foothills. Timber was thankful he had filled his canteens at the farm and had given Scout his fill of water before leaving there. He had a canteen with him as he figured he would be up there for some time. There was precious little shade, only a little from the bush he was lying under. Timber pulled his hat further over his face and settled down to look around the camp. He had his spyglass with him which he used to take a good look at every man he could see down there. It was a good place to watch from as it gave a full uninterrupted view of the entire mine workings.

He found the man he figured was Crazy Jack easy enough. He was up on the veranda of the office talking to the man in the suit. Jack was pointing and obviously explaining something rather animatedly.

Whatever it was Timber couldn't see how it would change his plan, the plan he hadn't got yet but he was working on. Moving the spyglass around he found an outlaw holding a rifle, he looked bored as he oversaw three men working at a vat. It looked like hard work and it would be hotter down there than where Timber was. Moving across he saw another armed man at the mine entrance. There were other armed men wherever there were workers and he saw two men at the entrance to the valley. The two cabins in the middle of the valley weren't guarded but Timber guessed they would be later when the miners and workers went back to them. He stayed where he was through the afternoon watching to see the pattern of work and if and when the guards were changed over. By early evening he had it all figured out. What he wanted now was to talk to the miners again and that would mean waiting until they were all locked in the two cabins. He made his way back down to Scout to ensure all was well with him and he used up some more of his cold supplies before going back up to the ridge.

Jack wasn't happy, he found Doug and complained to him, "Where the heck is Thomas and Billy, they've been gone too long now?"

Doug had been wondering the same thing, "Beats me Jack. I can only think they've gone to town and gotten themselves drunk in some saloon or other."

Jack wasn't so sure, "It's not like Thomas to do that."

"You want me to send men out looking for them?"

"No, we keep all we have here tonight. They should be back in the morning and they'll get the rough edge of my tongue when they do," Jack stormed off leaving Doug in thought.

Timber thought again of how many outlaws were left at the mine. He got it to eight men, the odds were getting better. There was sure gonna be some bounty money for him when this thing was over, if he made it out alive of course. He now had to wait for dark again to go down to the cabins so it was time to ride around to the other side where that would be easier to do. He got down to Scout and took the long route around the valley to get back to the same place he had used last time. He left Scout ground reined in case he needed him in a hurry and then got to the place where he could climb down. Looking around it looked safe enough and all the guards seemed to be in their places. Taking his time he climbed down to the valley floor and as last time he made his way over to the two cabins. Creeping along the wall of one of them he came again to the window where he took a look inside. Again men in there saw him and he had to put a finger to his lips to stop them making a sound that might alert the guards.

"Hey Marshal, you came back, are you getting us out tonight?" Casey asked him in a low voice.

"Maybe yeah. How many are in here?"

"There's ten of us here Marshal the rest are in the other cabin."

"Are you all being forced to work here, do you all wanna get out?"

"We are being kept here, and you bet, of course we want out."

"Okay, hang in there while I check the other cabin," Timber then carefully crept across to it and found a window that was open a crack, none of the windows opened very far, not far enough for a man to get out of. It would make a lot of noise forcing any of them open any further. He got to the window and looked inside. No one noticed him until he hissed at the men he could see. Then they crowded around to see and talk to him.

"Hey Mike?" Timber whispered.

Mike came to the window surrounded by other men.

"Are you all regular miners in here and still working as forced labor?"

"We are now. We were all miners here before Jack and his crazy outlaw friends arrived and we worked for Jeff Collins and James Underhill. Now we still do the work but without any pay. We've been waiting on you coming back, what's your plan?"

"I figure on getting everyone out, one cabin at a time and I'm doing the other one first. Once I let you out get everyone away to a safe place then get to the horses."

"Are you alone?"

"Do you see anyone with me?"

"You must be as crazy as Jack to think you can manage all this."

"We'll see. This mine, is there just the one entrance?"

"Yeah but there are a couple of holes to the outside along the way, too difficult to get out of though. We've looked into that thinking we could get away from there."

Timber, pursed his lips, "Okay it was an idea. I still need to check it out though, good to know there are holes in there to the outside, now just stay quiet and wait for me," Timber slipped away and back to the first cabin window where men were waiting for him. He signed for them to be quiet and then he crept around to the front where he knew a man was standing guard. He was pleased for a sandy ground that his boots made no noise on then he drew a gun and carried on to the corner of the cabin and took a peep around it. The guard was standing close by the door. As Timber watched he stomped around a little no doubt getting bored. Timber waited until he was facing away from him then in a mad dash he got to the man and slugged him over his head with his gun sending him to the ground in a heap.

Listening carefully to make sure any sounds he had made hadn't set up an alarm he then unlocked the cabin door as it was simply bolted across. He opened the door to find all ten men ready to go.

"Follow me one at a time and stop coming out if you hear an owl call," Timber told them then he set off back to the cliff face. Once there he turned to watch the men come out after him. Casey led the men out and when he got to him Timber said, "Climb to the top, there's a bunch of trees a few yards off, wait for me there."

He then went back to the other cabin and opened it up, "Come on Mike get the men out there."

Mike was out in a moment and was stopped by Timber, "The other men are out and going up the cliff where they should be safe. You get these men together and take this man's gun. Hide out by the vats and get to the horses when you can then get out of here," Timber didn't want all the men to go to the same place.

Timber then left them and made his way stealthily over to the mine entrance. He would have to go past it to get to the corral for the horses. It was a few yards up from the valley floor approached by a well-worn path. That was the only tricky part for him but it was dark and he figured none of the guards would look that way anyway. As he walked up he kept on looking out for anyone but arrived at the entrance okay. With one more quick look around he went inside looking for something he wanted.

Unfortunately for Timber he had been seen. One of the guards just happened to look around and see Timber on the path and then go in the mine entrance.

Casey led the ten men with him up the cliff where Timber had shown them. It wasn't to hard to climb especially as it was starting to get light but as more and more of them tackled it they gradually loosened the soil and rocks along the way and some of it slipped down. The first few made a noise as they slid down causing everyone to stop and wait to see if the sounds had raised an alarm. They waited a few minutes then carried on more carefully then before. They all managed to get up and Casey took them to the trees that Timber had mentioned. There he got them all to sit down and stay quiet while they waited for Timber.

Mike took the outlaw's gun and stealthily led the way over to the vats and machinery. There was a lot of it so it was easy for all the men to hide among it. The corral wasn't that far away but Mike knew they would need time to get the horses ready so he would have to wait until a man he could see holding a rifle had moved away from them.

13

Timber walked in a few feet and was soon in pitch darkness. He had seen some kerosene lamps and matches on a bench at the entrance so he got one of them and keeping away from the entrance he lit the lamp, then he could carry on.

Outside the man who had seen Timber enter the mine started shouting waking everyone up. Jack came running out of the shack he was in demanding to know what was happening.

"There's a man going in the mine," the man shouted at him.

Jack looked in the direction but Timber was long gone, "You sure about that?"

"Sure I'm sure, a man in deerskins just went in the mine."

Jack nodded and looked around to see Doug coming over to him, "Get some men up there Doug," then he turned to the man, "Go keep an eye out," Jack then took another look up at the mine and started off for it. He hadn't got very far when the man called out again.

"Hey Jack, Marty's out cold here."

Jack stopped and looked back as the man opened the cabin door to find it empty.

"Hey, they've all gone," he looked back as Jack turned around to take a look.

"Go find them, they can't be far away," he could see that the horses were all safe in the corral so the miners couldn't have gone far.

As men came out of the tents and shacks Jack got them all organized in either looking for the escaped miners or going with him to the mine. He shouted out orders and got the men running around to where he wanted them then with Doug beside him and two other men he ran on to the mine.

"It's that pesky Marshal Timber Doug, we have him trapped in the mine," Jack gave Doug an evil grin as the hurried on.

Timber had walked on some way into the mine. He was interested to see just what was in there and whether any purified silver was stored inside as he hadn't seen where it was stored yet. He went on a few yards and then he heard voices being raised coming from outside. He cussed and made his way back. He figured the miners had been seen. He hurried back towards the mine entrance.

Jack got close to the entrance and ducked down behind a pile of barrels and buckets to take a look while the men with him scattered around to find cover for themselves. Jack then took another look and decided to call out now that he had Timber trapped.

"Hey Marshal, come on outta there, there's no place for you to go."

Timber stopped and looked carefully to the outside and then at two men who made a dash for the entrance where there were tools and buckets they could hide behind. He wasn't going to let them get that far. He drew his guns and fired at them. One of them ducked down but with the other man being in the open and silhouetted against the night sky he was an easy target so Timber shot him down.

He then called out, "I know what you are doing here Jack and I'm going to stop you. You and your men are all going to jail or hell, your choice so just give yourselves up now."

Jack laughed back at him, "You're hardly in a position to call any terms Timber and don't look for help from the men you've let out, my boys are rounding them up right now."

The other man was crouching down where they kept some dynamite for blasting and thinking it would be a good idea he lit a stick and threw it at the entrance as he called out, "That'll take care of him Jack."

It did a lot more damage than the man thought and as it exploded it brought the ceiling down in an explosion of falling rock and dust blocking the mine entrance.

"What the heck did you do that for?" Jack said rounding on the man.

"I didn't think it would cause that much damage, but heck we can dig it out again, the Marshal should be dead in there now."

Jack considered that. Once the miners had been rounded up again then yes they could dig the Marshal out, he grinned at the man, "Okay, go help get the miners up here."

Casey Williams had taken control of the workers early on. He had been one of the first men to be taken to the mine and had naturally been the man for the others to turn to. All the men respected him and looked up to him. Now he had the job of trying to organize the men and keep them where he wanted them.

He made them all gather together in the trees just as Timber had told him. Now they waited keeping as quiet as they could. Not all the men were happy however. One man in particular just had to speak up.

"Maybe we shouldn't have done this Casey. Jack's gonna be mad at us if he finds us."

"We'd better make sure he doesn't then."

That didn't appease him, "What if Timber gets caught or killed or just can't get the horses for us?"

"If you want to go back I'm not standing in your way," Casey said. He looked for other unhappy men and although there were some serious faces here was no other dissent. The man shut up as he realized he was on his own with his complaints.

Casey was concerned and he kept to the side of the ridge where he could look out. There was nothing much to see but then he heard gunfire and then an explosion. That could only be bad news what was he to do now?

14

When the dynamite exploded Timber was flung back amid a cloud of dust. He was lucky and thankful that the lamp kept alight, partly because he had put it down behind a boulder when he had arrived back at the entrance. He had only gone a short way into the mine before he'd had to go back and he hadn't found the one thing he'd been looking for, now he knew why; it was kept outside.

He got up and dusted himself down as best as he could with his hat now that the worse of the dust had settled. He picked up the lamp and walked up to the wall of rock and checked it out, there was no way he was going out that way unless men from outside dug their way in. He turned around and started walking. He had to bow his head against the ceiling, which was supported on strong wooden poles that Timber hoped hadn't been loosened by the blast. As he carried on he walked past tools, buckets and items the miners obviously used. He wondered if he would be able to use some of them to dig himself out if he could find even a small hole to the outside but then he considered that to be very unlikely. He kept on walking until he came to a fork in the tunnel. He hadn't been told about that, he stopped and sighed, which way was he to go? Both were black unwelcoming holes, both slightly lower than where he was.

He remembered having been told that there were small holes to the outside along the tunnels but which one? Although he studied the two directions there was no way he could work out which way to go so he just took the left fork and carried on. It became worse when the tunnel spilt again into two. Now he was getting worried about losing his way and getting lost forever underground. Timber was an open-air man, being constricted in any way went against everything that he was. Already he was beginning to sweat and he could feel a panic way down deep inside him wanting to rise up. He pushed the thoughts back and focused on finding a way out of the tunnels that were turning into a labyrinth.

Step after step he carried on occasionally swirling the kerosene around in the lamp to gauge how much he had left. The tunnels ran pretty straight but they did turn now and then. He came to a corner and going around it he stopped amazed to see it was a dead end. There was a rock face in front of him. He turned around thinking hard on what turns he had taken. Could he remember the way he had walked to get here? There was nothing he could do except go back and stop at each junction to try and remember the way he had come and hope to find a way that would lead him to a hole to the outside. Water sometimes dripped on him making the ground wet and slippery. Again Timber had to quell the feeling of panic at being trapped underground, he just had to find a way out

He got back to the last junction he had turned off at and then took the other tunnel. He looked now for signs of use, footprints, anything to tell him which tunnels were in use although he knew that it might not be a case of that and that any tunnel would be as good as any other for what he wanted. All he could do was carry on and keep searching for a hole that he hoped he would be able to squeeze out of in spite of what Mike had said. As he carried on he tried different tunnels until he began to lose where he was. He stopped and shook the kerosene lamp again and only heard a faint noise coming from it. It wasn't going to last him very long and without it he was going to be in serious trouble. He began to worry now. Not many things worried Timber. In fact there were very few things that could worry him. The worse thoughts he had were in his dreams when his wife and daughter came to him.

They were his entire life until a man he had thwarted when he tried to rape a girl took his revenge by killing them. Timber had found the man and had then subjected him to a brutal murder. That resulted in him going to jail where he stayed in a state of hell until the territory governor offered to get him out in return for doing the job he did now which was hunting out outlaws and bad men which he then dealt out his form of justice, usually from the barrel of his gun. It was also very lucrative for him, not only did he get paid by the governor, he also received pay for his old job of being a sheriff, on top of that he got the bounty of the men he caught and whatever they had on them. This resulted in him having thousands of dollars in the bank which he didn't need but thought he might do something with one day. Right now he had to get out of this mine.

As he carried on along the tunnels he looked for any kerosene or other lamps but he didn't come across any. It got to where he turned the wick down very low to save the oil. He came to another junction but he couldn't remember if he had been here before or not, there was only one thing to do and that was to take the turn and hope for the best.

Mike was in a quandary. Having heard the gunshots he didn't know now whether to go and investigate, try and get the horses with the miners or even go back to the cabin knowing how angry Jack would be if he came and found them. The men were beginning to talk amongst themselves and he knew he would have to take control of the situation and soon. He just had to make a decision.

He didn't know who had shot who or even what the shots for. Then the explosion had come as a shock to him. Looking over at the mine he could see the rubble around the entrance and clouds of dust beginning to settle. He wondered now where Timber was and if he was still alive?

What he did know was that Marshal Timber had put his life on the line to save them and that he must now do what he could for him. He turned around to face the men.

"We gotta go and find out what's happening over there and see if we can help Timber."

Not all of them thought that was a good idea and said so.

"Okay, so some of you just stay here, now who's with me?"

Only eight men came forward while the rest hung back. Mike nodded to the eight then turned to the others, "I understand why you don't want to risk yourselves. Just stay hidden and if any of you do change your minds at any time then I'll be glad to have you along," he then spoke to the eight men as he held up the outlaw's gun, "We take this slow and easy, I got this here Colt off the man Timber slugged and we need more if we can get them, now just you follow me and keep quiet," Mike then led them off towards the mine.

Timber was getting increasingly worried. The mine was oppressive, it was dank and would be black if it wasn't for the lamp. Here and there more water dripped down to make the tunnels more miserable for him. He didn't want to die in here. He wasn't used to being in enclosed spaces. The open air was for him. All he could do was carry on and hope for the best. He took a few more turns and stumbled along in the near dark as he had the wick on the lamp turned down as low as he could to preserve the oil. It was as he came around a bend that he stopped and looked ahead. A thin shaft of light was showing just a few yards further on. He hurried on over to it.

He got under the hole where the light was shining through to find it was too small for him to get through just as Mike had told him. He had looked for tools as he had walked through the tunnels and all he had found was a battered shovel that he had brought along with him. Now he put the lamp down and began to hammer away at the hole just above his head with the shovel trying to make the hole bigger. He worked and worked until the sweat was pouring off him. He had to take a rest and examine what damage he had done. It wasn't a lot and certainly not big enough for him to get through. He kept on working, gradually chipping more and more stones and slivers of rock away. As he worked he suddenly heard a cracking sound and a lump of rock fell from the side of the hole, now it was a lot bigger and he reckoned he would get through the to the outside. All he had to do was get himself up there to pull himself out. He jumped up to get a hold of the rock around the hole but found he slipped back off again, after a few tries he realized he needed help. He got up as far as he could and then gave a whistle. He dropped down then jumped up and whistled again, and then he waited before he did it again.

Just a few minutes later help arrived. Timber looked up through the hole to find Scout looking down at him. Timber spoke to the horse so that he moved around until his reins dropped through the hole. Timber took hold of them in one hand, jumped up and grabbed the rock with the other and with a huge effort he was able to pull himself through enough to be able to grab rocks on the outside and pull himself out as Scout pulled back on his reins giving Timber the help he needed. He collapsed on the ground as he smiled up at Scout thanking his lucky stars he had spent time training him.

15

Timber mounted Scout and looked around for the way back to the mine then he urged Scout to a lope to where he had left the workers in the trees. He arrived there to find them all waiting for him. He slid off Scout and asked if they were all there.

Several of the men began to speak at once so Timber raised a hand to stop them then Casey answered him.

"I wasn't sure what to do Timber. We heard gunshots and an explosion. We didn't know if you were alive or dead. I was about to try and move out."

"As you can see I'm alive and I'm glad to see all of you are too. Keep everyone here a little longer Casey, I'll let you know when it's safe to come down," Timber called to him as jumped back on Scout and rode off below the skyline to get closer to the mine.

Once he was close enough he left Scout ground reined again and got to the edge to look over at the mine entrance. He could see men were there digging away at the pile of rock. He smiled thinking that they considered he was still in there. That being the case what he did now was going to come as a big surprise.

He could see the men working were all outlaws so that must mean they have discovered that the miners had all been let loose and they hadn't found them or they would have made them do the work, so where was Mike and the men with him? As he looked he then saw Mike and a bunch of men creeping around the vats and machinery and it looked like they were trying to get weapons of some sort and looking n the direction of the mine. He had to get down there before they got themselves killed. He hurried down the cliff face keeping well out of sight of the outlaws who looked like they were all now at the mine entrance.

Once down on the valley floor Timber made for where Mike was getting the men with him organized. Mike saw him approaching so he stopped and waited for him. Timber ducked down low over an open area and got to where the men were hidden from the outlaws.

"Timber, I thought you might be dead," Mike said as he got up to them.

"It will take a lot to kill me, now listen, you keep the men here, no sense in any of you getting hurt."

"Timber you can't take all those men on by yourself, we are going to help you."

"No you're not. Now all of you stay here and keep an eye out for me. I figure all the outlaws are at the mine but some of them might not be, shout or fire that gun you're holding to alert me if any others show up."

As soon as Mike promised he would Timber took off for the mine entrance. He got so far then stopped at a pile of buckets and barrels where he took a good look at what the outlaws were doing and how many there were. What he needed now was an angle as there were too many for him to go in there gung ho. Looking around he then grinned as he saw just what he needed, it was just a question of getting it. To get to where it was meant him running across an open area of ground but then it wasn't that far. He waited until all the men he could see were looking away from him and then he ran over, a gun in his hand just in case. He dropped down again at a pile of boxes, and taking care not to be seen he reached into one and grabbed a handful of sticks. Then he moved around the cases out of sight and bent over he ran a few yards to the cliff face where there were piles of rock and soil no doubt from the mine that he could use as cover. Once there he lit a stick of dynamite and threw it at the mine entrance. It arched its way across the sky and fell right at the entrance where men were digging away. The explosion blew men into the air as well as bringing down soil and rocks again all around the entrance.

The men that were left covered their heads and ran off a few yards, which meant that Timber was able to pick another one of them off before they realized what was happening and dived for cover so they could return fire.

Jack and Doug had stayed away from the men working as they weren't going to get their hands dirty. Now they looked across the mine and saw where Timber was in total shock.

"How the heck did he get out of that mine?" Jack asked.

Doug was as amazed as he was, he shook his head, "He's a clever one and no mistake."

Jack huffed, "Clever maybe but not clever enough, he has himself boxed in now."

Doug looked at where Timber was by the cliff face and agreed with him, "Now we can finish him," Doug moved forward drawing his gun.

16

Jack had been beside himself with anger when he had seen his man throw the dynamite that blocked the mine entrance. He had been angry and pleased at the same time.

"That's trapped the Marshal in there and maybe killed him but now we gotta get it all dug out again," he said to him.

The man looked sheepish at Jack, "Better than having us all shot up."

"Maybe, we need the miners up here to dig it out."

The man looked unhappy knowing the miners had all fled having been let out of their cabins.

"Get down there Joe and help find them, I want them back up here," Jack had that crazy look n his eyes so Joe was happy to hurry away from him.

Joe ran off still happy with what he had done. He had been by the entrance and a possible target for Timber. He went on down to the cabins to check them again and he took a look at Marty who was now sitting up and holding his head. He shouted up to Jack about him then took a look at him.

"You gonna be okay Marty?" he asked.

"I guess, just give me a minute and I need a gun," Marty answered slowly.

"There are some over at the corral why don't you go get one, I'm looking for the miners?"

Marty said that he would do that. Joe was about to leave him when he saw a movement over at the vats which were near the corral.

"Hey, there are the miners. Come on Marty, you can get a gun there. I'll hold them up while you get one."

Marty struggled to get up then staggered along with Joe towards the miners. Joe helped him along some of the way, "This mining job is getting out of hand," Marty said, "That Marshal is sure getting to be a real pain and that's the truth."

"Maybe he is but he's not going to get out of there alive. He should be dead now in the mine," Joe said, "Come on we need these miners to go check for us," he hurried on with Marty as fast as he could.

Jeff Collins had been at the mine office most of the time. The only occasions he got back to town were when he had some of Jack's men along with him and then they would go to his house to stay where he lived alone. Now he was in the office having spent an uncomfortable night there as he often had to. The shooting and the explosions took him outside to the veranda to see what was going on. He was amazed to see the situation, the mine entrance blocked, dead men lying around and Jack with Doug shouting instructions out to the remaining men to clear the mine entrance and then other men running around shouting about the miners.

Something major had happened but he had no idea what it was. He wanted to talk to Jack about it but the man was far too busy for that. As he watched he saw Mike come around the vats with a group of men and he wondered what he was going to do. It looked like Mike had a gun but the others were unarmed apart from hand tools. It looked like they were going to join in with whatever was happening. He went back in the office to get the gun he kept in the drawer of his desk.

Mike was waiting for his chance. He longed to get back at the men who had caused them so much misery but he knew he had to take care so that none of the men with him got hurt. Looking around the valley he saw men running around and then two of the outlaws saw him. He stopped and was about to cry out when one of the miners threw a hammer at them. It was a very good throw and it hit Joe on his head knocking him down. Mike looked on as the men with him went over to get Marty who looked unsteady on his feet. He didn't fancy the man's chances against them.

Mike looked around for another man they could attack and saw two coming towards them and then suddenly they weren't there anymore as an explosion erupted right where they were. Timber had seen them going for the miners and had thrown a stick of dynamite their way.

Timber knew there weren't that many outlaws left. He drew both of his guns and looked for targets. He soon saw two men not far away who were coming towards him. The first one was easy as they had open ground between them. The other one dived down for cover as his friend fell. Then he tried to shoot Timber from where he was. Timber took his time and waited for him to show himself. The man raised up trying to get an aim on Timber. It was a big mistake and Timber was able to shoot him in his forehead.

Jack and Doug were up by the mine entrance, which was now partly cleared. They watched what was happening and got more angry and frustrated.

"That man has the luck of the devil," Doug said.

"Yeah he does, we need to take him out," Jack looked over to where Timber was crouched down hidden by waste from the mine.

"You got any ideas?"

"Maybe," Jack looked to see just how many men he had left. He didn't see any, "Seems like our time here has come to an end Doug. Come on, get your horse, I'm going to the office," Jack made off for the office keeping well out of Timber's sight. He didn't want a stick of dynamite coming his way. He was pleased he had his horse with him.

Doug went to the corral and got his horse but then he knew he had to keep Timber busy while Jack got their money from the office.

Jeff saw Jack coming towards the office from a window and put the gun into the belt of his trousers out of sight.

Jack leapt off his horse at the office and ran up the stairs. He burst into the office to find Jeff standing at the far end. He turned as Jack came in, "So what's happening now?"

"We got a problem."

"I'll say, it looks like a war zone out there,"

"That's exactly what it is," Jack strode across to a strong box and opened it.

Jeff watched him, "I'm guessing you're leaving now?"

"You got that right. You can have what's left of the mine."

Jeff had to smile, at last an outcome, "What's brought this about?"

"Would you believe one man?"

Jeff shrugged, "What kinda man?"

Jack stopped and turned to Jeff, "Marshal Jake Timber. I never saw a more determined man."

"He sounds like quite a guy."

"Don't you get any ideas now, he ain't about to get friendly with you any time soon."

Jeff was happy to take his chances; in fact he figured he would get on very well with a lawman.

Jack got busy taking sacks of money out of the strongbox then once his arms were full he headed for the door, "The mine is all yours," he said as he went out.

Doug wasn't happy at being left but he was determined to get rid of Timber. From where he was Timber wasn't that far away so he began to go over there keeping to cover as best as he could.

Timber looked around from the safety of where he was. It had gone quiet and he couldn't see any more outlaws. Then he saw Jack riding off for the office. He was about to go after him when from the corner of his eye he saw a movement. Looking towards it he saw Doug coming at him fast. Timber turned to shoot him but Doug had timed his run well and he leapt onto Timber causing him to drop his gun. Doug was then trying to trip Timber up as he grabbed hold of him. Timber was about as big as Doug and about the same weight so they were evenly matched. Timber managed to stay upright as he drove a knee up into Doug's groin. Doug stepped back as he went for his gun. Timber was ready for him and drew his. At the same time Doug launched himself forward colliding again with Timber. They both fell dropping their guns.

Doug rolled away then drew a knife and went again for Timber, "It's all over for you Marshal," he shouted as he ran.

Timber always carried a long hunting knife and he drew it from his belt. They squared up to each other both holding their knives out. Doug was confident; he had won many knife fights before and considered himself an expert. Timber had used a knife on occasions but usually relied on his guns. Now here they were both of them unable to search around for dropped guns as they looked at each other in the eye waiting for a chance to attack. Doug drove forward first just as Timber expected. For a big man Timber was light on his feet and nimble. He slid away to the side with no problems and lashed out with his knife at the same time drawing blood through Doug's shirt.

"We can end this Doug, just drop the knife and take a short spell in prison, you don't need to die," Timber said as Doug rounded on him again.

"Oh it's you who's gonna die," Doug said making a dash forward.

They grabbed each other's knife hands and it became a struggle and a trial of strength as they both tried to win over the other. Doug pulled Timber around hoping to trip him up while Timber started to twist Doug's arm to make him drop the knife. Doug began to feel that it could happen so he pulled back and almost fell over as his foot hit a rock. Timber fell into him as Doug released Timber's hand to save himself and Timber found his knife going deep into Doug's chest. Doug fell mortally wounded. Timber pulled his knife free as blood spurted from the wound. Doug looked down at it, then up at Timber before he collapsed into the dirt. Timber wiped his knife on Doug's shirt then retrieved his guns. It was time to go looking for Jack.

17

Jack had taken all the money from the office strongbox but he knew there was some purified silver still in the mine, which he intended to take as much as he could with him. It was obvious he couldn't keep on working the mine now. With nearly all of his men dead and the miners loose it was time to move on to someplace else. He stood on the veranda and took a look around. He was pleased to see two men at the bottom of the stairs.

"Hey Jack, we've been looking for you, that Marshal has sure taken a lot of us out."

Jack walked down the stairs pleased to see the two of them; Wayne and Bruce, "Doug is seeing to him right now," he called down, "I reckon it's time for us to go but I want to get the silver from the mine first, it would be a shame to leave it here."

"It sure would," Wayne was happy to hear that from Jack as he was keen to go as was Bruce.

Jack got down to them keeping a tight hold of the money bag, "Okay, I'll ride over to the mine, you two get your horses and meet me there."

The two men ran off while Jack mounted up.

Timber walked around the rocks and was about to whistle for

Scout when he saw Jack riding towards him and across to the mine while two other men were coming across the open ground. It made sense to Timber to wait for the two of them to get closer; he tucked himself away again among the rocks to wait for them.

Jack arrived at the mine entrance and looking down from there he was amazed to see Doug's body lying on the ground a few yards a away. So it was just the two men and him left. He hoped to be able to see to Timber once he had got what he wanted from the mine.

Timber watched as the two men changed course and went to the corral which told him they intended to ride out, well he could scupper those plans, he moved off towards them.

Mike had got the men with him to calm down and stay where they were as he figured they were pretty safe at the vats. He looked out and saw Jack ride to the mine entrance and Timber heading for the two men who were in the corral. There didn't seem to be any other men around so he thought about going to help Timber. It seemed a pretty safe bet so he got the men to go with him.

Timber got to the corral as the two men were saddling up, he got among the horses and close to them without them realizing he was there. Then he came in the open and challenged them.

"Going somewhere boys?" he called out.

They both turned to him shocked to hear his voice, Wayne was the closest to him and he called back.

"You the Marshal we've been hearing about?"

"That's me yeah, Jake Timber. I want you two to just drop your guns and put your hands where I can see them."

Wayne glanced at Bruce who nodded back to him then both of them went for their guns. Timber had already gotten hold of his and he brought both of them out. Before either of them could fire, Timber's right hand gun was spitting lead at Wayne taking him down. Bruce had been behind Wayne and he now came into view and stopped trying to aim at Timber seeing both of his guns pointing at him. He slowly lowered his gun back into its holster.

"It's all over for you now, so tell me what is it with this mine, does the man in the suit own it?"

Bruce glared at Timber then answered, "Jeff Collins yeah, course he ain't happy about us being here but then he don't seem that unhappy either."

"You saying he's in on something here?"

Bruce shrugged, "You'll have to ask him."

"I will, now I need you to drop that gun nice and easy."

Mike had decided to get over to Timber fast and help out, he was tired of waiting around. He hurried on with the other men behind him. As he approached the corral he called out, taking Timber's attention just for a second. It was the chance Bruce had been waiting for and he went again for his gun. It nearly worked as Timber had holstered his right hand gun and Bruce had seen that but he hadn't noticed Timber was still holding the one in his left hand which he now brought around so that just as Bruce cleared leather with his gun Timber shot him.

Mike came running into the corral with the other men, "Timber, are you okay?"

"Yeah, fine Mike. Keep a lookout for any more men will you and make sure any you see don't get away, there are some guns here for your men."

Timber left them there and started off for the mine entrance. He knew Jack was there somewhere having seen him ride up to the mine. With no one else to stop him Timber got to the mine entrance quickly. He stopped there at the side of the entrance to listen and take a peep around to see inside. The entrance now was a lot smaller than it had been but the outlaws had done well to open up a space to get into the mine. It was dark apart from a faint flicker which was obviously some way inside. Timber grabbed a lamp from the collection there and went in. He didn't light it yet but had it with him just in case he needed it. He carried it in his left hand while holding a gun in his right.

Jack had found some purified silver and he put it near the entrance ready to take away. He knew there was some more further in and figuring he had some time he went off to get it. He had just found some when he heard a noise. Looking back he could just see a shape at the entrance which disappeared as it came inside into the gloom. He shouted out asking who it was hoping it to be one of his men come to find him.

Timber shouted back at him, "It's Jake Timber Jack, U.S. Marshal. You're trapped in here just like I was so you may as well just give yourself up and come on out."

Jack had no intentions of being caught and he still figured the two men outside would come to his rescue so for a reply he fired two shots at where he thought Timber was. The shots came close to where Timber was standing beside the wall. He had his answer so it was now a question of winkling the man out of there. He wondered if Jack knew of any way out, were any of the holes being big enough? It was possible he would find the hole where he got out so he would have to follow him in to be sure he wouldn't get away. He fired a shot down the tunnel and then advanced a few yards to where there was a pile of stout poles he could take cover at.

Jack knew there were holes to the outside on the outside tunnel. He didn't know how big they were but it was worth trying them so he carried on deeper into the tunnel. He found a junction and took the outer one then he stopped to look back and listen. He could hear Timber some way behind him coming along so he risked another shot at him.

The shot went wide but it gave Timber a good idea of where Jack was and he could see the faint flicker of his lamp. He carried on stumbling along not daring to light his lamp but relying on the faint flicker from Jack's.

Jack got to where there was a small hole to the outside. It allowed a ray of light to enter the tunnel so he set the lamp down and tried the hole for size but he couldn't get his shoulders through. He also heard Timber getting close. He dropped down and fired at him again hoping to hit him.

Timber had seen the light in the tunnel from the hole as Jack had done and he narrowly avoided being hit by Jack's bullet. He got down onto the ground and fired back to keep Jack busy as he couldn't see exactly where he was. Jack wasn't about to go any further. He had some light and he figured Timber would keep on coming and show himself so he could kill him. He got down low and then as he saw a shape approaching he fired again.

Timber was lucky not to be hit and he dived to the ground again. Knowing now where Jack was he fired at him. The first two shots ricocheted off the rocks and hit the ceiling over Jack's head. As Jack fired back there was a groaning creaking noise then a few rocks fell around Jack. As Jack looked up a whole section of the ceiling came crashing down burying him completely. Timber watched open mouthed then realized it hadn't finished yet as more of the ceiling dropped closer to him. It was time to get out. He ran back as fast as he could as he heard rocks falling behind him. He could see the circle of light at the entrance so he dropped the lamp and ran for it, fearing to be buried as well as more rocks fell, the sounds telling Timber they were getting close to him. He got to the entrance and burst out just as there was a rumble as dust and rocks came flying out at him. He rolled on the ground then slowly got up. The mine entrance was gone again to be replaced by a pile of rocks. He dusted himself down with his hat as Mike and the men with him came running up.

"That was close Timber, where's Jack?"

Timber nodded to the mine, "In there."

18

Mike sent men up to where Casey was still hiding out and brought him down with the miners then together they began to clean everywhere up of dead bodies. As soon as Timber was ready he got up on Scout and rode off to the office. As he got there he saw Jeff coming out.

"Not had a chance to talk before but I'm guessing you are Jeff Collins," Timber said as he climbed up the stairs to him.

"Marshal Timber, Jack told me about you."

"I bet he did, we need to talk," Timber got right up to him and stood waiting.

Jeff could see Timber wasn't going to move out of his way so he sighed and went back in the office. Timber followed him in.

"I'm guessing Jack is dead?"

"Yeah and all the rest of the Crazy Jack's. So we need to straighten this out just what was going on here."

Jeff gave him a look before going behind his desk and sitting down heavily into his chair. Timber remained standing up a few feet back from him.

"Word is Jeff that there were two of you who owned this mine, where's the other man?" Timber asked.

"James was killed by Crazy Jack because he wouldn't agree to his terms."

Timber nodded, "Just what were his terms?"

"That we carry on getting silver ore out of the mine, purify it and sell it on in town with Jack and his men getting most of the money for it, only without paying the miners to do it and obtaining more labor to get a lot done quicker as Jack was in a hurry not to hang around here too long."

"So you still made something from it?"

"Of course, it is my mine. Jack wanted all of the silver but I worked a deal with him in that I'd do the arrangements for the sale."

"Just where did you store the purified silver?"

"It wasn't stored anywhere much. There was a small amount in the mine but mostly as soon as it was ready it was taken off to town."

"To the assay office?"

"Yes that's right."

"Then sold by Jacob."

"Yes that's how it worked."

"And he got his cut?"

"Of course."

"I've met the miners who dug it out and prepared it and they sure aren't happy with the arrangement. It still seems a bit much to kill James for that, was there no other way?"

Jeff squirmed around on his chair, "Jack didn't see one. James was very pig headed."

"He must have been, where is he now?"

Jeff squirmed around again, "Jack left his body over at the spoil dump."

"You know what gets me Jeff, is why you are still here? Why you were in conversations with Jack and why you didn't get away and bring the law in if he was stealing all the silver?"

"It wasn't that easy Timber. There were men with me all the time."

"All the time?"

"Some nights I had to stay right here in this office. If I went home they went with me."

"You expect me to believe that in all this time you couldn't have made a run for it or got word out somehow?"

Jeff was getting red in the face, "Hell Timber, they were crazy killers, what was I to do?"

Timber studied Jeff for a few moments, "How about you just tell me the truth Jeff, it will go a lot easier on you?"

Jeff was pleased he'd got the gun from his drawer and shoved in his belt. His hand went to it thinking he may well need it soon, "The truth, why I just told you the truth."

"This purified silver, you had it checked out at the Assay office in Little Bend."

"Yes, what of it?"

"That man is as bent as a screw eyed skunk."

Jeff stared at Timber as his fingers closed around the butt of his gun, "I don't know a thing about that. He always seemed okay to me."

"I don't doubt it. I'll be interested in talking to him later."

"Look Timber, I was between a rock and a hard place. Jack would have killed me if'n I hadn't gone along with him."

Timber looked at him waiting.

"Okay yeah I had to agree to certain things to stay alive. The idea was to work with him and get the silver sold off so he could take the money, him and his men. The miners and men he roped in to work here weren't going to get anything. In return I stayed alive and kept the mine after they had gone."

"Not much of that left now. You are still an accomplice to the murder of James and kidnap of the workers, maybe there'll be other charges in due course." Timber was watching Jeff very carefully.

Jeff sat back in his chair as though resigned to his fate, "So what happens now?"

"Now you come with me back to the sheriff's office in Little Bend where we can straighten this whole thing out."

Jeff could imagine what charges would be brought forward especially as the whole story hadn't been told yet, he decided to try his luck. His hand closed around the butt of the gun and he brought it out and over the desk to aim at Timber but he was way too slow.

Timber was very experienced in such things and his gun was aimed at Jeff's heart before he could aim his gun.

"Just put it down Jeff, I'd hate to have to kill you."

Jeff sighed again and put it on the desk then he stood up, "Let's go and get this finished."

Timber followed Jeff down the stars to find Mike and a few other men waiting there, all of them now armed with the outlaws guns.

"You got him then Timber," Mike said.

"Yeah, I got him, you hold him here for a spell okay," Timber turned and walked back up to the office. After a while he came down again.

"We can get off to Little Bend now," he said taking hold of Jeff.

On the way to town Timber left the men to take Jeff with them while he went off to visit Don's farm again. He rode up to find both Don and Maggie waiting for him.

"I was hoping you would come back for the mens bodies from the shed Timber," Don called to him as Timber rode up.

"I said I would," Timber answered as he dismounted.

"Yeah I know but we wondered if you'd get back here alive."

"Here I am."

"And we're very pleased to see you," Maggie told him.

Timber went to get the bodies while Maggie and Don prepared the outlaws horses. As soon as he was ready to go Timber said, "You'll have no bother here now," then he was up on Scout and leading the two horses away.

Later that day found Timber in the sheriff's office with Nathanial and Mike while Jeff was locked in a cell. Timber had asked Nathanial to write out bounty tickets for him and had taken the bodies down to the undertaker. He also had the sheriff write out other bounty tickets for him on those men they agreed that Timber had taken out.

They all talked about what had happened while Nathanial took notes. Jeff conceded his involvement in kidnap and James's murder in return for a shorter sentence.

"The mine will have to be closed down," Nathanial said, "Until all the legal proceedings have been completed."

That didn't worry Jeff; there was nothing to go back there for anyway. Once that was all done Timber excused himself and took a walk down the street to the Assay office. He walked in to find the same man behind the counter. Jacob looked up at him and gave a sly grin as he waited for Timber to walk over to him.

Timber stopped right in front of him, "Jeff Collins is locked up at the sheriff's office."

Jacob glared at him, "So, what's that got to do with me?"

"Oh I reckon quite a lot. You valued the silver."

"Sure you know that."

"And then you sold it on?"

Jacob shuffled his feet, "So what of it?"

"There is no proof of any transactions between you. All I could find was a list of silver sold at prices higher than they should be, now why was that?"

Jacob didn't know what to say, he shook his head.

"It wouldn't be for you to cream off a fat fee and get more money for the silver for Jeff because there were no taxes or fees being paid?"

Jacob gave a silly grin and tried to laugh it off before Timber reached across the counter and grabbed him by his shirtfront and almost dragged him over it.

"You're coming with me, you can keep Jeff company in the next cell then you can explain where the money went and who bought the silver," Timber pulled him out of the office and took him to Nathanial.

That night was a happy one in Little Bend. Everyone who was anyone was there in Grady's Saloon and the man of the moment was Timber. He had all his drinks paid for and was given all the food he wanted. It was very late when he got to his bed at the hotel. The next morning though he was up at dawn as usual. He took breakfast at a cafe then shortly after he was riding Scout out of town.

Don saw him approaching well before he was close. Maggie joined him and waited for Timber to ride up to them.

"I hope you bring good news?" Dona asked.

"None better," Timber said as he dismounted.

Maggie gave him a big smile and waved him to sit on the porch with them. Timber was pleased to do so out of the burning sun. They waited for Timber to speak.

"The outlaws are all dead. The mine is closed and the owner Jeff Collins is in jail, so you can relax here it's all over."

Now that is good news," Don said. He waved a finger and went in the house. He came out again with a bottle of whiskey and a handful of glasses, "This calls for a celebration."

When Timber rode off it was as inebriated as he had ever been and it was a feeling he wasn't used to. It would fade, until then he kinda liked it. He reached into a short pocket and brought out the wanted notice he had left. He'd had it when he arrived in Little Bend, now it was time to go looking for the outlaw whose picture was on the notice.

THE END

VOLUME THREE

CONSPIRACY IN THE LONE STAR

1

The town of Idle Butte wasn't that big but it was a bustling place. Situated as it was with cattle ranches all around that wasn't surprising and no doubt it would get bigger as it was doing day by day. However building work had slowed down and that was all because of one man. Carlton McAllister was a cattle baron. He owned a lot of land with many more cattle on it than a man could count in a month. The thing was that he wasn't happy with that, not by a long way. He wanted the town, the farms, and the land all around as well and he paid bad men good money to get it for him. Right in the middle of the main street a part of that was being arranged by two of his strong-arm men against a storeowner.

Nash Hanson had built the store himself and stocked it with his hard earned money from towns to the east. There was no way he was just going to hand over any of the money he earned from selling his wares to anybody just like that.

Rowdy Brogan was arguing it out with him, "You know Nash this could go easy or it could go hard, your choice."

Nash looked up at him. He was a lot shorter than Rowdy and definitely a whole lot weaker. Rowdy was built like a brick outhouse and it would take as much force to knock him over as the outhouse. He had black hair that could hardy fit under his hat and a stubble to go with it. Nash then looked to the man standing next to him. He was nearly as bad. Cole Henderson wasn't as big as Rowdy but not that far off either. Both of them were the best that Carlton employed. Both men wore a Colt .44 strapped to their waist and tied down over black trousers. Both men wore white shirts as if they were a uniform under leather waistcoats and from where Nash was standing they virtually blocked the sun out from him, but still Nash wasn't moving, he still refused to pay up.

Rowdy was losing his patience, "Now look here Nash. You know the arrangement. You give us twenty five percent of your profits and we make sure you don't get any bother and we ensure no Indians or outlaws come to get anything from the town either."

"You give me bother. You give me bother every week coming to my store and wanting my profits," Nash turned to nod at the general store behind him where the two men had stopped him when he had come outside.

"That's not very polite Nash," Cole said in that slow annoying way he had, "Just pay up."

"You know what, I'm not going to. Not this time, not ever so there," Nash stood with his legs apart and his hands on his hips showing his defiance of any arrangement Carlton McAllister had made.

Cole carried on, "You know the boss gives the town a cow every so often. A full cow so you can all have a party, yeah right out on the street here, to show his appreciation."

Nash was only too well aware of the cow McAllister gave now and then, "I don't care if he gives each and every one of us a full cow every week, I ain't paying you fellas another godamn cent."

Cole looked at Rowdy and Rowdy looked at him then Rowdy looked back at Nash and he pointed a finger at him, "Now that is downright rude Nash. I'm warning you now, we want that money and we ain't going nowhere without it."

"You go anywhere you damn well like, I don't care."

Rowdy glanced at Cole again and then he sent a ham sized closed fist straight into Nash's face. The blow sent Nash off his feet to land a few yards further away on his back with a crushed nose and a broken jaw. Blood spurted out in a fountain over his face, what was left of it.

"I did warn you Nash, he said as he rubbed his knuckles, "Come on Cole we'll get it ourselves." Both men just left Nash lying there in the dirt unable to get himself up while they went in the store and raided the cash tin Nash kept under the counter. They then picked a few things from the shelves that they took a liking to before walking out again. Nash was still lying where he was. A few people had come close but none of them would go to Nash while the two men were around.

"See you around Nash," Rowdy said as they walked past him to their horses. Once they had gone the people standing around ran over to him and helped him up.

"Oh my, Nash," John Walker said to him as he knelt beside him. John owned a barbershop and he'd had Rowdy go to him as well but he had paid up, "We gotta get him to the doc," he said trying to get him up. Two other men joined in and helped to half carry him to the doctor's office.

As the doctor stitched him up he told Nash he should go to the sheriff.

"Huh, some sheriff he is why old Don Johnson ain't gonna do nothin' he never does. Why sometimes I reckon he's in with those dirty coyotes."

"I'd still go see him, when you feel up to it that is," the doctor told him as he carried on working on him."

"I'll consider it," Nash replied through the pain he was receiving.

"It was the following day before Nash was able to go over to sheriff Don Johnson's office. He stood and told him all about him being attacked as Don just sat in his chair on the opposite side of his desk.

"You know I can't go up against them two hoodlums Nash. I'd get the same as you and probably worse."

'What kind of sheriff are you Don? We need those men stopping."

Don cocked his head and sucked in his cheeks, "I knows that Nash. But until I get some help around here it ain't gonna happen."

"So what help are you waitin' on?"

"I've sent for a marshal and some men to come on over here, they'll sort them out you'll see."

Nash shook his head as he leaned on the desk for support, "Well I don't know Don, those men better get here soon or we're all done for," Nash slowly made his way to the door and went out.

Don Johnson sat up straight and grinned as he watched him go.

2

Nash was going to take some time to recover. Luckily he was married and his wife took over the store. She had been horrified to see him when he came back in helped by the two men. She took him in the back and made him tell her all about it, then she let him rest while she saw to the customers who came in although most of them were in there just to ask how Nash was holding up.

Carlton McAllister or his men had approached most of the businesses in town and they always started off friendly explaining the benefits of joining the scheme as they called it. It was only if the businessmen decided not to join that they got aggressive sometimes extremely so that one way or another everyone who was asked to join did so. They all knew it was a farce and a scam but Carlton McAllister wanted it that way so he could argue his case if it ever came to him needing to.

The talk about Nash was soon all over the town with everyone being angry and upset over it. If it could happen to Nash then it could happen to any one of them. Ten of them got together and stormed off to see the sheriff. He wasn't pleased to have so many angry townsfolk in his office at once all wanting to know what he was going to do about McAllister and his men?

Don Johnson got up from his desk and waved his arms at them pushing them back from him, "Now just hold on there folks, just what do you expect me to do?"

"Why go out there and arrest McAllister of course," John shouted back at him.

"And get myself killed? Look I have already said that I have asked for the marshal to come over here with some men to straighten this all out, I cant do it alone, unless you all wanna go out there and help me," he added.

That stopped them as none of them wanted to risk doing that, "We got families Don," one of them said, "we can't go doing that."

"And neither can I. You all just keep a low profile until the marshal comes."

"And just when will that be?" John asked him.

"Oh I dunno, when he gets here I suppose, now go on get out of my office," Johnson pushed them all out amid a lot of grumbling from them. Once they were gone he went back to his desk, opened a drawer and took out a bottle of whiskey from which he poured a generous measure into a glass. He put he feet up on his desk, had a little chuckle to himself and drained the glass.

Don knew that McAllister hardly ever came to town and it was rare that he met him, which suited him very well. So long as the money kept on coming in he didn't care. Don had met up with McAllister on one of his rare visits to Idle Butte when the man had made a point of calling in on him. He had laid down straight away what the situation was and gave Don a choice; let his men have their way around town or get shot. Don chose to turn a blind eye to their activities.

It wasn't as though McAllister just wanted the town. In fact that was just a bonus for him. What he really wanted was the farms outlying his land and the other ranches that bordered up to it. Over time he was building up a team of paid men to get it all for him.

3

Jake Timber had been riding for a few days now. He had come out of Eagle Pass having thwarted a gang of Road Agents there and now he was on the trail again in search of any man who had a bounty on his head or any other outlaw, bandit or wrongdoer he could find.

That had been his job for some time now and one he had gotten into very well. It paid him well along with ridding Texas of as many bad men as he could. The territory governor, The Honorable Robert Pierce Fullerton had given him the task and had authorized him to do it in any way he chose. He had given Timber a badge and the necessary papers to prove it. He was heading east away from the border and back into the territory he was used to. This was wide-open land with grass for cattle of which he saw a lot of as he rode along. He knew cattle ranching was a big thing in these parts.

He was pretty much always alone. He didn't mind being alone, he was alone most of the time as he didn't much like having company with him so it was a good thing he was happy with his own company, that and his faithful big bay horse; Scout. He often talked to him and he could swear that the horse understood every single goddamn word. So it was that he carried on and came across the town of Idle Butte.

As he rode in he could see it was a reasonably sized place and there seemed to be a lot of building work started so the place was prospering and that was no doubt down to the cattle. The main street was wide enough to turn a wagon around on and it was dry and dusty which was better than the mud the streets often turned to when it rained. Timber rode on looking for the sheriff's office. It had become somewhat of a habit for him to go and check the sheriff out first. He was most likely to know if there were any outlaws in the area or at least have some wanted notices for Timber to take a look at. Before he got there he saw a confrontation taking place with loud words being spoken as he rode past a saloon. It sounded bad so Timber stopped and looped Scout's reins around the hitch rail to go and see what all the fuss was about.

He stopped just inside the door to let his eyes adjust to the dim light then he saw what he took to be the bartender in a deep conversation with two men in the middle of the room.

"You can't just keep on taking money off me like this, it's ruining my business here Rowdy," Timber heard the bartender say.

In front of him with their backs to Timber were two men, two big men. Timber stayed where he was to hear more of the conversation.

"Maybe you should work harder to sell more booze," Rowdy told him.

The bartender shrugged his shoulders his anger showing through, "It's hard enough to sell what I need to survive never mind you taking more off me and for what? Nothing that's what."

"It looks like you need some persuading," Rowdy said stepping closer to him.

"Why don't you try and persuade me first?" Timber called over to him.

Rowdy and Cole turned around to look at him. Rowdy saw what he took to be a mountain man in deerskins, scruffy, needing a shave and he didn't see any threat from him although the man was nearly as big as him and was wearing twin guns. He laughed at him as did Cole then he took a pace forward.

"You wanna make something of this fella?" he snarled at Timber.

Timber shrugged, "Why not? I'm sure the bartender won't mind my standing in for him."

Rowdy couldn't believe his ears. No one had ever spoken to him like that. He gave a big smile as he called back, "Okay, no guns, just me and you," Rowdy intended to throttle Timber to death in his hands not just shoot him down to show how big and strong he was to the men in the saloon watching.

Timber was going to announce who he was but then changed his mind. It wouldn't make any difference to men like these anyway, he just stood his ground, "Whenever you're ready, but make it soon, I ain't got all day to toss the breeze with the likes of you."

Rowdy's mouth opened in surprise at the comment. He glanced at Cole and waved a hand to tell him to keep out of it then he stepped forward his arms curling out ready to encompass Timber but he didn't get that far. As Rowdy then advanced a lot faster Timber kicked out with a size thirteen leather boot with steel toe caps. It connected exactly with Rowdy's knee cap with a sharp snapping sound that reduced Rowdy to a shivering wreck on the floor screaming out and trying to support his broken knee.

Cole was amazed and instinctively went for his gun to shoot Timber but he was way too slow. Timber was already drawing both of his guns at the same time, a well practiced maneuver and he shot the gun out of Cole's hand taking most of his fingers with it. Both men were now screaming in pain as blood began to pool on the saloon floor.

Timber was pointing a gun at both of them, "Now I suggest you help each other and crawl back to the hole you came out of."

Neither man was able to talk back at him and it took Cole a lot of doing to get Rowdy up so he could lean against him to hobble out the saloon, no doubt heading for the doctor's office.

Timber holstered his guns amid smiles and clapping from the men in there.

"Well done," one man shouted, "It's about time those two got their comeuppance."

"Just what's going on here?" Timber asked.

The bartender walked over to him, "Mister that was quite something. Why I ain't seen nothing like it before, who are you?"

Timber pulled a badge from a pocket in his deerskin shirt and held it up for all to see, "The name's Jake Timber I'm a U.S. Marshal and it looks like I got here just in time."

"You can say that again," the bartender paused a moment, "You figure on staying around a while?"

"You think I oughta?"

Several men came forward all talking at once. Timber had to hold his hands up and call for them to talk one at a time. The bartender called for silence then had them speak as he pointed to them. Gradually Timber learned about Carlton McAllister and what he was up to.

"We would sure appreciate your help Timber in getting rid of McAllister," the bartender said to him when they had all had their say.

Timber pursed his lips and thought for a minute, "I'd need to know more."

"More? What more is there to know," a man asked him.

"I've always found its good to get all the information you can before taking action."

Another man thought that was a good idea, "You do that Timber. I just hope your actions don't bring more trouble to us."

"I'll sure do my best to avoid that. I'd better go start but I'll have a beer first."

The bartender rushed to give him one on the house. Timber sat and heard more stories from the men in there then once he had all the information he could get he finished his beer and walked out.

4

Out on the sidewalk Timber looked around for any more of McAllister's men now he knew that they came in town to run a protection racket. He didn't see anyone who looked like they might be and anyway he had been told that it was normally just Rowdy and Cole. He began to go down the businesses one by one asking them to tell him their experiences, who had been to see them and when. It was while he was walking along when he saw a young woman come out of a shop and a man followed her, they were having some kind of an argument.

With what he had found out so far he carried on up to them. The man was standing with his back to him while the woman was behind him. Timber carried on until he was just a couple of feet away from him. He didn't look to be one of McAllister's men judging by the suit he was wearing. He waited to catch some of what was being said.

"The woman was angry, "Look I've told you before, so for the last time just leave me alone, okay?"

"But..." was all the man said before Timber interrupted.

"You heard the lady mister now just you leave her alone."

The man turned around as he stepped to one side so Timber could now see the two of them. The woman was a lot younger than him but mature, she was especially attractive with shiny almost black hair around her face to fall in curls about her shoulders. Her face was long and sculptured and she looked agitated. Timber took to her in an instant. The man was a different matter. He was well overweight with hardly any hair at all. He looked untidy, scruffy even although he was clean-shaven. That just helped to show off his mean ugly face.

"I'll thank you to mind your own business," he said to Timber as he was about to turn around again.

"I'm making it my business, now leave off or I'll make you."

The man turned around again, "Do you know who I am?" he asked rather indignantly.

"Yeah, I know who you are. A fat busy body who's bothering this lady now move those big feet of yours," Timber took a menacing step towards him and the man stepped back nearly tripping over the step of the shop. He stumbled awkwardly then walked off the sidewalk grumbling and shaking a finger.

The woman laughed, "Thanks mister. Oh look at him?"

"I'll shake more than his finger if he bothers you again miss," Timber said but his eyes were on her.

She turned back to him and looked up into his face, "Who do I have to thank for my rescue?" she asked with a smile.

Timber tipped his hat, "Jake Timber, U.S. Marshal."

"Oh I'm honored. Sarah McAllister," she said still looking straight at him.

Timber cocked his head to one side, "McAllister as in...?"

Sarah sighed, "Yes as in Carlton McAllister, he's my step father."

Timber stopped to take that in and was about to move off when she continued, "But I don't have anything to do with him. I don't like him, in fact I hate him. That was his cheap busy body he has spying everywhere for him, Elias Sykes, a horrid little man."

Timber couldn't deny he was horrid, "I see. I have heard some stories today about your step father."

"I can imagine," she had turned to watch Elias waddle off but now she turned again to Timber, "But you're a Marshal, have you come to arrest him?"

Timber had to smile at her serious face, "No, well not yet. I need to find out more and look into things here first."

"We should talk," Sarah looked around then said, "Would you like to talk there is a cafe just along here...?"

"Sure, why not," Timber stepped beside her and let her lead the way to a cafe which was small and intimate just the place to sit quietly and discuss things.

They sat almost facing each other at a table and Timber ordered coffee for both of them. Then he waited for Sarah to begin.

"What do I call you, Marshal or..."

"Timber will do just fine."

"Well Timber. I know a lot about what Carlton is up to. He's a very pig headed man and no one can tell him anything he doesn't want to know."

"So what does he want to know, or do?"

Sarah took a drink of her coffee before she answered. Timber noted that she was wearing a long green dress that matched her eyes much as they did his.

"It's hard to know for sure what he wants. He has always been a keen businessman since before I met him. He owns a ranch a few miles out of town; it's a big one but he always wants to add on to it. He has this thing about money too although goodness knows he has enough of it already but when anyone mentions it he always says you can never have too much and he goes after more. He'll never spend it all of course."

"So why does he keep on accumulating it?"

Sarah looked at him, "Honestly, I don't know. He married my mother when my father died. He was a farmer and a good one. The funny thing was he got bitten by a rattler and died. Mother couldn't be without someone with her so when Carlton began calling round flashing his money she just went with it. Oh Carlton was sweetness and light to begin with but gradually he changed into the monster he is now. He has men working for him, bad men, gunslingers and hard men who will do anything for a buck. They do all his dirty work for him. I wonder sometimes if he knows all the things they get up to," she saw the question in Timber's eyes before she asked so she carried on, "Mother died of consumption a year back. I couldn't stand things at the ranch after that with the new wife he found all to quickly who hated me being there so I moved away. I've been over in Dallas but I've come back to visit friends I have here to see if they are okay, only for a little while though now I see how things still are at the Royal Oak Ranch."

"A grand sounding name."

"For a grand looking ranch. He has everything there and its all top grade stuff too."

Timber pursed his lips, "He lives well then?"

"Very well, unlike the men who work for him or the folk in this town with his rackets and scams."

"A real charmer by the sound of him."

"Yes but there's something more Timber, I can feel it."

Timber waited for her to carry on.

"He's up to something else I know."

"In what way?"

"I don't know, it's just the way he spoke to me when we met briefly when he saw me off the stagecoach here. I need to know what it is."

"Well if you need help, I'm here."

Sarah smiled at him, "That would be wonderful thanks, but how?"

"We start by doing what I was doing, asking around, try to get some leads."

Sarah smiled at him, "Okay thanks, looks like we are a team."

"You bet, let's get started," Timber got up and dropped a bill on the table.

5

Timber found Sarah to be very useful in finding out things. As they walked around town he realized that she knew quite a few people. Some of them weren't friendly at all, distrustful of the family connection but fortunately, probably due to Sarah's open friendly personality most people they met were happy to talk to them. One person in particular had things to say.

"McAllister sure is draining this town but isn't he more interested in getting more land?"

Sarah had to agree with that, "He has always said he wants as much land as he can get," she said turning to Timber.

"Then maybe we should ride out and see if any land owners to his boundaries have had any bother from him?"

Sarah only had to consider that for an instant, "Okay sure yeah let's do that,' she thanked the man for the idea then stood with Timber as the man walked off, "My horse is at the livery stable."

"Fine, I'll get Scout and walk along with you."

"Okay, I'll wait here."

"No need," Timber gave a whistle and Scout pulled on the special knot Timber had used on the hitch rail and trotted over to him.

"My that's some well trained horse you have there," Sarah said impressed.

"Oh he knows more than that," Timber said taking his reins and walking along with Sarah to the stable, "You know any of the rancher's around your step father's ranch?" Timber asked her.

"Some yeah, most probably. I guess we should visit the ones I really do know first."

"That would be good and take me past McAllister's spread, I wanna see it for myself."

"Sure, no problem."

Sarah's horse turned out to be a black gelding smaller than Scout. Timber waited while she saddled up then they rode out together for the first ranch which was owned by Joe Caruthers. It was nowhere near as big a place as McAllister's but still covered a lot of acres. Joe was busy doing some branding when Timber and Sarah arrived. He knew Sarah from previous visits so he stopped work and went over to them.

"Sarah, howdy it's been a while," he said as he got to them.

"Sure has Joe. I have a friend with me, this here's Jake Timber, he's a marshal."

Joe looked up at him surprised, "A marshal huh, you come to arrest me," he laughed.

"No sir, we're here looking for information," Timber answered.

"Oh, what kind of information, I'll help if'n I can?"

"Its about Carlton Joe. We think he might be up to something regarding land and we wondered if you'd been approached about it?" Sarah said.

"About land, well no. I got mine here and it does join onto your step pa's,' he stopped then squinted up at them in the bright sunlight, "You think he might have thoughts on getting it for himself?"

"It's only a thought Joe," Timber said, "we just gotta check things out. He has the town pretty well sown up."

"I know about that, a bad thing. Carlton has enough not to need to be doing that."

"Yeah well, if he or his men call round asking let us know," Timber began to swing Scout around to ride out.

Sarah gave a farewell to Joe and rode out with Timber.

The next ranch they came to was more interesting. Sarah took Timber to one owned by an older man. Frank Willis was getting on in years and he had no one to leave his ranch to as his only son had died recently from a heart attack. Sarah made the introductions again and Timber asked the question.

"Now ain't that strange. I done got asked that very question just yesterday."

Timber grinned, now they were getting somewhere, "Care to tell us about it?"

"Sure thing. A couple of McAllister's men came to see me, asked how I was getting on and all and did I want to sell up to him?"

"What did you say?"

"I said I'd think on it. Is there more I ought to know?"

"Only that McAllister may be trying to get land, did they talk money?"

"Hmm well they gave a price yeah, but I would never sell out for that. I figured if they really wanted it they would up the ante?"

Timber didn't think that would happen, if they come again give an excuse, say you need more time, we need to look into what he is up to."

"If you say so, it seems odd to me though."

"Don't you worry Frank, we'll get back to you," Sarah said as they left.

It was a similar story at other ranches they called at. Apart from one. Alex Hughes, place wasn't that big but it bordered onto McAllister's at an important place. If McAllister had the land he could move his cattle more easily out of the area. Sarah explained this to Timber as they rode so they were keen to hear what Alex had to say.

Timber found Alex to be a slow talking sensible kinda man. They told him the reason for their visit and he took a deep breath before speaking.

"Yeah, I had a couple of men call round a couple of days back. They tried to convince me to sell the whole damn ranch to them. They said McAllister would pay the going price."

"Did they give you a price?" Timber asked.

Alex paused to spit on the ground well to the side then he turned back, "The price they offered wouldn't even cover the cost of the house, so I sent them on their way."

"Did they say if they'd be back?" Sarah asked him.

"Yeah, as a matter of fact they did. In two or three days time they said McAllister wanted the land and that he would get it eventually. "

"You just hang in there Alex, I'm working on straightening this all out," Timber said.

Sarah and Timber left him and talked about it as they headed back to town.

"McAllister is certainly looking to buy them out but at rock bottom prices," Timber said.

"Yeah, it seems like Carlton is after more land all right," Sarah said.

"I wonder what he's prepared to do to get it," Timber added.

Sarah gave him a look before answering, "I have an idea it will be whatever it takes."

Timber had no argument with that. They rode on pretty much in silence, each with their own thoughts. When they arrived back in town Timber told Sarah he wanted to go visit the sheriff.

"Don Johnson? You'll be wasting your time there Timber."

"Now why might that be?"

"Well he's a lazy good for nothing that's why. In fact it wouldn't surprise me if he was in Carlton's pocket."

"That doesn't sound like a very good opinion of him, I'll go see him anyway."

"Okay whatever. I'll be heading to the hotel. I'm figuring on staying a night or two before I go home."

"And home's in Dallas."

Sarah grinned at him as she answered, "I've been living with an aunt at her place over in Dallas, a few days stagecoach ride from here."

"Okay, I'll check out the sheriff then call on you later. I'll be looking for a room there myself."

"You do that, maybe we can eat together."

Timber doffed his hat and left her to ride on to the sheriff's office.

6

Timber found the office and leaving Scout at the hitch rail he went inside. Don Johnson was idly cleaning a rifle at his desk. He looked up at Timber.

"Can I help you Mister?" he asked.

"It's more that I can help you," Timber said as he showed the sheriff his Marshal badge," Jake Timber."

Don was intrigued, "I don't quite understand you marshal, how do you think you can help me?"

"Oh with a certain rancher in these parts who has a protection racket that I know of and is intimidating other ranchers to sell up to him, and that's just the things I know about."

Don nodded his head, his mind working overtime, "If you are referring to Mister Carlton McAllister then I'm afraid you're mistaken marshal, he's just a clever businessman."

"He's clever I'll give you that, and maybe he's a businessman too but there's no doubt that he is involved in unlawful activities."

"No how'd you figure that?" Don was thinking hard and trying to buy time.

"I know he employs men here to work a protection racket because I've met two of them who won't be working for a spell."

"Ah it was you then at the saloon."

"You heard about it then, so why didn't you take those boys down?"

Don knew he wouldn't have been able to if he'd wanted to. Looking at Timber he had to wonder how he had done it. Sure he was a big man not as big as Rowdy and to take him and Cole together, well that was some feat. Timber looked more like a drifter or a mountain man than a lawman, that was until he looked up into the man's face then he changed his mind, "As I said, I figured they were just conducting business."

"If you are as naive as that Johnson you shouldn't be wearing that star and if you're not that naive I still reckon you shouldn't be wearing it."

"Look Timber, I'm one man here. I can't take down McAllister."

"I'll tell you what you do, first off you don't tell McAllister I'm here. I want that to be a surprise for him. Second when I call for you to help you come a running, otherwise we might not get on too well," Timber didn't wait for his answer, he just walked out the door. He rode Scout down to the livery stable and got him booked in for the night then he walked on from there to the hotel where he went straight up to the desk. A scrawny man was standing behind it.

"A room for tonight," Timber said.

"Just the one night?"

"For now."

"Okay Mister, if you could just sign in here," The clerk spun a register around for him and left him while he looked for a key on a board.

"A room with a street view," Timber said as he wrote.

The clerk turned to him, "Those rooms are more expensive."

"Whatever, give me one."

The clerk changed the key and took the money off Timber, "You want anything else?"

"Yeah, which room is Sarah McAllister in?"

The clerk pulled a face, "Well I shouldn't..."

Timber had to flash his badge then the clerk told him. As it happened she was in the room right next door.

Timber got settled in his room and checked the view from the window then he went and knocked on Sarah's door. She answered it almost immediately.

"What kept you?" she asked.

"Oh I had that chat with the sheriff and I took Scout to the stables. I see your horse is there too."

"Yes, Bill Hodges is the hostler there, he's a good man, your horse will be well looked after."

"I'm glad to hear it. Well are we gonna eat or not?"

Sarah smiled at him and stepped out of the room, "I know a good place to go," she said leading the way.

"So long as they have steak that'll be fine."

The restaurant Sarah chose was the best place in town and soon they were sitting down with plates of food. They both had steak, potatoes and gravy. They finished the food before they began to talk again.

"So what brought you to Idle Butte?" Sarah asked as she stirred her coffee.

"I just drifted in here I guess."

"But you're not a drifter, why would a marshal just drift into here?"

Timber sat closer to her, "I can understand your doubts Sarah but I am who I say I am."

"I have no doubts about that Timber, just why come here?"

Timber took a sip of his coffee before he answered, "I have a job to do Sarah it was given to me by the territory governor. He wants me to help clean Texas up so he can apply for membership to the Union as a safe outlaw free state."

"That sounds like quite a job."

"It sure is, but I've been doing it for quite a while now. I seem to find trouble pretty easily."

"And now you have your sights on Carlton."

"You got a problem with that?"

"No way, he is a hateful bully of a man, he deserves all that's coming to him."

Timber quizzed her some more about her step father and became convinced that she was genuine in her feelings for him. Time passed by until they decided to leave. Timber offered to take her for a drink but she refused, preferring to go back to her hotel room. The night was still young and Timber took himself off to a saloon for a beer before turning in. He found one he liked and ordered his drink at the bar then he found a table and sat down. His entrance hadn't gone unnoticed.

A man in particular watched him sit down. He waited a while to see if anyone went to him but no one did so it was time for him to make his move. He had been propping the end of the bar up but now he walked slowly and steadily towards Timber's table.

Timber had taken a pack of cards from a pocket intending to have a quiet game of Solitaire when he saw the man approaching. Timber was never really at rest; he was always alert for who might come up on him. A lot of men had and there were not many left to tell the tale. He watched as the man got closer. From under his hat he took in the size of the man, the swagger, the tied down gun. He looked pretty well dressed so he must make money somehow. He had a chiseled face and he looked to be sure of himself. Timber let him come on as he slowly put the cards away again.

The man had been informed about Timber being in town and that he could prove to be a real nuisance so he had been asked to prevent him from doing that, in fact to prevent him from doing anything again, ever. The man had no name and never gave it out. He walked to within a few feet of Timber then stopped. He took a good look at him and smiled.

Timber took a good look at the man but he didn't smile. He waited for him to speak.

"You know mister we've had nosy busy bodies in town before,"

"You looking at me?" Timber answered.

"Sure I'm looking at you. I reckon you should just get back to the hills where your kind belong."

"My kind?"

"Yeah, stinking hillbilly's or mountain men or whatever you are."

"I'm not a hillbilly, or a mountain man, as for stinking," Timber raised an arm and did a mock smell of himself, "Maybe I'll take a bath afterwards."

"After what?"

"After straightening out whatever it is you intend to do, and if you do intend to do something hurry it up will you, I'm ready for another beer?"

The man just stood where he was hardly believing that Timber had said that, no one ever talked to him like that. For a few moments he just froze. Moments that Timber made full use of. Then he went for his gun. He was fast and if Timber had waited he might just have beat him but Timber was too experienced for that. In those few precious seconds he had drawn a gun from under the table and he shot the man down just as his gun cleared leather. The man collapsed with a look of sheer amazement on his face.

Timber had no doubt that the man had been sent to kill him, but by whom? The sheriff knew he was in town, maybe McAllister had been informed and then there was Rowdy and Cody. Maybe he'd find out later but for now he called on anybody to go get the undertaker then he called out, "If the sheriff comes tell him it was Jake Timber who shot this man," Timber then searched the man's pockets and took the money and things he found then he relieved him of his gun which was a fine specimen and would fetch a good price. He then walked out and made for the hotel only he didn't get that far.

On the other side of the street four men were waiting for him. One of them was sitting down with his leg stretched out. One had his right hand all bandaged up. Only the other two were in good health, for now.

"That's him right there Dakota," Rowdy said as Timber came out the saloon.

"Okay Rowdy leave it to us," Dakota said, "Come on Buck we can do this easy," he stepped into the street with Buck beside him.

Timber carried on thinking of the killing he had just done in his mind so for once he was off guard. It was getting dark so Dakota and Buck found it easy enough to cross the street and follow him.

As Timber walked along he became aware of footsteps behind him so he turned around to see who it was. He was nearly in time but the two men ran the last few yards and caught him just as he turned. Dakota was in front and he threw a punch at Timber which caught him on his chin knocking him backwards. Then Dakota and Buck were on him punching him anywhere they could. Timber was dazed by the first blow and although he fought back he wasn't making any headway, the two men were big and strong and gave hard punches. There was no time to lose. It occurred to Timber as to why they hadn't gone for their guns but then maybe they were just too confident in themselves not to need to do that. Timber didn't waste another second he drew both guns at once and shot the one in front of him then he spun around to see the other man going for his gun but way too late, Timber shot him as well. Once the gun smoke had drifted away he looked around for any more men coming for him. That was when he saw Rowdy being helped to hobble away with Cody. He couldn't resist going over there.

"In a hurry to get away are we?" He called out as he closed up on them hobbling along a little like Rowdy. He ached all over and he had some cuts which were bleeding but he wasn't about to just let them go.

With Rowdy not being able to walk very well they had been slow moving off. Cole turned around to him, "What if we are?"

"You saw what just happened, now you wouldn't have put those boys up to that would you?"

Rowdy turned as well still being held up by Cole with his left arm. Rowdy's arms were free however. Seeing Timber was so close and he was wearing a gun he just had to go for it as he was partly hidden from him by Cole.

Even in Timber's weakened state he saw the action before it even started and he drew on Rowdy. As Rowdy brought his gun around Timber shot him then he pointed his gun at Cole as Rowdy fell to the sidewalk.

"I told you two skunks to go back to the hole you came out of, its not my fault now Rowdy is dead, probably done him a favor," Timber said glancing down at him, he'd never have walked again or rode a horse."

Cole just stared back at Timber and didn't speak, he just raised his arms to show he wasn't wearing a gun.

"Okay, now you can go back to whoever pays you which I reckon is McAllister. Oh and tell him to give it up, I'll be seeing him soon," with that Timber waited as Cole went to his horse. As he got there he called back.

"What about Rowdy?'

"Oh I think we'll just leave him there like the vermin he is."

Cole shrugged, mounted up and rode out. Once he was out of sight Timber went to the hotel and up to his room.

Sarah heard him go in and she went to his room, knocked and walked in, she was surprised to see Timber, "What the heck happened to you?"

"I ran into more of your step father's paid bullyboys."

"Sit down," she ordered then she took the jug, bowl of water and a cloth from the top of a cupboard and got to work on cleaning him up.

It took Sarah a while to clean him up. She took off his shirt and bathed his bruises and cuts. She also saw other small wounds there and a big scar across his side, "My you have been in a few battles."

"A few," Timber winched as she worked on a particularly bad cut.

After she was done she had Timber lie on the bed to rest and she lay next to him. She touched the flesh wound on his side, "That looks quite fresh."

"Picked it up from the last outlaws I dealt with."

Sarah took a look at it, "You got any other things I ought to see."

"That rather depends on you."

It was later that night when Sarah returned to her room. Timber always tried to keep clear of women knowing he couldn't get close to one with what he was and what he had become but sometimes things just happened.

7

They met up again the following morning when Timber knocked on her door, it was early, the sun was nowhere near up yet. Timber didn't sleep much, just a couple of hours at a time. That was ever since he'd had to kill a man who had killed his wife and daughter. He had been especially brutal with him and that had got him into jail. He'd still be there now if the territory governor hadn't decided to make use of Timber's obvious talents for the good of the territory. The events though had made an effect on Timber. Sleep didn't come easy and when it did it was often with dreams of what had happened that woke him up, sometimes in a cold sweat.

Sarah had been awake fortunately and after a couple of minutes she let him in, "It's not even dawn yet," she said to him as he entered.

"Use all the time you have," Timber answered.

Sarah could see he was still hurting so she got him to sit on the bed, "You were beaten up pretty bad Timber, Carlton is going to have a lot more men like him, you can't take them all on by yourself."

"It's not stopped me before," Timber said trying to get himself comfortable.

"Maybe not but I think you, that is we need some help to finish this."

"What are you suggesting?"

"I know of a man who would help us. He's a retired lawman Timber, you'd like him."

"And why would he want to help us?"

"For one thing he has a score to settle with Carlton, some bother he had with him, you'd have to ask him what."

"I don't know, I prefer to work alone."

"But he could be useful if only as back up, let me talk to him see what he says?"

"Okay, if you have a mind to. I'll want to know more about him and meet him before we decide on anything."

"Agreed," Sarah went up to him and planted a kiss on his cheek, we can go find him this morning."

"After breakfast," Timber got up and took her arm to lead her out of the room.

While they were eating breakfast the sheriff walked in to them, "You had a busy night Timber," he said as he stood close to their table.

"Busier than yours I expect," was Timber's answer.

Don looked to Sarah, "You wanna be with this man?"

"I wouldn't be here if I didn't want to."

"He's a killer."

"I only know about him killing vermin Don," she stared at him until he turned back to Timber.

"Just take it easy can't you. What you've done is going to infuriate McAllister as it is."

"I can't see anything wrong with that."

"You will when he sends his men in here after you."

"And how will he know where I am?"

Don colored up and stormed out, "You'll see, you'll see," he said as he left.

"That's got him worked up," Sarah said.

"He needs working up. So who is this lawman you think will help us?"

"His name is Winston Gage. He's about your age I would say, very experienced but he ran into trouble with Carlton and now he doesn't do anything much as far as I know."

"And where do we find him?"

"He lives out of town, he has a small farm now, I've been there a couple of times."

As they were talking a man came up to their table, "Sorry to interrupt but I couldn't help but overhear. I heard you say something about having it out with Carlton McAllister?"

They both turned to him but it was Timber who answered, "So what if we are?"

"Well I'd like to help. You see I've got a grudge against McAllister as well."

Timber pointed to a spare chair at the table and the man sat down. Then Timber said, "Explain yourself Mister...?"

"It's Giles Hounslow, I think I heard the name Sarah raised?"

Timber told him their names and that he was a marshal. Giles reacted to that.

"A marshal! My my, things must be bad around here."

"So come on Giles spill the beans, what do you want?" Timber asked.

"I want to help you. That scoundrel McAllister set me up, got me in bother with the law."

"And just how did he do that?"

"Well I'll tell you the truth. I was a little out of the law at one time..."

"A little?"

"Yeah, let me finish, I did a few petty crimes yeah okay, I had to in order to survive. Anyway McAllister gave me a job, it wasn't much, just cleaning the stables and general things no one else wanted to do. Then he had me join with some of his boys to come to town getting money from the townsfolk. Now I swear I thought that was all above board. Anyway the sheriff came out for us. And this was before old Johnson joined up with McAllister. Johnson he had it in for us only McAllister swore blind it was just me doing the deed. He locked me up and my other crimes came to light and I did six months in jail."

Timber turned to Sarah, "So it looks like we will have a retired lawman and a reformed convict helping us, quite a mix wouldn't you say."

"Add us to the list and I would say you're right," Sarah answered.

"We should go see this lawman now, Giles you can ride along with us," Timber got up to go.

Sarah led the way out to the farm where she knew Winston Gage lived. The place was set in a quiet hollow with a few trees growing close by. The farm itself consisted of a wooden house with a two smaller buildings to the side. There was a henhouse and a small corral with a horse in it. Apart from that there were tools and wood for kindling lying all around the place. It looked like Winston Gage wasn't the tidiest of men.

They heard Winston chopping wood before they saw him. As they got up to the buildings the sounds were coming from around the back so they all rode around there.

Winston stopped when he saw them and leaned on the long handle of his axe to greet them.

"Howdy Sarah, who's this you've got with you?" he called to her.

"Winston this is Marshal Jake Timber, and that's Giles Hounslow."

"Winston frowned, "Giles I know, Timber I don't. Why don't you step down and tell me your business?"

They all dismounted and gathered around Winston who stayed where he was but he did put the axe down. Timber let Sarah get things started.

"Winston, my step father Carlton, who you know of course is up to some unlawful things. Things that are also causing a lot of grief in Idle Butte. Timber here has already straightened out some of his hired guns and hard men but there are more. We intend to put an end to his ways and we are looking for help."

Winston stood for a few moments taking all that in, "Well now, that's sounds like a good thing to do Sarah, won't be easy though I know. I've been keeping an eye on McAllister and I know he has some rough men working for him. As you know Sarah I have a grudge against him as well which is one reason why I've been keeping an eye on him. He conned me out of a good piece of land he still hasn't paid me for."

"Sounds like you should have done something earlier," Timber said interrupting.

"You reckon I haven't thought about that? As I say I know the kind of men he has with him. I'd most likely have gotten myself killed if I'd gone in there alone."

"Now you don't have to, now you have us."

Winston looked at Giles, "With him? He's a robber who I have caught at least twice."

Timber gave Giles a quick glance before looking back at Winston, "If there is anyone in Texas who doesn't hold with outlaws it's me. However, I reckon this man really is looking for redemption and I for one am prepared to give him the chance."

"Winston shook his head, "On your head be it. Okay, I'm in what's your plan?"

8

Carlton McAllister was pacing around the large living room in his ranch house as he listened to Cole telling him of his meeting with Timber.

"This marshal fella, you say he just gunned Rowdy down?" he had heard Cole recite it twice now but he still didn't believe it.

Cole's right hand had a big bandage around it and he sure wasn't happy, "That's what happened boss yeah."

"So you're telling me that this Timber or whatever his name is got the better of both of you in a straight fight?"

Cole didn't like admitting that but he did, "He's pretty good boss, we didn't stand a chance against him."

"So just how many men d'you figger I gotta send to straighten him out?"

Cole didn't want to answer but he mumbled, "Can't rightly say,"

"No, I guess you can't at that. Looks like I'm gonna have to go and see this fella for myself. Okay you can go now. You're not much use to me now as you are. Go and see my foreman see if he can find anything for you to do."

Carlton grinned as Cole walked out. His foreman, Brady Simms was a hard man and he didn't fancy Cole's chances with him. He thought a while longer then he went out to make some arrangements.

Timber spent most of the day getting to know the two men who were now going to help Sarah and him. It was a question of coming up with a workable plan to get to McAllister and see what they could do about him and his men. To do this Timber wanted to ride out to his ranch for a look see.

"We can do that, no problem, but not too close mind. McAllister has men around there looking out all the time," Winston said.

"So long as I get to see the lie of the land and a brief look at the buildings that will be enough," Timber answered.

Winston led them all out to McAllister's ranch but he didn't get close to it. He pulled up at a rise some way off where they then had to crawl to the top to take a look over at the ranch. Timber took his spyglass and lay down on the ridge careful to mask any reflections from the glass. He had Sarah to one side of him Winston to the other and Giles next to him.

"You've been to the ranch before," Timber said, "Explain it to me?"

Sarah knew it best of all so she took Timber through what all the buildings were for giving special attention to the buildings where men may be, the bunk houses and tack rooms.

"The ranch house is big as you can see. Carlton lives there alone now but he employs a couple of men to cook and clean for him."

"No women?"

"He doesn't use them very often, he reckons men can do other work as well to get his moneys worth."

Timber took a good look all around with his spyglass and took in as many details as he could, asking questions about the things that interested him. Once he was happy he got them all to creep back to their horses. Then they rode back to Winston's farm. Timber had been thinking all the way back. Winston invited them all into his farmhouse which was rather cramped but still big enough for them to sit around a table to discuss Timber's plan of getting to McAllister hopefully without having a war with his men.

Carlton very quickly organized a trip to town with a cow for the residents. He sent a couple of men on ahead to get the tables ready on the street and to announce it to everybody. He wanted to get this done fast to give him a look at Timber before anything else happened.

Timber completed his plan then left Winston and headed back to town with Sarah and Giles. As they rode in they saw tables being erected in the street, Sarah knew immediately what that meant.

"It looks like you'll get to see Carlton quicker that you thought. He's bringing a cow to town for a beef roast for everyone. He does this from time to time as a peace offering of some sort."

Timber grinned, guessing that Cole had been to see him and that was the reason for McAllister doing this, so maybe he wouldn't need his plan after all.

"It'll be tomorrow Timber and will last pretty much all day. He'll bring all manner of other food as well to have with it but he won't provide any booze. Everyone will have to pay for that at a saloon of which he'll take half the money for."

They chose a saloon close by to watch them from and having bought a beer inside they then stood on the sidewalk along with other people. Some of them commented on what was happening and Timber tried to get into conversations with them while Sarah stayed with Hounslow.

"You all looking forward to this?" he asked a group of men standing close by.

"McAllister likes to do his bit as he calls it," one of them answered.

Another spat on the ground before saying, "A small reward for all he takes."

Timber found that they would all attend, frightened not to as McAllister would expect them there at some time during the day.

"I guess he'll have men working on sharing it out?" Timber said.

"You can bet on it and plenty of his bully boy gunslingers too. He never comes to town without them."

Timber took it all in as he watched the street being laid out in preparation for the next day. The men working there didn't look like any threat apart from one who stood by wearing a gun while the workers weren't. Timber was happy for them to get on, he'll see McAllister tomorrow and work out what to do then. After a while they decided to move off and he paid for all of them for dinner at a cafe.

Giles was pleased to be with them and to be included. He talked on and on about the situation and McAllister until Timber told him to give it a rest. Later on Hounslow went to the house he lived at where he paid for a room while Sarah and Timber went back to the hotel.

9

Timber was awake early as usual the next day and he woke Sarah. Then while she got herself ready Timber went out the hotel to take a look along the street. The tables were all laid out further up the street and while he was looking around Sarah joined him.

"It could be an interesting day."

Timber turned to her, "It could be," as he spoke he saw Giles coming towards them.

"You can't leave me out now," he said as he got up to them, "You got a plan for today yet Timber?"

Timber had to smile at him, "Glad you're with us. No I don't yet. I reckon we'll just see how it pans out, we can always use any plan I make tomorrow if we have to."

"We know how these cow roast days usually work out Timber, it will get busy here later," Sarah told him.

"The busier the better for me. That will give me a chance to check men out easier."

"And McAllister," Giles added.

"No, not forgetting the main man."

"He'll have men with him."

"I'm sure he will but he will have heard about me now from Cole so I reckon he'll be searching me out."

"We'd better keep an eye on you then Timber," Sarah said, "We don't want his men to get you alone."

"No worries there Sarah, just keep your eyes open for his men and keep me informed where they are, I'll handle the rest."

Sarah was concerned for him for all his bravado, she had seen her step father's men work before and she was sure she wasn't going to let him out of her sight. She was wearing a shirt and trousers today with a jacket so it would hide the gun she had underneath it.

Giles was keen to be of help, "Just say where you want me Timber?"

"For now stay close while we wait for them to come into town, then I might just have a place for you to stay at but first, breakfast." Now that Timber had seen the situation on the street he took them all back to the same cafe where the same waitress served them. They all ate their fill then Timber took them out again to see there was some activity in the street. A couple of wagons had arrived with ten riders to set out the cow they had brought with them to cook over fires in metal bins. Giles began to wish he hadn't eaten breakfast and had left room for some beef, but then it was going to be there all day so he reckoned he'd have room for some later. Timber and Sarah looked out for McAllister to arrive.

"I guess he won't be here until everything is set up and selling," Sarah said.

Timber agreed with that but now that everything was taking shape he could see better where McAllister would most likely be when he did get to town and he wanted them all to be in good positions at that time in case any trouble started. He got Giles up the street on the same side as the cow to keep a look out. Sarah was to be further down the street on the same side while Timber would be across the street to watch the proceedings. While he waited for the main man he took in the men that were already there. Most of them were wearing guns apart from the men who were acting as chefs or waiters. They looked hard men, Timber wondered just how hard they were.

It was an hour later when a lot of townsfolk were getting their share of the cow that McAllister arrived. He had just two men with him, one to either side, both were big men and both had their guns tied down to their legs. It was the first time Timber got to see Carlton McAllister. He was shorter than Timber and was putting on weight although he looked as though he was once a fit man. He had grey hair, lots of it. Timber watched him ride up on his Palomino horse and leave it at the hitch rail at a saloon just up from where the cow was being roasted. The two men with him did the same thing and never left his side as he walked around checking that all was well and smiling at townsfolk as he called out greetings to them, which some men answered, others just turned away. McAllister's eyes were everywhere looking to see just who was there. The first face he noticed was a man who had worked for him, Giles was standing leaning against a porch pole in the shade but McAllister's sharp eyes still recognized him. The second person he recognized was Sarah. She had got into conversation with a couple walking past so as to not to look out of place but McAllister was still surprised to see her. He knew she had come to town but he thought she had left some time ago, so why was she still here? That was something he was interested to find out. He looked around for Timber. He had been told he was a big man in deerskins with a wide brown hat wearing long black boots with sliver toe and heel caps. He also knew that Timber carried two Colt .44 guns in a holster.

Timber had stayed in the shade of a porch up against the building opposite the cow tables as far out of view as he could be but he wanted a better look at McAllister and the two men with him so he stepped out and mingled with some townsfolk to get closer to them. McAllister saw him straight away. He took good looks at him through the people as they moved around as he told the men with him where he was. Timber had caused him some grief already and he didn't want him to cause any more. He had men around town now who should be able to take him down. He grinned to himself about that then he would see to Giles who was obviously in with Timber somehow by the way they nodded to each other and then there was Sarah, he was going to have to talk to her later. He could see that Timber was looking at him just as much which suited him just fine. He didn't want the two men with him to leave his side so he signaled to two other men he had there as to who Timber was. They both started off towards where Timber was now walking.

Timber had decided to get around McAllister and closer to Giles for backup. He got around to the sidewalk before he noticed the two men walking purposefully towards him. He stopped and looked around for a suitable place to meet them. He could see there were other men of McAllister's around and he counted them to be five men to worry about, the chefs and other men were no threat to him. Next to him there was a wide alleyway between the buildings and that's where he went. The two men smiled figuring he was trying to get away from them so they paced on looking forward to some fun.

Timber got into the alleyway and walked down a few yards to be clear of the street then he stopped to wait. The men walking in were strong arms that McAllister had hired for just such an eventuality of persuading people not to mess with him. Billy Evans was with Archie Downes. Both of them were big strong men who were used to street fighting. McAllister saw them walking off and had a little chuckle to himself then he began chatting to town residents although they didn't want to talk to him.

Billy and Archie walked into the alleyway side by side and between them they virtually filled the width of it. They saw Timber standing a few yards further in. He was in the middle of the alleyway and facing them.

"You looking for me?" Timber called to them.

They both stopped amused at the sight of him, sure he was big but no bigger than one of them.

"We are and we've found you," Billy looked around, "Nice n' quiet here too."

"Yeah well I don't want to upset the party out there too much."

Billy wanted a fist fight not use his guns, "What say, you and me huh?"

"While your friend watches on?"

"Oh he won't get involved, just you and me, come one," Billy advanced a few feet.

Archie stood as far to one side as he could with a wide grin on his face, this was going to be fun.

Timber let him come on a few feet, "You work for McAllister?" he asked.

"Yeah we do his dirty work for him."

That was all Timber wanted to know. As Billy advanced with his arms wide ready for a fight Timber pulled a gun and shot him down. Billy's mouth opened to speak and then he dropped heavily into the dirt.

Timber cocked his head at Archie, "I ain't got time to play games," he holstered his gun hoping Archie would draw which he did. Timber figured with arms his size he'd be slow which he was, and for insurance he already had his other gun halfway out of its holster so it was easy for him to beat Archie's draw and shoot him as well.

Timber checked them both out. Neither had much on them only a few dollars which he pocketed. He stuck both their guns in his belt and then walked back out to the street.

McAllister had been looking over at Giles, wondering what he was just standing there for but he wanted to talk to Sarah so he made his way towards her. As he did Sarah saw him coming and stood waiting for him. Before he could get to her Timber came out of the alleyway in front of him. They stopped a few yards apart. McAllister had his men to either side of him so he wasn't particularly worried but he realized what had happened.

"I heard two shots, I thought they were for you. You're quite a hard man Timber, you could have a job with me anytime."

"No way McAllister, and if those boys to either side of you want to try anything I'd advise against it."

"Because you're wearing two guns?"

"That and the man behind you with his. That makes one gun for each of you."

McAllister allowed himself a glance behind him, "Giles, I might have guessed."

"You did me wrong McAllister," Giles said.

Sarah was standing a little way back and she walked forward but kept her distance behind Timber, "Why can't you just be happy with what you have Carlton?"

McAllister looked around Timber to answer her, "Because you can never have enough. It's always the way to make more."

"Because you need it or for the fun of it?"

McAllister grinned, "Both I guess."

The men to his sides were getting restless, "Do you want us to finish this boss?" one of them asked.

"Not yet I want to talk to the marshal here," he turned back to Timber, "So what will it take to make you go away?"

"Give up on the protection racket, pay back whatever you have taken, let these men you have go and then get back to your ranch."

"You know that's not going to happen."

"In that case I won't be going anywhere."

"Your choice. I can see we have a standoff here, maybe we can talk again?"

"Any time," Timber kept his eyes on the two men with McAllister as he turned around.

"Come on boys, we'll continue this later," he then walked off with them.

Giles and Sarah joined Timber as they watched them go.

"Is that it?" Giles asked.

"For now I guess, there'll be another time."

Sarah sighed, "How is this gonna end?"

"Happily for some, not for others," Timber answered.

10

Timber watched as McAllister got back to where his men were still cutting up the cow and handing the meat out to the townsfolk. Although they all didn't like McAllister they took what he gave them. McAllister was in conversation with five men then he left them and went to his horse with the two bodyguards then left town. The five men he left behind moved around to keep an eye on things. Timber watched to see where they went but he lost sight of them quickly among the townsfolk there. He did however see another face he knew.

    Winston had been thinking. He had things to do on his farm but he was worried about what McAllister was doing and for Sarah's safety. She had this marshal fella with her now and that beat up outlaw for what good he would be but he was still concerned and decided to take a ride into town to see what help he could be. He arrived in time to see McAllister riding out. The cow party was closing up as he looked around for Sarah and Timber. Then he saw them all together down the street so he rode on up to them.

    "Have I missed anything?"

    "Only if you count two of McAllister's men dead in the alleyway just here," Timber told him.

Winston looked at the alleyway, "You killed em?"

"Yeah, I guess we should tell the undertaker."

"You checked em out yet?"

"I need to visit the sheriff again to see what wanted notices he has. They don't match any I have on me."

"Let me take a look," they all walked into the alleyway and Winston took a look at their faces, "I know both of these, Archie Downes and Billy Evans, they are known outlaws. The sheriff should have notices on them."

"Thanks. In that case I need their horses and you can help me drape them over their saddles."

Giles said he would go get the horses while Timber and Winston would drag the bodies to the end of the alleyway.

Giles had seen the men come into town and he knew exactly where their horses were. He walked up to them and unlooped their reins from the hitch rail. Unfortunately for him he was seen by more of McAllister's men, two of them walked over to him.

"Just where are you going with Billy and Archie's horses?" one of them asked him.

Giles had put himself into a spot of bother. He looked around but Timber and Winston were still in the alleyway. He could see Sarah on the sidewalk but she wasn't looking his way.

"Just taking the horses down to them," he said hoping to bluff it out.

"Seems to me they would come for them after they have finished the job the boss gave them to do," the men stood firm boxing Giles in.

"No, they asked for them," Giles had the reins in his hands and tried to walk past them but they stood in his way.

"We'll take a walk with you," the same man said.

Giles began to panic, he didn't feel able to tackle the two men and he had seen other men of McAllister close by so he had to just walk along with them and hope for the best. They had only gone a short way when one of them said, "Hey wait a minute, you used to work for the boss didn't you?"

"Yeah that's right."

"And got let go?" The men had stopped making Giles stop as well.

The man who had been quiet too another look at Giles, "Say Wayne I saw this man hanging around that marshal."

Wayne grabbed hold of Giles making him let go of the horses reins, "Yeah, I remember now, so have I. Now just what are you up to?"

"Nothing, I'm with Archie and Billy just taking their horses to them."

"Naw, you're up to something so come on out with it?" Wayne stood very close to him while his friend Rocky stood behind Giles.

Giles didn't say anything, which would have been difficult anyway as Wayne had him by his shirtfront and had pulled him up nearly off his feet with his shirt choking him.

"I think we need to make him talk," Wayne grinned at Rocky.

Rocky gave Giles a hard punch to his stomach driving what wind he had out of him. He was about to give him another one when a voice came from behind them.

"Let him go."

They turned around to see Sarah standing a little way behind them leveling a gun at them. They grinned at each other but Wayne did let go of Giles so he could turn to see Sarah better. Giles collapsed onto the sidewalk trying to breathe again.

"So what have we here, a woman coming to this little man's aid," Wayne said smiling at her.

"And succeeding. Just stand way from him," Sarah said in as stern a voice as she could muster.

Wayne stood in front of Rocky so Sarah wouldn't see Rocky draw his gun, then he stood back again. Sarah saw the gun in Rocky's hand and she didn't hesitate, she fired a shot which hit Rocky's forearm sending the gun spinning from his hand. She then turned the gun onto Wayne.

"I said stand away."

They both slowly and reluctantly did with Wayne's smile now turned into a scowl.

Timber and Winston had heard the shot and looked up the street to see Sarah holding the men up. Timber set off up the street followed closely by Winston. They got there just as Wayne was figuring that he might draw on Sarah. When he saw the two men arrive he stood back.

Timber had a gun out as he got beside Sarah. Rocky was holding his arm and cussing at Sarah.

"That's no way to talk to a lady, now you two get going, you can leave your guns here."

Wayne reluctantly dropped his gun then helped Rocky away from them.

"Another job for the doctor," Timber said as he turned to Sarah, "You did well but you should have called for me."

"You were busy, I handled it."

They looked down as Giles got up, "I don't care who saved me, I'm just thankful."

Winston had been looking around, "I see three of McAllister's men coming up."

They looked to see the three men walking down the street. It was obvious they were all gunslingers and it didn't look like they were going to back down.

"Stand behind me or well to one side Sarah," Timber told her.

For once Sarah did as he asked her but she kept a hold of her gun. Winston and Giles stood to either side of Timber. They then waited as they men advanced towards them.

The three men were hired guns who were paid very well by McAllister to keep him safe. He had left them in town to hopefully take Timber out without him being involved. They lined up in the street and stood firm.

"Any time you've ready," the middle man called.

Timber was reaching for both of his guns before the men had even stopped walking. He then fired in quick succession hitting and killing two of them as they were drawing their guns. The third man had his gun out as Timber was shooting the second man and he fired back at Timber. He was an experienced gunman but Timber was cleverer. As he fired he moved to one side so the man's bullet just bore a hole through Timber's shirt. Timber then fired again and killed the third man. Winston and Giles had their guns out by that time but found that they didn't need them.

Winston looked over at Timber in amazement, "That's some clever shooting Timber."

"Never wait for a draw. If you've got to do it, do it early, why give them a chance?"

Winston had to agree with that as they walked up to make sure they were all dead. At that minute sheriff Don Johnson arrived. Timber gave him a look.

"Better late than never sheriff," he said to him as scornfully as he could manage.

"Like I said McAllister's men are a hard bunch to go up against. I heard the shots and came over."

Timber shook his head, "Well now you're here, I want you to check these men out and two more by an alleyway against any wanted notices you have and if any match I want tickets for the bounty on their heads."

"I dare say I can do that," Don said as he checked them out.

Sarah stood beside Timber now it was over, "You did well, thanks, maybe now he has lost his men Carlton will give it up."

"I'm not sure of that but I reckon it will help," Timber then turned to Winston, "Thanks for turning up, maybe we can use your help again."

"You mean when you go to see McAllister?"

"Yeah."

"I'll be waiting, just call on me," Winston said then walked off.

"That's it for today Giles, I may need you tomorrow though," Timber told him.

"I'll call at the hotel, early, maybe not too early," he said looking at Sarah then him."

"Just after first light will be fine," Timber said, giving him a smile.

Timber and Sarah called at the cafe to eat before they returned to the hotel talking through the days events.

11

Carlton McAllister rode back to his ranch with his two trusted men full of thought. He wondered just how much Timber knew and how long he could keep his secret for. Things were moving fast and the marshal was sure being a thorn in his side. He had to make sure he was safe at the ranch so he was going to have to bring more men in to help him.

    He had been at the ranch a good few years now. He had started it off when he was married to his first wife. He had loved her with a passion, she had been married before but her husband had died from a snake bite. Carlton had seen her in town when he had an immediate attraction to her. He had gradually wooed her and then married her. She'd had a daughter with her first husband, Sarah who Carlton tried to get on with although he found that hard to do. Time had gone on and his wife had died from consumption. He had been devastated at her death and on a bounce back he had taken up with another woman, one his step daughter Sarah just couldn't get on with. What made it worse is that the woman pushed Sarah out until she decided to leave. The woman only stayed with Carlton for a short while after that until they began having rows then he sent her out of the ranch. She had been pleased to go and took the money that

Carlton gave her. Sarah hadn't got back with her step father as she found it hard to reconcile how he had let his second wife drive her out of her home. She also didn't like what he was doing so there was no way she was going back. She knew he had employed men who had killed and beaten people up for him. It was just too much for her to bear so she had gone back east to an aunt there to stay with. Her trip back had been to see friends and she had no idea of how her life was going to pan out now.

Over time McAllister had assembled a team of men to help him get what he wanted. With no woman left in his life he had gone completely off the rails and was now just getting everything he could from whoever he could. Two men he had employed early on were the ones with him now. He trusted them and paid them well and he provided food and board for them. He had found them in town when they were robbing a store. He talked to them when they came out and offered them the job which they had taken. McAllister didn't know how long they would stay but he was happy to have them now. He had to find a way to get rid of the marshal then he could get back to his ways and finish off the plan he had started. It looked like Timber wouldn't be easy to kill, he had to think it out and find a way.

That night he thought it through over a glass of whiskey in his favorite chair in his living room which was fitted out with the best furniture money could buy and decorated to a high standard. He sat there and figured the best thing to do was just to go and meet Timber head on. He would take his two bodyguards with him but he would try to reason with the marshal first, maybe he could find a way to get him to move on and leave him alone? He would find out tomorrow.

The next morning Timber woke Sarah up early as was his custom. They got ready and went out to look for Giles. He wasn't around so they went down to the stables to get their horses ready to ride out to Winston's place. They saddled up and led the horses out of the stable after Timber paid the hostler for their feed and board.

McAllister was also up early. He had told his two bodyguards to be at the ranch house ready to go before dawn which they were. He'd also had a man get his horse ready so all he had to do was walk out the ranch house and mount up. The men had a rough idea of what was expected of them but McAllister laid it on for them while they were riding to town.

"All we need to do today is take out Marshal Timber. I don't care how we do it or who sees us I just want it done and I've come along with you to see that it is done."

Doug Walker was riding to his right hand side and he wasn't sure if what his boss had said was a remark on their competence. However he let it go, it was better not to antagonize McAllister especially when he was in a mood such as he was in today.

Jasper Copeland wasn't so bright, "You can trust us to do it boss, no need for you to come with us."

McAllister slowly turned too him, "When I want your opinion or advice I'll ask for it until then just shut it."

Jasper scowled and shut up, letting his horse take a step backwards from where he was riding alongside McAllister.

McAllister finished the ride into town in silence. He was thinking of the men he had lost to the marshal and hoping that the two men he had with him would be good enough to take him out. He was prepared to help them out if necessary. They arrived and walked their horses down the main street looking for him. They looked to both sides of the street and McAllister sent them off at intervals to check saloons and cafes and to ask people they met if that had seen him no one was helpful which was to be expected so the carried on. It wasn't until they got right down the street that they caught sight of him with Sarah outside the livery stable. McAllister smiled thinking that was a perfect place for what he wanted to do.

Timber was facing up the street as he talked to Sarah so he saw the three men riding down towards them, "Go and find Giles will you Sarah?"

Sarah looked around and saw the men, "You sure you want me to leave you here?"

"I'm sure, now go."

Sarah mounted up and rode off keeping to the far side of the street without acknowledging Carlton as she passed him and his men.

Carlton ignored her, his mind was on Timber. They got a little closer before McAllister stopped and nodded to his men. Doug and Jasper got off their horses and walked on a few yards side by side. Timber had left Scout safely at the stable entrance and he had walked out into the street to face them.

"Marshal," McAllister called out, "It doesn't have to end this way, we can talk and find a way around it."

"That's not gonna happen McAllister. The only way around this is to give up your unlawful ways and pay back what you have taken from these townsfolk and maybe others," as Timber spoke his eyes flashed to and from each one of them while his hands were down beside his guns. He could see he was up against hired gunslingers who were probably faster than him and maybe accurate shooters but he still wouldn't back down. He kept his eyes looking up the street. He was pleased to see the gunslingers had advanced as far as they had towards him.

"Last chance Timber, I can't keep my men waiting on you all day," McAllister said.

Doug and Jasper were standing waiting for the command from McAllister to shoot Timber, both of them feeling very confident.

Timber saw McAllister nod and that was the signal. Timber drew his guns and flung himself towards the stable as he fired both guns at once. Doug and Jasper drew their guns and had to make rapid adjustments to their aim as Timber suddenly moved. One of Timber's bullets flew wide but the other one caught Doug in his stomach taking him down. Jasper fired at Timber but narrowly missed him not expecting him to dive down like that. Timber had also shouted a command at Scout as he dove down. The horse responded immediately and came charging out and barged straight into Jasper's horse before carrying on into McAllister's horse spooking both of them before carrying on. It prevented both men from doing anything and gave Timber the time he needed to get a bead on Jasper as he got clear of Scout with difficulty and looked for Timber his gun at the ready. He didn't have a chance to take a shot before both of Timber's guns roared again. Both bullets caught Jasper in his chest and he was dead before he hit the ground.

McAllister was amazed at what had happened and he drew his gun as Jasper fired but he stopped as a voice came from behind him.

"I wouldn't do that McAllister," Giles said cocking his gun as he spoke. McAllister heard the sound and looked around to see Giles pointing a gun at him with Sarah at his side.

"Give it up Carlton, this has gone far enough," Sarah said.

McAllister noted that ever since Sarah had left the ranch she had always called him by his first name not as pa.

"I'll go Sarah, but this ain't over yet," McAllister roughly pulled his horse around and trotted off up the street.

12

Timber walked over to Doug and kicked his gun away from him not that he was in a fit state to use it. He checked his wound then stood back.

"It's not good is it?" Doug said in between coughing up blood.

"No it isn't. You wanna tell me how many men McAllister has at the ranch"

"Why should I?"

"I can leave you here or call the doctor over."

"Call him," Doug gasped.

Timber waved at Sarah who hurried off to get him.

"So tell me."

"He has two more paid gunslingers over there and another ten men he can call on to do his dirty work," Doug grinned through the pain up at him, "More than even you can handle at one time."

"We'll see about that," Timber picked up his gun and went over to Jasper as the doctor arrived with Sarah. He took Copeland's gun and emptied his pockets just as sheriff Johnson arrived.

"I see you've been busy again Timber," Don said.

"Not my fault, these man attacked me."

"We can vouch for that Don," Sarah said to him as she stood with Giles.

"I guess you will at that. These two are known to me. Come over to the office when you ready Timber, I'll have all the tickets for you."

Timber thanked him as he walked off and looked over to where the doctor was working on Walker who then turned to Timber and gave a thumbs down signal. Timber just nodded.

"I wasn't happy with McAllister just riding off like that. Nothing is really straightened out yet. We need to go after him and get this thing finished," Timber said.

"I'm happy to go with you Timber," Giles told him.

"I'll go as well Timber and I reckon we should call for Winston on the way," Sarah added.

"Someone call my name," Winston said as he walked up to them, "Two more men less I see."

"Around twelve more to go up against, so I'm told" Timber answered.

"So if I heard right you are going off to see McAllister again?"

"We are Winston but I'm not happy about the sheriff. It seemed to me he left pretty quickly. I would like you to stay in town and keep an eye on him and the town while we are away."

"If you're sure then yeah, I can do that."

"Thanks Winston, we'll be back later," Timber moved off with Giles and Sarah hurrying after him. They got their horses and rode off out of town with Sarah trying to get Timber's thoughts from him. Winston hoped he would be coming back.

"Sometimes I have a plan, sometimes I work it out as I go, this is one of those times," Timber was keen now to get his work here finished before McAllister had time to get any plans he had in motion.

They got to where Timber had stopped the last time on the way to McAllister's ranch where there was some cover for them to hide in while they took a look down at the ranch. Timber then worked out his plan.

"There is a lot of men there Timber," Giles said as he lay down with Timber and Sarah at the rise edge.

"Just as many as Doug said."

"So have you got a plan yet Timber?" Sarah asked.

"It's coming. It seems to me that most of the men are at the front of the ranch house. I can count seven there and one at each end so where are the other three?"

"Beats me," Giles said as he looked all around the ranch laid out in front of them.

"Carlton could have them in the house with him," Sarah offered.

"I'd have thought one maybe. I need to get a lot closer. Sarah stay here will you. Giles get around the far right hand side of the buildings there then close in on the back of the ranch house. I'll go from the left."

"And what do I do when I get there?" Giles asked.

"If you can take a man out silently then do it. If not wait close by for my call then come ready to use your gun."

Giles nodded, happy to do that. He could see a couple of men down there he had a grudge against he would like to straighten out."

"You want me to just stay here?" Sarah asked.

"You'll be safe here and you can keep an eye out for us."

"But Carlton won't hurt me."

"Maybe, maybe not but I wouldn't trust his men not to, so stay here," Timber then crawled back to Scout and mounting up he took a wide sweep around the rise to where he could leave his horse out of sight then go in from there. Giles did a similar thing in the opposite direction. Sarah stayed where she was fuming at being left out.

Timber got Scout safely hidden away then from there he was able to make his way towards the ranch house, then stopped. There was a man holding a rifle just a little way from him guarding the rear door of the ranch house. Now Timber had to find a way of getting to him without alerting the men at the front.

Sarah watched Timber get close to the house and Giles doing a similar thing at the other side and decided to do something herself. She reckoned she would be safe enough and decided she would go down there and distract the men so allowing Timber and Giles to get to Carlton. She wasn't sure what Timber intended to do when he got to Carlton as he hadn't said. It was maddening that the man kept so much to himself but she thought he would try talking to Carlton again and then maybe arrest him for his crimes. That seemed like a good alternative to her and would be for the best. After a short time he would be free again with hopefully everything straightened out. She moved back then mounted her horse to go down there.

Instead of trying to creep up on the ranch house she just rode straight down to it. As she got closer she saw the men moving towards her away from the ends of the house which she guessed would be helping Timber and Giles. She rode on right up to them and sat there waiting on them.

McAllister's men gawped at her, wondering what on earth she was doing. Most of them knew of her and that she was estranged from their boss if not actually antagonistic towards him. They walked out to where she was, all of them interested and now losing interest in guarding the ranch.

Sarah sat where she was making them come to her. As they got close the leading man called out to her, "You Sarah McAllister?"

"Yes I am."

"What are you doing here, the boss won't be happy about it?"

"No? Well I'm here anyway."

"You haven't said why yet?"

Sarah tossed her hair trying to get time to think of a suitable answer, "I've come to see just who Carlton has here and I can see a lot of wasters," she wasn't sure about antagonizing them but she had to keep their interest and keep them where they were to give Timber and Giles a chance.

The leader looked around at the men there smiling, "I'd say the lady needs taking in hand boys what do you say?"

He was given a lot of encouragement then three of them surged forward with him and pulled her from her horse.

"Hey what do you think you're doing," she cried as she was unceremoniously pulled off and then dragged towards the house surrounded by rough men laughing and making comments.

Timber heard Sarah call out and as she did so the man he was watching walked around to the corner of the building right in front of where Timber was lying on the ground hidden by tall grass. He leapt up fast drawing a gun which he used to smash down onto the man's head, knocking him out cold. He took his gun and rifle and flung both of them yards away into the dust and grass where they wouldn't be easy to find and then dragged the man into cover out of sight just in case, then he went to the corner to take a look around at the front of the house. There he could see Sarah being man handled into the house.

13

McAllister had a man with him in the living room for protection; James Younger as he figured that Timber would be coming for him now that Doug and Jasper had been taken out. As they sat there talking they heard the commotion as Sarah complained in a very loud voice at being forcibly taken into the house. He got up with his man to go take a look. He was surprised to see her being carried in by three men.

"Put her down," he said.

The men let her go and Sarah took time to rearrange her shirt that had come out of her trousers, "Keep your bully boys hands off me," she shouted at McAllister.

"What the heck are you doing here Sarah?" he said as he waved his men away. They went but sorry to miss out on the conversation to come.

"I came to see you," she answered looking him straight in the eye.

"A strange way to do it. Why upset my men like that?"

"Upset them! How do you think I feel?"

"Come on in," he led the way with his man waiting for Sarah then following her.

Carlton gestured for Sarah to take a seat where he could see her from his favorite chair.

"Been a while since you were here," he said.

"Yeah and I reckon it needs a good clean," she said looking around.

Carlton grinned at her, "I don't have a housekeeper I use men I employ here, maybe they need some lessons, you could give them some."

"No way Carlton, I'm going back east now."

"Not yet you're not."

"'What do you mean?" Sarah didn't like his attitude.

"Not unless you and Timber give up this vendetta against me."

"Vendetta. Carlton we are just trying to get you to see sense and stop what are you doing to the town and farms around here."

"What I do is my business Sarah, you shouldn't have come here or bring that marshal. Now I have to keep you here."

Sara was confused, "Keep me here?"

"Yes, your being here will bring Timber to me then I will have him and settle this then you can go."

"You can't keep me here."

"Oh yes I can," he called a man in and said to him, "Brandon take her to the store shed, lock her in and post a guard there."

Brandon went to take her hand but she pulled it away, Brandon beckoned to another man and between them they marched her away and outside to the shed where they pushed her in, bolted the door and then the man Brandon had beckoned stayed there while he walked off.

Giles had got around the other side of the ranch house quite easily as the guard there hearing the sounds from the front went to take a look meaning that Giles could get to the back wall. Once there he waved at Timber but then he heard the guard coming back. He waited for him with a gun in his hand but as the guard came around Giles was too slow in hitting him. The guard dropped his rifle in surprise then struggled with Giles until Timber arrived and knocked the man out.

"Get him over there," Timber said nodding to some rough ground. Giles dragged him over while Timber disposed of the rifle. As they got back to the ranch house they heard the sounds of Sarah complaining loudly and then saw to men virtually carrying her around the far end of the ranch house. Both Timber and Giles got around the other side in time not to be seen by them. They then watched as Sarah was locked up and one of the men left the other on guard.

"They have Sarah," Giles whispered.

"But not for long," Timber whispered back. He took another peep around the corner to get a good look at the guard. He had propped his rifle up against the shed and was now leaning against the door. He was only a few yards away. Timber picked up a stone then threw it passed the guard to clatter on the ground. As the guard turned to see what it was Timber launched himself around the corner and as the guard turned back he sent a large fist straight into the man's face causing him to collapse like a sack of flour

"Drag him away and the rifle," Timber whispered to Giles who was now with him. As Giles did that Timber threw back the bolt and opened the door. Sarah was amazed to see him but she had the forethought not to cry out.

"Come on out of there we need to get you safe." Timber said.

As Giles returned Timber said, "We get Sarah back to town Giles then think again. Where's your horse Sarah?"

"I saw a man take it to a corral," she pointed to the side of the house.

They all went for a look and saw it was alone in a corral to the side of the house where it would be unseen from any men at the front. Quickly Timber got it for her.

"Go with Giles, I'll meet you on the ridge."

Both Sarah and Giles were happy to hear that and walked off leaving Timber to go off for Scout. They all rode around the ranch to meet up on the ridge.

"Now we ride for town," Timber said.

"But what about McAllister?" Giles asked.

"We'll see to him later," Timber then had them ride off.

14

Sarah didn't say much on the ride back to town. She was in shock about what had happened. Much as she hated Carlton she never thought he would lock her up like that. She had been worried about being left alone with his men knowing what kind of people they were but now she was safe riding along with Timber and Giles. She had thanked them both profusely and had now gone quiet. No one spoke much at all until they arrived back. Timber was keen to go and see Winston so they looked for him first.

Winston had gone to the sheriff's office and made sure the man was there. He knew him to be pretty useless anyway and to be in McAllister's pocket. He didn't bother going in as he thought it best just to keep an eye on him. He wandered around the town looking for any of McAllister's men and for once he didn't see any which was a good thing. Having nothing to do he sat outside a saloon to keep watch. He saw Timber coming down the street so he got up to meet them.

"How'd it go?" he asked.

"Not as expected. You got someplace you can look after Sarah for a while?" Timber said.

Winston gave them all a look, "You'd better tell me what's

happened," he looked around, "In here's as good as anywhere," he said pointing at the saloon.

They all went in and Timber related to Winston what had happened. Winston then looked at Sarah, "I'm sorry it worked out that way."

Sarah was recovering from her shock and sorrow, now she was feeling angry, "Thanks but it's okay, I should have known really."

"Well now look, I got me the farm, why don't we go out there and Sarah stays with me until this thing is all over huh?" Winston looked at Timber as he spoke.

Timber nodded to him letting him know that he would stay around until it was all over, "We'll ride with you to your farm then we'll go on from there."

"Thanks Winston but maybe I would still be of help to Timber with Carlton," Sarah said not wanting to be out of it.

"I doubt you would be now Sarah, I think it will be better if just Giles and me go this time."

"You reckon you can handle the rest of McAllister's men?" Winston asked.

"If not I'll coming racing back for you."

Winston wasn't sure if he was joking or being serious so he just said, "I'll be there if you need me."

Timber just grinned at him and stood up to go.

Within a little while they were back at Winston's farm. Sarah still wasn't quite happy at being left there but she agreed meaning that Timber and Giles could set off back for McAllister's ranch.

McAllister was suddenly alerted to something being wrong by one of his men coming shouting at the door. He got up to find the man full of what he had found out back.

"Boss, we got trouble. Three men have been knocked out and left hidden out here and Sarah's gone!"

"What do you mean gone?"

"I mean the store shed is empty and her horse is missing."

McAllister cussed himself. He should have taken more care and now that he thought about it he should have had her horse taken somewhere safe.

"Get some men together and get off for town. Find her and bring her back," he told him. He watched as the man ran off then he went back inside.

"It looks like we haven't seen the end of that marshal," he said to James.

James Younger just smiled. He had been within McAllister for some time now and knew him pretty well.

"Would you like me to go get her?"

"Naw, you stay here. I might have need of you yet."

James hoped that he would do. He got paid whatever, but something fun to do now and then wouldn't come amiss for him.

The man who had told McAllister about Sarah found three other men keen to go with him so they mounted up and galloped off. They had no idea how long Sarah had been gone other than they knew she had been put in the shed about two hours ago.

Timber and Giles rode along with Giles asking what Timber intended to do now?

"We need to find a way into the house around his men and get to McAllister. I'll give him a chance to give himself up."

"And if he won't?"

"Then I'll arrest him and take him back to town."

"That sounds like one hell of a tall order to me."

Timber grinned across at him, "It is, you still coming along?"

"You bet. I can't wait to see his face when you arrest him."

Timber stopped talking and looked ahead to where he could see four riders coming towards them.

"It looks like we may be doing this piecemeal," Timber said.

"Could be, those are McAllister's men," Giles added.

"Move out Giles," Timber said as the riders closed in on them.

Two of the men had seen Timber in town and they shouted to the other two alerting them as to who he was. That made them all excited that now they were able to try and kill him, get out of him where

Sarah was and go back for McAllister's praise. They also knew Giles beside him but they weren't worried about him.

"Circle around them," the leader called out.

Timber didn't wait for that to happen as he saw the riders drifting apart. He snagged his rifle and took the far right one out of his saddle before sending another round into the breech. The men scattered out wide around them and began to fire back. They were only just coming into range of hand guns so Timber took the opportunity to take another one out of his saddle. Giles took three shots to bring a man down which just left the leader who was totally amazed at how suddenly the tables had been turned. He slid off his horse and got down in the rocks and hollows and letting his horse go he looked for the two men.

Both Giles and Timber had got off their horses and as usual at times like this Timber sent Scout running off to somewhere safe, he didn't want a stray shot or one on purpose to hit him. Giles had done pretty much the same thing and got down in the same way as the McAllister man had done. Timber didn't want to waste any time here so he got down and aimed his rifle at where he knew the man was and waited. Seconds later he saw enough of him to take a shot. The man had lifted himself up having seen Giles getting down from his horse and aimed at him. Timber could see enough of the man so he took the shot and was pleased to see the man fall. He then carefully made his way over to him as did Giles.

Timber got there to find he was still alive but bleeding profusely. He picked up the man's gun from where he had dropped it and looked down at him as Giles arrived.

"That was a pretty stupid things to do coming up on us like that," Timber said.

The man grimaced in pain as he looked up at the two of them, "You might be a big man Timber and a marshal but you ain't as clever as you think you are," he said the words in between gasps of pain with his hands over where Timber's bullet had hit him but they didn't stop his blood from pouring out between his fingers.

"You got something to tell me?" Timber asked.

"You're on the wrong track thinking its all about the town with McAllister, you need to look further afield," the man was pleased to let McAllister's secret go. If it wasn't for him he wouldn't have got shot and he knew he hadn't got long. His voice faded out as more blood came out of him and Timber had to lean in close to hear the last words.

"Land," is all the man said then he collapsed into the dust.

15

Giles looked at Timber, "What did he mean, land?"

"Can't say for sure but it looks like McAllister is up to more tricks than the town protection racket."

"So what now?"

"We take these men to town and check them against wanted notices picking up Sarah on the way. Before I go and see McAllister again I want more information to take with me," Timber visited each man one by one and searched them taking what he wanted then he had Giles help him put the men over their saddles to take back with them.

As they were doing it Giles asked, "Shouldn't we take them to McAllister?"

"No. The sheriff in town can organize them. I want to check if they have bounties on them and I don't want McAllister to know about this just yet," Timber stroked his nose and Giles took the hint.

They rode back to Winston's farm who was surprised to see them so soon. He went out to meet them with Sarah right beside him.

"That was quick, how did it go?" Winston asked, "And who are these men?"

Both Winston and Sarah were surprised to see the four bodies draped over their saddles.

"These four attacked us as they were coming this way, presumably after you Sarah. McAllister must want you back bad," Timber said.

Sarah grunted, "I can't think what for except maybe to winkle you out to go there, I can't think of any other reason."

"Do you have any connection with McAllister now, anything in a will or a trust or anything like that, maybe from your ma?"

Sarah shook her head at him, "No not that I know of, why ask me that?"

"Oh it's just something one of these men said that got me thinking that's all. What about land, I'm guess he has a lot of that?"

"Too much really, he can't handle what he has got and I know he wants more if he can get it but folk are hanging onto what they have."

Timber pursed his lips in thought, "We're going to town now, I have a few questions to ask."

"It all sounds interesting Timber I reckon I'll ride along with you," Winston said.

"Can you leave this place for long?"

Winston spread his arms, "What you can see is all there is, it don't take much looking after and yes it can manage by itself for a spell."

"Okay, so let's go."

They rode back in and on to the sheriff's office. Don was not pleased to have Timber walk into his office. He was even more unhappy when going out with him to see the four men together with Winston and Sarah.

"Have you any idea how much bother this will bring us?" Don asked rounding on Timber.

"Some, but don't you worry about that, we'll see to any that happens," Timber told him.

"Now look here I'm the sheriff of this town and I don't want any more bother, in fact I think you have over stayed your welcome."

"I said not to worry Don. I'm going nowhere until this whole mess is straightened out. As for you being the sheriff here I suggest you try harder at doing it and stop taking handouts from McAllister."

Don looked as though he was going to explode and didn't answer.

"We have things to do Don so, I'm going to, leave these men with you to organize and don't forget to check them out and get tickets ready for me for their bounty's, I'll be back by and by to collect them," Timber then turned away from him, "Winston take Sarah to the hotel will you and stay with her, you too Giles I'll come to you soon," Timber didn't say where he was going but left them there and strode off. He made his way to the town council office which he had seen before on his walks around town. He walked in to find four men inside sitting around at desks. They looked up at him and one spoke to him.

"Can I help you mister?"

"I sure hope so. I hear there is a certain person buying land up around here and I want to know if there might just be a reason for that, apart from the obvious?"

The man looked around at the others who all looked back at him.

"Is there a reason for you to ask that question mister and who are you?"

Timber showed them his badge, "I'm Jake timber U.S. Marshal and the reason is I've just been battling with the man."

"Ah yes, McAllister. Timber I'm Jason Morrison, leader of the town council here. Yes we know about McAllister's activities but as yet we haven't been able to stop him," he looked down for a second, "Are you here to change all that?'

"Oh I'll stop him, right now I'm looking for information to help me with that."

"Marshal we are very lucky here in that there is a major event happening soon that will change this town forever."

Timber looked at him and waited.

"The railroad is coming through right by here," he said with a big smile, "Isn't that great?"

Timber nodded his head, "And the price of land will go up."

"You'd better believe it, ain't that good news?"

"I guess. So where exactly is it coming through?"

"It's not common knowledge Timber as these things sometimes

fall through and it may go elsewhere but look at this," Jason took him to a map of the area which showed a red line going across it, "That's the route," he said pointing to it.

"So now how would McAllister know of this?"

"Oh he doesn't, he can't do. Only council members are aware of it. We won't make it common knowledge until we are dead sure of it."

"So how many councilors are there?"

"Us four and two more."

"I'm going to need names."

Jason wasn't happy about giving them all out but he did and where to find them all. Timber thanked him and left. Just when he thought it was getting easy it had just got a whole lot harder.

16

Timber made his way down to the hotel. He asked at the desk which room Sarah and the men were in then he made his way upstairs to the room. It was opened by Winston. Sarah was sitting on a chair by the window while Timber joined the men to sit on the bed.

"Where've you been Timber?" Winston asked.

"I've had an idea that there is more to this since that man died with us out there. Now the council have let me in on a secret."

"Oh yeah?"

They all stared at Timber waiting for him to tell them what it was, instead Timber asked Sarah a question.

"What do you know about McAllister's activities Sarah, you did say he wants more land?"

"Well that's right yes. He has a big spread but he has always tried to expand it. I haven't been back in town that long but from what I've heard he's been buying up as much more as he can."

"Then he knows about it."

"About what Timber. Are you going to tell us or not?' Sarah was getting frustrated.

"I've been told that the railroad is going to pass close to Idle Butte.

When it does the price of land around here will go right up, especially if you have it first to sell rights to them to cross it."

They all sat around taking that in until Sarah spoke up.

"So that's why he's doing it."

"It also explains the robberies from the townsfolk here with his scheme, that's giving him the money to buy it with," Winston added.

"I always knew that man was a bad 'un," Giles added.

Sarah gave them a look, "So what are you going to do now?"

"It's not that simple. McAllister is in this with someone else, otherwise how did he find out about the railroad. There are six men on the town council and any one of them could have told him."

"And expecting a pay out?" Winston said.

"If not already getting one."

"So you're saying you want the corrupt councilor as well as taking down McAllister?" Giles said.

"Exactly."

"Okay but which one is it?" Sarah asked.

"I don't know, yet but I intend to find out."

"But how can you do that?"

"This is where I need your help Sarah. What friends does your step father have in this town? Who does he know that he gets on with? The councilors all have jobs of some sort he could have met the man I want anywhere."

"Well now let me see. I've been away for a while as you know but before that he had contact with lots of other ranchers and people in town."

"Anyone specific, anyone that used to call round?"

Sarah thought for a few moments then she looked up at him, "Well yes now that I come to think about it there was one man who came to see him quite often, they seemed to be very friendly."

"And he is..?"

"A man called Samuel Longstone. He has a small ranch bordering Carlton's but he leaves it to his men to run, he works here in town at the bank."

"Well that sure all figures, I need to go see him."

"We'll come with you Timber if you want us to but right now I can see trouble in the street out here," Giles said. From where he was sitting he had a good view out of the window.

They all turned to see two of McAllister's men arguing with a man in the street.

"Looks like McAllister needs more money," Giles said.

"I need to stop that," Timber said as he left the room. They all got up to follow him out anxious to see what was going to happen and to be there to help out if need be.

Timber got out in the street to find the men still arguing with the man. He could hear the words being said and it was looking like it was getting out of hand. McAllister's men had their backs towards him as he hurried over to them. Winston and Giles weren't that far behind, both of them keeping Sarah behind them where she would be safe.

"Just hold it right there," Timber called when he was close enough to the men.

McAllister's men turned around to see him while the man stepped to one side, also to see who had called out. He smiled when he saw Timber.

The other two men didn't smile, "Just keep out of this, it's none of your business," one of them said.

"Oh but it is and even if it wasn't I'm making it my business," Timber replied.

The two men turned around fully ignoring the townsman so he hurried off to the sidewalk to watch while well out of the field of fire.

"You really want to do this?" the same man said to Timber.

"Do you?" Timber called back.

"We're just picking up our dues here mister?"

"No you're not, you're committing a robbery so as a U.S. Marshal I am here to stop you."

That was enough for the men and they went for their guns. Timber was already drawing his and beat them by a part of a second. Both of his guns thundered out smoke and fire and both of his bullets hit their mark. The man who had been speaking now had a broken right arm, his gun dropped to the ground. The man with him had been hit in his side which had made him drop his gun and fall down. Timber kept his guns aimed at them.

"Difficult though it might be, you two help each other and get back to McAllister when you can and tell him not to send any more men here."

With great difficulty the men hobbled away towards the doctor's office. Timber wondered just what kind of service they would receive there? He turned to see his friends waiting for him.

"Two more out of action," he said to them.

"A good job done Timber, be a while before they get back to McAllister with the message though," Winston said.

"Who cares, if any more men come here I'll see to them as well."

Sarah began to realize that this marshal was a hard man.

17

"Time to make a visit to the bank," Timber said.

"You want some company?" Winston asked.

"No, you and Giles hang around here, keep an eye out for those two leaving the doctor's office, make sure they go and look out for any other of McAllister's men, Sarah can come with me."

Sarah walked off with him leaving Winston and Giles to themselves.

"So what will you say to this man then Timber?"

"I'll find out just how deep he is in this conspiracy with McAllister then I'll act on what I find out."

Sarah nodded as she tried to keep up with him. They soon arrived at the bank and went inside. Timber stopped for a look around then they went up to the counter where a clerk greeted them.

"I'm looking for Samuel Longstone," Timber said to him.

"Mister Longstone, I'm afraid he isn't here sir, can I help you?" the clerk said looking at both of them.

"That's too bad, do you know where we can find him?"

The clerk looked around before answering, "I can't really give out that kind of information sir without some kind of authority."

"Will this do it," Timber said showing the man his Marshal badge.

The clerk had to agree, "Er, yes sir, well now Mister Longstone has gone off to see one of our clients, one of our best clients, a Mister McAllister at his ranch."

"Thanks," Timber turned to go.

"Don't you want to know where it is?" the clerk asked.

"Oh we know where it is," Timber moved off with Sarah at his side.

"I guess it's another trip out to Carlton's ranch then Timber," Sarah said, wondering how that will pan out.

"I guess so," they walked on until they saw Winston and Giles waving to them along the street. They all met up on the sidewalk outside a cafe.

"He's gone to see McAllister," Timber said, "So that's where I'm going next."

"You'll need us with you," Winston said.

Timber looked down at Sarah, "Well I'm thinking that you two ought to stay here and look after Sarah while I go and see him."

"Now you can't keep us out of all the fun Timber, I want to see the look on McAllister's face when you tackle him about all this, Giles said.

"Timber, I'm going with you," Sarah said standing with her hands on her hips.

"With what happened last time I don't think that's a good idea, you stay here with Winston."

The thing is Timber, I reckon I ought to go with you as well," Winston said.

Timber stopped and looked at all of them," Dang me, okay if that's what you want I reckon we should all go in that case."

That was met with smiles and nods of agreement. They had their horses down at the livery stable so they all went down there and as they walked Timber asked about the two men he had wounded.

"They came out the doctor's office with only bandages around them, I guess he sent them packing with minimal help. McAllister has a man at the ranch that will have to see to them now," Winston told him.

Timber nodded and walked on.

18

Timber had got to know the way to the ranch pretty well by now and he also knew where to stop close to it which is where he went with the others bunched around him. They got off their horses to creep up to the ridge and look over at the ranch.

"It looks pretty quiet down there," Giles said.

"Except there are a few men around the place," Winston added.

Timber and Sarah were lying side by side watching. Timber was counting the men and taking note of their positions. They walked around a little bit, more to stretch their legs Timber thought.

"You going in through the back again Timber?" Giles asked.

"It might be easier, but I'll need to see around there first."

"So it's another ride around there then."

"I guess yeah."

"So how are we gonna work this Timber?" Winston asked.

Timber wanted Sarah to stay where she was safe but now he had the problem of wanting the two men with him so it was what to do with her, he quickly made up his mind.

"We go down as before Winston you go with Giles to the right, he knows the way. I'll go to the left and Sarah you come with me. I'm hoping you have your gun with you this time."

"I sure have Timber and I don't mind using it either."

"Good girl so let's go."

They all rode off in their different directions and got down to where they could leave their horses just like last time. Timber had Sarah stop to tell her to keep behind him. He was happy that she agreed to that. He began to work his way around keeping in cover as best as he could, the outhouses helped with that until he could see behind the ranch house. There was a man at each corner like last time but also there was a man at the back door, they were all holding rifles and had guns strapped to their waists.

Timber got a glimpse of Winston beyond the other end of the house, so they were all in positions it was just a question now of how to remove the guard at the door. He was bound to see them come across from either end of the ranch house. Timber had thoughts of taking out the guards at the end of the building much like last time but not with him there, whatever they did they needed to do it quietly so as not to bring all the men from the front around to them. As it happened Sarah came up with solution.

"You want the man at the door taking out Timber?" she asked as Timber explained the situation to her.

"I need to find a way yeah."

"No bother," she got up and brazenly started to walk towards him taking no notice of Timber warning her to stay. The three guards immediately saw her and watched her walk to them.

The guard at her end watched her walk past him calling out, "Come to see us again so soon lady," he laughed as he said it.

She just glanced around at him and kept on going. She got up to the guard at the door and stopped, "I know you, you were here the last time I called round."

The guard was numb struck, "Why, er, how, what are you doing here?"

"You mean why have I come back here after you locked me up in a shed?" as she talked she glanced in both directions to see the two other guards watching her. She kept the attention of the guards giving Timber and Winston time to come up to the house on both sides. She now had to get this man's full attention.

"So yeah why have you come back?" the guard asked her.

"I want to see Carlton," Sarah stepped right up to him then said, "Let me in."

She then got the chance she had been looking for as the man turned around to show her that the door was locked. She had her gun out in no time and pointed it at him.

"No noise," she said as she took his rifle and flung it aside and then took his gun.

As she did that Timber came up behind the guard nearest him and told him much the same thing while relieving him of his rifle and gun while Winston did the same to the one at the far end. They then marched the men to the same shed Sarah had been locked in to lock them in it.

"No noise now y'hear or I'll come back and kill all of you," Timber told them as he closed the door and pulled the bolt across.

"Now for the house," Timber said walking to the back door, "Just me and Sarah inside, I'll holler if I need you, stay out here and watch for anyone coming," he told Winston and Giles.

Winston and Giles took a guard's rifle each and stood at either end of the house, thinking they could be mistaken for McAllister's men if anyone did come around the building.

Timber got to the door with Sarah right behind him then he opened it carefully and looked inside. There was a corridor that went a short way in to where another corridor ran across the end of it. He stepped in and let Sarah in.

"You know this house, where will McAllister be?"

"I would expect him to be in the living room, especially if he has someone come to see him. He has a den but doesn't let anyone in there."

"Lead the way," Timber kept close to her as they crept to the corridor then turned right along it. Doors led off from it which were all shut. Timber hoped the rooms were all empty. They crept along until Sarah stopped at a door.

"This is it," she whispered.

Timber got up to the door and Sarah got behind him. He put his ear to the door and as he did so the door moved open very slightly. He got hold of the handle and listened. They could now both hear the voices in the room.

"Carlton this has been a damn fine plan of mine as you know but we gotta hurry things up now. There is a U.S. Marshal in town stirring things up."

"I know about that Sam, the man has been up here."

"Really? So what does he know?"

"Quite a lot," Timber said as he entered the room.

Sarah would have been happy to wait a while longer and hear more but Timber reckoned he'd heard enough and he didn't want to hang around too long in case any men came and saw them.

Samuel and Carlton looked at him in shock.

"How the hell did you get in here, you're trespassing?" Carlton then saw Sarah behind him, "You brought him here?"

"No, he brought me. We want to hear all about this secret plan you have Carlton."

"Plan, what plan?" Carlton got up from his chair and paced towards them leaving Samuel still sitting where he was.

"We know about the railroad coming through. We know there is something between you two here and now I want hear just what plan you have?" Timber said.

As Timber mentioned the railroad they both knew the game was up. They gave each other a look then Samuel turned to Timber.

"Seems like you have us at a disadvantage Marshal Timber."

"I would say so councilor now why don't you just tell us what is going on here?"

"Sit down Carlton, the cat's out of the bag we may as well just tell them."

Carlton made a grumbling noise and sat down, "When this is over Sarah, we need to talk."

"Really Carlton? We haven't talked properly for a long time. So come on how did this plan of yours work?"

"It started out with me actually Sarah," Samuel said, "I heard about the railroad coming through and I knew that would put the price of land up to sell to folk who would want to come here and the railroad would pay to cut through it but I hadn't got any land and not much money to buy some but Carlton here..."

"I had the land but then the more we could get the better so I started buying it in."

"And needed more money, from the townsfolk?" Sarah interrupted.

"Yeah well, I suppose yes it helped."

"And working at the bank must have helped," Timber said to Samuel who colored up.

"If you hadn't have spent money employing all these rough men you have you might not have had to steal so much," Sarah said.

"Ah but I needed them to do the work. With the land bought Samuel was going to ensure the railroad went through what we have and that they pay a high price for it. Then we were gonna split the profits."

"And if you hadn't done that?" Timber asked.

"Well then the council would have got the money from the railroad to build a station with and more buildings for the town."

"So you were going to take the money the town would have had?' Sarah asked.

"That's about the size of it but it was all just business," McAllister said.

"Business!" Timber had to correct them, "It was fraud and theft. You are both guilty of various crimes."

"So what happens now?" Samuel asked.

"Now we all go to town to straighten this all out and you make sure we get past your men McAllister or I will start shooting."

19

As Samuel and McAllister got up Timber said, "Remember you are both under arrest, any funny business and you won't get to town."

McAllister had sent his man James out of the room while he had a talk with Samuel and now he hoped that he would be able to do something to help them. That was until they walked out the room into the corridor to find Winston and Giles there both pointing guns at him. McAllister gave up then to accept his fate, still hoping that he could get out of this mess somehow. He had men around the ranch who might just arrange that for him. He had no cares about Samuel, what happened to him happened.

Timber got McAllister to walk out first while he stood right behind him. Sarah was behind him, Winston had Samuel and Giles brought James out. Once outside the guards there all looked at them. One man called out to McAllister and asked if he was all right.

"No bother boys. We are leaving here for town, just put your guns down," he said that feeling the barrel of one of Timber's guns digging into his back.

They got well outside and McAllister called for their horses to be brought to them, all except Timber's, he just whistled for Scout who came trotting up. They mounted up with guns kept on McAllister and Samuel with Giles letting James go so he could cover them mounting up then they rode out.

They got to town without incident and with hardly any talk as everyone had their own thoughts. Once there they rode straight down to the sheriff's office and pulled up outside. Don Johnson came out having seen them through the window. McAllister was pleased to see him, maybe there was a way out of this after all.

"What's going on Mister McAllister?" Don called to him.

McAllister was about to answer when Timber butted in, "Johnson these two men are under arrest and I need to lock them up in your cells."

Don didn't know what to say, "I, I don't understand."

"Yes you do now get those cells open," Timber slipped off Scout and with the help of Winston and Giles he got both men into a cell each where he locked the doors and took the keys back to hang on a hook near Don's desk.

"Just how long do you want me to look after them Timber," Don asked seeing that he couldn't do anything to help McAllister.

"I don't."

Don looked at him.

"If you think I'm going to leave these two men in your control then you're losing your senses."

"Timber, I am the sheriff here."

"Yeah, a corrupt sheriff in McAllister's pocket, well you're out of here, I'll deal with you later," Timber took a hold of him then flung him outside.

"You can't do this Timber," Don shouted back in rage.

Timber looked out the door at him, "I just have now scram, vamoose," he then shut the door.

"Now Winston. Would you like the sheriff's job here, for a while at least."

"You got it Timber," Winston was very pleased with that and he moved over to Johnson's desk to see what was there, "I'll need to organize the circuit judge to get over here," he said while looking through the pile of paperwork on the desk.

"What would you like me to do?" Giles asked.

"Well now I ain't got nothin' for you Giles. You've kept your end up and done good. You can do just whatever you like."

"Well I was thinking of keeping Winston here company for a while."

"Suits me," Winston said, I need a deputy to get the coffee, do the errands..."

Giles groaned, "Me and my big mouth, you still got it Winston," he said smiling at him.

"That just leaves you and me then Timber," Sarah said looking up at him.

"Ah now I got things lined up for you. First off you're coming with me to see the rest of the council then we'll get some grub. I guess you two can organize that for yourselves," he said to Winston.

"Sure, I can send my deputy out," Winston said winking at him.

"Just make sure you swear him in then. Come on Sarah we still got things to do."

Timber looked over to the cells where McAllister was talking to Samuel in low tones, "Don't you two start making plans now, the next time you come out of there will be to see the circuit judge."

"You need a case against us for that," McAllister hissed back at him.

"You think I won't have one?" Timber called back. He opened the door for Sarah and they left as Winston talked to Giles. They walked on up the street to the town council office. Timber didn't knock he just walked straight in. He was lucky, all five of the other council members were in there having a meeting. They weren't happy to have the interruption. One of them got up to complain but Timber waved him down flashing his badge as he spoke.

"We won't hold you up for long, I'm Jake Timber U.S. Marshal and this is Sarah McAllister, we're here to tell you that Samuel Longstone is cooling off in a cell in the sheriff's office waiting trial for fraud and theft. McAllister is in there with him."

"What are you talking about marshal, Longstone is a council member, that can't be right."

"Oh I assure you it is. He was working with McAllister to buy land and then sell it for a high price when the railroad comes through."

"The railroad, how did you hear about that?"

"From him. This will all need straightening out, oh and I've turned out sheriff Don Johnson as well as he is corrupt, taking hand-outs from them for turning a bind eye to the protection racket they were running."

"That's a lot of accusations marshal."

"Oh there'll be more yet. So you can now do whatever you have to do about all that, come on Sarah."

Outside Sarah smiled up at Timber, "You don't mince your words do you?"

"No point in doing that. If something needs saying, say it otherwise keep your mouth shut."

"I'll bear that in mind," she said as she walked along with him.

"Okay, enough work for today, let's go eat," Timber didn't wait for a reply he just headed off for the restaurant they had used before.

20

James was upset as he saw Timber take his boss away, that meant the money would now dry up and his job was gone. He had to do what he could about that. He hadn't been able to do anything at the time but now it was different. He began to shout at the men grouping around outside to gather around him. He looked around as four men came from around the back to join them. One man had heard noises from the shed and had gone to find the three men in there. He let them out then they picked their guns up from where Timber had thrown them near the shed before they went around to the front of the house.

"We need to go get McAllister back, without him there ain't any money, so who's with me?" James called out.

A few hands went up and cries of assent came from others. James was pleased and counted up who was with him, he reckoned the nine of them could make a difference and get his boss back. How hard could it be against one marshal and two other men? Once organized if they all struck at the same time it should be a breeze.

"Okay, now we wait till dark, it'll be easier for us then. We need to go find McAllister who looks like being in a cell at the sheriff's, we're going right in there and get him out, if we have to kill the marshal and whoever he has with him to do it then so be it, you all got that?"

"Sure we have James but how are going to get him out alive, won't that marshal just shoot him?"

"That was something James hadn't thought about, "We'll worry about that when we get there and see what the situation is now get ready we go soon," he walked off to get his horse and to think of a plan. It was a couple of hours later when they all rode out from the ranch.

As they rode into town James still hadn't got a plan of action, all he knew was he had to get McAllister out of jail whatever it took. He knew there wouldn't be much opposition, okay the marshal was going to be a hard one but apart from him there was just a beat up sheriff and an ex convict so he figured it wouldn't be too hard to do however he tackled it. He had some hare-brained ideas thrown at him as they rode in, all of which he rejected. His idea was simply just to storm the place with all guns blazing.

Timber and Sarah were in the cafe enjoying being together and talking in between eating. They had been together quite a lot and had got to know each other a little although Sarah could see that Timber had hidden depths she knew she would never get to know. She was however happy in his company and he made her feel safe.

Winston had made some ground in getting the sheriff's office organized. He had completed most of the paperwork that needed doing and had looked through the pile of wanted notices there, he knew a few of the faces he saw. Giles helped around the place and got food and water for the prisoners and coffee for them and their food. He was good company and Winston got to like him.

"Be good if we could be the sheriff and deputy here all the time wouldn't it Winston," he said to him.

"I'm not to sure about that Giles, I have my farm to run and the town council would have to approve that anyway."

"Just an idea," Giles stood by a window looking at the street until he said, "Hey we got company coming, lots of it."

James was pleased to get into town with the nine men. It wasn't very busy being late which pleased him as he rode straight down to the sheriff's office. He got off his horse as did two others when they got there while the other men all waited around on their horses.

"Hey in the office, we've come for Mister McAllister, you'd better just give him up to us."

Winston leapt up from his chair where he'd had his boots resting on the desk, "Get us a rifle each," he said to Giles as he hurried to a window. Outside he could see James with two men beside him and the others waiting, "Where is Timber now I want him?" James said to himself. He opened a window to shout back, "Just go and leave this James, you're not going to do any good."

"We ain't going without McAllister so you'd better just open up."

Winston closed the window and pulled the wooden blind down leaving just a slot to fire through. Giles was busy doing the other window. As James saw them doing that he fired shots at them which came close to hitting them. The two men with him took up the cue and fired as well. Winston and Giles were lucky to secure the windows with their lives.

Timber and Sarah weren't that far away so they heard the gunshots.

"Sounds like trouble Sarah," Timber got up and threw a bill on the table then raced out, Sarah wasn't far behind him. They hurried down the street to where they could see riders outside the sheriff's office.

"Oh no, Carlton's men, they've come for him," Sarah said as they hurried on. Timber drew his guns and ran until he was within shouting range of them.

"You men back off from there," he stopped on the sidewalk with some cover from porch posts. He waved for Sarah to get back. She still had her gun and got it out ready to use.

James turned around with the two other men and fired at Timber. Timber fired back and one of the men fell. Winston and Giles began to fire as well from the windows making everyone scatter. Some rode off a ways while others just left their horses and ran for some cover.

Inside the office McAllister and Longstone gripped the bars of their cells anxious to see how it would all pan out.

"I told you my men would come for us," McAllister said turning to see Longstone.

"Let's hope they can do something," Longstone replied.

Winston and Giles had heard Timber's shots and had seen the man fall so they knew he must be out there somewhere.

James had the men all start firing at the door and windows hoping for a lucky shot. He had a man with him where he was crouched behind a horse trough.

"We need to get to the door, cover me," he then ran out and dodged around to get under a window and to the door. He tried the handle but Winston had locked it. He tried to see in through the window slot in the door and fired twice through it. Winston then knew someone was there but daren't go to it, he stayed where he was knowing it would be a hard job to get the door open.

James got another man to join him then another while the next man was shot down on the way then they began shooting at the door lock and used a bench as a battering ram against it. The other men gave covering fire as townsfolk kept their distance and watched. The door was giving way much to McAllister's cries of joy. Winston and Giles weren't so happy but they couldn't leave their windows to do anything about it.

Timber had taken two of the men out and was now trying to get Sarah to back off as he was worried about going off and leaving her and he sure didn't want her with him. The trouble was that Sarah wanted to be in on it.

"Just stay here and if you have to come stay right behind me," Timber didn't have time to say or do anything else as he went a few yards closer to the men, firing as he went. He took one out straight away but others fired at him making him and Sarah dove down onto the sidewalk

Winston heard the door cracking open so he took one more shot which thankfully hit its target then he went to the door.

"It's going to break open soon Giles can you shoot any of them?"

Giles was at a window where that might be possible. To make it easier he pulled up the wooden blind to lean out but he was then met with a barrage of shots so he had to close it again.

Timber looked to see how many of them there were left. It looked like there were three at the door and two left outside. Timber was about to fire at the three on the door when it suddenly burst open and two of them went inside, the last one was too slow and Timber shot him down. The men outside concentrated their fire on Timber now that James was inside. Sarah had managed to get up on a barrel beside a porch pole unseen by the men which gave her a good view down onto them. She aimed carefully and took the shot. The bullet struck a man in his head and finished him. The man next to him jumped up to shoot Sarah but now he was showing more of himself Timber easily shot him.

Inside the office James stumbled as the man with him pushed against him to get inside. Winston was set to shoot James but he suddenly dropped down behind the desk. The man with him stormed in and shot Giles before he turned his gun on Winston but he was too late as Winston had time to aim at him and fire. The man was taken in his throat and he fell back in the doorway. James got up only to look down the barrel of Winston's gun. He still thought of taking the chance when he saw Timber come in also aiming a gun at him.

"Drop it James, I won't ask twice," Timber told him.

James dropped the gun and stood there. Then he looked over to McAllister, "I tried," he said.

McAllister nodded then sat on the bed dejected as did Longstone.

"You're under arrest James," Winston said and took him to lock him up with McAllister as he only had the two cells.

"That was a hell of a day," Winston said as he walked back.

"There's a lot of organizing to do out here," Sarah called as she looked in.

Winston called back, "You're right. He went to look at Giles with Timber then he turned to him, he's alive, get the doctor."

Sarah heard him and ran off only to meet the doctor a few yards away.

"I guess I might be needed," he said and went back with her.

They stood around while the doctor worked on Giles. After a while he said, "He'll be okay, he'll live."

"That's good, thanks doc," Timber said.

"He'll need some care for a while."

"I'll make sure he gets it," Winston said as he walked to the cells with Timber and Sarah to check on the prisoners.

"I guess we won't have that talk now," McAllister said looking straight at Sarah."

"I guess not," Sarah turned away not wanting to be with him any more.

"You three will all stay here until the circuit judge arrives then we can finalize all this," Timber told them" Can you manage everything?" Timber asked Winston.

"Sure, no problem."

He seemed happy to do it so Timber took Sarah away to a saloon after making sure Scout was okay where he ordered a whiskey for her and a beer for him which they took to a table.

"You did very well out there," Timber told her.

"Uhuh, first time I ever killed a man," She looked glum as she emptied the glass.

Timber waved at the bartender for another whiskey for her, "It was still the thing to do, they were bad men, paid assassins."

"I know, its still a big deal though."

"Sure, but you probably saved my life and gave me time to save Winston's so don't beat yourself up for long over it."

Sarah smiled at him, "Thanks. So what's next for you?"

"I need to go see the council again in the morning and get them to straighten the mess out McAllister has made then I guess I'll be free to ride on out of here, how about you?"

"I'm going back east to my aunt. I've had enough of it out here."

Timber stayed with her for a while until she excused herself to go and get ready to leave. Timber ordered another beer and took a pack of cards from a pocket, it was time for some relaxation before he went to the hotel for a night in his room before calling on the council tomorrow.

THE END

VOLUME FOUR

REVENGE IN THE LONE STAR

1

Jason Archer stood back and looked at the men he had with him. All of them were strong hard men and all of them were almost as merciless as he was. They had stopped at a stream where there was a grove of trees for shade against the burning sun in the barren lands of Texas. It wasn't the best place to be but they were there to avoid being caught by a posse who had been chasing after them.

They had raided and robbed a store in a small town and hadn't expected to have the response they'd had of a posse being rounded up. They had been lucky to avoid it so far. Sure they had robbed the store of supplies and money and they had killed the store owner in the process but even so it was a surprise to have men come after them. They might have been caught as well if it hadn't have been for Jason's brother.

Ashley Archer was younger than Jason by two years and Jason never let him forget it. Even so on this occasion it was him that had saved the day. He had been riding drag and looking around every now he had seen riders coming towards them. He had no doubt who they were and gave the alarm for them all to run. It had been Jason even then who had decided where they would run to and at least for now he had been successful.

Ashley had teamed up with his brother who already had three outlaws with him. Over time they collected three more who were hardened criminals as they all were. The brothers had come along the Upper Road Trail in Texas looking to find somewhere they weren't known to carry on with their lives of crime and had decided on the area to the north of San Antonio.

Before either of the Archer brothers had become outlaws they had started out in wagons with their wives having given everything up in Galveston. Unfortunately on the way Ashely lost his wife; Betty to consumption and then they had more bother when a group of bandits found them. They appeared from nowhere and attacked them. Jason had a friend with him who was killed as the bandits rode in firing their guns. The bandits then had them step away from the wagons while they ransacked them breaking things and throwing everything out laughing and joking as they did so. They took what they wanted while the men stood helpless with guns aimed at them. It was Lucy, Jason's wife who shouted out to them to stop which only made things worse. They grabbed her and pulled her onto one of their horses behind a bandit and they rode off taking her with them.

Once they had gone Jason got his gun which the bandits hadn't found in the wagon. Ashley got a shotgun he had stashed away then they set out after the bandits. It was a hard fast ride until they came across them where they had stopped to take a proper look at what they had got. They had Jason's wife off the horse and she was struggling against them. Jason was in a rage and shot the man closest to her. That got everyone shooting. Ashley with his shotgun split two men in two while Jason took out two other men, he was so incensed he didn't care who he killed. One bandit got Lucy around her neck with a gun to her head. As Jason tried to find a clear shot at him the bandit could see it was all over for him being the last bandit left so he shot her dead then fired at Jason which almost hit him. Jason shot him and emptied his gun of bullets into the man's quivering body.

They buried Lucy where they were and left the bandits for the critters and buzzards while they took all the things the bandits had so they now had horses, guns and some supplies. It changed their ideas of what they wanted to do. They gave up on the plan they had of starting a ranch as they sat around a camp fire that night.

Jason suggested that they take up a life of being outlaws and take what they wanted and needed from anyone they could. Jason was pleased that Ashley agreed with him.

"You know what Jason, it sounds like a damn good idea to me. Why should we toil and graft at a ranch now that Betty and Lucy are gone?"

"You sure you wanna do that?" Jason really wanted to be sure of his brother.

"Sure, I'm sure. Why we can shoot well enough and what else is there for us now?"

Jason nodded his head, "It won't be easy or a bed of roses. Being outside the law means we will have to keep riding on and watching our backs the whole time."

"So what? We have been badly wronged Jason and who is going to help us now. I don't want to be a rancher anymore. I say we go on the road and get what we can until we have enough money to buy a ranch already built with everything we need."

The talk carried on into the night and then they slept on it. By the morning the decision was made and from then on they searched out places to rob trying to get that money together while having men join them along the way. They found that to get it they often had to kill as well which strangely came easily to them. Within a short time they had made a name for themselves as the 'Archers' traveling around a large area robbing and killing while keeping away from the occasional posse that came after them. That was until they were offered a job they couldn't refuse.

They had been in a one horse town when they had been approached by a man who recognized them from wanted posters he had seen but he had no intention of handing them in, on the contrary he went to see them because of what they were. His offer of work in getting money for him the way they were doing was just too good to be true and they accepted it as the reward offered was so great. They needed more men to achieve what the man wanted from them but they were easy to get together, very quickly they had six men working with them.

Jason had a mug of coffee as he stood at the stream watching his men. Carter was almost as tall as he was at six feet. He was broad and he had that crop of black unruly hair just like his that would never quite stay under his hat. He was a sensible clear thinking man, that was different to his younger brother, Emmett. He was shorter and not as broad he was also less of a talker, more of a thinker but when he did talk it was normally good to listen to him. Carter was with a man called Ryder as he often was. The two men got on well and Jason was pleased as the two men were fast reliable gunmen.

Ashley was with four other men around the fire where they were drinking coffee. Troy was dimmer than all the others, he was always slower to catch up on what was being said or to understand a joke. That didn't make him any better or worse than the others though. He was just as good with a gun and he didn't mind using it, it just didn't matter to him, he would shoot without thinking and often while putting himself in harms way. Ashley had often thought he would get killed doing that but so far he hadn't. Walker was very much like Ashley. A calm man who thought things through. Gideon was the last man to join them, he was talkative and liked to make jokes about the others which sometimes didn't go down so well. Together they made an eight man outlaw gang intent on getting as much money as they could as easily as they could to pass on to the man Jason had met in return for freedom and riches.

2

Jason called them all together. He waited until they gathered around before he started talking.

"Okay, now we all know what we've got to do and I've been thinking, we ought to try our luck with the stagecoaches. We've seen them coming through and we all know they carry a strongbox that could contain valuables for the taking and then there's the passengers valuables and their luggage."

Ashely nodded, "Been thinking along those lines myself, what do you say boys?"

Carter was the first to speak, "Yeah sure that sounds real easy."

Troy couldn't help but add to Carter, "I'd love to shoot up a stagecoach."

"It'll be more than just that Troy," Jason said, "We need to plan it out and each man have his place and do his part of the job if it's gonna work for us."

"Sure okay," Ryder said, "That sure sounds like a good idea though. We'd only have the driver and shotgun guard to deal with."

"Better than a town full of folk," Ashley said.

"Okay we need a plan, so first thing we do is take a ride into the next town which must have a stagecoach office as we have seen them passing close to here. We find out what and when is coming through then we go and hold it up."

"Sounds good Jason, we should have done that some time ago," Ashley said.

"Well we can do it now. Pack up here let's ride."

It was a day later when they rode into Angel Creek and took a good look around the town. It was a bustling place with plenty of targets for them to rob but Jason didn't want any of that.

"We stick to what we are doing here. We don't want any folk to get to know our faces or anything about us," he said as they rode along the streets.

They found the stagecoach office pretty easily as a stagecoach came squeaking and rattling past them so all they had to do was follow it. When they arrived they saw the sign above the office which told them it was part of the Butterfield Overland Mail Company. They stopped at the building next door which very fortunately happened to be a saloon. They hitched their horses then took a good look at the stagecoach. Two men were getting down from the box which they took a good look at.

"If those two are on the ones we get it's gonna be like taking candy from a baby," Troy said.

Ashley gave him a hard look, "I said to keep quite about our business," he told him.

They stood in silence as they watched the men go into the office while other men came to replace the horses.

"Y'all wait here I'll go in and ask a few questions, see what you can see while I'm gone," Jason said before moving off.

They all watched him go then Troy spoke up again, "Let's take us a look inside it," he moved off before Ashley could stop him to go right up to the stagecoach and opened the door from the sidewalk to take a look inside it.

"That man," Ashley said as he moved off after him.

They all began to move towards the stagecoach until Ashley waved them away then he grabbed hold of Troy's shirt collar and pulled him back as he was about to climb inside.

"Hey," Troy called out indignantly.

"Hey nothing, you keep your big nose outta there. We don't want anyone here to see you enough to recognize you later, now git," Ashley shoved him away to where the rest of the men were standing a few yards away. They couldn't resist a laugh at Troy's misfortune. Ashely pushed him along so they all joined up again.

"Carter and and Ryder take a look around the back, the rest of us will stay here," Ashley told them.

They walked off while Ashley noticed a sign on the office wall which he wandered over to take a look at. It gave a list of the weeks stagecoach times and destinations.

"Huh, will you look at that, it's all here for us?"

"No need for Jason to go in there then," Emmett said.

As Emmett talked Jason came out the office again and walked over to them.

"You see the sign," Troy shouted to him.

Jason nodded and walked on taking them all with him to the saloon sidewalk.

"I've had a talk with the superintendent in there and yes I have seen the sign Troy. There is a stage coming in tomorrow from Houston which will fit the bill for us exactly. It's going to be full of passengers all of which sound like they will have money for us. I got out of him which trail it's coming in on without giving him any clues as to why I wanted to know."

"So we can get out there ready for it?" Ryder asked.

"We can but first this place looks of interest to me," he nodded at the saloon behind him and he didn't have any complaints. They all walked in and up to the bar which was already quite full. Troy was about to push his way in when Jason got hold of him.

"Remember and all of you," he said as they gathered to him, "We are not to be noticed so play it cool."

Troy calmed down and took a space there was at the bar while the others stood behind waiting. They got what drinks they wanted and then looked around for a table to sit at. They were all taken but one of them only had one man sat at it with spare chairs around it. Jason went up to him and stood beside him until the man paid him attention.

"Would you be happy to sit someplace else so me and my boys can sit together?" Jason asked.

Jake Timber looked up at him and at the men stood around him, "Seems to me there are other tables here you can go harass folk at."

Jason didn't know whether to take it further or not. After all the man looked like a drifter sitting there in deerskins with a wide floppy brown hat on. He then noticed the twin gun holster with Colt butts sticking out of it. What drifter wears two guns he thought? If it wasn't for the fact that he wanted to keep a low profile he might well have taken it further but he just smiled at Timber.

"Okay mister, you got it," he said and turned away to find that Troy and Emmett had persuaded two men to leave a table without any fuss so he walked over to join them.

Timber took a good look at the men then he turned back to his beer and the pack of cards laid out on the table for a game of Solitaire.

He had been in town for only a few hours having ridden east from a town where he'd had a big job of straightening out a cattle baron who had terrorized a town. Since then he had ridden east in Texas to arrive in Angel Creek. He'd been to see the sheriff earlier as he usually did when riding into a new town to check up with him on any outlaws Timber was looking for or to find out what wanted notices he had and if there was anyone special he needed to look out for. The sheriff hadn't been that helpful but he had shown Timber the wanted notices he had. None of them were of especial interest but Timber had taken a copy of those he thought he might look into.

All the outlaws stayed at the table they had, drinking and quietly discussing the raid they would be doing tomorrow and they paid no more attention to Timber.

Timber only paid a small amount of interest in them. He had noted that they were all wearing guns but then that by itself didn't mean anything. He had taken an instant dislike to all of them, they seemed far too sure of themselves and they appeared rough and rowdy. Even so he wasn't worried about them. He finished his beer, put his cards away and walked out. He had his horse; Scout at the hitch rail and mounting up he rode down to where he knew the livery stable was. Once there he booked him in for the night then went off to book a find at the hotel.

3

Jason talked for a while with everyone about the stagecoach raid they were going to do the following day. He felt quite safe talking about it in the saloon as it was noisy and they were all gathered close together. Once he had outlined his plan and they had finished drinking he took them all out again.

"You got any thoughts on where to stay tonight?" Ashley asked.

"I guess we move out of town, as agreed we don't want anyone to remember us," they all nodded at that totally forgetting about the man in deerskins.

The rode out of town for a few miles towards the place where Jason had already thought of holding up the stagecoach. Along the way they found a suitable area to stop at close to the trail they had been following. There was a grove of trees perfect for them to get behind off the trail. Together they soon had a fire going with food and coffee heating up on it.

"I can't wait to get us some real money together," Carter said.

They all agreed as they finished eating and holding mugs of coffee.

"We won't get that much from the stagecoach Carter," Jason said smiling at him.

"No but it will be a start. All the money we get we seem to spend."
There was no disagreement with that.
"Maybe we should try a bank," Ryder said.
"That's an idea," Jason agreed, "maybe after this stagecoach job."

It was something for them all to think about that night. The next morning they were up and ready to ride early as Jason didn't want to miss the stagecoach and they had some miles left to ride. Eventually they came to a bend in the trail that went around a high rock outcrop which Jason considered to be as good a place as any for the hold up. Just around the bend was a long straight that they could use to stop the stagecoach on.

"Okay, we will do it here. Ryder, get up these rocks and warn us when it reaches the far end of the trail then we can all ride out. Don't worry Ryder you'll get back down in time to join us."

Having that organized they all found themselves a place to wait. Jason had already discovered that the stagecoach should be where they were before midday so they didn't have too long to wait.

The stagecoach was a few miles away and making good time for Angel Creek. The driver was an older man but an experienced member of the Butterfield line. Doug Evans had done the run many times before. He knew about the bend in the trail but he'd never had any trouble there before so he carried on towards it.

Sitting next to him was his shotgun guard, Carl Harlow also an experienced man. He sat with the shotgun handy across his lap. He'd only ever had to use it once and that was a while ago so he also wasn't worried about the upcoming bend.

Inside the coach was a bulky businessman who kept a bag on his knee when he could just as easily put in in the net above the seat. He sweated continually which didn't do anything for the smell of bodies. Robert Earl just couldn't rest, his black thin hair was slicked down flat on his head and his round glasses kept on slipping off his nose.

Sitting next to him in the middle was Jon Baker. Jon was a tall scrawling kinda man, slow in his actions and his speech. At the end of the bench was Wyatt Stanley. He hardly spoke the whole time but he looked around him and gazed out the widow on occasions by pulling the blind up that was stopping the dust from coming in. His clothes were neat and close fitting and he wore a jacket the whole time even in the heat.

On the opposite bench sat two people, Mister and Missus Austin McKenzie. Austin was a big man dressed very smartly in black jacket, trousers and white shirt. He was sitting quietly holding hands with his wife Emma who was dressed in a fine long blue dress. She had her long blond hair tied up in a bun and a small white hat set on top.

Ryder had got up on top of the outcrop to keep an eye out for the stagecoach approaching while the rest of them waited at the bottom. Jason couldn't resist an occasional peep around the bend to look for it. Ryder saw the dust before he saw the stagecoach. It was coming along fast so he quickly got down the rocks to say that it was coming.

Jason had spent some time telling everyone of how he thought it best to handle this and where all of them should be. No one had any complaints and as soon as Ryder gave them the news they all pulled their bandanas over their faces and prepared to ride out. Jason told Ryder to take a look around the bend while keeping out of sight and let them know when the stagecoach was at the distance away they wanted it. Ryder gave the word a little early so he could get back to his horse before they all set off towards the oncoming stagecoach, racing around the bend straight towards it.

Both Doug and Harlow saw the outlaws approaching and Carl brought up the shotgun. Jason saw him do that and he fired at him. The shot went slightly off from where he wanted it and it caught Carl in his shoulder making him drop the shotgun and grab his shoulder where blood began to leak out. Doug could see there was no way he was going to get past the outlaws riding towards him and there was no way off the trail he was on because of the high rocky outcrop on one side and the small outcrops on the other so he had to pull up. He looked across at Carl as the outlaws rode up and asked him how he was.

"I guess I'll live," Carl answered holding his shoulder trying to stop the blood from coming out.

Jason pulled up at the side of Doug while Ashley went to Carl's side. The others all stayed a few yards away on both sides of the stagecoach. Ryder was beside the door on the driver's side while Carter took the opposite door. Emmett stayed with Carter while Troy and Walker were with Ryder. Both Ryder and Walker got off their horses while Troy stayed on his which was to keep guard and was Jason's idea of keeping him where he couldn't mess things up.

"Just hold it there driver, don't you go trying to move off now," Jason called to him. He could see the shotgun guard was no longer any threat and the shotgun had fallen to the ground. He then moved out a little so he could see the stagecoach doors from an angle while still able to see the driver. Ashley did the same on the other side.

"You people inside just all come on out this side now," Jason called to them.

The first person out was a man who took his time and looked around before coming down the steps to the ground. Jon looked at the outlaws before he slowly got to the ground without speaking. Wyatt followed him and had to duck low to get out of the door. Next out was the business man Robert who protested all the time as he huffed and puffed his way out. As they gathered around Ryder got them to stand in a line beside the stagecoach. After a few seconds Austin came out blinking to get his eyes accustomed to the bright light. Once he got down he then leaned back into the coach where Emma looked out then took his hand to help her get down before they joined the line where Austin kept her to his side closest to the other passengers.

Once they were all out and standing still Jason and Ashley rode their horses back to the front of the stagecoach.

"Throw the strongbox down," Jason called out to Doug. Carl wasn't going to be of much help sitting back as he was holding his shoulder. Doug tried and found it hard to shift it until Jason left his horse and went to help him. The box then fell easily to the ground and Jason shot the padlock off it and opened the lid while Ryder stood close by.

With the attention of those two taken Wyatt shuffled around a little to make some space between him and the other passengers. He could only see Walker and Troy from where he was and he decided to take a chance. He stepped out further from the other passengers and pulled a gun from under his jacket.

"Drop the guns," he called out.

The words shocked the outlaws and came as a surprise to the other passengers as well. Ryder spun around as Walker and Troy both turned their guns on him.

Wyatt saw that they weren't going to do as he had asked and as he aimed to take down the closest outlaw all three of them shot him down in a welter of bullets.

"What the hell did he do that for?" Ryder shouted.

Everyone was too shocked to answer then Jon decided to move towards where Wyatt had dropped his gun. Jason saw him doing that from where he was and not wanting to take any chances he shot him.

"Whoa hold it fella, no need to shoot us all," Doug said to him but Jason took no notice of him.

Robert stood with his eyes closed shaking with fear still holding on tight to his bag. Austin had Emma in his arms who was now shaking and crying.

"No need!" Jason said, "If they hadn't tried anything they would still be alive. Ashley come and help me here." Jason looked back down at the strong box as Ashley rode up. Carter and Emmett also rode around to help. They all dismounted to assist Jason to empty the contents of the strongbox into cloth bags which they then began to hang onto their horses.

Ryder walked up to Robert and stood just a couple of feet in front of him holding his gun, "Give me the bag," he said.

Robert didn't move. He just stood shaking his eyes still closed mumbling to himself.

"I said, give me the bag," Ryder then poked him in his belly with his gun.

Robert opened his eyes and looked at Ryder suddenly understanding what he had said, "No, no way you can't have it," he gripped it to his chest even tighter.

"Give it me, you fat idiot," Ryder said snatching it out of his hands.

He dropped it on the ground as Robert begged him to give it back then Ryder grinned and knelt down to open it watched by Troy and Walker both aiming their guns at the passengers.

Ryder gave a look of surprise when he opened the bag, "Wow, yeah fat guy, this will do nicely."

"But you don't understand, the money isn't mine, I'm just delivering it for a client," Robert sobbed at Ryder.

"Just tell him you lost it," Ryder said jabbing Robert again as he stepped forward to try and get the bag back. Ryder fastened it to his saddle and then looked at how they were doing at the strongbox. They had finished and looked back at Ryder who then nodded at Austin and Emma.

"What about these two," he called out.

Austin stepped in front of Emma, "Now you leave my wife be, y'hear?" Austin said in as stern a voice he could manage.

"We'll do just as we please mister and while we're at it we'll have what you've got and we'll get everyone else's things," Ryder held his hand out.

Austin stepped forward again his anger boiling inside him. Ryder saw the look on his face and decided to do something about it. He reached forward to push Austin back but Austin punched him in his face making him stagger back.

"Why you..." Ryder said as he recovered his balance and he fired his gun once hitting Austin in his heart killing him.

Emma screamed and dove down to hold Austin, "Austin, no, no," she cried as she saw he was dead. She looked back up at Ryder, "You murdering scum, I'll get you for this."

Ryder wasn't happy about what he had done but he put on a brave face now, "He shouldn't have hit me."

"What do you think he would do, you were threatening us," Emma wept as she said the words.

Jason came up with Ashley and saw what had happened.

"You heard what Ryder said now hand over your valuables," Jason advanced on Robert and Emma so they did as he asked. Ryder checked the bodies and robbed them. Emma watched on horrified as her husband was searched and his money, ring and his knife belt was taken as well as his gold watch.

"Get on your horse Ryder, we're riding out," he gave Emma a look then went back to his horse. Soon they were all riding off in a cloud of dust.

4

As the outlaws rode off Emma stayed sobbing over her husband's body. She was inconsolable by Doug who jumped down from the box to be with her. Whatever he said made no difference to her she sobbed and swore she would get her revenge.

Robert found it hard to come out of his trance but eventually he did but he was of no use to Emma at all, he just wandered around in a dream as Doug tried to get Emma up.

"Come on now miss we gotta get back to town and tell the sheriff about those men," Doug said to her touching her shoulder.

Emma then did get up and dried her tears, "Yes we must, but we can't just leave him here."

Doug turned to Robert, "You're gonna have to help me to get these men into the coach. Never you mind miss, you can ride up on top with me and Carl."

Carl was of no use and it took Doug together with Robert's help to get the bodies into the stagecoach. Emma was of more use than he was. As they worked Doug had something to say.

"You know that Wyatt fella who started things, well he was an employee of Butterfield's, an extra guard we have with us by and by."

"Pity he didn't shoot at least one of them," Emma replied.

Doug nodded, agreeing with her.

Emma went to see Carl and she climbed up to him and helped to dress his wound as best as she could, "We need to get him to a doctor as quick as we can," she said seeing how pale and weak he was. She got what coats and rugs she could find and wrapped them around him and wondered if he would be better off inside the coach but it was rather full in there and anyway he was adamant about staying where he was.

The ride back to the town of Angel Creek was not a good one. Robert had to ride inside with the bodies which he was not pleased about. Emma sat in between Doug and Carl her mind in a whirl the whole way back. Doug drove the horses as hard as he could wanting to get Carl back to town and the doctor as soon as possible but he still had to slow down at big ruts so as not to jolt him too much. As soon as Doug pulled up outside the Butterfield office he jumped down to get help. Very soon the stagecoach was surrounded by men all trying to get Carl down from the box and empty the coach. For a while it was pretty busy there. Emma was escorted into the office and through to the inner office of the superintendent where she was sat down and a glass of whiskey offered her which she took.

The superintendent Alfred Masterton had hurriedly provided her with the drink then he sat on a chair in front of her, "Now miss you must tell me all about what happened."

Emma waved a hand at him as she finished the whiskey, "Oh really, my head is in such a whirl."

Alfred could see that and he had to stop as Doug came into the office, "She needs rest, we can talk to her later, I can tell you all about the outlaws and what happened," he said.

Alfred beckoned him in as two townsfolk women came in to take Emma away to look after her. She was taken to the hotel where a room had been provided for her by the proprietor in view of what had happened. She was made comfortable and offered food and drink which she refused. They stayed with her for a while to make sure she was okay to leave then they gave her some time alone.

The rest of the day was taken up with the bodies being taken to the undertaker, Carl to the doctor and discussions about what had happened all over town.

Sheriff Dusty Colby was all over it. He checked in at the Butterfield office to learn what he could there then he visited the hotel to see Emma. She wasn't in a good place when he entered her room accompanied by Sue Ellen, the woman who had specially been looking after Emma.

"I hear you've had a bad time miss and I'm sorry about your husband," he said to her as Sue sat next to her on the bed and put a protective arm around her.

"Bad! You have no idea of the horrors I've seen. Three men were shot down in front of me including my husband, how can you even imagine that?" Emma felt the tears dripping down her face again as Sue whispered words to her and tried to comfort her.

Dusty stood back, lost for words as Emma looked back up at him, "So when are you going after them?"

"Well now er, that's a maybe."

"A maybe?"

"Sure, they will be long gone by now and getting a posse here will be hard to do."

"Of course they'll be long gone but surely sheriff it's your job..."

"It's my job to keep the law and order in this town Emma yes but to go out there..."

Emma glared at him with almost as much hatred as she felt for her husband's killers, "If you won't do something about them then I will."

"Now now, you know you can't do that. Those men will be caught sooner or later you mark my words."

"Just how much later do you think that will happen sheriff?" Emma spat the words out.

Dusty had no answer, he just shrugged and walked out.

Emma stayed in the room for some time until Sue managed to persuade her to go and eat with her. In the restaurant Emma found she could only manage a few mouthfuls then she excused herself and prevented Sue from going with her as she walked out.

Her first call was at the undertaker to ensure he husband was being taken care of and to arrange his funeral. The second was back at the hotel where she emptied her bags on the bed that had been taken up for her and she changed into a white shirt, black trousers and jacket, under which she buckled on her husband's gun belt and stuffed his Colt .44 into the holster which he had taken with him in his bag. She went down to the desk and paid for the clerk to look after her things for her saying she would be away for a few days then she headed down to the livery stable.

She had come to town with her husband for him to take up a job at the bank with hopefully a job for her too. The bank was going to arrange some accommodation for them until they got settled, well she had no use for that now. At the stables she looked at what horses the hostler had for sale and she was able to buy what she thought was a good black gelding together with a saddle, bridle and all the bits and pieces she needed. She was determined to find the outlaws and kill all of them. She had used her husband's gun often before after he had taught her how to use it figuring you never knew when that knowledge might be useful, well now it was.

5

When Emma had left Alfred found he was very busy with men coming in and out all wanting to know what had happened and his own men busy trying to straighten out the stagecoach. The sheriff had been of little help and soon disappeared. Alfred had been keen to find out whether the sheriff was going out after the outlaws but found he wasn't interested in doing that. At least Doug had managed to bring the strongbox back. He had persuaded Robert to help him put it back under the box. He had taken a quick look inside it to find there were only a few letters and paperwork left in the bottom of it. He had no idea what else it had contained. Alfred now had the job of straightening that all out.

Timber heard the news about the hold up while taking a beer in the same saloon as last time, 'Barney's Saloon'. He couldn't help but hear when a group of men strode in telling tales of what had happened and how the outlaws had killed so many men and that none of the outlaws had been killed. They were full of it. Timber took it all as their wistful thinking and moved out to the sheriff's office to get the facts. He walked in the office to find Dusty Colby sorting through some paperwork, a job Timber knew was the bane of any sheriff.

Dusty looked up as Timber walked in and looked around then got impatient, "Can I help you mister?"

"I sure hope so," Timber said while taking the man in, so far he wasn't impressed, "I hear there's been a stagecoach hold up."

"You heard right, early today on its way here, so what's it to you?"

"Oh, it may well be of interest," Timber pulled his marshal badge from a pocket and showed it him, "Jake Timber U.S. Marshal. I have the sometimes unenviable job to round up criminals in Texas and these boys sure sound like good candidates to me."

Dusty calmed down, "Okay, why didn't you say you are a marshal when you walked in?"

Timber shrugged, "I've told you now," he stood waiting on the sheriff.

"Yeah okay. A band of outlaws held it up at Comanche Bend. They emptied the strongbox, stole everything worth anything from all the passengers and ended up killing three of them and injuring Carl the guard."

This was a watered down version of what was going around the saloon as Timber figured, "Any survivors?"

"Yeah the driver Doug, a businessman and a woman, Emma McKenzie. Doug may give you some information, he's a steady guy. Carl's with the doc, I'd try him later. The business man had his eyes closed the whole time apparently so I'd give him a miss which leaves you with Emma," Dusty shook his head and looked down.

Timber waited then asked, "What's with Emma?"

Dusty looked up at him, "She came with her husband to start work at the bank, he was one of the men who were killed."

Timber nodded and pursed his lips as Dusty carried on.

"She's taken it very badly. Okay I know anyone would but, well there's something different about Emma. She's one strong lady and she is determined to bring them to justice," Dusty grinned, "of course I told her that ain't gonna happen, she will have to wait until they are caught doing some other job."

"Not necessarily, where will I find her?"

"Last I heard she was gonna get a horse from the livery and go after them herself."

Timber nodded and walked out without another word. He took a walk down to the livery stable and saw a woman checking over the tack and a horse as he walked in.

"Your name Emma Mckenzie," he asked her.

Emma turned surprised to hear her name being called out. She was even more surprised to see a big man standing there dressed in deerskins wearing a brown wide brimmed hat, black boots with silver toe and heel caps and most of all the fact that he was wearing twin Colt .44 revolvers at his waist. At first she wasn't going to answer him but something made her change her mind.

"Yes, I'm Emma, who's asking?" She stood her ground looking straight at him which confirmed the impression that Dusty had of her.

"The name is Timber, U.S. Marshal," he showed her his badge to confirm it then put it away, "I heard about the hold up, would you like to tell me about it?"

"I've already told the sheriff and the Butterfield line superintendent," she turned away as she began to saddle up.

"Maybe, but you haven't told me. Why don't you just leave that for a spell and fill me in?"

Emma turned bak to him, "I don't know mister, its been a long day."

"That I can believe and it's Timber. Leave the horse, come and eat with me, I want to know all you can tell me if I'm going to get those men."

"What you'd go after them?" Her face was suddenly full off hope and surprise.

"Sure, why not?"

"Well that's a lot more than the sheriff will do," Emma made her mind up, "okay you got it, where?" She asked looking around.

"Not here, come on there's a good restaurant just up the street, my treat."

Emma had to grin at his serious face in spite of everything, "Okay, lead on."

Once they were seated and had a plate of food in front of them Timber let Emma eat. It had been a while for her and although she thought she wouldn't, she cleaned the plate. Afterwards over coffee she began to lighten up as she got to know Timber a little better. It was harrowing for her to recall the death of her husband and she skipped over it but Timber got the idea of the whole hold up.

"What names did you hear?" he wanted to know.

Emma didn't have to think, "Ryder was one. Ashley was another."

"But you didn't see any faces?"

"No sorry, they all wore their bandanas up over their faces the whole time."

"What about their horses, did anything stand out to you?"

"Now that you mention it yes. There was a pure black; a bay with four white socks..." she went on to describe all of them.

"You have an eye for detail," Timber said.

"I can tell you what most of them were wearing too."

Timber was impressed and he let her tell him all she could remember.

"That will all be very useful for me when I get out there thanks."

Emma paused, "When you get out there?"

"Yeah, I'll go to where the hold up occurred and see what I can pick up, maybe there will still be some tracks to follow."

"But I'm going out there Timber but you can ride along if you wish."

Timber smiled at her, "This is work for me Emma."

"No way, I'm going and you can't stop me. I have my husbands gun and I sure know how to use it."

"You killed anyone with it?"

"Well no, but I sure know how to shoot."

Timber looked at her serious face, "So if I leave you here you'll just ride out after me huh?"

"You got it."

Timber sighed, "Okay ride with me but be prepared to do as I say if things get rough?"

Emma, smiled, the first time all day.

6

Timber wasn't sure about taking Emma along. He preferred to work alone and having a woman with him when chasing after a gang of dangerous outlaws didn't seem like a good idea. However he could see how determined she was and he sure didn't want her trailing along after him. He just had to hope after some time she would give up and go back to Angel Creek. He then let her go back down to the livery stable with him.

"Finish saddling up," he said to her and went to get Scout ready to move after finding the hostler and paying for the horses's keep. The big bay horse was pleased to see him and Timber soon had him ready. He led him out to find Emma waiting for him.

"So are we off now?" She asked him.

"Not yet, two calls to make first," Timber didn't say what they were but rode off leaving Emma to ride after him. The first call was to the Butterfield Overland Stagecoach office. They pulled up outside and Timber led the way inside. Alfred saw them come in from his inner office and he walked out to greet them.

"Who's your friend Emma?" He asked.

"This is Marshal Timber, he's going to help me find my husband's killers."

Alfred looked shocked, "Are you sure that's a good idea?"

"No she isn't," Timber interrupted, "but she's going with me anyway. I want a word with the driver and guard from that trip."

"I'm surprised to see you here marshal."

"Yeah, I just got in, so where will I find them?"

"Doug's over in the cafe just up the street, Carl's laid up at home."

"Where's home?"

Alfred gave him a look so Timber flashed him his badge and asked again. Alfred wrote it down for him. Timber took it and walked out then he went off with Emma looking for the cafe. They found it easily enough. Doug was sitting close to a window and easy to see from outside. Timber went in followed by Emma. He was surprised to see them and stopped eating as they walked up to his table.

Emma got in front of Timber and explained to Doug who he was who then looked up at Timber and waited.

"You were the driver on the stagecoach so you had the best chance of seeing those outlaws, I'm hoping there is something more you can remember to tell me to help find them?"

'I already told what I know enough times marshal, now if you don't mind I'm eating."

Timber pulled up a chair facing Doug and sat down, "You see Doug, I do mind. This lady here has lost her husband, other men have died today and I want to hear every little thing you can remember about the whole hold up, so start talking."

Doug sighed and pushed his half finished plate away, "From the beginning yeah?"

"That will work for me."

Timber listened to the whole story from Doug's point of view and angles and learned nothing more than he had from Emma. He thanked him and got up. He took Emma with him to find Carl's home which turned out to be a small house tucked in between two others in a street behind the Butterfield office. He knocked on the door and had to wait until an elderly woman answered it. She was surprised to see Timber standing there.

"What do you want?" She asked.

Timber showed her his badge, "U.S. Marshal Jake Timber. I'm looking into the stagecoach hold up and I need to talk to Carl."

The woman backed off and let them in, "He's not well marshal, please don't stay long," she guided them to an upstairs room where Carl was lying on a bed, his chest and shoulder wrapped in bandages. He recognized Emma when she walked in. Again she quickly explained who Timber was knowing Carl would be shocked to see such a man enter his bedroom. Carl just lay still as Timber asked the same questions as he had Doug. Carl was hardly in a situation to say much, but he did add something they didn't know

"As they rode up it was obvious one man was in charge. I heard his name being called; Jason. He was bigger than any of them. I noticed he was riding a pure black horse, no white socks or blaze just black."

Timber quizzed him further but that was the only extra thing they learned. They left him then and went to their horses outside.

"Can we get after them now?" Emma said as she mounted up.

"You wanna eat don't you? We go get supplies first, then we go," Timber mounted Scout and then rode with Emma down to a general store where Timber bought all he thought they would need and shared it out between their saddlebags. Emma bought a rifle at Timber's suggestion. Once they were ready Timber then led the way out until Emma rode up to him.

"Do you know where you are going?"

"Pretty much. The superintendent gave me directions, and you should know anyway."

"I know the trail we came in on so yeah I do," Emma pushed her horse slightly ahead of Scout as Timber grinned at her and let her take the lead.

The day was already well advanced but Timber was still pleased to get away from town and out into the open. They rode on until they managed to get to the place where the hold up had happened. It was now dusk and Timber didn't want to go walking all over it in the poor light.

"Its good to be here Emma but we'll wait until first light before we look it over," he told her.

Emma wanted to get a move on after the outlaws but she saw the sense of that. She stopped with him short of the location and just stared at it. It seemed strange to her that Austin had been killed just a short way from where she was. Seeing the place brought it all back to her and she had to wipe tears way from her eyes. She was angry with herself for breaking down. All that could wait until she had found the men responsible and had brought them to justice in whatever form that might take.

Timber saw the tears but he didn't say anything, he climbed down from Scout and set about preparing a camp for them. There was plenty of brushwood around to make a fire with and soon he had one burning. Emma helped in order to take her mind off things. She got tins of beans, some biscuits from her saddles bag and began to heat them up while attempting to make some gravy. Timber got busy with the coffee pot. It wasn't until it was all ready to eat and the horses had been seen to that they began to talk. Emma's horse had been hobbled but Scout was so well trained he was just let free.

"You think there may still be tracks of those men to follow?" Emma asked as she spooned beans into her mouth.

"Could be but they could be messed up some by now, I will see in the morning," as he spoke a wind sprung up and they huddled closer to the fire, it was going to be a cold night.

Emma shuddered and pulled a blanket around her, "Tell me something about yourself Timber, have you always been a marshal?"

Timber didn't normally get involved in conversations but somehow it all came out, "I was a sheriff once. Then I got involved with a man trying to rape a bargirl. I stopped him and in revenge he killed my wife and daughter."

Emma winced as she realized other people had bad happenings too.

"I found the man and subjected him to a particularly gruesome death which landed me in jail. I spent some dark days and nights in there in total despair and I would still be there if it hadn't have been for the territory governor the Honorable Robert Pierce Fullerton. He saw the potential in me and gave me the job I currently have of hunting down outlaws and bringing them to justice."

"You take them in for trial you mean?"

Timber had to smile, "No not usually. Usually I kill them but yes some do go to jail. It all depends on them really."

Emma nodded at that, pleased to hear it.

"So what about you Emma?"

She sat back and sighed before speaking, "I lived with my husband Austin back in Houston. He was in banking as I was and we got offered the job here which was a promotion for Austin and more money so we upped sticks and came out here, well kinda. Our things are still back in Houston all ready to bring over. We came out first to get the job organized and stay at the hotel until our things arrived. Austin had arranged a house for us to buy through the bank. Now I don't know what to do about any of that and I won't decide until those men have been dealt with," she looked at Timber and he could see the fire in her eyes.

"I ain't about to direct you either way. See how you feel once we get them."

"We will get them won't we?"

"I'll give it a danged good try, now get some sleep, it's gonna be a long day tomorrow."

Emma got into her bedroll and snuggled up while Timber settled himself down. Sleep never came easy for him and when it did he only slept for a couple of hours or so at a time. Often he would wake up in a cold sweat after a nightmare of what happened to his family.

7

Jason had ridden off fast from the stagecoach shocked to some extent at the murders they'd had to commit. The irony was if they had all just given in at first then they would still be alive. At the same time he was glad it had happened as it made a lot less people to give information about them to a posse or anyone else who decided to try and do something about it. He rode on for some time before slowing down to let his horse breathe. All the others had kept up with him and there hadn't been any talking. As they slowed down Ashley rode up alongside him.

"We sure straightened them out didn't we?" He grinned across at his elder brother.

Jason grinned back at him, "We did and we got the strongbox contents."

"Yeah, we need to go through all of that."

"In good time Ashley. We need to find a good place to hole up for tonight and check it all out plus what we got from the passengers."

"You figure we'll get a posse after us?"

"Could be, depends on what the folk of Angel Creek decide to do, hopefully nothing."

"Let 'em come," Carter said as he rode up to them, "We can take them on, no sweat."

Jason looked at the man. He had grown close to him over time. He was a man ready to fight for his freedom and for the things he wanted. Jason was pleased he was with them. He agreed with what he said but even so he still had words to say.

"That would depend somewhat on who came. A platoon of solders might be awkward. Best not to encourage conflict Carter, you never know how they might turn out."

Carter shook his head, "There ain't no soldiers near here. The best they may send out is a posse led by one sheriff and just a bunch of townsfolk."

Jason was going to give an answer then thought better of it, there wasn't going to be any pursuit, they were virtually home free. He would ride until dusk, camp out then carry on, no one was going to find them.

It was two hours later when they finally stopped for the night. Jason decided on the location. He found a canyon with a grove of trees at the bottom where they could hide away, just in case he had said. They built a small fire with hard dry wood for little smoke and settled down to rest and eat. They were all tired and it was only once they had eaten that they wanted to look through what they had taken. Jason had it all laid out on the ground for them to see.

"There it is boys, some letters and paperwork of no interest. Some money envelopes but also," he had to smile, "Bags of money, coins and bills, lots of them."

They all looked through as Ryder said, "We got some good things from the passengers too," he held up a gold pocket watch as an example.

"You keep that safe Ryder, could be worth a good few dollars," Jason told him.

"Don't worry, I intend to."

They shared out what there was and then Jason had an idea, "I say we stack the loot here to come back to when we need to, then if any of us get caught the rest get the full amount." Thee was some discussion about that but in the end they all agreed and found a good place under a jumble of rocks to leave it then they sat back down to chat and drink coffee.

"So you got any ideas on what's next Jason?" Ashley asked him.

"That stagecoach was a good target. I say we do another one, the money will be useful."

They all agreed with that, Carter then asked, "How do we find one?"

Jason rubbed his nose, "Ah already organized, you need to keep ahead. I got information on some others while in town."

Carter laughed as they all did, "Sounds good, so come on where and when?"

"There is one coming out of town tomorrow. We can wait for it out here to come to us. I heard some rich folk will be on it so it could be a good hit for us."

That information went down well with Ashley saying, "Trust you to come up with something."

"You know me, I'll look after us. Now that stage will be coming through here maybe late afternoon so we need to be ready for it."

"Plenty of time then."

"Maybe Ashley but it's not just here, we have to get to the trail and find a good place to ambush it from so we still need to be away tomorrow early."

"No problem with that. Here's to another good hit."

They were all happy with the arrangement although Jason knew he would have to finalize how to take the stagecoach once he found a good place along the trail tomorrow.

They all settled down thinking of what tomorrow was going to bring them.

8

Timber only slept for a couple of hours that night. He had the nightmare again of his wife and daughter being murdered and he woke up in a cold sweat. He sat up knowing no more sleep would come to him. It was still dark, the sun wouldn't come up for some time yet. He sat thinking of what he was currently doing. Chasing after a gang of outlaws was normal, having a woman tag along with him wasn't. She seemed a hardy kind of girl who said she could shoot but he wasn't putting any strength into that. She was going to be a liability for sure. He just had to see what he could do and how he could handle things to keep her safe and get the outlaws, no mean feat.

As dawn came Timber stoked up the fire and got some coffee heating up then he woke Emma who eventually stirred especially when Timber handed her a cup of hot coffee. Then he left her to go and cook some bacon and heat some beans he'd brought from town. Emma soon joined him and made short work of the food. Once it was all finished they got ready to go. Emma had to go get her horse while Timber just whistled for Scout. It wasn't long before they were right up at the hold up location.

"Just wait here Emma, let me take a look around," Timber said getting off Scout. He looked all around the area then went back to her and mounted up on Scout. "Seems like they headed off west so that's where we'll go."

Emma just nodded, thankful at last to be on their trail. They rode on for a while with Timber checking the ground as they went. He realized they were working their way around in a wide circle. It took some time but he found where the outlaws had made camp the night before. Emma was surprised.

"But that's not far from where we stopped last night."

"No it's not," Timber wondered what the outlaws intentions were. He had expected them to keep on riding in a straight line, at least for a while.

Timber carried on letting Emma ride beside him or behind, wherever she wanted. They carried on until Timber had to stop. He got off Scout and looked around again then went back to Emma.

"The tracks have become very confusing, all mixed up, there are two directions now they could have gone in," he mounted up as Emma looked around.

"So what are we going to do, split up?"

"No, we take the most likely route and hope to find fresh tracks soon," Timber took off in a direction that he knew would take them back to the stagecoach trail.

Jason had everyone out on the trail early. He knew they had a good few miles to ride to get around back to the stagecoach trail and then they would need time to organize the place they would hit the stagecoach from when it arrived. He kept the men going until they arrived at a place where they could see the trail laid out before them. They were on a slight rise which gave a good enough view in both directions.

"Not much here in the way of cover to attack it from," Ashley said as they sat on their horses looking at it.

"No. We'll have to ride until we find somewhere suitable," Jason carried on with the rest of them following on. It took him another couple of hours to find a suitable place. He pulled up where there was a bunch of trees just off from the trail. Some distance to the other side of the trail was a raised rocky area which would have been perfect but it was really too far away.

"This will have to do," he said as he rode into the trees.

"Not bad at all. We can hide in here and ride out at the last minute," Ashley said.

Ryder was interested in the rocky area, "Looks like we have someplace to ride off to as well."

Jason looked across to it and estimated how long it would take to get there and smiled, yes they had their escape route all right, "Okay take a rest and be ready for when we see that stagecoach approach."

They all settled by a tree in ones and twos to wait. They drank water from their canteens not wanting to start a fire. They didn't have long to wait as the stagecoach came into view earlier than expected which suited them all very well. Jason had them mount up in the cover of the trees and pull their bandanas up ready. Then as the stagecoach got close Jason took them all out with their guns drawn ready to hold it up.

The driver and guard didn't see the outlaws until the last minute as they came out of the trees. The guard raised the rifle he was holding and as the outlaws all got closer he took aimed and fired at one of them. For saying he was on a swaying stagecoach that the driver was still pushing the horses along and the outlaws were riding it was a pretty good shot. It took Ryder's hat off to go flying out behind him. He took umbrage to that and fired back. His third shot took the guard off the bench to roll in the dust as the stagecoach carried on.

The outlaws were all close to the stagecoach now and the driver could see he was going to have to stop or get killed. He reined the horses in and gradually stopped. The outlaws all surrounded it and keeping their guns leveled Jason called for the passengers to get out. Ashley was close to the driver who he warned not to try anything and throw down the strongbox. The driver having no choice did as he was asked letting it thud to the ground.

Ryder and Carter were at the doors of the coach and waited as the passengers all got out and lined up as they were told to do along the driver's side. Walker got the job of getting off his horse to collect what valuables they had into a bag he held out.

Timber and Emma were riding along towards the trail and saw the stagecoach traveling along then they were surprised to see the outlaws come out of the trees and hold it up. They were still a little way off so he slid off Scout letting him run on as he snagged his rifle. He called out to Emma to get on the ground as well then he lay behind a few rocks and leveled his rifle. Emma did as he asked and lay down with him having snagged her rifle as well. She knew she should have practiced with her rifle before to ensure it fired straight but it was too late for that now.

"Timber these could well be the same men," she said excited to have found them so soon.

"Whatever, they ain't getting away with it this time," Timber could see what was happening and the fact that they had already killed the guard. He aimed his rifle and fired a shot off.

Jason and Ashley watched open mouthed as Walker suddenly spun around and fell dead from his horse to the ground. They looked over to where the shot had come from as they all did to hear another shot which very narrowly missed Jason. The shooter obviously wasn't worried about the passengers being hit and he was tucked away where they would have difficulty getting him. They all realized that riding off to try and shoot him would result in at least one more of them being killed so they all responded to Jason saying they ought to ride out. They were encouraged more when two of the passengers produced guns and started shooting at them. They were lucky to get away as they rode off to the rocky area.

As they rode away Timber whistled for Scout and jumped up on him when he arrived and rode off for the stagecoach. Emma took longer to get her horse and ride off after him cussing at Timber for not waiting for her.

Timber rode up and shouted out as to who he was holding up his badge so he wouldn't get shot. He arrived to find a passenger kneeling down by the outlaw he had shot. He left Scout and went to join him. As he got there the passenger got up, "He's alive," he said.

Timber got down to him and saw then that he had winged him in his side, even so there was a lot of blood. He was now lying on his back and he scowled up at Timber, "Who the heck are you?"

Timber told him as he checked how bad he was, his chances weren't good, "I want to know who you are?"

"Sure you do."

"Who runs the outlaws you are with?"

Walker coughed up blood as he laughed, "Wouldn't you like to know. I ain't telling you who the main man is."

Timber cocked his head to one side, "The main man?"

"We ain't just a band of outlaws, there's more to us than that," Walker was keen to talk to brag about himself.

"You're in pretty bad state here mister, you tell me what you know and I'll get you fixed up."

Walker looked at him and wondered how much he could say without giving too much away, "We work for the main man, I don't know his name, he's high up in the territory and has organized a syndicate in town."

"I'm going to need more than that, just what is he up to?"

"I don't know any more than that, no one has told me," Walker's eyes closed and his breathing became erratic.

The passenger beside him looked at Timber, "This man needs help marshal?"

Other passengers came to him and the driver who took a look then said, "We need to get him to the doc in town if he is going to be in any shape to say more."

Timber could see the man was now drifting in and out of consciousness so he had to agree. They got him inside the coach, there being room for him while the guard's body was put on the coach roof. Emma took a good look at Walker but she didn't recognize him but she had recognized some of the horses, enough to know this was the same gang that had killed her husband.

She rode back with the stagecoach alongside Timber telling him that these were the same men.

"That seems most likely, I wouldn't think there would be many gangs in this area doing the same thing."

"Why are we going to town not going after the rest of them?" Emma asked.

"They won't be far away if they are working for this main man fella. We need to try and find out more about him and that will lead us to them."

Emma nodded and accepted that.

9

Jason had led the rest of them off fast to the rocks and with a backward glance he had then carried on for a few miles before stopping in the hidden canyon where he felt safe. They all gathered around and got off their horses to talk. Ashley was the most upset.

"Walker's dead," he said looking around at the rest of them, "who was that man that shot him?"

They all shook their heads, "He was a good shot whoever he was and that means he wasn't just a townsman," Jason offered.

"I wish he'd been a bad shot, he killed him all right," Ashley looked at Ryder and Troy who were both upset about losing one of them but then that was always a risk.

"We should have stayed and killed him," Ryder said.

"We would have lost more of us. A marksman like him in cover over open ground, how many more of us would he have killed and then the passengers drawing guns didn't help."

"So what do we do?" Ryder carried on.

"We keep on doing what we were that's what," Jason told him.

"Do you reckon that's the right thing to do Jason is it really worth carrying on?" Ashley said.

"Look I'm sorry about Walker too, he was a good man but we all knew we were taking chances when we started out on this thing. The man did warn us."

"Yeah I know Jason, but it still hurts."

"Sure it does."

"We need to look out for that shooter," Ryder said, "I reckon I'll know him if I see him again."

"You got that good a look at him?" Ashley asked.

"Pretty much yeah, the fact he was wearing deerskins anyway and there was a woman with him."

They all looked at Ryder, "A woman?" Carter asked him.

"Yeah, I swear I've seen her before too."

"What recently?"

"Yeah Carter."

"There can't be many of them around who'd come out here with him," Carter said.

Jason asked, "You don't mean the woman who's husband we killed at the last stagecoach raid?"

Ryder stared at him, "Say yeah, that's her."

"So she got herself a man to help her out in looking for us." Ashley said.

"Could be. Okay look we need to get ourselves together and carry on. We still have to get the money we need to take to the man, then we're done," Jason said.

"Then we get our land, our pardons and start a good life but without Walker," Ashley said.

They all looked down at that. Jason put an arm around his brother, "What's done is done, we have to carry on."

Ashley nodded, "Okay we need to plan the next raid and get this over with quickly."

Jason said, "We set this thing up with the man to get the money he needs then he will ensure we all get a free pardon, land and money to set ourselves up with, the deal is just too good to walk out on."

They all agreed with that.

Timber and Emma talked a little on the way back to Angel Creek. They had been interested to hear what the outlaw had said to them and wanted to know more.

"We must ask him the names of those outlaws when we get back Timber," Emma said.

"We do, just as soon as the doc has him in a shape to do that."

Emma hoped now that they would learn more from him, enough to find the rest of the outlaws and either kill them or arrest them for trial and then the hangman's noose. They carried on into town and as soon as the stagecoach stopped outside the office Emma went to find out how the man was doing while calling out for someone to bring a doctor. As she got to the stagecoach the passenger who had been with him got out and stopped her.

"It's no use, he died on the way here."

Emma groaned, "Oh no, now we're back where we started from in finding them."

Timber got to her, "Not quite."

Emma turned to him, "How do you mean?"

"We know there is some syndicate at work here, they must be in league somehow with whatever it is they are planning."

"But how do we find that out?"

"All in good time. First I want the sheriff to give me a ticket for the bounty on this man then we visit the town council. I reckon this is all centered around this town, maybe we can find out more about it from them."

Emma took that in and waited while Timber found the sheriff and had him come take a look at the dead outlaw.

Sheriff Dusty Colby was as keen as Timber to go take a look at the man. He sighed when he saw him and turned to Timber, "Yeah I know of him, Walker Brady, he's one of the Archer Gang. They've been tearing up the territory for a while now."

Timber was pleased to get more information as Emma was, "So you know them?" She asked.

"Yeah, it's a well known gang, but I've never got close to them."

"Thanks for that sheriff. I'll be along to pick up the ticket on him and maybe you can show me any wanted notices you have on them?"

Dusty gave him a look, "Sure come along when you're ready."

It then got busy as the men in the Butterfield office came out to see what was going on and the passengers in the stagecoach wanted a ride out to where they had been going. Timber and Emma left them to it and rode off up the street to a saloon Timber liked the look of to get a drink, something to eat and to talk

Emma wasn't used to going in such places and she hung back but then followed Timber in figuring she ought to find out what saloons were like especially as the men she was after would no doubt frequent them. She kept close to Timber once inside and followed him to the bar. He bought a beer for himself and gin for her and ordered what food they had then motioned for them to sit at a table near a wall.

"I hope you have a plan as to how we get the information we need Timber," Emma said as she sipped at her gin.

"We rest, eat and drink then we go find the town council and see what they can tell us."

The food came and they had a couple more drinks before Timber decided it was time to go. He asked the bartender where to find the council office if there was one and got directions. They walked the short distance up the street to where Timber had been told to go. It was just a small office and was even smaller when Timber and Emma walked straight in. There were four men inside sitting around a table who all looked up at their visitors then one of them stood up.

"Is there something we can do for you?"

"Maybe, maybe not. I'm Jake Timber U.S. Marshal," he said showing his badge, "this lady here is Emma McKenzie, her husband was killed by outlaws who robbed the stage yesterday."

"I'm sorry to hear that," he said looking at Emma," but you need to see the sheriff about that."

"Just who am I talking to?" Timber asked looking at the well dressed tall man.

Emma sighed getting tired of not being included in anything.

"I'm Ernest Wells, head of the council here and I have several businesses in town," he turned around to face the other three men, "Frederick Johnson," he said, "also the owner of several businesses here." The man nodded to Timber. He was overweight and almost bald, "Rusty Evans, he's into real estate," Ernest continued, then he pointed to the last man.

"Thomas Redmile, who has his finger in several pies, isn't that so Thomas?"

Thomas straightened up in his chair. Timber could see he was quite a big man, obviously fit and about his age.

"I have interests in various establishments yes," Thomas answered.

"Would one of them be a syndicate?" Timber asked.

Thomas shifted in his chair, "A syndicate, what kind of syndicate?"

"Oh I don't know, one that involves hiring men of shall we say dubious characters?"

Thomas stared at Timber for a few seconds as the other two men looked on, "Just what are you suggesting, that I'm involved some wrong doing, because if you are...?"

"Don't you go upsetting yourself, it's just a question. I have a job to do that involves asking questions."

"Just what job is that marshal?" Ernest asked.

"One of bringing outlaws to justice and ensuring nothing underhand is going on."

"Now look here," Thomas got up from his chair.

Timber grinned, hoping now that the man would say something to his advantage, "Go on...?"

Thomas stopped and calmed down, "I, that is we, are all genuine businessmen here Timber, there is nothing for you to bother yourself about."

"Then there's no need to continue our conversation, good day gentlemen," Timber walked out pushing Emma in front of him.

Outside Emma was not happy, "Why end it so quick, I thought he might say something useful."

"He almost did, but he won't with the other men there. He looked guilty to me so we just walk away from here and wait somewhere until he comes out, then we follow him."

Emma smiled and nodded her head. She was just beginning to get to know Timber.

10

Timber took Emma a few yards up the street to where they could hide between two buildings. It was in the shadows and as dusk was approaching it was dark enough for them not to be seen. They waited there for a while before Thomas came out of the office. It had been boring just waiting there but now they both took an interest. Timber didn't know which direction Thomas would go in so he was pleased that it was away from them. They waited until he had walked off before they came out and began to follow him.

Thomas didn't have any thought about being followed he carried on at a good pace. He had somewhere to go and now information to give, he hurried on. Timber and Emma followed him on foot as he walked down the street. Timber made sure he was in front, keeping Emma where she would be safe just in case anything happened. They carried on and Timber began to wonder where Thomas was going. They got to the end of the street and he just carried on out into the open ground after the livery stable which was the last building in the town.

Emma stayed right with Timber and as Thomas left the town she said, "Shouldn't we have got the horses?"

"No, he would have noticed them, we keep on staying in the shadows and no noise."

Emma took the hint and shut up. Timber was walking as fast as Thomas was while staying a good way back and she was having difficulty keeping up with him. They kept him in sight as he approached a little draw where there were some trees, then he disappeared into them. Timber raised a hand to warn Emma to keep back as he kept going and then just before he trees he stopped.

"Keep well behind me," he whispered to her as he carried on into the trees. He stopped just inside as he made Thomas out walking through to the other side. Very carefully Timber followed on. He saw that Thomas had stopped at the far end of the trees and was looking out as though he was waiting for someone. It was easy then for Timber to get a lot closer and hide. He was interested now in who Thomas was waiting for? Emma stuck close to him and waited behind the same tree as him.

After what seemed like just a few minutes Timber and Emma heard and saw two riders going up to Thomas. They listened hard to hear their voices. All they caught were a few words but it was obvious the men were in on whatever Thomas was trying to hide.

Thomas was explaining something to them and they were talking back. They heard the words syndicate and how the secret had better not come out. Thomas was remonstrating with them until they finished talking and rode off. Timber and Emma had been trying to see the mens faces and look for markings on their horses but it was very hard as it had now got a lot darker. Now that Thomas was alone Timber made a decision and ran over to him just as the riders left. He grabbed hold of him and spun him around. He had seen he wasn't armed so he felt safe in doing that. He then flung him against a tree driving the air out of him. Thomas just stood there held tight in Timber's grip.

"Just what the heck is going on Thomas and don't tell me you don't know?"

"Timber I swear I don't know. They just pay me to keep a look out and tell them what I see and hear."

"Who pays you and to tell them what?"

Emma came up then and Thomas saw her, "You'd be best to keep the lady out of this, it could go badly for her."

"Thomas you'd better explain yourself and soon," Timber let go with his left hand and balled it up into a fist that he aimed at Thomas's face.

"Look you got it right that there is a syndicate and some of it is in town but not all of it. These are bad men Timber, they wouldn't hesitate to kill to keep their secret safe."

"Just what is this secret?"

"You'd better tell him Thomas, Timber doesn't have much patience," Emmas told him.

"I don't know all of it."

"Then tell us what you do know," Timber clenched his fist tighter.

"It goes a lot higher than the town council..." Thomas began. He didn't get to say anymore as there was a gunshot and Thomas groaned and fell dead to the ground.

Timber and Emma both looked to see the same men had returned and shot him. Timber reached for his gun and fired at them joined in by Emma. The riders just raced away leaving them no wiser as to who they were.

"Come on, I need my horse now," Timber shouted as he ran off for the saloon.

Emma ran with him and as Timber mounted Scout she got up on her horse.

"What are you doing Emma, I'm going after them alone?" Timber shouted to her.

"No way, I'm in this too deep now to stay here, I'm going whether you want me to or not," Emma said in that stubborn way Timber was getting used to.

"It's too dangerous for you especially at night, now you stay here."

"No way Timber I'm coming." Timber could tell she was close to tears so he left it knowing she would follow him anyway. In a few short minutes they were away from the saloon and riding off in the direction the two men had gone.

11

Timber rode out fast not waiting for Emma to catch up. He still hoped she would give up in the dark and go back. He rode on being careful where he put Scout but he knew the horse would find his own way, he just had to point him the right direction. He got back to the trees easily enough then set off in the direction the two men had taken. He couldn't go too fast but then he knew they wouldn't be able to either.

The two men weren't that far in front having stopped after riding a little way beside a bunch of trees. One of them was keen to talk to the other. Matt Hampton was a small weedy kinda man and although quite hard he wasn't sure about what they had just done.

"You sure the man's gonna be pleased with that Charlie?" He asked as they pulled up.

"He might not be but he would be more upset if Thomas had spilt the beans to the marshal and that's for damn sure."

"That man sure did look like the marshal we were told about."

"Yeah, it was a good thing we were told about him."

"Sure was, good to have that contact, so which one of us is gonna tell the man?"

"I guess I'll do it, you can relax."

While they had stopped to talk Timber had been able to narrow the distance on them and he saw them silhouetted against the sky, he urged Scout on to catch up with them. The two men didn't notice him and stopped to talk some more figuring no one would be coming after them, least of all Timber.

Timber carried on and stormed into the open area beside the trees. Coming in from behind them the trees had hidden him right up until he was close up to them. He drew a gun as he pulled up and then the other one as he stopped before either man had a chance to do anything.

"You two just hold it right there and pull your guns out with thumb and finger and let them drop," he said to them.

Matt and Charlie were too dumbstruck to do anything but what Timber had asked. As soon as they had done that Timber relaxed but kept his guns aimed at them, "Now I know you killed Thomas but I want to know why and who you are?"

Charlie answered first, "So you must be Marshal Timber?"

"You got that right, now who are you?"

"That's none of your business. You ought to just keep your nose out of things marshal, this is bigger than you can possibly handle."

"Now that's the thing you see. I heard that before, so just what is going on?"

"To answer that I'll have to kill you," Charlie was taking a big chance hoping that the dark would help him. He had another gun, a smaller .38 hidden away that he suddenly brought out and aimed at Timber. Unluckily for him Timber had been watching very carefully and saw the action, then he fired at Charlie and took him out of his saddle to land heavily in the dirt. Timber then looked at Matt.

"Looks like you're gonna have to tell me the story on your own now."

Matt was so shocked he just sat on his horse staring back at Timber until he found his voice, "I can't tell you much, no one tells me anything except what to do."

"Just tell me what you know?"

"We got together to make money, steal it, as much as we can for the man in return for favors we want. We work for men in town much as Jason and his men do," as he spoke he saw Emma riding up. She had been left behind and had cussed Timber for doing so, now she rode up to be with him. She rode right up making Timber glance around for just a second at her. It was enough for Matt who leapt off his horse for his gun he could see lying on the ground. He managed to pick it up before Timber got a bead on him. He called out for Matt to drop it but Matt was too far gone and brought the gun up. Timber couldn't risk being shot so he fired and hit Matt in his chest killing him.

Timber turned to Emma, about to reprimand her but he stopped knowing no good would come from that so instead he said, "I thought you would stay away."

"Timber I had to come and I'm sorry, I can see you were talking to that man."

"Yes I was, he was about to tell me what is going on."

Emma was sorry then angry, "If you hadn't left me behind it wouldn't have happened."

"If you had stayed behind like I said then it wouldn't have happened."

Emma stared at him and felt the tears coming again. Timber relented.

"Get down and help me here. I need to search them, see what they have, maybe there will be something for us then you can hold their horses while I get them over their saddles."

Emma did as he asked so it wasn't long before they were all ready to move out with Timber not finding anything of use.

"We take these men back to town Emma, see if there are wanted notices on them, if there are maybe their names will give us a clue as to who they are with."

Emma agreed and rode alongside him, her mind a whirl of emotions.

12

It was very late when Timber and Emma rode into town with Timber leading the horses with the two mens bodies draped over them. They carried on down the street until they reached the sheriff's office where they stopped. Timber left Emma outside with the horses while he went inside. He was lucky to find Dusty still in there working on his paperwork with lamplight. He looked up as Timber walked in.

"Back again?" he said.

"Just like a bad cent. I have two bodies outside for you."

Dusty stared at him, "Who have you killed this time?"

"Come take a look, maybe you can help identify them. Oh and have you found Thomas Redmile yet. He was killed by them at a copse of trees just outside town?"

"No I haven't," he sighed, "I guess I'll have to go check. You have some explaining to do Timber, but yeah I'll look at the two men outside first."

They went out and under the light of lamps Dusty looked at the two men then shook his head, "No sorry, I don't know these two."

"You sure of that?"

"Sure I'm sure and there's no point in going through the wanted notices, I'm telling you they won't be there. They need taking to the undertaker but he'll be all shut up by now."

"He'll open up for me," Timber said taking the reins of the horses and mounting up. He didn't say another word until he pulled up at the undertakers office. Then he banged on the door until a window opened upstairs and a head appeared. Timber shouted at him to come down and take the two men off him. The undertaker wasn't happy about it but Timber persuaded him. He then came down and took the men off Timber grumbling the whole time.

Timber and Emma saw Dusty riding down the street towards them as they finished with the undertaker and they joined him in going down to where they knew Thomas had been killed. It was dark in the trees and Timber had to get off Scout to find the body. Dusty went to join him and cussed as he saw Thomas.

"You say those two men you brought in killed him?"

"That's what I said."

Dusty looked down again at him, "Now why would they do that?"

"Now that I can answer. They killed him because he was about to explain to me just what is going on around here."

"Going on, what do you mean?"

"I mean there is a syndicate in town, or close by that is up to something and I'm danged if I can find out what or who is in it."

"That's the craziest thing I've heard in a while. I don't know of any syndicate. Is that all you have?"

"Right now yes, unless you have something to tell me?"

"I just told you, it's all news to me."

Timber nodded and watched Dusty's face. He turned away and reached down for Thomas.

"Are you gonna give me a hand with him?"

Dusty helped Timber pick him up and drape him over his horse. He was going to have to go back with him and wake the undertaker again.

"I still need to know all that happened tonight," Dusty said as he began to walk back leading his horse. Timber walked along with him leading Scout while Emma rode beside them.

"I went to see the town council with Emma here as I had heard something about a syndicate from the last man I killed. Thomas here looked very shifty and we followed him to the trees here where he was having a meeting with the two men I brought to you. They killed Thomas to stop him talking then rode off. I was lucky to catch them up. As I tried to get information out of them they pulled guns on me so I had to shoot them."

"That's damned strange and we can't now talk to any of them," Timber thought Dusty looked pleased about that but he didn't comment. He walked to the undertakers with the sheriff then left him there and mounting Scout he joined Emma.

"So what now?" She asked him.

"Now we get to the hotel to get some sleep but we see to the horses first."

They took the horses down to the stable to find no one there but they put them in stalls anyway with Timber saying they will straighten it out with the hostler in the morning then they walked back to the hotel.

There was no one at the desk when they walked in so Timber had to bang on the desk to get attention. The clerk came out to him a little flustered but he gave them keys for two rooms anyway as Timber paid for them. They then went upstairs and Emma invited Timber into her room so they could talk.

"Isn't it a little late to talk?" Timber asked as he stood in the doorway.

"I'm not tired and I do think we should talk," Emma walked right inside and sat on the bed where she patted it next to her. Timber took the cue and walked in, he shut the door and sat bedside her.

As soon as he sat down Emma said, "Don't you think that sheriff was a little strange?"

Timber grinned, "Yeah, most sheriffs are but yes I know what you mean. He didn't seem upset about the murder of Thomas or about me killing the two men."

"Exactly and the way he looked at you, there is something not right there."

"You think he's in with whatever is going on?"

"Could be. I wouldn't be surprised and just what is going on Timber?"

"I don't rightly know, something big that's for damn sure and it's being kept a secret."

"Which means its bad?"

"Bad enough to murder folk yes and then there's the stagecoach raids, they have to be connected to it somehow."

"I know but I just can't get my head around it."

"Neither can I, yet. We need to see the sheriff again which we will do in the morning."

"Sounds good to me Timber," Emma paused then said, "Do you think we are safe?"

"You're safe as long as I'm with you."

"And what about you?"

"No need to worry about me. I've been in these kind of situations for some time now and I'm still here."

Emma rested her head on Timber's shoulder, "I wish Austin was here, I could always rely on him."

Timber nodded and allowed her head to remain against him, "Are the arrangements done yet for him?"

"Oh yes, tomorrow morning, so whatever you're doing I won't be with you."

"You want me along?"

"No, I'd rather go alone but thanks."

Timber got up to go but Emma stopped him, "Will you stay in here tonight, I'd feel safer?"

Timber sat back down again, "That's fine by me."

13

Timber woke early as usual. He turned over and looked across at Emma who was still asleep. It wasn't usual for him to get involved with women, not after what had happened to the first three women in his life. There had been an occasional dalliance with ones that came into his life but he always made sure any relationship didn't last, how could it with the work he did? Yet again a woman had come into his life but this one had just lost her husband and she was going to need time to get over that before forming another relationship and then certainly not with him. He would help her find the killers but then he would be moving on.

He got up and when he was ready he woke Emma and told her to come down when she was ready. He sat in the foyer thinking things through and came to the decision to have breakfast then go see the sheriff again, see if he could find out any more and figure out just who's side he was on.

Emma came down flustered that he had got up and left her but she soon smiled again when she saw he had waited for her. Timber took her to a cafe for breakfast and paid for just about everything that was on the menu.

"Always pays to set yourself up for the day, you never know how it's gonna turn out," he told her. He then spoke about going to see Dusty and Emma agreed.

"I've been wondering about him, I'm sure he's up to something or he's trying to keep something from us."

"Then we go and find out."

"I have Austin's funeral first Timber."

"Yeah of course. You go ahead, I'll catch you later."

Timber waited until Emma had finished then he got up and laid some coins on the table before walking out. Emma found she had to follow him, again.

Emma went off on her own to be joined by Sue at the undertakers' office. Timber took himself down to see Scout and make sure the horses were all right.

Some time later he walked over to the undertakers office and saw Emma return. She said her goodbyes to Sue then went to him.

"I'm ready now she said.

Timber didn't question her they set off for the sheriff's office. As they got close they saw Dusty come out and walk off up the street.

"Ah no, we've missed him," Emma said.

"Maybe, but I wanna see where he goes," Timber kept on walking but not catching Dusty up. They watched as he walked to the council office and went inside. Timber then increased his pace to get there.

"There is window on the side wall which was open last time I was here, I hope it is now," Timber went between the buildings to where there was a window high up on the wall and it was open. They stood underneath it and listened.

"I can't hear a thing," Emma said.

"Neither can I."

"Why don't we go in and talk to them?"

"Because they might be saying things right now that they wouldn't want us to hear," Timber looked again at Emma's small frame, "I could hold you up there then we'd find out."

Emma looked up at the window then grinned at Timber, "Okay."

Timber lifted her up easily so she was right up against the

window and could see partly into the room and hear every word being said. Emma kept still and listened carefully.

She clearly heard the sheriff talking, "Just how many men do you need?"

The question was directed to one of the council members, Ernest Wells.

Emma listened as Ernest answered, "The Archer's should be well enough."

"With one dead already and we don't know if he spoke to marshal Timber?"

"No we don't but seeing as Timber hasn't come storming in here I'd say he knows nothing so we carry on."

"Okay we carry on, so they're in the area now and what's their next job gonna be?"

"You don't need to know that Dusty, just let them do their job."

"But I do need to know Ernest. I'm the sheriff around here and folk come to me for help and information. The more I know about what the Archer's are doing the better I can protect our interests."

Ernest took time to reply and Emma could hear him talking in low tones to the others but she couldn't catch what the words were. Then Ernest turned again to Dusty.

"Okay well I can't actually tell for certain. They have got this thing now about getting the money from stagecoaches which I guess they will do for a while but I can't say which one or where."

Dusty nodded, "Okay well that's something anyway."

"Yeah, so just keep your head down and if that nosy marshal goes to see you again don't tell him anything you understand?"

"Oh yeah I understand. You know Thomas Redmile has been killed?"

"Yeah we were told. We do have others we can call on to do work for us."

"Not Charlie or Matt any more, Timber killed the two of 'em."

It went quiet in the room until Ernest spoke again, "How do you know that?'

"Because Timber brought them to me draped over their saddles."

"Did he say anything about them, what they said maybe?"

"No, only that they killed Thomas Redmile and he had to kill them."

"Okay, like I say he hasn't come here since so he can't know anything, just go about your business."

Dusty didn't answer he just turned for the door. Emma saw him doing that so she waved at Timber to put her down.

"He's coming out Timber, he's in on it, we should tackle him about it now."

"Whoa there, I think not. You tell me all you heard then I'll think on it. Even if'n he's in on it I think it might be better to let him think we don't know, for now anyways, that could be to our advantage."

Timber guided Emma out onto the street and kept her to the shade of the sidewalks under the porches, "Now tell me what was said?"

Emma poured it all out almost word for word as they watched Dusty walk back to his office. Timber listened and nodded his head now and then. Once she had finished Timber took a look down the street.

"I guess we need to go back to the Butterfield office then and find out when and where the next few stagecoaches are coming and going then we need to decide on which is the most likely one they will hit."

Emma had to agree with that and walked off with him to the stagecoach office. Outside they saw a sign stating when the stagecoaches were arriving and leaving. They stopped to take a look at that before going inside. The three people in there seemed quite busy but they stopped when Timber asked to see the superintendent. Alfred came out of his inner office to see who wanted him. Timber told him who he was and showed his badge before asking about the stagecoaches.

"Just what do you want to know?" Alfred asked.

"We know there have been some stagecoach robberies and I'm thinking there will be more so the question is just what are the next few days of stagecoaches carrying that might be of interest to outlaws?"

"I sure hope you are wrong about any more hold ups marshal," Alfred said then he carried on, "None of them have anything much different from each other. They all carry a strongbox which holds mail which can be valuable depending on what's been sent, there could also be valuables in there I guess. Then there's the passengers themselves and what they may have on them or in their luggage. I don't know of any special passengers coming or going over the next few weeks never mind days."

"Okay, well thanks for that."

"So what are you intending to do," Alfred gave him a look, "Do you know something I should?"

"Let's just say I'm keen to stop any hold ups on any stagecoach. Do they all use the same trail out of town?"

"Not exactly, most do use the trail going east out of here for a few miles but then they branch off south and north, you can see the turnings easy enough."

"I guess I'll take a look east of here then."

"If you think one is going to be held up you let me know," Alfred said as he loosened his shirt collar.

"You'll be the first to know," Timber said as he walked out.

Emma had stayed with him the whole time and hadn't made a comment, now she did.

"So you're thinking of just riding out on the trail east of here on the off chance?"

"Sure, you got any better ideas?"

"No, we might need some food though, we could be in for a wait."

"I could you mean."

"No Timber we, I'm not leaving you until this thing is over and those men are all caught, or dead."

Timber noticed the gap between the last few words, "Okay, we get the horses then call in at a store."

Emma smiled at him and walked with him to the livery stable.

14

The outlaws stayed in the canyon for the rest of the day while they pondered the loss of Walker and planned their next holdup. They ate what they had with them intending to get more supplies once they had robbed the stagecoach. Jason went to spend some time with his brother. He found him sitting alone on a rock slab and sat next to him.

"We knew this might happen Ashley, in fact it could happen to any of us."

"I know that Jason, it just brings it home to you that it could happen."

"We just have to take more care next time and look out for that man. He has that woman with him from the stagecoach where we killed her husband so she's obviously out for revenge."

"So it looks like she has hired a gun to try and do that, well he's going to have a job on his hands to take out all of us."

"That's a fact, so now we need to plan the next job and get this all over with, we need a lot more money yet."

"Yeah Ashley we do and I'm thinking we stay with easy targets for a while and try another stagecoach."

"That's fine with me," Ashley looked at the other men, "and I'm sure they won't mind."

"Okay well I made a note of the stagecoaches coming through this area and there is one tomorrow we could take."

"Ain't it a bit much to keep on taking stagecoaches in this area, shouldn't we move out aways?"

"I reckon we can take one more. Any coming into this area won't be aware of the ones we have already taken so I don't see a risk there."

Ashley considered that before answering, "Yeah okay then, one more. You got a time for it?"

"The sign in Angel Creek said it won't be arriving there until two in the afternoon so I reckon if we get up the trail we could take it at around midday."

"That sounds good to me, let's tell the others," he got up and walked over to them with Jason following on.

Emma walked with Timber to the livery stable where they then went to get their horses. Scout whickered as Timber walked in. The horse was always pleased to see him as Timber was him. He went into the stall and stroked the horses muzzle while he talked quietly to it. He met acquaintances along the way but since his last woman Scout had been his only friend. He could talk to it and he swore it understood every damn word. He had trained it from a foal and it knew plenty of tricks, some of which were very useful. In doing them the horse had saved his life at least twice and Timber was always very careful to make sure Scout was out of the way when he was involved in any shootings. He saddled up then led him out to meet up with Emma. He looked for the hostler who noticed him walking out and hurried over to him. Timber paid him what he owed for Scout and for Emma's horse then he mounted up.

"Next stop the general store," Timber said to her as he urged Scout on.

In the store they chose enough things for a few days not knowing how long they would be out of town. Once again Timber paid for everything.

"You don't have to keep on paying Timber, I have some money," Emma didn't like the idea of always taking from him.

"Emma I have more money than I'll ever spend so let me do this for us," Timber's expression made Emma smile and relax.

"Okay Timber thanks anyway."

"You're welcome, now we ought to move on out."

They put they supplies into their saddle bags and having mounted up they walked the horses out of town. Emma still wasn't sure of Timber's intentions.

"So what's your plan?"

"I ain't got a plan, just an idea."

"Which is?"

"Which is to follow the trail the stagecoaches take to come into town and hope to catch it as it comes in, then hopefully your outlaws will try to hold it up."

"Hopefully?"

"Yeah, that's what we want isn't it to catch them? As we don't know where they are this will be the best way to do it."

Emma nodded, she wanted to catch them yes but she was very concerned as to how it would turn out if they did attack the stagecoach and they were there with it. She just had to hope that Timber knew what he was doing. They kept on riding out of town and onto the trail.

Although they had plenty of time the outlaws were still up early the next morning heating food and brewing coffee. Within a short time they were all ready to go and find the stagecoach. Jason and Ashley had told them about it last night.

Troy had been especially pleased to hear it, "That sounds good to me, I can't wait to see the passengers faces when we get them lined up and take what they have."

Ryder kept quiet, he knew it was his fault that the woman had got herself a gunman and that he had killed Walker. He was going to be a lot more careful this time.

Carter was pleased as Troy was, "I'll be at the front this time and make sure the guard and driver don't do anything foolish."

"Whatever you want Carter, I'll be there with you otherwise all of you take the positions you did the last time." Jason didn't get any argument with that, "okay let's go"

The stagecoach was on its way to Angel Creek then it was going on to San Antonio. Angel Creek was just going to be a stopping off place on the way. It was being driven by a young man who had worked hard to get to where he was. Duke Henderson figured he was just as good as any old timer who'd been doing it for years. Sitting beside him was an older man, a lot heavier than him. Willie Carson had a lot of experience and he didn't carry a shotgun like some guards did, he had himself a Winchester rifle and he carried a Colt .44 in a holster around his waist. He had heard tales of Road Agents holding up stagecoaches and he wanted to be as ready as he could be if any tried to hold up his stagecoach.

Traveling inside were two men and two women. The women were middle aged sisters going to visit family while the two men were businessmen going to San Antonio to look at any land they could buy up.

Jason got quite a way up the trail with his men wanting to be as far away from Angel Creek as he could be to have less chance of any interruptions. What he wanted was to find somewhere they could lay up and wait for the stagecoach to come by and surprise it. It took him some time to find anywhere and that was just a hollow where they could just all get into. He led them all into it then he sent Ryder to lie at the top to keep a look out for it coming. Ryder had hardly got himself settled before he saw a cloud of dust that gradually took on the shape of the stagecoach. He hurried back down to tell them.

"Okay, here we go and make sure you all go where you're supposed to," Jason called as he urged his horse up out of the hollow.

Timber also saw the cloud of dust which he reckoned would be the stagecoach. He looked all around to see if there were any riders around who could be the outlaws. Emma saw the dust as well and noticed what Timber was doing.

"There's no guarantee the outlaws will attack this one Timber and maybe they are behind us waiting for it if they are."

"That would be true Emma but look," Timber pointed ahead.

Emma looked to see riders coming up out of a hollow and making off for the stagecoach, "Oh my, yes it is them I'm sure."

"Okay now you stay back here," Timber snagged his rifle as he spoke.

Emma almost complained as she wanted to be in on the outlaws being caught but she could see that it would be dangerous for her to go with him but before she could say anything Timber told her to get her rifle.

Emma pulled it from its holster unsure of what he wanted her to do.

"You get down here and wait. You say you can shoot, well you might just have the chance to prove it. If you think you can take any of them out then do so. If you see I'm in trouble then shoot at them anyway. You are far enough back to be able to run for town in front of them if it all goes wrong."

Emma got her confidence back, "Sure okay I can do that," even so her hand holding the rifle was shaking. Timber rode off and she got to the ground a few yards from her horse and lay down leveling the rifle at the outlaws. As she lay there her confidence came back, she gritted her teeth and waited.

15

Jason and Carter took the front of the stagecoach while Ashley and Ryder took the left side and Gideon, Emmett and Troy took the right side. They all had their bandanas up over their faces and drew their guns as they got closer to the stagecoach which was still rattling towards them. However it stopped as the outlaws stood in its way.

Duke didn't know what else to do. The thought flashed through his mind as to what a more experienced driver would have done but he couldn't see what else anyone could do, he was facing two gunmen with more gathering around the coach. He pulled on the reins and called at the horses to stop. Once they were at a standstill he looked across at Willie for guidance. Willie was to engrossed as to what he was going to do to take any notice. He was still holding his rile and considering using it until Jason called out to him.

"I'd just lay that rifle down if I was you."

Willie only thought about for a second before he did exactly that. He still had his gun at his waist if a chance came along to use it. He sat still waiting.

Carter was keen to get the job done, "You two throw down the strongbox, and don't get any funny ideas," he shouted up to them.

Willie looked at Duke, "Just toss it down kid, this ain't the time for any heroics."

Duke was pleased to have the responsibility taken from him and he reached down for the strongbox under the seat. Willie helped him to throw it down. Carter was pleased and slipped off his horse to go check it out while Jason kept his gun trained on the two men on the box. He shot the padlock off it and opened the lid to find the usual pile of envelopes and paperwork. He got busy bagging it all up.

As he did that Ryder called the passengers to get out on his side of the stagecoach. They were reluctant but they did as he asked. Ryder had them line up so he could keep an eye on them. Ashley stayed on his horse holding them all at gun point while Ryder got down to relieve them of their valuables.

The men stood firm as Ryder went up to them. He had a bag and told them to drop any rings, watches, money or anything else of value into it. Neither of the men were armed and they were not the sort to argue with anyone who was, so they gave up what they had. The two women kept right back beside the stagecoach and wrapped their arms around each other as they shook with fear. The two men noticed this only after Ryder had robbed them, they then edged closer to the women to offer support. Ryder ignored them and turned to the women.

"Come on ladies give it up, we ain't got all day."

They were too frightened to do anything and Ryder got more impatient, as he was about to grab hold of them he heard Ashley shout to him,

"We got a visitor."

Ryder spun around to see who it was and saw a single rider racing towards them and he had a rifle to his shoulder.

Timber was happy to leave Emma behind, he was worried about her with a group of outlaws ahead of them all with guns, all no doubt happy to shoot them. He brought the rifle to his shoulder knowing it would be hard to aim well from his horse but he was able to let go of the reins and direct Scout just by talking to him. He pulled the butt of the rifle tight in and took a bead on the closest outlaw then he squeezed the trigger. From the angle Timber was coming in Emmett was the closest to him. With the distance and the galloping horse it was a pretty good shot and it caught Emmett high up on his shoulder but it was enough to knock him off his horse. He fell screaming in pain at his broken collarbone. All the outlaws stopped what they were doing and looked over at Timber.

Ryder had been busy trying to get the women to listen to him but now he ran to his horse and jumped up on it. Jason was shouting at everyone to shoot Timber as they all rode up to the front of the stagecoach. They all aimed their guns at him but none of them had a chance to fire before Timber suddenly leaped from Scout to scramble behind a hollow where some rocks lay on the rim. As he jumped he yelled at Scout to move off. True to form the big bay ran off at right angles following a well known command. Timber quickly levered another round into the Winchester and took aim again at the outlaws.

As Timber dropped down Jason shouted out to go get him. He didn't give a thought to the driver and guard figuring they were unarmed. It took the men a few seconds to get organized and in that time Timber fired again and his shot was followed by one from Emma. Timber's shot flew true and took Gideon out of his saddle. Emma's shot flew harmlessly over Jason's head but it was enough to spook him. He could see he was against at least two people with rifles in cover. They had got most of what they wanted anyway from the coach, it was time to go.

"Come on, we need to get out of here," he called as he spurred his horse away towards hills he could see across to the side of the stagecoach.

As they rode off bullets whizzed around them but none made any contact until one of Timber's caught Ryder in his left arm then they were out of range.

Emmett slowly managed to get up and he began to stagger towards his horse until Willie stopped him. He pulled his gun and dropped down from the box.

"You hold it right there or I swear I'll plug you good."

Emmett turned and his hand went down to his holster to find it empty, his gun had slipped out when he fell. He stood with his hands to his sides.

"Go on then shoot, go on do it," he held his hands out to his sides knowing it was all over for him whatever the guard did.

Timber whistled for Scout who came back at a lope to him. He looked back to Emma as he mounted up. She was already riding towards him. Timber set off for the stagecoach and got there just ahead of her to find the guard pointing a gun at the man he had wounded.

"I'll take it from here," Timber said getting off Scout.

"Who are you?" Willie asked still not lowering his gun.

"I'm Marshal Jake Timber," he said showing his badge.

Willie relaxed as Timber went up to Emmett.

"You wanna talk to me?" Timber asked.

"I ain't got nothin' to say to yah," Emmett turned to spit on the ground.

"Suits me, you want it the hard way," Timber advanced towards him.

"It's either die now or hang later, I got nothing to lose and nothing to say."

Timber could see the man was in pain and probably wouldn't give in if he gave him more pain, "Okay have it your way, you can go back with us for the hangman's rope, unless you do talk of course, then we can cut a deal."

"There'll be no deal," Emmett reached behind him with his good hand and brought out a knife that he threw at Timber. Just as he threw it Willie shot him dead as he still had his gun trained on him.

Timber shook his head, "Pity, he might still have talked."

"I had to kill him or he would have killed you," Willie said with no remorse.

Emma had no remorse either, "Good, that's two more of them dead, I reckon just five to go."

"We have to agree with the lady marshal," one of the ladies said to him now that they had come out of their fear and shock.

"Yeah, thanks for coming along, shame it wasn't before they robbed us though," a business man said.

"Yeah well whatever, but at least you can all get back to town now with your lives. Come on Emma we have some riding to do," Timber pushed past them all and mounted up on Scout. As they rode off Timber told Emma the dead outlaws could be taken in by the stagecoach. Normally he would have taken them in himself but today he was more concerned with bringing down the rest of them. The stagecoach team will take them in and he could see about getting any bounties on their heads later.

16

Jason had been shocked to see the rider coming to them, then to have him shoot Emmett. Jason wondered if was alive or dead. In the circumstances he wished he was dead so he couldn't say anything about the rest of them or what they were doing. He cussed himself now for not finishing him off while he was there. Then there was Gideon. He had seen him shot too but he was sure he was dead. Whatever, there wasn't anything he could do about it now.

They all kept on riding until they were into the hills where they felt safe enough to stop to talk and check out what they had got from the stagecoach.

Ashley wasn't pleased, "You know what Ryder you should never have killed that woman's husband, look what trouble you have brought us all now."

They were all standing around and opening the bags of items to take a proper look at them Ryder stopped emptying the bag he had. His arm hurt but as he examined it he found it was just a flesh wound and would heal.

"That husband you talk about was going to cause trouble maybe even kill one of us, I had to do it."

They all looked at Ryder who was looking around for support and not getting any.

"You were a mite early Ryder but what is done is done, we have to just get on with it now. One things for sure we will all be looking out for that man now," Jason had to say something to calm things down. He gave Ashley a meaningful look as he spoke.

Ashley shook his head and got busy looking at what they had. It wasn't bad. There was money from the strongbox and a few valuables. Ryder had done okay from the two men, it was just a shame he hadn't had time to rob the women as well or go through the luggage but it was the best they could have done.

"We need to put this with the rest of it now and then work out just how much more we need," Jason said.

Ashley and Ryder were packing it all away again as Carter said, "Shouldn't we go look for this gunman the woman has and kill him?"

"Not a bad idea Carter if we know where to find him." Jason then paused before carrying on, "but he must be in Angel Creek surely?"

That gave Troy something to say, "Yeah of course, great, so let's go over there and find him."

"We get this stuff back first then yeah we can go and do that," Jason helped pack it all away then they mounted up again and set off for the place they had stashed the rest of the money and items they had stolen so far.

The place wasn't that far from Angel Creek which wasn't surprising in that they had been employed from there. The canyon they used was more like a deep hollow. It was a rocky place and there was a bunch of trees in the bottom. It was there under a pile of boulders that they had been keeping the money and items they had been stealing. They got back there uneventfully although they all took glances behind them just in case. They rode into the trees and to the pile of boulders then Jason and Ryder got down to put the takings under there from the stagecoach. Once that was done they all relaxed feeling safe where they were and settled down for a rest and to talk over what had happened again. Jason let them all talk while he heated up some coffee for them, he figured it wouldn't hurt to let them rest a while and get things off their minds.

Ashley still wasn't happy with Ryder and ignored him most of the time not that Ryder was bothered about it he just kept on talking to Carter. Jason worried over the man who had caught them at the stagecoach. Somehow he had found them twice and each time he had taken at least one of them out, Jason was keen to find out who he was. A ride to town was now essential.

"If you boys have stopped your nattering we should be on our way. We need to find out who that man is at least if we don't find him in town."

"Is that wise," Ashley said, "I'm guessing you mean calling in at the office to get that answer?"

"Sure unless we run into him first."

Ashley shrugged and got up from where he'd been sitting with the others, "Okay let's go."

The ride into town was done mostly in silence as they all thought of their position, how they had got where they were and what the rewards would be if they could just finish what they had started.

They rode in nervously. They'd worn their bandanas over their faces the whole time they had held up the stagecoaches but even so it seemed like a risk to all of them. Jason began to have doubts about coming in, maybe he should have just stayed away but he really needed to know who was on their tail and shake him off. They rode past the Butterfield Overland Stagecoach office which didn't do anything to settle their nerves then on to the council office. All the time they looked around them for the man in deerskins without seeing him.

At the office they all stopped and Jason and Ashley got off their horses to go inside. The rest of them were happy enough to wait outside keeping watch.

Inside the office they only found one man working there. Ernest looked up at them from his desk the he stood up, "What the heck are you two doing here?"

"We need information Ernest and now," Jason said.

"Yeah, we're losing men like there's no tomorrow and we need to know who's doing it," Ashley added.

Ernest looked from one to the other, "So you've met the marshal then?"

"Marshal?" Jason looked at his brother who shrugged.

"U.S. Marshal Jake Timber, he's been in town a while, wears deerskins."

"Wait a minute," Ashley suddenly took his brother's arm, "That man we saw in the saloon."

Jason looked puzzled at him then suddenly he nodded his head, "Yeah I remember now he wouldn't leave his table."

"So Jason we know what he looks like."

"This Timber has been roped in by Emma McKenzie who's husband you shot," Ernest said, "and he's after your blood. Seems he's on some kind of mission to rid the territory of everybody who's outside of the law."

"Is he now, well then maybe we'd all better watch out for him," Jason said giving Ernest a look.

"You're right about that, so you ought to stop him, be good if you could."

"You mean do more dirty work for you?"

"For you Jason and your brother here. I don't know about the men you have with you."

"Yeah well we will. I guess you don't know where he is right now?"

"No I don't but maybe you'd better go look?"

"Oh we will, come on Ashley, we got work to do," Jason led the way out without another word to Ernest.

17

Timber and Emma rode off in the direction the outlaws had taken. Timber hoped they would keep together and not drop one off somewhere to ambush them. He kept on looking around as they rode on keeping to a lope to try and catch the outlaws up. They arrived at the canyon and saw the remains of a fire and that the place had been used to camp out at. Timber look around while Emma stayed on her horse.

"See anything of interest?" she asked.

Timber gave her a wave while he carried on looking then he walked back to her, "Naw, nothing much. This place has been used a few times though I would guess. We could just wait here for them to come back."

"But what if they don't? What if they rob another stagecoach and kill more people while we wait here?" Emma was very keen not to wait but to carry on after them.

Timber just shrugged, "Okay, we can always come back later let's ride," he got up on Scout and they headed out carrying on following what sign the outlaws had left behind them.

Jason and Ashley went back to the rest of the outlaws and told them what they had learned. Troy was happy about it.

"So now we have a name and yeah I remember him as well now. What do you know, he was right under our noses."

None of them missed the irony of that. Ashley wanted to get on, "Okay, we know now so let's go find him."

Jason and Ashley mounted up and then all together they rode down the street until they reached the end.

"Well he ain't about that I can see," Jason said.

"How d'you figure that, we ain't checked out any places yet."

"I didn't see any big bay horses outside any of them that matched the marshal's, did you?"

Troy stopped having not thought of that, then he carried on, "So what now?"

"We ride back up but just in case this time we check out the likely places where he might be."

Troy was happy with that as they all were so they began to ride back and called in at some shops, a cafe and saloons. Jason was as thirsty as all of them were so he allowed a stay at one of them to down a few beers and get the trail dust out of their mouths.

Timber and Emma rode side by side following what sign they could find and they began to realize just where they were heading.

"It looks like we're going to Angel Creek," Emma said.

"Yeah it does, that's interesting."

"Interesting? Why on earth would they do that?"

"Beats me, they must have a reason though."

They thought about it while they carried on and soon they were riding down the main street. Emma was concerned now, "Shouldn't we take care Timber, after all there are a few of them?"

"Never bothered me before, just get out of the way if they show up."

Emma still wasn't happy and she looked all around her constantly expecting to see them at any second coming for them.

Timber looked around as well but he was also looking for the mens horses, he stopped when he saw them. Emma stopped with him and then noticed why he'd stopped.

"What, they're all in the saloon?"

"Seems so," Timber got off Scout and looped his reins around a hitch rail at the next building.

"What do you want me to do?" Emma asked as she secured her horse there too.

Timber looked at her and thought for a moment, "I guess take your rifle across the street and cover me."

Emma nervously did as she was asked, at least Timber wasn't keeping her out of things. She crossed the street and leaned behind a porch post where she could see the saloon doors. She had the rifle ready to fire.

As Timber headed for the saloon he stopped as he saw men coming out and one of them pointed at him.

Jason had finally managed to get the men to leave the saloon. Troy was the first man out and he saw Timber and he couldn't help but cry out and point at him.

"It's him, that marshal he's here," he pulled his gun as he spoke.

Timber took it in and immediately drew his guns. As he saw Troy aiming his gun at him he fired making Troy double up and drop his gun as Timber's bullets hit him.

The rest of the outlaws scattered as they drew their guns as well. Timber had to move fast off the open street to find cover at the side of the next building.

Ryder stayed close to the saloon doors looking to get a bead on Timber, his arm hurt but he could still use his gun. Emma saw him from where she was and something about the man told her who he was. It was the man that had shot Austin in cold blood. She brought up the rifle and took aim at him. Her hands were shaking but she held the rifle steady and once she was sure she squeezed the trigger.

Ryder suddenly noticed Emma across the street and knew immediately who she was. He began to change his aim to her but too late, Emma's bullet struck him in the middle of his chest and took him down like a sack of flour.

Carter screamed across to Jason and Ashley, "We gotta get out of here," he ran out to the horses shooting wildly as he did. Jason and Ashley had no choice but to go with him. Together they fired their guns towards Timber and Emma as they mounted up and spurring their horses raced off.

Emma ran across the street to check on Ryder. She got there to find him lying on his back. She knelt down and could see that he was dead and with mixed emotions she got up from him. Timber arrived at the same time.

"You did well," he said as she went to him. He could see tears in her eyes, "Don't worry about shooting him, he deserved what he got."

"Oh he did. It just brought it all back to me."

"Sure. Look the last three are getting away, I'm going after them."

"Not without me you're not," Emma brushed her tears away on a sleeve and went for her horse. Timber shook his head and walked to Scout. Then they were off again riding up the street and out of town at a lope.

Jason and Ashley caught up with Carter and together they kept on riding towards their camp while shouting to each other at the same time.

"They really mean business," Carter called as they joined him.

"Yeah, we need to finish this business and soon," Ashley answered.

"Look hold up a minute," Jason had them stop so he could talk to them, "Timber might come on after us. It is possible with them being so keen on trying to kill us. You two stay here and ambush him if he comes. I'll ride on and get all we have made so far. I'll wait there a spell then if you're not back I'll meet you later at the trail out of town on the rise where we hit the first stagecoach."

Ashley and Carter weren't sure but Jason convinced them that it was the best thing to do then he rode off leaving them to it.

18

As Jason rode off Carter looked at Ashley, "You reckon that marshal will come on after us?"

"Can't say but he has so far. There's no harm in hunkering down and waiting on him a spell."

Carter nodded, "What if he has the woman with him?"

"What if he has. She shot Ryder so she's a target as well now."

Carter accepted that and looked around, "So where d'you wanna do this?"

Ashley had already decided, "We passed a place that will suit us," Ashley turned his horse and rode back a short way to where there was a slight rise and a pile of rocks they could get down behind. There was a bunch of trees a few yards away where they left their horses and snagging their rifles and canteens they went back to the rocks where they got down ready to wait a while.

Timber could see the route the three men had taken and he followed it for a good way then he slowed down.

"What are you doing Timber, they're getting away."

Timber went down to a walk, "Now are they? Looking ahead there are a few places that would be good to make an ambush from."

Emma pulled her horse up, "What? You think they will?"

"Could be. Best not to take the chance."

"So what do we do?"

"We ride a good ways around this track they are on. We can get back to it further on."

"But what of they aren't planning an ambush and we lose them?"

"We won't lose them forever, we'll find them again," Timber didn't waste any more time talking he turned Scout around and headed off to one side of the track.

Emma kept close to him glancing over at the track several times wondering if she would see any signs of an ambush set for them. Timber took a wide loop around using what rises, trees and rocks there were to keep out of view from where he figured the outlaws track was. As he continued he began to circle around. Emma became more concerned then.

"Have we gone far enough yet Timber?"

"I figure we have, now keep quiet," Timber carried on at a walking pace back to the track he knew the outlaws had been heading along. They rode for a while until Timber stopped again. Emma pulled up alongside him.

"See ahead, those trees," Timber whispered.

Emma took a look and then gasped, "Horses."

"Yeah two of them, hidden from anyone approaching from the other direction."

"So they have laid an ambush for us."

"Seems so. Now like last time Emma you wait here. Keep your rifle ready and cover me again," Timber slipped off Scout and left him there then he quietly moved off keeping bent over low.

Carter and Ashley were getting bored. They had lain in the dust for some time with nothing happening.

"He ain't coming," Carter said.

"Keep your voice down, you know how they travel. He may still do, we'll give it a little longer."

They both then froze as they heard a voice coming from behind them, "You boys just let go of your rifles and turn around real slow."

Both of them looked around before moving then seeing Timber

standing behind them with a gun in each hand they knew they would have to do as he asked. Once they were standing up Timber got them to drop their gun belts and then make three steps towards him.

"Okay, now we can talk."

"Talk about what?" Ashley said angry at being caught out so easily.

"About what you boys are up to, where the other one of you is and where you've stashed what you've stolen?"

"That's a lot of questions."

"So get answering. Where the other man is first."

The two men exchanged glances then Ashley answered, "He's long gone. Took his share and skedaddled."

Timber wasn't sure of that but he let it go, for now, "So where are your shares?"

Ashley had to smile now. He knew Jason should still be at the camp and would wait a while so it was an easy answer, "It's not far from here, I guess you want us to take you there?"

"Better than dying out here I guess."

"I guess so," Ashley glanced again at Carter who gave a slight nod of his head.

Timber turned and waved for Emma to join them and waited while she rode up keeping the two men covered as she did so. He kept his eyes on the men.

"So just what is going on?" He asked for the second time.

"We're just taking what we can, we have no other way to live."

"I know its more than that so come on what is it?"

"I done told you marshal, that's all there is."

Timber nodded. It was a long way back to town and he wanted to get the money and items they had stolen, he could always question them again later.

Emma arrived and Timber had her collect the outlaws guns and stash them on her horse then he had her go and get their horses.

"Okay you two now mount up and you ride in front of us, any wrong move and you're dead."

That was okay by them, they were happy to take him to where

they knew Jason was so he could kill Timber then they could take the woman afterwards.

They rode slowly as Timber told them to which also suited the two men. Gradually they approached the camp. As they got close Timber knew where they were going and remembered that he had been there but he hadn't found anything so this was going to be interesting.

Jason had got there easily enough and he had gone to the rocks where their stash was and took it all out. He put it in his saddlebags and what was left into a cloth bag he tied to his saddle then he looked around for his brother and Carter to come to him. He got out of the trees and up the canyon to the top to be able to look out more easily although he still kept himself below the skyline. He waited there listening out for any gunshots but he didn't hear any. Time went on and he wondered what was happening. The marshal should be with them by now if he was coming at all and if not then he figured they would have given up waiting for him and should be here soon. Then he saw riders approaching, more than two. He couldn't tell who was with them but he was sure the first two were Ashley and Carter. Something was wrong. He settled down into the trees just below the canyon rim to wait and he snagged his rifle.

Timber pushed the men on. He was happy they were indeed going to where the money was but he still wondered about the third man. It was very unlikely he would have just left them so he could well be around someplace and most probably at the camp. The two men had been too willing to take him there. He let them get a little closer before he stopped them.

"Okay hold it right there," he called to them.

They both stopped surprised by the order, "We ain't there yet," Ashley said.

"I know that. Emma we got a situation just like twice before. We'll do the same thing again. You wait here with your rifle until I holler for you."

Emma was now well used to doing that so she got off her horse and pushed it away to the side while she snagged her rifle.

"Okay now we walk in from here, get off your horses," Timber told the two men.

This was not what they had expected so they weren't happy to do so but Timber made them get off. Once they were on the ground Timber got off Scout and sent him away then he got up behind them.

"Okay now walk on and remember I have a gun at each of your backs."

Ashley shrugged, he still knew that his brother wouldn't have left the camp yet and would be close by so they walked on knowing Jason would have seen them by now.

Jason had seen everything and now that they were closer he could see the marshal. He still wasn't sure who the other rider was having stopped some way back. He now saw Ashley and Carter walking straight towards him with the marshal behind them. He didn't know what had happened but knew he just had to take Timber out. He stayed on his horse figuring the height would help him and he rode slightly around the trees to try and get a bead on Timber from the side as they passed by where he was.

Emma was on the ground again thinking this was getting to be a habit. However it suited her well enough. She lay the ground and had her rifle to her shoulder as she scanned the trees ahead of where Timber was heading. Then she saw a glimmer of light which she knew immediately was the glint from a rifle barrel. She squinted down her rifle sights to lock onto it.

Jason only had to move a little way now to be able to see Timber when they got closer and he waited. Emma then saw him and realized what he was doing. There was no way she could allow that so she aimed as carefully as she could and then took the shot.

The rifle shot reverberated around taking everyone by surprise. The bullet raked across Jason's side making him lose a grip on the rifle and drop it. The pain was intense and he now knew his cover was blown. At the same time Ashley took his chance and stopped, whirling around to try and grab hold of Timber. Carter then tried the same thing. Neither of them got close. Ashley tried to grab Timber's gun but Timber fired at the same time tearing a hole right through

Ashley's middle. As he dropped Carter swung a fist hoping to get Timber off balance but Timber swayed backwards firing at the same time. Carter fell shot through his heart. Timber then dropped to the ground taking cover behind the two bodies. He heard another rifle shot at the same time as Emma tried again to hit Jason. It was all too much for Jason who then urged his horse down into the canyon and some cover. Seeing Jason ride off Emma swung up on her horse and hurried over a lot closer then leaped off it again as she got up to Timber.

"He's gone down the canyon," she yelled as she got down still keeping a firm hold of her rifle.

"We need to get him alive if possible I have questions for him," Timber looked at Emma. It wasn't usual for him to get any help but this woman was proving to be very useful, "Stay in cover of the trees, see if you can get through them and keep an eye out for him. I'm going around to try and get him," Timber didn't wait for a reply but left her there and crept off into the trees.

Jason was totally horrified and upset at seeing his brother killed. He wasn't worried about Carter except for the fact that it now left him alone with Timber and the woman who he had now recognized. He rode down into the canyon to keep clear of the woman and her rifle and then he left his horse and got down among the rocks figuring Timber would come down for him and he could then shoot him.

Timber kept very low to the ground and got through the trees to take another look into the canyon. Having been there before he had a good idea of the layout of the place. He could see the outlaw's horse and figured the man wouldn't be far from it. There was a jumble of rocks there that he figured he would be hiding behind. He crept on keeping the same distance from him to get around behind him.

Emma saw Timber go and she also saw the horse. She got down among the trees and looked down to the rocks. She saw odd movements in one place and finally the place where Jason was. She stayed still and waited.

Timber carried on and got clear of the immediate area then he ran around the end of the canyon to the other side and began to work his way along. Jason took odd looks over the rocks wondering where he was. Emma watched and waited looking for any sign of Timber. She saw him then making his way down right above where Jason was. She was concerned the man might hear Timber and shoot him so she took his attention by firing a shot at him. She knew the chances of hitting him were very small but that wasn't the intention.

Jason wasn't happy about being shot at and he looked for the shooter but he couldn't make out where he was as he figured it would be Timber shooting at him so he was very surprised to hear him call to him.

"Drop the gun and stand up with your hands wide," Timber said while keeping a close look at him.

Jason dropped his gun and turned around to face Timber as he stood up.

"You're under arrest," Timber told him.

19

Jason couldn't see any way out of his predicament. He had lost his brother and all the men who had been with him, now he was alone and arrested by the marshal who had been after him since Ryder had killed the woman's husband. There was nothing he could do, for now. He just had to hope that a chance would crop up for him to get away.

Timber had him step away from his gun and down out of the rocks. Emma hurried over to them to take a good look at Jason.

"You killed my husband in cold blood," she hissed at him.

"It wasn't me that did that. It was Ryder. You shot him at the saloon."

"Don't you think I know that and I was happy to kill him but if it hadn't have been for you coming to rob the stagecoach it wouldn't have happened."

Jason didn't have an answer. He could have explained the situation he had with his brother as to how they had no choice but to take to crime and how they had been given a job to do but he knew it wouldn't cut anything with her so he just kept quiet.

"Okay Emma, don't get too close to him, go and get his gun will you," Timber was worried he might try something and that was a way to get her from him then he looked at the outlaw, "So what's your name?"

Jason saw no reason to lie so he told him then he followed on with, "You have just killed my brother Ashley."

"If he hadn't have got involved in robbery and murder he would still be alive," Timber said with no remorse.

While Emma was away Timber took Jason to his horse and whistled for Scout to come to him. Then he got Emma to get her horse and mount up. She then covered Jason while Timber checked Jason's horse and found the money and items he had stolen with the others. He got Jason on his horse before he mounted Scout, then they were ready to go.

All the way back to town Jason looked for a chance to ride off but he knew that would only get him killed as Timber kept a gun on him pretty much all the time and Emma had kept his gun belt. Timber had thoughts of his own. This man looked like he would be hard to break down and confess as to what he was involved in which was obviously more than just robbery. He knew something wasn't right at the council office either so he decided to take him there and kill two birds with one stone.

20

They rode into town and Timber kept on straight down the street until they arrived at the council office, then he made Jason stop. Jason was surprised as he had expected to be taken down to the sheriffs office and jail. He looked questioningly at Timber.

"Get off your horse and stand there," Timber told him before he got off Scout to join him then he turned to Emma, "go get the sheriff Emma and bring him here."

Emma rode off and Timber leveled a gun at Jason, "Okay, go in there," he said waving his gun at the office door. Jason's mind was racing now, he couldn't believe Timber had brought him here. There was nothing for it, he had to go in now and try to bluff it out, he walked to the door, took a deep breath, opened it and walked inside. Timber walked in right behind him and shoved him further in where he could keep an eye on him, he was also pleased to see the three council members all there sitting around a table. They all looked up amazed at their visitors.

"What's the meaning of this Timber?" Ernest asked glancing at Jason at the same time.

"It's time to get to the bottom of what's going on around here councilor and this man is going to help us."

Ernest looked again at Jason, "And just who is he?"

Timber grinned, "What you don't recognize him?"

Ernest gave a look of horror, "No of course not, what are you saying?"

As he spoke Jason shuffled round looking at the three men there and giving them hard looks."

"I'm saying there is some kind of conspiracy going on here and I want to get to the bottom of it. Now you all just stay calm here, there's two more people to join us."

Everyone looked at each other shocked to have this happen. It was only a couple of minutes later that the door opened and sheriff Dusty Colby entered followed by Emma.

"Now we're all here we can start," Timber said.

Dusty looked around, "Now look here Timber, I object to having Emma bring me here like this, just what is it you want?"

Emma stood way back from everyone at the side of the room so she was able to see them all from a different angle to Timber. She had her hand down by her gun if need be.

"Now this man here, Jason is the only outlaw left of the gang that's been robbing stagecoaches as well as making other trouble, that I know, who he is working for I don't."

"What are you saying, this man is robbing and killing for someone?" Frederick asked.

"That's exactly what I mean and I'm thinking that at least one of you here knows all about it."

Rusty wasn't happy, "That's quite an accusation Timber, you got any grounds for that?"

"Only what I've heard, what we've both heard," Timber nodded at Emma.

"That's right. I was listening at this window when you sheriff were here discussing the robberies and the men that were doing it and you seemed to be on their side to me."

"Whoa now, don't bring me into this, I ain't got nothing to do with it," Dusty held his hands up as he spoke.

"I heard you sheriff, you can't get away from that."

"Well now we seem to have us a situation here," Ernest said sitting back in his chair.

"That we do, now tell us sheriff just what is going on?"

Dusty was aware that Timber's gun was pointing towards all of them and now was the time to talk, "Okay you heard me talking in here that time, but what you heard wasn't the truth. I'm not in on the syndicate here, you need to talk to Ernest or Frederick or Rusty for that matter, they're all in on it."

"The thing is sheriff we don't know yet what 'it' is?"

The councilors all sat upright in their chairs and scowled at the sheriff. Ernest was most indignant, "Now don't you go shooting your damn mouth off, there ain't nothin' to say."

"Ah but there is," Dusty paused then looked straight at Timber, "As soon as I saw you I knew this would be straightened out. I've been trying to get to the source of what's going on but I've not been able to. Jason here is the man you need to talk to," Dusty waved a hand to him and stood back.

"So what of it then Jason?" Timber asked.

"I'm not telling you a damn thing," he stood resolute, his face stern.

"Okay well then let's see what these councilors have to say shall we?"

"We don't need to say anything either Timber," Ernest said.

"Ah but you do. You see you're not dealing with a sheriff the council pays now, you're dealing with me and the territory governor the Honorable Robert Pierce Fullerton has given me the job of straightening out any injustice in Texas. Now I ain't concerned about the well being of any of you men. I'm quite happy to take you all to jail and keep you there until you talk, or I can make things much harder for you," Timber pulled his other gun and cocked it.

"You ain't gonna shoot us Timber," Ernest sneered.

"No?" Timber fired and grazed Ernest's arm. The sound of the shot was loud in the room. As the smoke cleared they all saw Ernest clutching his arm and cussing at Timber.

"You can't do that, why I'll have you arrested and thrown into jail."

"I don't think so. Now that was just for openers, you want me to continue?"

"You'd better believe him gents I've seen this man work and he don't give a damn. The governor has given him the power to dish out justice any way he wants to," Emma told them.

"So who's next for a warning?" Timber asked.

"Okay, okay," Fredrick said, "It's all down to him," he pointed straight at Jason and all eyes went to him.

Timber cocked a head at him waiting for an answer.

Jason scoffed at them, "You think you're all high and mighty Timber huh? Well sometimes you gotta do things you wouldn't normally."

"Like murder and robbery?"

Jason scowled at him, "You don't understand."

"No I don't so tell me."

"We had to do what we did. We needed money, lots of money. The man we are working for hadn't got enough to set up a committee to rival the governor."

Ernest was getting worried, "Just leave it Jason."

"No I won't. I've lost my brother, no doubt my freedom and all my dreams and for what? To fuel some mad mans scheme to change the future of Texas."

"Just who is this man?" Timber asked.

"His name is the Honorable Milton Westbrook. He works for the territory governor but he's trying to bring him down and change all his decisions and plans and he needs money to pay people to go on his side."

"And he employed you to do it?"

"Yeah, through these men right here. We were promised a pardon, land and money if he won over the governor which was much more than we could have got from a life of crime. I don't know what these men were getting out of it."

"And this Milton Westbrook, he set this all up?"

"Yeah. He doesn't want Texas to join the Union and he has been getting people together with him to oppose Robert Pierce Fullerton, the governor and get it overturned. It's a big deal and would be worth a lot to him with what he could then do so he was prepared to pay men like us. The thing was he didn't have enough money of his own to bribe, pay, whatever these other men to side with him so he brought Ashley and me in on it and some others to help get the money and keep a lid on things with promises of pardons and great wealth later."

Dusty had been listening intently, "I thought so, I knew something was wrong here. What you heard at the window was me trying to get closer in with them to find all this out."

Jason glanced around at Dusty, "That's right, he was. He did try to smoke them all out."

Timber looked at the three councilors, "So come on what was it you were going to get out of this?"

Ernest was going to stay silent but Frederick decided to talk knowing that would help his case later, "Simply put Timber it was money and a chance for us to maybe climb up the ladder a little way. Milton Westbrook would have helped us with that."

Timber sighed, "Okay, you men are all going to jail to await the circuit judge. I'm sure Dusty here can accommodate you and organize something with the robbery takings we have outside."

"You bet Timber," Dusty drew his gun and got them all to stand up while they protested about going to jail.

"You can tell the judge," Dusty told them as he marched them out helped by Timber while Emma followed on.

They walked down to the sheriff's office where he locked them up in his two cells, two men to a cell. Timber waited with Emma in the office until that was done.

"You know we thought you were a part of this Dusty but I'm sure glad you weren't. You hold them here. I will send the governor a telegram explaining things. I'm sure he will want to know about this Milton Westbrook character."

"I'm sure he will and thanks Timber. I wouldn't have got this done without you."

"Just remember to look for wanted notices on the outlaws, any bounty money is mine."

"Sure thing I will do."

"Now what about the robbery takings?"

"Bring them in let's take a look."

Timber got the bag off Jason's horse and his saddle bags and took them back into the office. Then they emptied them out and they were surprised at just how much there was. As they were looking through it Emma gave a cry and grabbed an item. They all looked at her as she held up a gold watch.

"This belonged to my husband Austin, I'd recognize it anywhere."

"Well good for you," Dusty said.

Emma kept a tight hold of it as Timber told Dusty to organize what he could with it all with the Butterfield line superintendent. He then left with Emma.

"You happy with that?" He asked her.

"As happy as I can be yes, and I did get the man who killed Austin."

"So what now for you?"

"I don't know maybe I'll still get a job at the bank?"

Timber nodded, "Worth a try. I'm hungry, let's go eat, my treat but I got a chore to do first."

Emma smiled at him and walked with him to the Telegraph office and waited while he sent a telegram then went with him to the restaurant they had used before.

Later they went back to the hotel for the night and the next morning Timber was back at the sheriff's office.

"You found any wanted notices on the outlaws?" He asked Dusty.

"Yeah as a matter of fact I did. The stagecoach brought some bodies back as you know, here's the tickets for them."

Timber thanked him, and turned to go, "I'll be on my way now, look after those men," Timber looked to the cells where four miserable men were sitting.

"You can count on it," Dusty said with a smile.

Timber then went back to the hotel and found Emma who was about to leave.

"I have something for you," Timber said as he stopped her in the foyer.

"You slipped out early this morning," she said looking up at him.

"Yeah I had things to do," he handed her the bounty tickets, "take these to the bank they will honor them, give you a start along with that job I'm sure you'll get."

Emma looked down at them then back up at Timber, "Thanks Timber, I really appreciate that. I guess this means you're leaving?"

"Yeah, I wouldn't be any good to you or to anyone here, I got a job to do."

"Good luck with it," Emma reached up and gave Timber a kiss on his cheek then walked out.

Timber shook his head then went out too and called in at the Telegraph office where there was a message for him. The governor was pleased and thankful for the information and he had appropriately seen to Milton Westbrook, and those who would have apposed him. He also told him of some bother he had heard about north of San Antonio with some settlers and he asked Timber to get over there to investigate. Timber was happy to go and do that. He got up on Scout and headed out of town.

THE END

VOLUME FIVE

OUTLAW SHOWDOWN IN THE LONE STAR

1

Jake Timber was riding along a dusty trail towards the town of Somerville in Texas. It was one of those hot days with no wind so it was really scorching. There were hardly any clouds in the sky to offer any relief in blocking out the sun. Timber was thankful he had filled his canteens at the last place he had been to and he just hoped they would hold out for him until he got to town. The last buildings he'd seen belonged to a young couple who were trying to make the beginnings of a small farm. They were immigrants from Missouri come down to Texas to take up on the Land Grants being dished out by the government. It was going to be hard work for them and Timber wished them well.

As the sun reached its highest point in the sky Timber stopped in what shade he could find beside a bunch of bushes and filled his wide brown hat with water for his horse, a big bay called Scout. There was hardly any water around and his canteens were getting low, he would be pleased to refill them when he got to town which he reckoned was still a few hours away.

Along the way his thoughts went gone back to the last few days. He'd had the job of taking out a group of men who had been terrorizing settlers coming south from Missouri who were all taking advantage of the free land grants in Texas. The men had been working for the land commissioner who was trying to swindle the immigrants out of their land. It had taken some time but Timber had finally managed to straighten it all out and he had sent a telegram to the territory governor the Honorable Robert Pierce Fullerton to inform him that he had settled all of the problems. Now though he wanted to send another telegram to him which was why he was headed back to the nearest town. He kept in touch with the governor frequently in case there was anything special he wanted him to work on. It occurred to him that he ought to check in again before he went riding off.

As it happened he got into town with half a canteen of water left and he rode straight down to the Telegraph office to send a telegram out. The boy there knew him from when he had been in before and dutifully wrote the message down then he gave it to the operator to tap out.

"That's a one long message mister, it's gonna cost you," the boy said.

Timber didn't care at all how much it would cost as he handed over more coins than the boy asked for and told him to keep the change.

"Gee thanks mister," the boy's face brightened up with a smile.

"That's fine, now there's more for you if you bring any answer to that telegram straight to me in Dukes Place saloon."

"No problem, you got it."

Timber left them to it and walked off to the saloon which was close by, so close he just led Scout to it and left him at the rail and went in the saloon. He knew it to be the best in town and being so near the Telegraph offie it suited him very well. He got settled in after buying a beer at the bar to wait for his reply. He figured he would have to wait some time so he took a battered old pack of cards from a pocket and laid them out on the table for a game of solitaire.

He had been there some time before he saw the Telegraph office boy come walking in carrying a telegram. He saw Timber and went over to him.

"Your telegram mister," the boy said.

Timber took it as the boy waited. Timber read it through then he handed the boy some coins telling him there wouldn't be a reply. The boy gave hm a wide smile as he pocketed the coins and walked out again. The telegram was from the territory governor and it told him that there was indeed a job that he wanted him to do. It had just come to the territory governor Robert Pierce Fullerton's attention and it concerned a gang of six men who had got together after breaking out of jail over to the west in the town of Helena. In doing so they had killed one guard and seriously injured another. They had also been on a robbery spree to get themselves set up with, guns, supplies and everything else they needed. All of the men were known to Timber as it had been him that had arrested them over a period of time and got them put away for crimes they had committed. Fullerton wanted them caught again and Timber was the man it do it - again.

Timber had worked in the area for a long time and he had indeed sent men to prison there as he had in other towns and areas too. He had been interested to read the list of names in the telegram. There was Jacob Simms, Nathanial Wilson, James Carter, Carl Evans, Gerard Dawson and Billy Benson. The names all rang bells in his head but he couldn't say for sure where he had heard them all or even where he had arrested them, maybe if he came across them he would recognize them. He was sure going to try and find them and if they weren't happy about going back to jail then he would just have to mete out justice from the barrel of his gun.

From Helena the men could have gone north, east or south so Timber was going to have to search around a good bit to find any of them again. He finished his beer and then went out to where Scout was waiting for him at the hitch rail. Timber never needed to secure him there, he just hung the reins over the rail knowing he wouldn't go wandering off and would come to his whistle if he needed him. He'd had the horse for a long time and he had trained him well. He then rode down the street to a general store and stocked up on supplies as it was going to be a long ride from where he was and he didn't know where he would end up or how long it would take him to find the men. He could have stayed the night in town but there was still plenty of daylight hours left to burn so he set off west.

He thought through the telegram he had received. It sounded odd that six men he had locked up should all break out together, but then maybe it wasn't like that. Maybe they had broken out in ones and twos and just ganged up. Maybe they weren't all men that he had sent to jail, he wouldn't know until he had found at least some of them to ask.

As dusk arrived he stopped at a place where there was a group of trees to give him some shelter from the wind that had sprung up from out of nowhere. It didn't take him long to unsaddle Scout and set him free. He knew the horse wouldn't wander far and would come back when he needed him, then he worked on getting a fire going and heating something up to eat.

A good many miles away six men were riding east. Jacob Simms was keen to get some miles under his feet before it got dark. It had been a long time since he had been locked up, caught by Marshal Jake Timber and the whole time he had spent behind bars he had thought of finding him and killing him. He had an idea where the man was as did the five men riding along with him. They had all been let out on purpose to achieve Timber's death by a man who had a strong grudge against him. The man knew just how good Timber was which was why he had arranged for so many men to be freed to get him. All of the men had a grudge or some reason why they also wanted Timber dead which worked very well for Jacob.

The man they were now working for had arranged it so they didn't just walk out of prison but had to do some work themselves. That resulted in a prison guard getting killed but the man wasn't concerned about a little collateral damage so long as the end result was achieved. Some of the men were in different prisons but the timing had been arranged for them to be out so they could all meet up in an area where Timber would be. At the last minute the man had learned where Timber was, it was disappointing for him that Timber was so far away but he was in no rush, the men that he had set up would just have to ride over to where Timber should be and find him. He wanted them to take their time over killing him and then report back.

It had been a big job for the man to work out how to get the outlaws out of prison and to find out roughly where Timber was so he could tell the outlaws where to go and find him. While he was in no real hurry he would be pleased when the deed was done and Timber was dead.

Jacob however was in a hurry, he had waited far too long to have a chance of taking his revenge and now he was free he was going to take it as fast as he could. The man had put him in charge as being the hardest and biggest one of them. He had been told where the others would be and to round them up into a group to go after Timber. That had proved to be quite an easy thing to do. He got them organized and had them steal the extra things they needed with him from the nearest town and then he had set out east with the men to the location where Timber was last seen. They were to get their revenge on Timber, telling him what the man wanted him to know before killing him. In return they would have pardons for their crimes and a cash bonus.

Jacob kept them all riding on into the dusk before the others convinced him to make a stop for the night. It had been easy to find the horses and a few things left for them once they were let out, that had all been set up for them. What they hadn't got they stole so when they rode off from the nearest town they were fully prepared. Jacob wondered just how much in bribes to the guards that had cost the man?

As dusk approached Jacob pulled up reluctantly and made a camp with the other men in an area close to a bunch of bushes for protection against the wind. Once the horses had been seen to, a fire made and food eaten it was good for them all to gather around the fire to talk, even Jacob found that to be useful. He knew they all had a reason for wanting Timber dead and that most likely they wouldn't want to talk about what their reasons were so he discussed where they were going and what their plans were for Timber once they had caught him.

"We don't kill him outright. He needs to know why we are doing it," Jacob told them.

"You got no argument with that," Nathanial said for all of them with a grin.

"No he needs bringing down a little first," James butted in with.

The others just grinned and murmured agreement.

It was Carl who asked, "Which one of us is gonna do the deed?"

They all paid attention and Jacob was quick to answer, he had been put in charge of the gang and he wanted to keep his authority, "I guess that will come down to the situation at that time."

Carl grinned again at all of them. Jacob knew this was the man he was going to have to watch the most. He was angrier than most of them and big and brash enough to cause problems between them. He calmed the situation down by talking about how far they still had to ride and asking for ideas of how to actually catch Timber. The talk went on into the night with most of the ideas way too far fetched to have any chance of working. Jacob had his own thoughts and of how he was going to enforce his idea when the time came. He went to sleep dreaming of how he would do that.

2

It was cold through the night so it was as well that Timber had left the fire well stocked with wood so that even at daybreak the ashes were still hot which made it easy to get it going again. He didn't linger long, only taking the time he needed to eat, drink coffee and prepare to ride out again. Then he was riding west as the day began to warm up. He knew he had a good way to go so he kept up as fast a pace as he could by walking a ways then a lope then a trot and back to a walk. That covered the most ground without wearing Scout out. For two days Timber kept this pace up getting further and further west while over to the west six men were riding hard towards him.

Timber came across a few one horse-towns on the way and at the end of the second day he figured he could take a short rest and give Scout time to recover as he rode into another one of them. This was a small place with the name of 'Rawlins'. Timber took that to be the name of the man or family that had started the town off, such as it was. There was a trading post sat by itself and then a little way on there were two lines of wooden buildings making a wide street. Timber rode past the trading post then along the street looking at the buildings to see what there was. It wouldn't be anywhere without a saloon and Timber pulled up at one of the three he could see there.

They all looked to be about the same from the outside and Timber wasn't really concerned anyway he just wanted a drink and to rest for a little while before looking to see if there was a hotel or a room he could hire in a saloon for the night. As he got to the door he could see it wasn't that big a place but it was set out well enough considering the size of the one street town. Maybe it would get smartened up as time went on. He went inside and slowly walked up to the bar while his eyes scanned around. There were only a few men in there and they all looked harmless. He ordered a beer and asked what food they had.

"I guess we can rustle you something up if you ain't the fussy type," the bartender said.

"Whatever you have will be fine," Timber was tired from the days of riding and roughing it out on the range. He was hoping now for just something to fill his belly, a drink and maybe a soft bed for the night. He knew he would need to organize something for Scout which he would get around to very soon.

Jacob had been pushing hard to cover as much ground as possible and like Timber he was looking for a town where they could get a drink and rest up for the night. He was pleased to see buildings coming up and then they passed a town sign telling him it was 'Rawlins'. They carried on into the one street riding past a bunch of tents where people were living as they built houses and businesses and where the workers lived. The place they pulled up at happened to be the same saloon Timber was sitting in. They left their horses at the hitch rail, dusted themselves down with their hats then walked up to the doors, all of them looking forward to getting a few beers. Going in the door Jacob stopped, surprised at what he saw, so much so that he pushed the men behind him back outside.

"Hey what's goin' on?' Nathanial asked who was right behind him.

"He's here, right here in this saloon."

Nathanial stared back at him as the others gathered around.

"You sure it's him?" Gerard asked, always being the one to question things.

"Sure I'm sure. He's big, wearing deerskins, wide brown hat, black boots, silver toe and heel caps, it's him all right."

"Okay, so how are we gonna handle this," Nathanial asked.

"You all know about him and have had trouble with him before so you know we aren't just gonna go in there to get him."

"We could Jacob. If enough of us go in there at once we could just shoot him down," Billy was the youngest and the most reckless.

"Except we don't to kill him outright now do we? We want to talk to him and make him suffer before we do that, besides I doubt we could do that without losing at least one of us."

"You're right, we've pretty much all seen the man work, we don't want to go straight up against him," James said this thinking back to when Timber had arrested him for murder.

"So what is the plan?" Nathanial asked.

Jacob had been looking around. Between the town and the trading post they had come past where someone had built an outhouse of some kind. There was a bit of a fence around part of it and a few tools left lying around. He had no idea what it had been used for but he began to think that it could be useful to them.

"Okay, here's what we do. We wait out here for him to come out. We'll have to wait around the sides of the saloon so he doesn't see any of us until it's too late. Okay it's been a while since he saw any of us but you can bet your life on it that he will recognize our faces for sure. Then we jump him from both sides at the same time."

"That's your plan?" Nathanial asked wide eyed.

Jacob looked at him, "You got a better one?"

Nathanial shut up while Gerard asked, "And what do we do with him then?"

"We get him out of the way, that little outhouse over there will do," Jacob waved an arm in its direction.

Gerard nodded, "Somewhere nice and quiet huh?"

They all looked over and agreed with what Jacob was saying then he carried on.

"Carl, you, Gerard and Billy take the left side, Nathanial, James and me will take the right. Now as soon as he's out here we all go jump him together y'hear, don't give him any time to act?"

There were no arguments with that so Jacob walked off as they all did to get into position. They had no idea how long it would be before Timber came out but having rode this far they could wait a while longer, the only downside was that they would have to wait for their beers.

Timber had been in there for a while and decided it was time to go. He put his cards away and walked off to the door. He paused there to take a look outside. It all looked peaceful enough so he stepped out onto the sidewalk.

3

Timber walked out into the bright sunlight and stepped across the sidewalk to get to his horse and that's as a far as he got.

Jacob was the first to leap on him quickly followed by the other five men, all of them punching and shoving him, pleased to be able to use some of their anger up on him. Timber retaliated immediately and managed to get one good punch in before one of them smashed him over the head with the butt of his gun and Timber went down.

"Okay let's get him to the outhouse," Jacob said.

It took four of them to carry him along to the outhouse while Jacob led Timber's horse with them. Jacob then tried the door which opened to show that there was nothing in it apart from a few old tools. He then took Timber's gun belt as he said, "Get him inside, we'll talk to him when he wakes up."

Timber came round very groggily as they tried to maneuver him inside, then he started to pull against them, which was enough for James who started punching him. Seeing him do that the other men joined in using up some more of their anger on him. Timber had no chance against them in the state he was and after a few minutes of that they shoved him inside where he fell on the ground almost unconscious again.

They all stood outside the outhouse to gloat at what they had achieved.

"We got him Jacob," Billy rubbed his hands together in delight.

"Yeah we got him, as soon as wakes up we will have a little talk with him."

"Yeah then we can beat him up some more," James added.

Nathanial took a look at Timber lying in the outhouse, "Then he has to die."

"But slowly, he has to feel our pain," Jacob told them.

"Ah you bet, I'm looking forward to that, he can take a few bullet holes afore we finish him," Carl said.

They all thought that was very amusing, then Gerard said, "Shame we didn't get a drink though."

"You'll get one soon enough, tie his horse to the fence there," Jacob said looking at Scout, "we'll get a good price for him later."

"And his guns Jacob these are sure good," Nathanial said picking his gun belt off the fence where Jacob had placed it.

"They sure are good looking guns, we might have to decide which one of us gets them," Jacob said with a smile.

"Hey he's coming round," Billy shouted having been keeping an eye on Timber from the doorway.

All the men went to the door to take a look as Timber tried to get up. He ached all over and pushing his fingers through his hair he found a big bump on his head. His eyes wouldn't quite focus and he was feeling sick so he ended up staying on the ground leaning up against the outhouse wall. He had got a couple of views of mens faces and some of them rang a bell in his head but he now wanted to know who they all were.

"Just who the heck are you men?" The words came out a little shaky and hoarse.

"You mean you don't recognize any of us?" Jacob leaned in as he spoke.

"Kinda, but your names beat me," Timber had a good idea who Jacob was but he was now fishing for information.

"You know what Timber, you ought to know all of us. We have

been waiting a long time to get to see you again and we do want you to know each one of us. I'm Jacob Simms," Jacob pulled back so that Nathanial could move in once he had given Timber a chance to take a good look at him. All of the men made sure that Timber knew who they were one at a time. Even in his befuddled state Timber took it all in. He remembered most of them as he tried hard to put the names to the faces. As they gave their names Timber realized they were all men he had jailed at some time or other. What he couldn't work out was why they were all here? He didn't have to wait long for an answer.

Jacob appeared back in the doorway. He looked down at Timber and smiled, "Not such a big man now are you?"

Timber squinted back up at him. He hurt all over but he felt his breathing getting better, he just needed more time.

"So are you gonna tell me what this is all about or not?"

"Oh we're gonna tell you all right," Jacob was going to enjoy this. The other men had gathered around so they could all see into the outhouse where Timber was sitting.

Jacob carried on, "As you might have noticed Timber that we are all men you arrested and locked up but now we are out and it looks to me like we have turned things around and it's you who is now locked up, or will be."

Timber looked around at the outhouse and reckoned it wasn't much of a jail, "How'd you all get together here?" He asked.

"Ah now that is the sweet part of it. You see Timber we were all let out just to come and find you. Some of us were a good ways apart but we got together and well, here we are."

Timber was finding that hard to figure in his current state, "Who let you out?"

"Now wouldn't you like to know? We'll keep that to ourselves for now, either way Timber you are gonna suffer just like we have and then we are going to kill you but not quickly," Jacob turned and laughed as all the men joined in.

Nathanial leaned in the outhouse, "That Robert Fullerton, the territory governor, he thinks you're infallible, well we're gonna show him that you're not."

Timber still couldn't figure out how the men had found him or who could have let them out of jail.

"Yeah then when you're dead we're gonna send your boots and hat to him to prove we killed you," Gerard added.

"The bonus on that Timber is that we will get paid for killing you," Billy laughed loudly at that thinking it was a huge joke.

"Yeah we will kill you but not yet. We need to tell you each of our stories so you understand why you have to die," Jacob said.

Timber was happy to hear them, it gave him the chance to put names and faces to the events that led up to him jailing them. It also gave him more time to come around. They had all been transferred to prisons in the area that Timber had arrested them in and had been let out to join up so they could find him and kill him. Timber still didn't know who had arranged that and the men didn't look like telling him.

4

Jacob waited until all the men had finished their say with Timber before closing the outhouse door. There was a rusty old bolt that he pushed across into place. It owed secure enough, then he stood back.

"Okay now before we do anything else we need to get to a Telegraph office and let the man know we have Timber and find out just what he wants us to tell him before we kill him."

"Will there one here in this one horse town?" Gerard asked.

"We can go and find that out, grab that drink we missed out on and get some more supplies all at the same time. We just need one man to wait here to make sure Timber doesn't get out," Jacob looked around for a volunteer.

Billy quickly answered, "I'll do it. I want to talk to him some more anyway and as soon as he's dead I can to go town and drink as much as I want to."

"That's great Billy. I dare say we will be a while though."

Billy just grinned back, "I don't mind that, me and Timber can have a nice long chat while y'all gone."

Jacob nodded, "Okay boys, let's ride," while they had been talking two of the men had brought all the horses over to the outhouse so they mounted up leaving Billy's horse next to Timber's at the fence then they rode off to check the town out for a Telegraph office. Billy was pleased to see them go as he had more words to say to Timber.

Jacob and the men were soon back in the town and as they rode down the street Jacob called out to a man riding up the other way.

"Say is there a Telegraph office here?"

"Not in this town no sir," the man replied. You need to go on to Indian Springs for one of those."

"How far is that?"

"Oh about two hours due south."

Jacob thanked him and turned to the others, "it looks like we got us some more riding to do, Timber will just have to wait for us, that will build up his worry nicely and get him to think on what he done to us."

"Someone needs to go tell Billy," Nathanial said.

"Yeah. You wanna do that, you can have some fun with Timber until we get back so long as you don't kill him," Jacob smiled across at him.

"Don't mind if I do at that," Nathanial said with a smile.

They rode off leaving Nathanial alone right outside a saloon. It had been some time since he'd had a drink and he needed one and seeing as there was plenty of time he decided he would do just that.

When they had all ridden off Billy walked up to the outhouse door, then not being able to see Timber as there was no window in the door and there was no way he was going to open it so he went to the outhouse side wall where there was a small window. It was slightly open and obviously stuck in that position. He stood there and looked in to see Timber and called to him.

"You know when you arrested me I had a friend with me, now I want to know what happened to him?"

Timber looked up at him and shuffled around to get a better view. He found his right leg hurt a lot from being kicked. He had never been exactly right from when he had suffered a minor gunshot wound in it, now it was giving him some grief.

"I remember you Billy, it was some time ago now."

"Yeah, too long thanks to you, so what about it?"

"You don't need to worry about him, I killed him and left his body were it was for the critters to have, which is what the scum deserved, after I had emptied his pockets of course."

Billy saw red, "Why you..." he went to the door and nearly pulled the bolt free but then he remembered that he was on his own and that he couldn't kill him just yet anyway.

When Billy had moved from the window Timber stood up. He had been moving his legs around and getting his head clear all the time and now was his chance. He knew that Billy was on his own out there and if he was going to act then it had to be before the others came back. He had been looking around the outhouse at the items inside it. Someone had left old tools lying around and one of them was perfect for what he wanted. A rusted old crowbar lying in the dirt. He could only see a part of it but he knew what it was, he had been loosening it with a foot for a while and he could now see that it was free to pick up. He reached across and got the end of it then used it as a prop to help him stand up. A second later he was at the door and the crowbar was rammed into the gap between the door and frame. He then used his two hundred and thirty eight pound weight to shove hard into the door as he pulled on the crowbar. The flimsy bolt didn't stand a chance and it sprang open allowing the door to slam out straight into Billy who was standing right up in front of it.

Billy was taken completely by surprise and was thrown to the ground by the door crashing into him with Timber's weight behind it. Then Timber was there looking down at him. Billy panicked and reached for his gun. Timber's guns were over on the fence but he did have the crowbar. It was either Billy or him and it sure wasn't going to be him. He launched himself down on Billy holding the crowbar in front of him. It went straight through Billy's neck pinning him to the ground. As Timber got up off him Billy twitched around as blood poured from his mouth and then he lay still.

Timber hobbled across to where his gun belt was hanging off the fence and buckled it on, then he walked back to Scout. He had heard that the other men were going to look for a Telegraph office, so now he had to search the town to see if they had found one.

Timber was in a mood to find them. He had figured when they had been locked up that it would be the last time he would see any of them so now to have six of them all at once ganging up on him and beating him up was really maddening. He still wasn't feeling well, he had bruises and cuts all over him and his right leg hurt but none of that was going to stop him giving out retribution as soon as he found them. He got to the town quickly and then slowed right down as he figured out where they would be. He didn't get far into the street before he found out there wasn't a Telegraph office there which didn't surprise him. He asked a man sitting outside a saloon and found out he would have to ride on to Indian Springs for one. Before he did that though he wanted to check out that they weren't somewhere still close by. The only obvious places to look were saloons and seeing as he was right outside one he carefully dismounted and leaving Scout at the hitch rail he painfully walked up the sidewalk to the door.

As was his normal way Timber didn't just walk in, he stayed at the door and let his eyes get adjusted to the lower light inside. He also tried to see just who was in there. All he could see were a few men, mostly with their backs towards him so he walked in and stepped to the side of the door before stopping for another look. He then recognized a man who turned around to see who had entered. That alone told Timber he was a man like himself either within the law or outside it. They both stared at each other for a second before it sunk in as to who they were both looking at.

Nathanial took slightly longer than Timber, it being such a shock to see him standing there. He cussed himself now for letting himself get a drink and he wondered what had happened to Billy. Whatever had happened he knew it was now just him alone to straighten this situation out. He considered himself a good man with a gun as a lot of dead men would testify if they could, but Timber was something else. As well as being good with a gun Nathanial knew he was clever and knew very well how to handle situations like this. He had to act and fast.

He went for his gun while at the same time knocking over the table he had been sitting at and diving to the floor. As he went down he fired at Timber hoping to surprise him.

It might have worked only Timber thought of a plan of his own at the same time. Just as Nathanial drew his gun Timber drew his right hand gun and fired at Nathanial as he went down, the bullet caught him in his thigh causing him to crash down on the floor a lot harder than he intended. Timber also moved just after firing to get around the table partly hiding Nathanial. Timber could have fired through it but he wanted to be sure of a direct hit with his second shot. Nathanial felt the pain and shock of the bullet in his leg which slowed him down by the second that Timber needed to get around the table and then he looked down into Nathanials scowling face and shot him again just as Nathanial was raising his gun. Timber kicked the gun away that had fallen from Nathaniel's hand and checked that he was dead then he stood up and looked around the saloon.

At the sound of the shots most of the men had fled for the door so there were only three of them left and the bartender who all looked shocked at Timber. He pulled his badge from a pocket and held it up.

"Jake Timber, U.S. Marshal," he called out which eased the mens minds somewhat. They then edged forward for a better look.

"This man is an outlaw and an escapee from prison," Timber told them.

"That's fine with us marshal, but would you mind getting him out of here?" The bartender asked.

Timber obliged by dragging the man out by his heels. He now had two dead bodies to dispose of together with the mens belongings and horses.

"You have a sheriff here and an undertaker?"

"No sheriff yet marshal, but we got us an undertaker, you'll find him down the street," the bartender told him.

Timber got a man there to help him drape Nathanial over his

horse, then led it back to the outhouse while riding Scout. With great difficulty in his current state Timber got Billy over his horse then checked the mens belongings and took what he wanted before he led the horses while he rode Scout down to the undertakers office. He handed the men over to the undertaker and left the mens horses as burial payment. Then he set out for Indian Springs.

5

Timber had been told that Indian Springs was just around two hours away. He still had plenty of daylight to burn so he hoped to catch up with the men by the end of the day. He knew there were six of them to start with and he had already taken two of them out so there was just four left, or so he hoped.

As he rode along his mind wandered to the four men left. He had seen their faces and had heard them tell him their names and where he had arrested them. That all seemed rather strange to him. Why didn't they just kill him outright or at least after telling him about them and why they wanted him dead? It was all down to this man they referred to and had to go send telegrams to. Who was he that it was so important that they had to send a telegram to this person and would they then wait for a reply? Timber sure hoped he would get some answers in Indian Springs.

Way ahead of him Jacob rode into town with James, Carl and Gerard, all of them keen to get the telegram sent and an answer received so that they could then get back to where Billy and Nathanial were keeping an eye on the man who had arrested them, the man who had ruined their lives and had stopped them from carrying on enjoying their work of murder and robbery.

Indian Springs was a bigger town than Rawlins with streets going off the main street. There were more people about and a lot more buildings, most of them businesses of some kind. It all looked a lot better to the outlaws as they searched for the Telegraph office. They found it halfway down the main street and pulled up outside.

"Okay now I'll go get the message sent, you boys just sit here," Jacob said as he headed for the door.

The others looked around and saw more than one saloon and all of them very close,

"I reckon we'll get that drink afore we leave," Gerard said.

The other two were of the same mind, "I reckon Billy and Nat can keep an eye on Timber a while longer," said James as he eyed up the closest saloon.

They hung around waiting for Jacob to come back out of the office. Jacob came out just a few minutes later and they looked at him.

"I've sent a telegram to him now we're waiting on a reply," he noticed the way the men were looking and he carried on with a smile," I asked for any reply to be brought to us in that there saloon." The man who had set them all free had given him an address to send telegrams to but he had been very careful in it being somewhere he could receive them while not giving away who he really was.

That brought smiles from all of them and together they walked over to it. They crowded in and were soon at the bar ordering whiskey and beers. Jacob found a table and they sat down but they soon had to get up again for refills. Then they sat talking while they waited for a reply to Jacob's telegram.

"Just what did you ask him?" Gerard wanted to know as the others listened for his answer.

"I told him we have caught Timber and we have him safely locked up, not in the best of health of course," they all laughed at that, "and I asked him what he wanted us to say to him from him and if he wanted anything special doing ?"

They all nodded at that knowing that it was something that had to be done before they could finish Timber off.

They were on their third beer before a lad arrived and handed over a piece of paper to Jacob. Jacob scanned over it then read it out:

To Jacob Wells.

I just need you to tell Timber exactly what bother he caused me and the people with me as discussed and that's all. Just make sure he knows. After that complete your assignment anyway you feel is fitting.

"Well that's simple enough, finish your beers and let's get back there," Jacob put the telegram into a pocket and stood up.

Although they had been pleased to spend some time in the saloon they were all now looking forward to getting back to the outhouse. Gerard gave a laugh as they mounted up.

"I can't wait to tell that marshal just what is gonna happen to him."

They were all in a good mood as they set off back for Rawlins.

Timber carried on riding towards Indian Springs. The man he'd got directions off had sent him on what he had said was a short cut from the main trail. It meant going over rough ground but it would save him time and seeing as he was on a horse not driving a wagon he would be fine. The ground was sure rough but nothing much different to what Timber had often ridden over. He took the route wanting to get to town while the outlaws were still there.

6

Jacob was more interested in getting back to Timber than the others. He had been the first prisoner to be approached by the man. It had come as a big surprise to have the man turn up. It took a while before he told him who he was, it was only when he got the guard to let him into his cell and the door had been closed that he did.

Jacob had been very surprised to discover who he was and he promised to keep that a secret as the man told him what he wanted him to do and what he would do for him in return. It took Jacob a while to get into his head what the man was saying. He had to hear it all a couple of times before it began to make any sense.

"Now look here this is the only chance you're gonna get of getting out of this place so you'd better take it," the man told him.

Jacob sat on his bunk and looked at the man sitting on his chair. He obviously had a dollar or two judging by his clothes, boots and hat. Jacob guessed him to be around fifty years old and his hair was certainly turning gray. He must be having a reasonable life judging by the size of him too. His face was rounded and he had a well trimmed mustache that turned up at the ends into points. He was very sure of himself and he had an offer that Jacob knew he was going to accept.

"So here it is Jacob. I know what crimes you committed and I know it was Marshal Jake Timber that arrested you and got you put in prison. Now it just turns out that the man did me a grave injustice too and I reckon we both have the same kinda thoughts about that man."

Jacob nodded, "I guess we do then, I sure have."

"That's what I want to hear, now this is what I want you to do. I can make the arrangements to get you out of here and have a horse waiting for you with hopefully all the things you're gonna need to do the job I got for you," the man paused to let the next part sink in, "I want you to go find Timber and kill him."

Jacob stared at him then laughed, "You want me to take on Marshal Timber on my own. It sure didn't work out the last time I tried it and that marshal, well he's gonna be a hard man to take down."

"You think I don't know that? Heck I know it better than anyone," the man leaned closer, "the thing is you don't have to do it on your own, I can get other men to help you."

"Other men?" Jacob gave him a someways glance not sure now about how this was going.

"Yeah, there are other men in here and in a prison close by that also have grounds for a big grudge against that man, I can get them all out for you to work with."

Jacob was now on the edge of the bed, "How many men? What grounds do they have?"

"I can get you five more men, three from here, two from elsewhere who can ride to meet you. The grounds they have for wanting Timber dead are much like yours Jacob. They have all been arrested by him and prevented from leading the rest of their lives because he put them in prison."

"Do I know any of them?"

The man shrugged, "I can't say, you'll find that out when you meet them."

"Where will that be?"

"There is a small mining camp north of here just follow the gap in the hills facing you. That will be your meeting place. Get to the nearest town from there which is Gordon Flats and send me a telegram to confirm that you are all together and set to go and I will send one back with Timber's current location. Once you have Timber you will send me a telegram again from wherever you are and wait for a reply in case I want to add anything to the message you will give him from me."

"What message do you want me to give him?"

"I want you to tell him about all the trouble he caused me," the man went on to tell Jacob exactly what he wanted to tell Timber before he killed him.

Jacob looked down after taking it all in then he looked up again at the man, "So when do I get out of here?"

"You have to realize Jacob that if you or any of the other men decide to double cross me and ride off then I will do everything in my power to catch you again, which I will do and believe me you will regret it. Do this job for me and I will ensure all records of your arrest and stay in here are burned, you will get pardons and a cash bonus."

Jacob sat back and smiled, the first time in a long while, "You saying you want me to run this job?"

"Yes Jacob I do."

"Okay so get me out of here and I'll get on it?"

"I'll make the arrangements and I'll get word to you about where Timber is. You may have to search around for somewhat but I'll give you his general position."

Jacob leaned forward again, "Do we really need to keep in touch?"

"Oh yes Jacob we do. You will send me a telegram at each stage and make sure that you do. I want to know when you have found him, then you need to keep him someplace safe while you let me know. I will tell you then what I want you to tell him for me if I have thought of other things to say and no doubt you will all want to make your own contributions to that. Then you send me another telegram when you have killed him. I will want some proof of that. So I expect you to send me his guns, hat and boots. If you manage to get those off him then you will no doubt have killed him. I'll send the address when you have them," the man leaned across and handed Jacob a piece of paper, "this is the address to send the telegrams to."

Jacob's eyes went wide when he read the address, "I can see now why you have the powers to get us out."

"Just do the job," the man got up and called for the guard.

That had been a few days ago now. Jacob had been let out just as the man had said and there had been a horse waiting for him. In the saddlebags was a gun and money to buy any other things he needed although he decided to steal those items and keep the money. He had made it to the mining camp easily enough and found he had to wait there as the other men found it as well. Once they arrived Jacob took pains to take control, although the man had told the others that he would be leading them. He took them to the nearest Telegraph office and sent the message. Very quickly a reply had arrived and he then knew where to ride to.

Everything had gone well so far for Jacob. He had found Timber, beaten him up and locked him in the outhouse where there were now two men guarding him. As with the others he was looking forward to getting back there and finishing the job.

7

Jacob led the men back to Rawlins feeling very confident with himself. He just had the one man to kill to get his freedom and money, a man he hated for locking him up and he was going to so enjoy making him suffer before he put him down. The men with him all began to talk about how they were going to kill him slowly and how they would enjoy doing that. Jacob wondered just how long Timber would last. He was a big man yes but a few bullet holes in him would soon weaken him and prevent him from doing anything but accept his fate. He rode on faster, anxious now to get the job done then ride away as a free man.

Timber was taking a while to get to Indian Springs although he was following the short cut. Shorter it might be but the route was hard in places and he wished he hadn't taken the man's advice now as it was taking longer than it should. So it was some time later when he arrived in town.

As he approached the street Timber kept well over to the shady side not wanting to advertise his arrival. The sun was well over midday making deep shadows where he needed them. He kept looking all around for any signs of the men who had attacked him. He knew that there were only four of them left but that they would be dangerous and would no doubt shoot him on sight now if they saw him. He needed to see them first.

He rode right along the street until he came to the end. On the way he had seen the Telegraph office part way down. There was only one horse tied outside and he doubted that it would belong to any of them by the look of it. He stopped where the buildings and tents petered out and wondered where they were now. Had they sent the message and gone on or had they gone back to where they thought he was? Either way it looked like he had missed them. He thought that was a shame but he wasn't unduly worried about it, he had found each one of them before and he sure was going to again. The thing was he really wanted to know who had set them up and he knew he couldn't kill all of them until he had got that out of one of them, that was going to make things harder.

Seeing as he was here he rode over to the Telegraph office and leaving Scout at the hitch rail he went inside. The office was small as they usually were. Inside was a desk area with wires everywhere and a Morse key where the operator sat tapping out a message. There was a man sitting on a chair close to him who must have asked for a message to be sent. There was also a young man there busy with paperwork at a small desk, he looked up at Timber as he entered.

"Afternoon sir, can I help you?" He asked.

Timber smiled at him, he was fresh faced and well dressed, "Maybe, I want to send a telegram," Timber told him.

"Then you've come to the right place," the lad said with a grin, "If you'd like to tell me what it is I can write it down and then Mister Longshaw here will send it for you."

There was another chair in front of his desk where Timber sat and told him what he wanted sending. Timber knew it was going to be a long message and expensive but he didn't care about that as money was no object to him. What with his wages as a marshal and his bonuses from the territory governor plus the bounty money he made and from selling on the mens things after he had either killed or arrested them he had accumulated a large amount of money, all safe in the bank.

The message he sent told the governor, the Honorable Robert Pierce Fullerton what had happened. He told about the men involved, their names and what he knew about them. As he thought, it was a long message. The lad wrote it all down methodically and then looked up at him.

"Mister that's gonna cost you five dollars," he looked aghast at Timber.

"Just get him to send it, I'll pay you," Timber reached in a pocket and brought out the money thankful he hadn't been robbed in the outhouse. The lad took it and put it away in a can under his desk.

The other customer had now left so the lad gave the message to the operator to send. Longshaw read it then he looked up at Timber, "You some kinda lawman?"

"Some kind yeah," Timber showed him his marshal badge."

The operator shrugged and started tapping the Morse key. Once that was done Timber stood up.

"I guess there may be a wait for a reply."

"I guess so. I can send Micky here with it if you're not far away like I did with the other man who came in here."

Timber's ears pricked up, "The other man, now just what did he say?"

"Well seeing as you're a marshal I guess can tell you. As I recall it was something about he had found his man and what did he want him to say to him."

Timber nodded, "Did he get a reply?"

"He sure did."

Timber stood waiting. The operator didn't like giving out such personal information but knowing what was in the messages and having Marshal Timber stood in front of him he obliged and told him what the reply said. It didn't help him in discovering who it had been sent to as it had been sent with just a number rather than a name to the Telegraph office. Timber thanked him as he walked out having agreed for Micky to bring the reply to the nearest saloon which was exactly what Jacob had told him for his reply.

Timber walked in the saloon having done his usual checks and ordered a beer at the bar. There were plenty of spare tables so Timber chose the one he liked and sat to wait for his reply. He put his right leg out which was hurting him after the beating he had taken. He could still feel where a bullet had grazed him across his thigh over a year ago now. At least he could rest it while he waited on the reply to his message. While he waited he played solitaire with his own pack of cards.

He drank his beer, then another before the lad looked in the saloon then went over to him with his reply. Timber took it and then sent him away. He opened it up and read it. The message told Timber to go and find them, arrest them if he could, if not then he was to mete out any justice he thought suitable. As Timber thought, the governor wanted him to find out who had set the men up if he possibly could. In the meantime he would try to find out who it was from his side and he would also look into the release of the men. Timber folded the message up and slipped it into a pocket. He finished his beer, put his cards away and went out to Scout.

Timber wondered now if the men would have gone back to the outhouse to kill him or if they would just ride off? There was an old timer sitting in a rocking chair outside the saloon, Timber touched his hat as he spoke to him.

"You been here a while?"

"Pretty much, not much else to do around here."

"Did you see four men come here, one or more go in the Telegraph office then ride out again?"

"I sure did, not the kind of men we want around here, you friends of them?"

"No but I need to find them."

"They rode off that way," the man waved an arm up the street.

Timber thanked him, so they were going back to the outhouse rather than just taking their freedom. Whoever had set them up was either going to pay them a lot of money or he had something over them. Whatever, Timber now knew which direction to ride out in.

8

Timber took the main trail this time back to Rawlins figuring it wouldn't take him any longer and he was now keen to get back as soon as he could to straighten those men out. He knew they would be going back to the outhouse and wondered what they would do when they got there and they found the place empty and their friends missing?

Jacob was pleased when the town buildings of Rawlins came into view, he skirted around them and made directly for the outhouse. He rode right to it and as he approached he looked to see where Billy and Nathanial were. The closer he got the more concerned he got until they arrived and realized that neither man was there. More than that the outhouse door was hanging off one hinge and Timber together with his horse had gone.

The four of them just sat on their horses for a few seconds taking it all in. Then Jacob cussed saying, "Now how in blazes did that happen?"

James slipped off his horse to go and take a look into the outhouse, he was soon out again.

"Naw nothing in there."

Carl had also looked around and he found something of interest, he held up a crowbar.

"Looks like this was used on one of them," he said showing where blood was on one end of it.

"If one of them is dead then the other one is most likely too," Jacob said as he leaned on the horn of his saddle.

"That marshal is sure one tough guy," Gerard said.

James had been thinking, "Wait a minute. What if they aren't dead? What if they killed Timber and put him someplace?"

That got them all thinking, they looked around hoping to see some sign but they didn't see anything.

"Don't you think they would be here if they had done that?" Jacob said.

That made them all think again.

"Yeah I guess so," James admitted.

"So what do you think we should do?" Gerard asked.

"I reckon we take a look around this one horse town first, to see if Timber is still here. I reckon he did manage to get out and kill Billy and Nathanial and maybe he is still around someplace, we need to go and find out."

They all agreed on that and rode down to the street where they rode along looking out for Billy and Nathanial if they were still alive and for Timber. There wasn't a great deal of places to look for them but they did try what saloons there were and it was at one of those that they got some information. They walked in together as they didn't like being apart now, worrying where Timber was. The saloon was quiet with only a few men in there and all heads turned their way as they entered. Jacob decided to just ask if any of them had seen Timber. He called out his name and description and looked around at the faces.

They all looked back at him and then just one of them spoke up, "Yeah, we seen that guy. Big man, he looked pretty beat up but he took on a man in here and shot him down, he reckoned he was a marshal."

Jacob was pleased to have the reply but not so pleased with what the man said.

"Any idea where he went?"

"He dragged the man out and took him down to the undertaker, after that I seen him heading east."

That was all Jacob needed to know, he thanked the man and then took the men with him back outside. He then stopped on the sidewalk to talk to them.

"Okay so Timber chased us on to Indian Springs."

"We never saw him there," James said.

"No well maybe we just crossed over someplace, the question is where is he now?"

They all looked at each other until Gerard said, "Maybe he's coming back here. He must have heard that we were going to Indian Springs and most likely what we were going to do there."

Jacob had to agree with him, "Yeah that sounds about right. So he'll get there and find we've gone again. He must know we will come back here thinking he will still be locked up."

"That's right he will," Gerard looked around again fearful of suddenly seeing him.

"I don't like this Jacob, the whole thing is going wrong," Carl said as he looked at the other men. He saw James agreeing with him.

"Yeah, it has. Timber is gonna be so sore about what we've done, if he comes here..." James said

"If he comes here we need to be ready for him. This is only a small place so we can stake it all out and wait for him to come then just shoot him down" Gerard said.

Jacob thought about that, "I guess we can but then we won't have that opportunity to talk to him and tell him what the man wants him to hear and then make his death slow."

It was Carl who answered that, "Does any of that matter now? Tell the man what he wants to hear. We've already told Timber most things and beaten him up, I say we shoot him on sight now."

Jacob had to smile at him, "You know, that doesn't sound like a bad idea at all," he looked at all of them to see if they agreed which they did, "okay that's what we'll do. Hopefully he won't be long coming back here then whichever one of us gets a bead on him first takes him out then we can send the man another telegram and send Timber's things on to him."

"And then we can all ride off free men," Gerard had a wide smile on his face.

"That's right so now we gotta figure out who is gonna wait where?"

They all looked around, each of them thinking where they would want to hide and wait for Timber. Jacob thought it best if he told them.

"James I reckon you should take your rifle over the street there and get between those buildings, you'll get a good view of the street from there." James looked over and nodded his head.

"Carl I reckon you should be over on this side, there is a building stepped back a little along the street where you can hide out at. Gerard I reckon you could get up on the roof of the building right down at the end of the street there."

Both men agreed with Jacobs suggestions as Gerard asked, "Where will you be?"

"I'm going to the other end of the street to watch out for him coming in from Indian Springs. Maybe that way I'll be the one to bag him."

No one had any objections with that, they were happy for Jacob to try and shoot him first. Then at least if he failed that would alert them all as to where Timber was. They all got their rifles from their horses and a water canteen and went over to their positions.

9

As he rode along Timber gave some thought as to what he would find back in Rawlins? The outlaws were no doubt going back there expecting to find him still in the outhouse. He had to smile to himself as to how surprised they would be when they got there.

The trail was easier going than the shortcut so it didn't seem long before Timber was coming up on the town with no sign of anyone along the way. As he got closer he stopped to take a look at the buildings and all around. The town for what it was looked quiet enough. There were just a few people walking around and it all looked peaceful. Timber knew for sure that the men would be there somewhere. They would want to go back to finish off the job of killing him. Having found him gone it was a question of what they would do? They could have given up and ridden out but Timber knew all of them to some extent and doubted if they would do that, not until they had lost a few more of them and lost the heart to carry on. Timber had to take care, he imagined them hiding out with rifles just waiting to pick him off as he rode in.

Timber set off again at a tangent to the town keeping well out of sight of it until he had got right around the town then he started back in from the other side but over and away from the street to keep out of sight as well as possible. Doing that he was able to get up to the outhouse from behind it. He then left Scout there ground reined so he would come at a whistle if Timber needed him, then he advanced on the town keeping down low, even crawling along open areas so he could get close to the buildings unobserved.

Not knowing where any of the men were and not totally sure they were there anyway it was difficult for Timber to advance. He had to check out every piece of cover he came to and he would have to check around and in each building too. What worried him most was if they were all together or waiting for him individually. He figured they would all be on their own making his job that little bit easier.

He got to the first building where he stopped as something had alerted him which had made the hairs on the back of his neck rise up. At times like these he took careful note of where he was and what was around him. There was no one at the building he was standing beside or across the street as far as he could tell but something was nagging at him. That was when he looked up. He stared out across the street before he allowed a smile to cross his face.

Gerard had got up on the roof of the end building easily enough and then laid down with his rifle. He knew Jacob had put him there to cover both ways into town but he was sure Timber would come from the west so that was the way he looked for him most of the time. Had he looked the other way the outcome could have been very different.

Timber had to either draw him out so he could see him and shoot him, although that would be hard with the sun in his eyes, the range and the man who he recognized as Gerard higher up than he was or he had to get up there. He looked around and decided that if he went back a few yards he would be able to get across the street where a rise would hide him from view of anyone down the street if he kept on the ground. It was slow work but it got him to the building where Gerard was. He then kept close to the building walls while he looked for an easy and hopefully quiet way up to the roof.

Gerard had used a ladder he had found close by among a pile of other building tools which he had left against the wall to get back down again. Timber came across it and figured out where it was in relation to where he had seen Gerard. He was happy that he should come up behind him so he began to climb. Fortunately the ladder didn't make any noise as he made his way up the rungs. As he his eyes reached the top he stopped to see where Gerard was and he was pleased to see he was facing away from him still looking down the street. Timber carried on climbing up and eventually got up onto the roof. Then drawing a gun he began to advance on Gerard.

10

Gerard had been lying in the sun for a long time. He had drank most of his water and he was getting tired. He knew he would have to abandon his position soon and go down to find some shade. His drowsiness made him slower than he normally would be so it took him a second or two to realize there were small sounds coming from behind him. He turned around to take a look and was amazed to see Timber up on the roof advancing towards him, he still had his rifle in his hands and struggled to bring it around to aim at Timber.

"I wouldn't do that Gerard, just put the rifle down," Timber called to him.

Gerard was too far gone to listen and he carried on bringing the rifle to bear on him.

Timber had no choice but to shoot him. He wanted to just stop Gerard from using the rifle and wound him but Gerard moved as Timber fired and the bullet went into his heart killing him.

Timber cussed and went to him to check that he was dead, then he looked down the street.

The gunshot had reverberated all the way down the street and all the outlaws had heard it. They all wanted to know who had fired the shot and whether one of them had managed to kill Timber so they all looked out into the street trying to find out.

From where Timber was he had a good view all along the street and he saw James come out from between two buildings and then Carl from further down the street. So he now knew where two more of them were which just left Jacob. He doubted if the two he had seen would stay where they were but at least he knew where they were now. He hurried back to the ladder.

James and Carl had both looked out at the same time but took a second to notice Timber standing on the roof. Jacob was hidden away at the end of the street where he had managed to climb up onto a roof there giving him views all around. As he turned at the gunshot he saw Timber immediately and ducked down so he wouldn't see him if he looked his way.

They were all shocked to see Timber there and they were sure now that the gunshot had been for Gerard meaning he was dead or at least of no use to them any more. Jacob considered working his way up the street to him but then decided to stay where he was and see what the other two would do, hopefully one of them would be successful in taking Timber down.

Timber got back down the ladder not wanting to be trapped up there then he hurried along a couple of buildings before he went back to the street between them and peered around the corner.

James was on the same side of the street as Timber and he slipped back behind the buildings Hoping to see Timber come down from the roof. He was late getting to where he would have seen him but he did see Timber slide between the buildings back to the street as he carefully made his way to the gap Timber had used with his gun in his hand.

Carl had got a better view of Timber being across the street from him. He knew that James was closer and he had seen him come out then hurry back, so he must have seen Timber and was going to meet him. Carl wanted to help him out but he had to take care not knowing where Timber was now or what he would do. He decided to creep along as best as he could towards him while he hoped that James would be able to shoot Timber before he got there.

Jacob had seen everything happen and he had no intention of moving as he felt safe where he was. He was going to let James and Carl do the job and hope that they managed to do it.

Timber stopped and waited at the end of the building. He reckoned one or more of the men would come his way and when they did he was ready to mete out some justice to them.

James got to where Timber had disappeared and looked down the gap towards the street. He could just make him out at the end almost hidden by a pile of barrels. He wasn't going to be able to shoot him from where he was so he took the chance of making his way along between the two buildings to get to where he would be able to.

Timber stood waiting, knowing he couldn't just stay there for long but he wanted to give the men a chance to do something. He was about to move off when he heard a sound from behind him. It was only a small sound and could have been the wind or a critter but it was enough to make Timber whirl around to see what had caused it. Seeing James creeping along came as a surprise, Timber figured James had done well to get that close undetected, but it was as close as he was going to get.

James saw Timber whirl around to him which was enough to get him shooting although he could only see a small amount of him.

Bullets flew into the barrels and one skimmed his hat forcing Timber to shoot back. He wanted one man alive to ask questions to but he wasn't going to risk being shot to do that. He fired twice hitting James both times. James dropped his gun, curled up in pain and then fell in the dirt.

Carl was further along the street when he heard the gunshots and again he wondered who had shot who? He had to carry on and find out. He didn't want to call out in case it was Timber who had shot James and give his position away so he just carried on trying to get to where he would see for himself.

Timber looked back into the street and saw Carl advancing towards him. He still didn't know where Jacob was but knew he had to work on getting Carl first and worry about Jacob afterwards while still keeping an eye out for him. Carl was in the shade across the empty street. Timber guessed that any townsfolk around would now be in cover wondering what the heck was going on? At least it meant that there shouldn't be any collateral damage caused to any of them. Carl saw Timber stepping forward no doubt trying to get a bead on him so he ducked down taking cover behind a water trough. He looked around the side of it for Timber but he wasn't there. Carl looked around wondering where he'd gone?

Timber saw Carl drop down realizing he was going to be hard to shoot him where he was so he quickly stepped across to the next sidewalk to get behind three horses that were tied to a hitch rail. What he needed now was a distraction in order to have a chance of getting Carl without being shot himself. The answer was just a little way off. He gave a whistle and Scout looked across to him and started to run over to him. Timber had spent many hours training the horse to do a good few tricks as he called them and now was the time to use one of them. As Scout approached Timber gave a command and a wave of an arm. The horse immediately changed course and ran up onto the sidewalk and very quickly barged into Carl. Timber knew that it was risky but he was pretty sure of the outcome.

Carl looked around for Timber and saw glimpses of him behind the horses, he tried to get a bead on him not looking down the street or expecting a big horse to come racing straight at him. He was taken completely by surprise as Scout got right up him so quickly. Carl raised up to get out of his way but Scout just barreled the man over. Carl fell out into the street where he anxiously looked across for Timber.

Timber knew Carl would give more attention to shooting him than his horse and as soon as Carl was in the open he fired at him. Carl fell over wounded in his side but not dead as Timber had intended. He squirmed around in the dirt and looked to fire at Timber his face a mask of anger. There was no way Timber was going to allow that so he shot him again and he went down.

It fell quiet in the street as Timber stayed where he was but he called out to Scout to make himself scarce which he did. Now there was only one man left to find, Timber hoped he would be able to arrest him or just put him out of action so he could question him about who had set them up and got them out of prison.

Jacob saw Carl shot. He had heard all the gun shots and knew that he was now the only one left. He started to think, hard. He knew that Timber was good and now he knew just how good. He figured he didn't have a chance against him in a straight fight. He wondered if he would be able to shoot him from where he was if he came along looking for him. Maybe he could but that also meant he would be trapped up on the roof if Timber saw him and staked him out. It was just too risky, he had to move and fast.

The way down was at the back of the building and he was quickly back down on the ground. He was thinking of what to do and the obvious thing to him was to get out away from town and to hell with it. The man who had arranged this would just have to find another way to get rid of Timber. He got to his horse, mounted up and rode out keeping out of sight of the street so Timber wouldn't see him.

11

Timber looked down the street and noticed a cloud of dust heading away fast which he figured would be the last man who he knew was Jacob Wells. He was going to have to go out after him but first he had the dead men here to organize. He left Carl where he was and then dragged James over to him. He had to climb up the ladder to the roof for Gerard and then dropped him over the edge before he then dragged him across to Carl. He searched each one and took everything of any use. He searched their horses saddlebags too and ended up with a small pile of things he could sell on.

As Timber worked, a few men began to gather around to take a look, one in particular was most interested.

"Mister I'm a lookin' to keep the law and order around here and I'd like to know just what you're a doin?"

Timber turned to see a well built middle aged man standing there wearing a gun. He reached into a pocket and showed his badge.

"Jake Timber U.S. Marshal, just doing my job," he answered.

"Are you the same man who killed two other men here?"

"Yeah I reckon I am."

"All bad men yeah?"

Timber stopped and stood up to face him.

"These are all bad men yes and one other has just ridden off. If you want to keep the law around here why didn't you come and help?"

"Shucks marshal I weren't sure about that, not knowing who was good and who wasn't."

"Well now you know."

"Sure well I only started this job a little while ago and we never had a killing here before."

"You've had three now. Look I need to get on after the last one of these outlaws, you can organize these men yeah?" Timber didn't wait for an answer, he whistled for Scout and was soon riding out of town.

Jacob rode on fast to get some distance between him and Timber, he had been taken aback by how fast and methodical Timber had killed the three men with him without getting a scratch. He reckoned now the only way he could remove Timber was to ambush him somewhere that he could just take him out with his rifle from a safe distance if he was going to do it at all. That was one idea he had, another idea was to just ride off and be done with it taking his chances of ever being arrested again.

He was riding back towards Indian Springs which gave him his third idea. He would go there and send a telegram to the man and tell him what had happened so that he could arrange for some other way to kill Timber. If the man did manage that it would mean that he wouldn't have to keep looking over his shoulder for the marshal. He rode on as fast as he could without burning his horse out so he got to town in record time. He rode straight to the Telegraph office and leaving his horse at the rail he ran inside. The operator was busy sending a message so Jacob had to wait until he had finished then he had Longshaw send a message out for him. The thing now was that he wanted to wait for a reply to know what was going to happen and if what he had said in the message would persuade the man to still grant him his freedom anyway?

The telegram arrived on the desk of a portly man in a small office. He was an angry and frustrated man. It seemed that whatever he did it was never enough to achieve his ends. He had arranged for the outlaws to be released from prison at great personal expense and now it had all come to nothing. The telegram was brief but it told him all he needed to know. The six men had failed, well five of them but he had no hopes of the sixth man being able to take down a man like Timber on his own. He was going to need someone else. Someone just as good, no someone better than Timber and he had just the right man in mind.

He had figured that getting suitable men out of prison would be the best bet in having Timber killed. He needed men who had a grudge against him and the men he had chosen certainly had, so what could have gone wrong? Six men against one would surely have been enough. He had arranged with Jacob, the man he wanted to lead them to keep in contact with him so he would know how far they had got and also he didn't want Timber to have a quick death, no he wanted him to suffer like he had and was still suffering now.

The thing was he knew the release of the men wouldn't become common knowledge with many people for a while of who he was so he had worked fast on getting the men released. After that he had set himself up as a lawyer in a town a little way off to the west from Austin, the town where he had lived before and had worked.

The man read the telegram twice to get in his head what it told him then he set off for the Telegraph office which was just down the street to send a reply. He was very annoyed to hear that only one of the six men was left, the rest all having been killed by the man he hated. Jacob may still be of help to him but he needed a back up, plus it was time he did something himself. He sent a telegram to Jacob then he sent another one out and asked for the reply to be brought to him then he returned to his office. He had only just set up the office which wasn't all that big but it served its purpose for him. He had been forced to go back to his earlier work of straightening out peoples legal matters after having left Austin, it wasn't something he wanted to do but there was little in the way of alternatives.

Jacob knew that Timber wouldn't take long in straightening out things back in Rawlins and would most likely come down to Indian Springs looking for him. He had done so before so he figured he would do it again and there was always the chance that Timber had seen him ride off anyway. He wondered just how long it would take the man to reply to him, or even if he would? He had to wait a while and hope he would and give him his freedom otherwise it would be back to what he had been doing and always had done. He thought on that and realized that he wouldn't change his ways anyway. To while away the time he rode his horse back to a saloon to get a drink and wait. He daren't wait too long but he surely had time for one whiskey at least.

12

Timber now knew he had just the one man to catch up with but this one was going to be more awkward than any of the others as he wanted him alive and well enough to talk so he could tell him just who the heck had broke them out of jail and set them on him and why? Another question was how did whoever it was know where Timber was well enough for the men to find him? So there was no way he was going to just shoot him if, or rather when he found him. He didn't want to wound him too badly either so the man could talk although Timber might hurt him more in the questioning.

He rode on knowing that Jacob had come this way. It was pretty much open land with just a few trees and areas where the land rose up and fell down again but it still gave places where a man could wait in cover with a rifle. Timber considered that possibility and thought what he would do in Jacob's situation? He would want to take him out as easily as possible and an ambush might just achieve that. He knew the men had wanted to talk to him before they killed him which was much like Timber wanted to do to Jacob but for totally different reasons. He figured that Jacob wouldn't bother with the talk now but just shoot him if he got a chance to do it so it was up to Timber not to give him that chance.

Timber decided to take the short cut route again down to Indian Springs as he doubted Jacob would think of that or even know about it. The ground was harder to travel over so Timber gave Scout his head to pick out the best way to go. He still kept his eyes wide open just in case Jacob was somehow just in front of him. He doubted it very much but there wasn't anything he could do about it anyway, he just had to take his chances taking the best precautions he could. He carried on east until he saw the town appear on the skyline. If Jacob was there he now had to take care so he changed course over to the north so he would be able to cut into the town from the side which he figured would be the safest way.

Jacob drank his beer sat in the saloon at table beside a front wall window which gave him good views of the street right up to the western end where he figured Timber would approach from. His eyes scanned the street outside as he emptied his glass and then another. He wondered how long it would take the man to send a reply to his telegram and it occurred to him that he might not reply at all, so he decided on one more beer then he was going, reply or not.

Timber rode well out away from the town before he turned Scout around back to the buildings. He took his time getting back watching very carefully for any movement. It was midday so coming in this way meant he had the sun behind him and would be in the eyes of anyone seeing him from the town. He arrived at the back of a building and left Scout there so he could sneak around to the street to look for Jacob.

Jacob finished his third beer and was about to get up and go when the boy from the Telegraph office appeared on the doorway. He saw Jacob and took a telegram over to him. Jacob took it and waved the boy away. He anxiously unfolded the piece paper to read it.

It told him that he was still going to have to kill Timber to get his freedom and also that he was sending another man his way to help out. The man's name was Luther Stein.

Jacob had no idea who Luther Stein was or when he would be arriving. He considered waiting for him but then changed his mind. He had hung around Indian Springs long enough as it was, it was time to go. Going up against Timber alone was not an option. Trying to ambush him was another option although dangerous. His thoughts were just on giving it all up and taking off on his own well away from here and Timber and let whoever the man was sending to straighten him out. Having thought it all through he decided that running away was the best option and to keep a good look behind him for a few days just in case he did see Timber and was able to shoot him with his rifle from a distance. He got up to go.

Timber got to the sidewalk from behind the street buildings and stopped in the shade to take a look up and down the street. It was quiet with only a few people moving around. He could see the Telegraph office just further down the street and there were no horses outside. There were some at the saloons though. He had looked at all the buildings when he was here last time so he knew pretty well what was where. He had to check out all the likely ones for Jacob just in case he was still here. He knew he had come here before to send a telegram, had he come this way from Rawlins to send another? If he had that would have been done by now. Of course he could have ridden straight off but maybe just maybe he had waited for a reply which meant he could still be in town. The most obvious places to look would be the saloons close to the Telegraph office. The nearest one was just a few yards away so Timber made his way towards it.

He arrived at the door and glanced inside. It was a good thing he hadn't just walked in because Jacob was inside just about to come out. He saw Timber and drew his gun and took a hurried shot. In his anxious state he missed by a hairs width as Timber ducked out around the door frame drawing his gun.

Jacob panicked as he remembered going up against Timber the last time and a shoot out with him was not something he wanted to do, he turned and ran knowing there was a back door in the saloon that led to an outhouse. He crashed his way out and ran to the outhouse where he hid around it just showing a sliver of himself waiting for Timber to come out of the saloon door after him.

Timber saw Jacob run for the back door and he stepped away from the saloon door and ran down by the side of the building and stopped when he got to the end where he carefully peered around the corner. There he could see Jacob quite clearly waiting for him to come out the back door. Timber aimed at him before he called out.

"Just drop that gun Jacob."

Jacob froze with horror at hearing Timber's voice, he looked across to where he was and he just couldn't help himself he changed his aim towards him.

Timber saw the action and fired. He had been careful where his shot would go and it tore into Jacob's right side. Jacob dropped his gun and doubled up with the pain before he slipped to the ground. Timber advanced on him keeping his gun aimed straight at him. As he arrived he kicked Jacob's gun away then looked down at him.

"That wasn't a good idea."

"You gonna kill me now?" Jacob asked through the pain.

"That rather depends on you. I know you are working for someone. Now you give me his name and I'll get some help for you, get you patched up then take you right back to jail. You keep quiet and you're dead."

Jacob knew Timber well enough to know he would do as he said. There seemed little point in protecting the man now. After all he hadn't given him his freedom, he had just put him in this situation.

"Okay, okay, I'll talk. The man you want is Milton Westbrook?"

Timber looked at him in surprise, "Milton Westbrook but he's the under governor for the state or at least he was."

"Yeah. I know you winkled him out before but he is still around."

"Are you telling me the truth? I told the governor about Westbrook's plan to overthrow him to stop the territory of Texas ever joining the Union. He was sacked from his position along with the men who sided with him."

"That's right but word didn't get around fast enough and he had time to arrange for six of us men who he knew had grounds to want to kill you to escape from prison. We got together and came after you. He was gonna pay us a good bonus and grant us our freedom with a pardon for our crimes," Jacob coughed some blood up which he spat onto the ground, "Look Timber can't we talk this over later, I'm bleeding out here."

"Soon. Where is Westbrook now?"

Jacob coughed up more blood before he answered, "He's in Coyote Flats,"

Timber nodded. He reached down to check on his wound as Jacob suddenly coughed up a fountain of blood then lay still.

Timber shook his head, maybe that shot to wound him didn't quite go where he intended it to. He stood up as he saw a few men hanging around.

"Go get the undertaker will you?" He called to them as he began to search Jacob's pockets.

13

Timber didn't find much on Jacob, just a few coins until he found the telegram from Milton Westbrook. He nodded to himself as he read it and then stuffed it into a pocket. He took what he wanted from the man and let the undertaker take whatever else there was.

Knowing what he did now Timber had to send a telegram out to the territory governor, the Honorable Robert Pierce Fullerton. The governor needed to know what was going on here and maybe do something more about the man who used to be the under governor, Milton Westbrook. He gave a whistle and waited for Scout to come trotting around to him then he rode him down to the Telegraph office. The operator had nothing to do when Timber walked in so he got straight to work on the message that Timber wanted sending out. When that was done Timber said he wouldn't be waiting on a reply as there was no need for one. He just got directions for Coyote Flats.

Coyote Flats was a larger town than Rawlins and was only a day or so ride away north east. Timber mounted up on Scout and set off, keen now to meet the man who had set him up and had caused so much bother to him before. He was sure going to straighten the man out when he found him.

Milton Westbrook returned to his office deep in thought. He knew

Timber was good but he still couldn't work out how the man had managed to take out six hardened criminals all of whom knew Timber and had big grudges against him. The fact that he had was very worrying, hence the telegram he had just sent out. He had a man waiting for him to call on. A man he had heard a lot about and had seen once. He knew him to be a paid assassin that some corrupt members of the government had used on occasions when there had been no other choices. Westbrook knew all about their activities and where to get hold of the man. He had already sent word to him to stay where he was for a while knowing he wasn't that far away in case he needed him and now he did. He wondered how long it would take him to arrive and he hoped he would be in time before Timber showed up?

Just a few hours ride away Luther Stein had got the telegram from Milton Westbrook. The news was good for him and he was sure going to take him up on the offer. It wasn't just for the money either, he had heard of Marshal Jake Timber and he reckoned taking him out would increase his own notoriety and no doubt bring him more work, maybe work that would pay better as well. He rode out pretty much immediately for Coyote Flats.

Luther was very confident in his abilities. He should be after all the time and effort he had put in practicing with his gun and after that working with outlaws to gain experience and knowledge. He had teamed up with two others that served him well in riding off on robbery sprees which sometimes meant having to kill those that tried to stop them. Gradually he honed his skills until he figured he was as good as he was going to get and then he started working alone. There had been the odd occasion when a man would come up against him when trying to stop Luther robbing him and sometimes for other reasons and that had given him the experience of fast draw shoot outs and so far he had always won. As his reputation grew he found himself being hired to take men out others wanted out of the way and work as a bodyguard. He found these jobs easier than stealing for a living and more profitable. That was how he been found by Milton Westbrook

Westbrook had worked with a group of men on the territory's council governments who were opposed to the territory of Texas joining the Union. They were a tough group of men working in secret against the Honorable Robert Pierce Fullerton and the men in his government. They needed money to bribe other men onto their side and money for men like Luther to remove others. As Luther was a known assassin they found him and persuaded him to work for them in between his other assignments. Milton had kept his contact information which was a telegram address in a small town to the south of Austin. Luther would call in there frequently to pick up any messages and if he knew he would be elsewhere he would arrange for messages to be sent to where he was.

Luther willingly took on Westbrook's request and wasted no time in riding over to Coyote Flats. Westbrook had told him exactly where he was in town so Luther had no difficulty in finding his office. He checked out the wording on the office door before going inside.

Westbrook looked up from his desk at the man who confidently walked in and sauntered up to him. He saw a tall well dressed man all in black, his trousers shirt and waistcoat were immaculately clean as he was. He was clean shaven apart from sporting a rakish mustache. His hair was cut short and stylish. He wore long black tooled boots and at his waist was a Colt revolver hanging in a black tooled holster. All in all the man cut a striking figure.

"Milton Westbrook?" Luther asked in a low smooth voice.

"Yes I'm Westbrook, so you must be Luther Stein?"

"The very same. You say you have an interesting job for me?"

"Oh I do, won't you sit down and we can talk it over?"

Luther pulled the chair away from the desk facing Westbrook and sat down, then he looked straight across at him. The look put Westbrook off his stride as he looked into the icy blue merciless eyes.

"I mentioned in the telegram that I want you to find a Marshal Jake Timber."

"You did and I know it ain't for a friendly talk?"

"Indeed not. In short Luther I want him dead."

Luther sat still and slowly nodded his head as though this was a normal kind of statement.

"I gathered that. It will cost you."

"I know and I am prepared to pay your normal fee."

"My normal fee just went up for this man. I need to take care with him."

"Well yes I appreciate that but..."

"No buts Westbrook, it's one thousand dollars for me to shoot him dead."

"That's way above your normal fee."

"It's well above a normal job, take it or leave it."

Luther started to get up so Westbrook quickly answered, "Okay, okay one thousand it is. Five hundred now, five hundred after I am sure he's dead."

Luther sat and slowly nodded his head waiting. Westbrook shuddered a little then opened a drawer and tossed a bundle of bills across the desk at him. Luther reached across and fanned through them.

"Its all there," Westbrook said.

"Oh I'm sure it is. Okay so how do you want me to do this"

Westbrook relaxed now that he could get down to the actual business.

"Timber will be be coming here to look for me of that I have no doubt. He has already killed some men I put onto him although one of them may still be alive. I just want you to watch out for him coming here and kill him before he gets to me, simple as that."

"Simple you say, these things are seldom simple. I need a full description of the man and his horse then I'll take a good look around the town to check it all out. Just when will he be arriving?"

Westbrook gave a description of Timber and ended by saying that he could well be here by the end of the day and that he would be leaving Rawlins coming into town from the west.

"I don't normally rush jobs like this. I like to weigh my target up and choose the place and time."

"You may not have that luxury with this one," Westbrook watched him with baited breath, he didn't want Luther to back out now.

Westbrook had to wait for Luther's answer, "Okay, I'll go with that but if I find the circumstances unsuitable then I'll return your money and leave you to find someone else."

Westbrook certainly didn't want that to happen, "Stay with the job and I'll throw in another five hundred."

"My you want this man dead bad," Luther said with a smile.

"Yes I do." Westbrook didn't want to explain any further or tell Luther all the circumstance that had brought him to this. He just hated Timber so much for wrecking his dreams, his plans and his life that he had to pay with his life.

Luther sat for a few seconds longer before he stood up, "Okay, I'll go check this place out."

Westbrook watched him leave thinking he had found the right man for the job and he relaxed back into his chair.

14

Luther stepped outside thinking of how he was going to complete this job? Taking out Jake Timber was not going to be easy unless he just holed himself up someplace with a rifle. He did think about that but decided against it, it just wasn't his way. He had never sunk down to taking targets out in that way and he wasn't about to start now. Besides he was looking forward to meeting Timber. He had heard a lot about the man and he was fully aware that the territory governor employed him as a special agent to administer justice to anyone working outside the law he came into contact with. He was just the kind of man Luther wanted to remove.

The town was quite busy which was a good and a bad thing both at the same time. What he wanted to know now was what lawmen there were in town and that was the next thing to do. He started to walk along the sidewalk down the street intending to cover both sides of the main street he was on to discover just what was in the town and come across the sheriff, if there was one. In a town this size he reckoned there would be one or at least a town council charged with keeping law and order. He walked past various shops and businesses and he could see that Westbrook would make a profitable business as a lawyer here. As he walked along he became aware of a building across the street with a sign proclaiming it to be a sheriff's office. He looked back to see how far away from Westbrook's office it was. It was a reasonable distance but anyone in the office was bound to hear any gunshots at that range. He needed to find out who was in there so he crossed over to it.

There were two windows into the office and Luther tried hard to see inside before going to the door but there were blinds coming partway down them that made that impossible. There was nothing for it he was just going to have to go inside. He got up to the door and listened carefully before he turned the handle. There were no sounds to alert him so he opened the door and stepped inside. He found a youngish man busily organizing a rifle rack who turned around to see him.

"Hey there, can I help you mister," The young man said, then looked carefully at Luther and his tied down gun.

Luther looked just as keenly back at the man. He was wearing a star but it wasn't that of a sheriff, "Luther Stein, who might you be?" He said.

"Deputy Jim Evans. I'm guessing you're looking for the sheriff?"

"Could be," Luther answered and waited for the deputy to carry on.

"He won't be back until late, if he gets back tonight at all. There has been some bother up at a ranch some ways from here he has gone to straighten it out, can I help you?"

That was good news to Luther, "Naw that's okay I just wanted to make contact with him that's all," then on impulse Luther continued, "I wondered if you might know of a Marshal Jake Timber?"

"Jake Timber?" The deputy pursed his lips and thought for a minute, "Can't say I've heard of him, sheriff might have though," he stopped then asked, "is there a reason for that?"

"He's a friend I'm trying to catch up with."

The deputy nodded his head, "I see, are you a lawman then?"

Luther couldn't help but smile, "No but I have a lot of contact with them."

The deputy didn't understand and cocked his head at him.

"So you are running this place alone then?" Luther carried on.

"Yeah, just for today," he was beginning to take an interest in Luther which Luther noticed not that it worried him. He could see that he could take him out anytime he wanted to.

"Maybe I'll call back," Luther said and walked out. Now that he had that information he carried on walking down the street then back up the other side until he had seen the whole street. Now he could work out where and how he was going to tackle the marshal. Westbrook seemed to think he would go straight to his office which did seem to be the most logical thing for him to do. So where was the best place to call him out. He thought about it, he knew the marshal was good with a gun but he doubted he had honed his skills in speed and accuracy as well as he had. So it was a question of whether to just call him out into the street or to kill him some other way. He wandered back to Westbrook's office and went back inside.

Westbrook sat up straight as he entered, "I'm glad you called back Luther, there is something else I want you to do."

Luther looked at him without speaking.

Westbrook hesitated then said, "This Timber has caused me so much trouble and bother that I would like him to know it was me that set him up to be killed before you do that."

Luther just kept on looking at him, "That makes the job that bit harder Westbrook."

"I know but just a few words would do it."

Luther walked up to the desk and placed both hands on it so he could lean right over to Westbrook.

"It doesn't matter how many words there are Westbrook it makes the whole thing much more dangerous."

Westbrook just kept on looking at him unsure of what to say, then he said, "Would another five hundred do it?"

Luther was very happy with the fee as it was and it would make taking Timber out a whole lot harder. However he always tried to please his clients to have them recommend him.

"Okay, I'll say some words, just tell me what they are - but if it comes to it being me or him I'll end it."

Westbrook looked up again into his icy eyes and just nodded his head, "Okay sure," he then went on to tell him what he wanted him to say, "Tell him it was Milton Westbrook who has arranged for his murder for his work in stopping me from preventing Texas keeping out of the Union. Something along those lines will do."

"Okay you got it," Luther stepped back from the desk, "I guess he'll be arriving soon, I'll wait outside for him," Luther then walked out.

Westbrook wanted to see what would happen and he thought that Timber wouldn't be long now in arriving, he stepped across to the window and saw Luther crossing the street. He hoped he would be able to take Timber down quickly because otherwise he was going to be in grave danger himself.

15

Luther thought it would be better if he was on the opposite side of the street when Timber arrived as that would give him a chance to get a good look at him. Although Westbrook was pressurizing him to make it quick Luther was in no hurry. He had found before that it was far better to weigh up his target and take his time to complete his contract, to ensure that he was in the right place and time to be sure of success. He found a place to watch for him from under the porch of a saloon where there was a bench outside he could sit on.

Timber was as sure as he could be now that there were no other men involved in all this and all he had to do now was get down to Coyote Flats and confront Milton Westbrook. He figured he had come down in the world a good way to be at a town like that instead of being in Austin where he knew the council and government offices were. It meant he wouldn't have to look around him so much, only as much as he usually did. The ride down there was fairly easy apart from the heat and the flies. Even so it seemed like a long time before he did eventually reach the town. He was keen to go and see Westbrook but at the same time he wanted to do that when he was fresh and able to concentrate on him so instead of going straight there he stopped at the first saloon he came across.

It looked like a lively place and it had a few people in there. He walked in taking as much care as he usually did and made his way over to the bar, not that he needed to do that as there were bargirls walking around serving. He found the bar was busy so he changed his mind as a table became free just in a position he liked. He went over to it and found it had a good view of the room and more importantly, the door. He hadn't sat down for more than a minute when a girl came up to him.

"Can I get you something mister?" She asked.

Timber saw she was a pretty girl of only around five feet tall. She had long golden hair and and a cute figure under the dress she was wearing which only just covered her. He smiled at her and ordered a beer, then he watched her disappear for the bar between the men standing around. The beer wasn't long in arriving and he gave her well over the price for it.

"Thanks mister, just give me a wave when you want another or give me a holler, the names Judy."

Timber just smiled at her and sat back looking around the room. There were plenty of men in there, most were just drinking while some were in card games, some others were there for a good time, maybe they had just got paid from some job or other and had come to town to spend it. Timber wasn't worried either way as long as they left him alone.

What he wanted next was some food and as the girl walked past him he got her attention and asked her what they had.

"We have some steak left, potatoes, a few greens and some gravy if you'd like some."

"That sounds great, thanks."

Judy leaned in to him, "It can be kinda salty but I'll see what I can do. Looks like you're ready for another beer too."

Timber had taken a liking to her, "That will be good and another beer would go down well yeah."

She brought the food to him and another beer and again Timber paid more than he had to which pleased her. He could well afford it, having more money than he could possibly ever spend. He was paid well by the governor for his work clearing the territory of outlaws and the bounty money he got from the men he either locked up or killed which all went into his bank account. Even then there was what he found in the mens pockets and saddlebags which he used as spending money.

He ate the food even though it was rather salty but it filled him up which was fine. He was finishing his beer when he heard some raucous laughter right behind him and a voice he recognized that wasn't in such a good mood. He turned around to find Judy being held in a clinch by a man who was groping her and laughing at his friends all around him as Judy tried to get free from him.

Timber stood up and took a look at the men with him then he stepped up to the man holding Judy and grabbed him by the collar of his shirt dragging him off her. The man nearly lost his balance and spun around clenching his fists and lashed out at Timber with a right which was not a very clever thing to do. Timber easily brushed his arm away and and hit him square on his nose with a gnarled fist of his own. The man fell back knocking a table over with blood pouring down his face.

His friends looked on shocked and one of them decided to draw his gun but not fast enough. Timber drew both of his and stood back.

"Any time you wanna try it, go ahead," he said in his deep resonating voice. The saloon room fell silent apart from the man on the floor moaning and groaning. No one tried to do anything.

"In future you just leave gals alone who don't want to be friends y'hear? Now pick your friend up and get out."

Two men struggled to get their friend up then without a word they hustled him out of the saloon.

Judy went up to Timber, "Thanks mister but you didn't have to do that?"

"Oh but I did and will do again if necessary."

Judy smiled at him and went about her work as the saloon became noisy again leaving Timber watching the men struggle out. The whole thing had been watched by Luther. He had got bored of sitting around and had gone looking for Timber. He had seen him arrive and go into the saloon so he had followed him and sneaked into the saloon while keeping well out of Timber's view as much as he could. He figured it would give him a chance to get to know him a little, well it had sure done that. He knew now to keep out of arms reach of him at least.

16

Timber waited until the men had left the saloon and then he looked at Judy again to ensure she was okay which she was, before he walked over to the bar and got the attention of the bartender who finally walked over to him.

"I'm looking for a Milton Westbrook, you know where I might find him?" Timber asked.

"The lawyer, sure. Just down the street here a ways on this side, can't miss it he has a sign over the door."

Timber thanked him and walked out into the dazzling sunshine outside. He mounted up on Scout and rode slowly down the street to the office of Milton Westbrook. He found it easily enough and pulled up outside to take a look at the office. It was small, smaller than Timber had imagined it would be. There was a sign over the door that stated it was his office and that he was a lawyer.

As Timber walked up to the door there was a small window he glanced through. He could see a portly man sitting at a desk busy with some paperwork. He didn't knock but tried the handle, it moved so he opened the door and walked inside. Westbrook looked up and sighed as he saw Timber.

"So you must be Marshal Jake Timber," he said as he sat up

straight and back into his chair recognizing him straight away from the descriptions he'd had of him.

"Which makes you Milton Westbrook, the former under governor for the territory of Texas," Timber paused as he looked around the room, "now a lawyer." Timber said it as a statement, not a question.

"That's right I am," Westbrook wasn't going to make things easier for Timber by giving more information away.

Timber walked closer to the desk and leaned over it a little so he could speak directly at Westbrook's face, "I've had some bother with men that you know."

Westbrook shrunk back seeing Timber's bulk, his rough stubble face and his deep green eyes that seemed to burn right down into his soul. He found he had trouble answering.

"I know a lot of men Timber."

"These men tried to kill me and the word is that you put them up to it," Timber stood square on to Westbrook, his face stern.

Westbrook wanted to just say that it was him but the words just wouldn't come out. His throat had suddenly gone very dry. Timber could see the effect he was having on the man and he wasn't about to lessen it.

"Don't you go thinking any of them is going to come and help you because they are all dead. I killed all six of them."

Milton took that in although he already knew the men he had released from prison must be dead.

"How did you do it Westbrook? How did you get those men out of prison? While you answer that put your hands on the desk where I can see them," Timber stepped back a little but kept his eyes on him.

Westbrook pulled his hands up onto the desk. He had a gun in a desk drawer but he wasn't going to try and get it with Timber watching him so closely. He could see Timber was waiting for an answer, well he could have one.

"Getting them out was easy enough. I was still the territory under governor as far as the prisons knew. It was going to take some time for word to get around. I knew a lot about you from when you arrested those men and I knew they would be keen to get their revenge on you, so I just arranged their releases so they could join up. You see Timber you stopped me and the people who were with me preventing the Texas territory plan about joining up with the Union, we wanted to keep it as a separate state with our own laws. Now it looks like it will be taken over."

"Just who else was with you?"

"No one you would know or that matters now, they are all gone and won't be seen in politics again."

Timber nodded, "I pretty much knew all of this, so you wanted revenge as well?"

"Sure I did, still do," Westbrook was getting his bravado back as his anger rose against Timber. Then he told him what he had been anxiously waiting to say, "when I heard those men hadn't been successful I got me another man to do the job," he smiled now watching Timber's face.

"Oh yeah, and who might that be?" Timber was intrigued.

"I may as well tell you 'cause you're gonna find out soon enough. The man's name is Luther Stein and he's the best gunslinger assassin there is. Your time is running out Timber."

Timber looked at the now grinning face of Milton Westbrook, "Foretold is forearmed. I'm guessing he's close by?"

"Oh yes, very close."

'Is this fella big?"

Milton just had to tell him, "Yeah he's tall, slim, all in black and he's good."

Timber had taken a good look around the office, small though it was and he had seen a door to the side of Westbrook's desk. Going straight outside now by the front door would be a big risk as Luther could be in hiding waiting maybe with a rifle to pick him off as he went out.

"I'm guessing that door goes outside," Timber said nodding at the back door.

Westbrook couldn't resist looking across at it and his face told Timber he was right.

"Okay, now you just sit there while I go and call on this Luther.

Don't go away now because I'll be back," Timber took a glance through the window into the street but didn't see anyone suspicious then he went to the back door waving a finger at Westbrook as he went out.

Timber was careful as he walked out. He'd had so called assassins onto him before and he knew they were usually good so he was going to have to take care if he wasn't going to get killed. Looking all around he didn't see anything to alert him and he guessed anyway that if Westbrook had set him up then the killer would be out in the street, maybe even now looking for him unless Westbrook had managed to warn him where he now was?

17

Luther had followed Timber out of the saloon and had crossed over to the opposite side of the street where he had watched Timber go into Westbrook's office. He doubted that Timber would do anything to Westbrook except talk. From what he had been told Timber had no actual evidence of wrongdoing so what could he arrest him on never mind kill him? He figured Timber would talk with him and maybe get to know that Westbrook had set him up. That being the case then Luther would have to find a way to take the marshal out quickly. He walked across the street to the window and took a look inside. He was surprised to only see Westbrook in there and that he was walking towards the door. Luther waited as Westbrook opened it.

"Timber came here, he knows you are out to kill him and he went out the back door," Westbrook said quickly then he shut the door again.

Luther wasn't happy about that, it was going to throw his plan out the window. Now he had Timber no doubt looking for him and he knew he wouldn't play fair as indeed he wouldn't, so where was he now?

Timber had moved along the back of the office to the corner and had then hurried up to the street corner where he peered around to see the front of the office. There wasn't anyone close by. He looked across the street for anyone who could be Luther but there were only a couple of people there who couldn't possibly be him.

Luther had moved off along the sidewalk and had slipped into the doorway of a general store along the street where he would be able to look for Timber. He grinned, pleased now that he knew where he was having seen him peer around the office corner. Now that Timber obviously knew about him he was going to have to change his plan. Instead of taking his time in weighing him up he was going to have to act faster so he could dictate the where and when. He decided to act now as he was very confident in his skills and seeing Timber dressed in deerskins with an old hat he figured the man wasn't as good as people had said. He had taken many fast gunmen down in his time in straight shootouts and he was sure of winning this one. He strode out into the street and walked a short way towards Timber.

"Hey Timber, come on out here," he called in a loud voice.

Timber watched him walk further towards him and got a good look at the man. He had been crafty in that if Timber walked out now he would have the sun in his eyes, he needed an angle and he was thinking one through.

"Be better if you just walk away Luther," he called back.

"Better for who? It's the end of the line Timber, no going back now."

Timber kept part of his body around the corner of the office as he answered.

"It sure is the end Luther, you sure you don't want to live for another day?"

Luther stopped and laughed. He was close enough now to Timber and as he was so sure of being a good shot that he left a greater distance between him and Timber knowing most shooters wouldn't be able to be accurate at that range. Timber saw that but it didn't concern him. He knew how accurate he could be at a given range. What he didn't want to do was just walk out into the street against a younger man who was renowned as being a fast gunfighter.

Timber was fast and very accurate but he still wouldn't do it, good as he was there will always be someone that little bit better.

Luther called across with his answer, "Strong words Timber and sure of course I do want to live another day and I will, so are you coming out or do I have to come and get you?"

Timber knew the words were meant to intimidate him and push him into a rash decision but he was wiser than that. He weighed up the distances then he left the building corner and walked to the edge of the sidewalk knowing Luther wouldn't try to shoot him where he was, there were too many obstacles in the way.

"If you're sure Luther then we can do this. I'll give you one last chance to just ride away."

Luther laughed again, "You sure are a caution Timber. It's almost a shame to have to do this."

"But you're being paid yes?" Timber said as he paced a little closer.

"You know that and by who."

"Milton Westbrook?"

"Yeah, you've met him."

"And I'll be meeting him again," Timber took a step off the sidewalk and called a command to Scout at the same time who was close by. The horse had been ground reined as he often was and now pulled away from the sidewalk at speed. Timber had taught the horse lots of tricks, some of which had saved him in the past now hopefully he would do again. It had worked with Carl so it was worth trying again. Scout ran out blocking Luther's view of Timber as he ran across the street. Timber had been ready for it and he had both of his guns drawn and ready to fire while Scout ran past Luther.

Luther had been taken by surprise. It took him valuable seconds to recover and as Scout ran past he saw Timber aiming at him. He drew his gun fast but he was now that split second too late as both of Timber's guns roared at him. The first bullet caught Luther in his thigh but the second was higher up and hit him in the centre of his chest. The .45 slug tore into his body sending him down into the dirt.

Scout had ran out of the way as Timber had told him to do so then Timber advanced on Luther keeping his guns aimed at him the whole time. Luther twitched as Timber got close and his gun was lying near his hand so Timber kicked that away then looked down at him. Luther was lying partly on his side but he was able to look up at Timber.

"Quite a trick you pulled there," he gasped.

"Scout is my friend and he's well trained."

"That I can see," Luther coughed up some blood then rolled over onto his back.

Timber checked the man's pockets and removed his holster which was finely engraved black leather. He took the gun as well being as it was a fine piece and would make a few dollars, then he stood up and looked down the street.

People were beginning to come over to him keen to see what had happened. The deputy had heard the shots and came out the office to look up the street then he too joined the people walking up to where Timber was standing beside Luther.

"What happened here?" The deputy asked. They didn't get many killings in town and he was already feeling out of his depth.

"I was called out, plenty of witnesses to that."

"I'll need more that that mister," the deputy said looking at him.

Timber pulled his marshal badge to show him, "Jake Timber, U.S. Marshal."

The deputy was surprised, Oh, er okay marshal," he looked down at Luther, "Say that man called in the office earlier."

Timber nodded knowing why he would have done that, "I have to go, the man's horse will pay for his funeral. Straighten him out for me will you" Timber then walked off whistling for Scout as he advanced on Westbrook's office.

18

Westbrook had watched from the open office window to see and hear Timber and Luther's clash of words. He could see it was going to be some kind of a shootout. He had a lot of faith in Luther but he also had a contingency plan, one that he'd had ever since he had heard about the men he had released being killed by Timber and that was to move out of town and go back to Austin where he used to live before he was thrown out of his position on the government by Robert Fullerton the territory governor. His things were still there and he hoped to get refuge from the man who's house they were now in that used to belong to him.

He had kept a horse outside ready to go with the saddlebags full of the things he would need for the journey. He had rooms in town he rented out meaning to get his own place eventually but there was nothing there to go back for.

He took the gun from the desk drawer and shoved it in his pants, then he went to the door which he opened and looked out. He watched in dismay as he saw Timber gun Luther down. It was time to go. He mounted his horse and spurred him off down the street away from Timber. He kept his horse at a gallop wanting to get as far away from Timber as he could. He hoped that he wouldn't follow him but he reckoned that he probably would. What he had to do was keep well ahead of him all the way back to Austin. He had friends there, friends he could rely on. They were men who had supported him in his ideas for stopping the governor, Robert Fullerton from taking Texas into the Union, if he could get back to them then he hoped that they would protect him or at least let him hide out with them until he could figure out a way of getting Timber off his trail.

Westbrook was worried now, everything he had done to remove Timber hadn't worked out and now no doubt he had the marshal gunning for him. He had been able to tell him why he wanted him dead but he guessed that would only make Timber want to get him more. Now he had to run as he sure didn't want Timber to get to him when he was alone.

He had pretty much all the things he needed with him. It wasn't much but then he didn't need much. There were a few things in the rooms he was renting but he could live without them. He also still had a quantity of things back in Austin. He had a house there which he had sold to make some money for himself but the new owner which was one of his friends had allowed him to leave his things there to collect at some time when he was able to. All he could think of now was getting there and keeping ahead of Timber.

Timber rode Scout down to Westbrook's office and pulled up outside. He thought he had seen the man riding out but he figured he had the time to check the office out. As he figured the room was empty when he walked in. He went to the desk and checked the paperwork laid out on the top. He found it to be all about petty legal stuff and of no interest. The drawers also drew a blank apart from one folder he did find to be of interest. It was about the house he owned up in Austin. Timber took an interest and read it through. He now had the address and the fact that there were still a lot of Westbrook's things there. He also figured that it was owned by a friend of his. Timber put the folder down and thought for minute then he figured that was where the man would run to, after all where else would he go? Timber grinned and walked out to Scout.

Austin was a two day ride away and although Timber was keen to run Westbrook down he was in no particular hurry as he reckoned he would get to him while he was still in Austin and maybe even at the house? He kept on riding north for Austin while keeping his eyes skinned for any sign of Westbrook along the way. He rode on for the rest of the day then stopped as the sun went down having found a place he liked the look of to spend the night. Timber always made sure before he left any town that he had the makings in his saddle bags for a couple of days food and coffee. He could always hunt for food and often game cropped up he could shoot but mostly he was in a hurry to get to where he was going and so often he needed to travel quietly and not announce his presence with a gunshot.

He settled down having set Scout free. Before he made a fire he took a good look all around for any tell tale signs for fire or smoke that Westbrook might have started if he was close by. With nothing to alert him he set about making a small fire with hard wood that wouldn't make much smoke and then he heated up the food he had brought with him. As night fell he sat looking at the stars and he began to think more about how this had all come about. It was a clear night and the sky was full of blazing stars, a coyote called breaking the peace otherwise it was a quiet and still night.

Timber had been involved in uncovering a conspiracy which was forcing immigrants from Missouri who had come down to take advantage of the land grants in Texas to move out again, with the man organizing that buying the land at rock bottom prices then selling it again at a big profit. He had straightened all that out and now here he was again after the same man that had set all that up.

Westbrook had stopped a few miles further on having driven his horse harder than he should have done. He had been so concerned about Timber catching up with him that he had carried on for as long as he could. With night approaching he had no choice but to stop. He found a stand of trees to hide among and like Timber he only made a fire big enough to cook on which he threw earth on to put it out as soon as he had eaten.

At the time he had organized for Luther to come to him he had known that it was possible Timber would come looking for him so he had then got himself prepared to move out if things went wrong which they disastrously had. His only real hope of getting through this now was in Austin where he would feel safe and have his friends around him. He had moved out of there when the governor had taken his job away and humiliated him in front of his friends and people he had worked with. Taking on the lawyer job was something he had used to do before he got his job on the government. When that was taken away from him he set himself up on his own and he still had the money to make a go of things somewhere else once he knew he was clear of Timber. He had his gun with him and still wondered if it might work out that he could kill the marshal himself, if it came to it he would sure try. He had an uneasy night stirring at any sound he heard so he roused before first light reckoning there was no point trying to sleep and he got ready to ride on.

Timber didn't sleep well either but then he never did. He would manage to get a couple of hours before his dreams would wake him up. The dreams would always be the same showing the horrors of having his wife and daughter murdered by a maniac who Timber had stopped from raping a bargirl. The man took his revenge by killing Timber's family. Timber had searched the man out and had subjected him to the worst death he could think of. The trouble was that he was found out and sent to jail. He would still be there now in his cell if it hadn't have been for the governor Robert Pierce Fullerton. He had heard of Timber and how well he had worked as a sheriff before he had been locked up and figured he was just the man he was looking for. He gave him the chance of working for him in searching out any outlaws and bringing them to justice by whatever means Timber thought best. He gave him a marshal badge and paperwork to show to anyone he needed to that he was authorized at the highest level. Not only could he straighten out any wrong doer but also anyone who stood in his way. He had been doing the job for some time now and saw no time when he would stop doing it. So like Westbrook he was up early and keen to move out.

19

Westbrook rode hard all day and arrived in Austin in the mid afternoon. He was pleased to have got there. All the way he had glanced behind him from time to time just to make sure that Timber wasn't coming up on him. He now had the choices of calling in on his friends first or going to his house to pick up a few things? He thought about whether Timber would in fact trail him all the way to Austin? Would he really want to do that? What would he gain from it? Some revenge against him for setting the outlaws on him maybe but then he had killed all of them. All he could do was hope for the best but he also had to be prepared. He knew he could hide out at one of his friends, or at least he thought he would be able to.

Thinking about it he decided to call on a friend first just in case he needed a bolt hole anytime soon. The man he decided on was someone he had worked with while being the under governor for Texas. It was a man who had first approached him on the subject of doing what they could to prevent Texas joining the Union. Westbrook warmed to the idea as it meant he would lose his job anyway if it happened and he liked things just as they were so he agreed to help out. There were a few men in the government with similar thoughts who were soon recruited. They soon discovered that they needed money and lots of it to make it work out for them. Certain bribes would be needed and money to put through the regulations they would need to do. It all had to be underhand and it had come down to Westbrook to organize it. He wasn't happy as other men weren't at immigrants coming south to take up land grants so it became obvious what they had to do.

He arranged for land grant certificates to have a small print put in which stated that if any immigrant left the land they had signed up for within a year then the land could be bought at a bargain price which Westbrook would then sell on for a big profit to get the money they needed. Of course he couldn't wait for a year and it was doubtful if anyone would leave in that time frame anyway so they would need to be persuaded. Ruthless men were recruited to do the job of persuading them to leave which worked out well until Timber intervened and stopped it all.

Not only did Timber stop the scheme he also informed the governor. Robert Fullerton had not been happy and he had cleared everyone out from their positions in the government with warrants for the arrest of some of them. Westbrook had avoided that by riding off and starting up his lawyer business but now he was back and wanting help. His friend wasn't far away so he went straight over there.

He got to the house easily enough and leaving his horse at the picket fence he walked up to the front door. It looked quiet but he knocked anyway and waited. He was surprised when a woman he didn't know opened the door and stood there asking him what he wanted. He asked for his friend and got an answer he didn't like.

"He ain't here no more," the woman said keeping the door only partly open, "he left, a week or so ago. We have the house now."

Westbrook stood dumbstruck not knowing what to say, he just apologized and walked back to his horse. If this friend had moved out then maybe some of the others had gone as well? It was time to go back to the house he had sold, maybe he could find out more about things there.

Timber rode along at a good pace. Scout was a big horse and he could keep going for long periods at a good lope. Timber looked out for any ambush sites along the way and he steered Scout away from them but they didn't have any bother or see anyone right up until they were close to town then they got onto a wide trail where people were coming and going. Austin was a big place so it wasn't surprising. Timber had the address but he still needed to find out where it was. It was the third person he asked who actually knew where it was to tell him. The street was a couple of streets back from the main street so Timber had to weave his way along to get to it.

Westbrook got to his house quickly. Although he had sold the place he knew the current owner wouldn't mind him calling round as they had agreed. Having heard the news from his friends house he approached with caution, after all Robert Fullerton had issued a warrant for his arrest. As with his friends house it looked very quiet. He got up to the door and having knocked he waited but no one came. He walked around the back and tried the door there and looked in the windows but the house appeared to be empty. That didn't bother him as he had kept keys for himself. He opened the back door and went inside. Lots of things had changed as he excepted it would have. He went upstairs to the room where the rest of his things were being stored. There were a few items of furniture, some clothes and odds and ends. What he was interested in was a suitcase he had. It was right at the back of the room where it wouldn't be noticed. He clambered over the furniture to get to it then carried it over to the window where he rested it on a cabinet to open it.

He wasn't concerned about the other things in the room although he thought he would take a clean change of clothes with him when he left. With the case open he looked inside and he checked that everything was there. He had put some things in it from when he had the under governor job but there were also things here he wanted. Tucked away in the bottom in a plain envelope was a bundle of bills he had kept there in case he'd been robbed while away. It had been a dangerous time and so this had seemed to be a good idea. There was also another gun, a derringer he pocketed. He still had his papers in the suitcase of when he was the under governor and his certificates showing he was a lawyer and a prominent member of the government that he figured might help him once he got far away from Austin. He filled his pockets with the money, the derringer and his certificates. He put the suitcase away and hurriedly got changed then he went back downstairs.

The friend he had sold the house to still hadn't returned which was fine, he could always send him a telegram sometime. As he looked out the window at the front of the house he suddenly froze. A man was riding up towards the house, a man he had hoped not to see again.

Timber had found a little difficulty in finding the house but now he could see it and there was a familiar horse waiting outside. Timber pulled up and looked at the house. It was in a row of similar others well spaced out. Some had picket fences around them while others just had an an open area. The one he was looking at didn't have a fence, the two story house stood alone. Timber guessed that Westbrook would be inside, he wondered who might be there with him, he would need to take care. What the house did have was stands of trees at the back and down the side of it. Timber didn't know if he had been seen or not yet but he knew he had to take the chance and somehow get to the house to confront Westbrook.

He rode Scout around behind the trees and left him there, then he edged through to the last tree which put him just a few yards from the house. With Westbrook's horse at the front of the house Timber reckoned that would be the way he would try to escape once he knew he was there so Timber made his way down to the front door to cut him off. He kept to the side of the building and crept along quickly to the front where he looked around. It was still quiet so he crept to the front and risked a quick glance up into the windows from underneath them. The room was empty so he carried on to the front door.

Westbrook moved out of the room into the hall wondering what to do? Timber was bound to come to the house and he was alone. He still had the two guns which were both loaded. His Colt was stuffed in his pants, the derringer in a pocket. He wondered if he could surprise

Timber and shoot him? He pulled the colt and cocked it as he wondered which door Timber would go to?

Timber got to the front door and took a look at it. It was a standard door, nothing really strong or thick and the lock looked flimsy enough to him. He drew a gun and lifted his size thirteen boot and slammed it into the door right beside the lock with all his force. The door flew open nearly going off its hinges.

The sounds and sight of the door crashing open dazed Westbrook for a second, then he began to raise his gun at Timber.

"Drop it Westbrook, or I'll shoot you dead where you stand," Timber said his gun aimed straight at him.

Westbrook sighed. Just looking at the hulk of Timber standing there with his gun was enough to make him drop his gun.

"So what now?" He asked.

"Now you are coming with me to face charges of attempted murder and the incitement of others to commit violence and murder," Timber kept his gun trained on Westbrook as he spoke.

Westbrook found it hard to reply. His mouth had gone very dry and his mind was racing.

"Whatever you are doing here will have to wait so come on out of there," Timber stood back to give Westbrook the space to walk out while keeping him covered.

With no other choice Westbrook walked outside as Timber backed away from him. Westbrook was thinking hard the whole time. He had to find a way out of this. He knew that once they got to a sheriff's office then it would be all over for him, there was only more thing he could try. He walked out with Timber and tried to keep close to him but Timber kept him at a few feet away.

"Now you wait right there Westbrook while I get my horse," Timber said.

As Timber whistled for Scout, Westbrook took his chance figuring it was the last one he was going to get. He reached into a pocket and pulled out the derringer then he turned to Timber bringing the gun up at the same time.

Timber was always very careful when in these situations and he made sure he never took his eyes off the man he was arresting even for a second, so he saw the movement and the derringer in Westbrook's hand. Timber wasn't going to get shot by him so he fired. He meant to just wound Westbrook but at that range and with Westbrook moving fast the bullet took him in his heart killing him instantly.

Timber shook his head as he looked down at the man. There had been no movement from the house so he guessed there was no one there. He bent down and took the derringer and searched Westbrook for anything else of interest. There was a roll of bills and coins which Timber took.

He then had to go and search for a sheriff to inform him of what had happened and organize an undertaker. It was some time before all that had been arranged. Timber wasn't concerned about the owner of the house he had taken Westbrook from apart for the fact that he wondered why he had gone there. Having got the sheriff and the undertaker there Timber wanted to go inside to search the house.

Sheriff Joseph Harper wasn't so sure about that, "Now Timber I know you're a marshal and all but that can't happen without permission of the owner."

"So where is he?" Timber was sure of getting in there one way or another.

"He's out of town so I've been told."

"Then he won't mind my taking a look around," Timber pushed his way past the sheriff and headed for the door only for the sheriff to run after him.

"Timber I said you have to wait."

Timber looked down at him and pulled out a piece of paper that had seen better days. He carefully unfolded it and held in under the sheriff's nose.

"Read that, I'll be back," Timber then went into the house leaving the sheriff with a surprised look on his face as he read the piece of paper.

Timber took a look around the rooms on the ground floor before going upstairs. The last room he checked up there looked like a storeroom with furniture piled up and a few boxes scattered around. That looked odd compared with the rest of the place so he looked around a little further. The boxes appeared to just have clothing in as well as a few other times but then a suitcase caught his eye. He reached around the furniture and pulled it out then he placed it on the sideboard as Westbrook had and looked inside. A few minutes later he was going downstairs smiling broadly.

Outside he took his authorization paper from the sheriff and tucked it away again in a pocket. The paper was his statement of authority signed by the Honorable Robert Pierce Fullerton as the territory governor and which stated that Timber was an independent law enforcement officer, who is above the law and reports directly to the governor. He has the power to arrest, detain, or execute criminal individuals as he sees fit. This included any local law enforcement, or locally elected or appointed official who attempts, in any way, to interfere with his official duties.

Timber then turned back to the sheriff, "Look after things here, I'm sure the governor will be talking to you soon enough about what to do with the things upstairs."

20

Timber then mounted Scout and rode off as he knew now exactly where he was going and just a few minutes later he was at the government offices. He had been there before, not for a long time but he knew where to go. He climbed the stairs to the second floor then along a corridor until he came to the door he wanted. Then he stopped and knocked politely. The door was opened by a woman he didn't know who asked him who he was and what he wanted.

"Jake Timber ma'am, U.S. Marshall to see the governor."

"Mister Fullerton is busy at the minute maybe you could call back later?" She wasn't keen to let him in as he was covered in trail dust over his deerskins and he hadn't shaved in days, added to that, he smelled of horses.

"That would be rather awkward ma'am, can't I wait here for him?"

Taken aback she opened the door wider saying, "Well I suppose so, but it could be a long wait."

"I'll wait," Timber walked in and seeing a fine leather sofa by a wall he went and sat on it.

The woman walked past saying she would let the governor know he was there. She went off through another door leaving Timber alone in the waiting room.

Timber sat for a little while but not for as long as the woman had intimated. The door to his left opened and she came out again.

"The governor will see you now," she said holding the door open for him.

Timber thanked her and walked in the office as the woman went out so Timber was now alone with the governor.

"Timber, it's been a while," Fullerton said as he came around the desk to shake his hand, "What is it that brings you here?" Fullerton waved at a comfortable chair facing the desk as he walked around to his chair behind the desk.

"Normally governor as you know I would send a telegram but as I was close by and because I have something for you I thought I'd drop by."

"That sounds intriguing Timber. It's good to see you again of course but what is it?"

Timber pulled a small bundle of paperwork from a packet and dropped it on the desk close to Fullerton's hands.

"For a while now as you know there has been some trouble from the under governor Milton Westbrook."

"Ah yes, Milton but that has been almost straightened out now. He has been taken down from his position and a warrant has been issued for his arrest," Fullerton leaned forward, "Are you saying you have found him?"

Timber smiled, "More than that. I have a list here of all the people involved in the conspiracy against you and full information of where the money came from and went."

Fullerton picked the bundle of papers up, "That's very good, how did you manage to do that," he talked as he flicked through the papers.

"I got on Westbrook's trail from the last job you gave me. He set up a group of outlaws he got released from prison to kill me."

"They would be the same released prisoners I sent you after?"

"That's right and they attacked me but I managed to break free and I killed the outlaws and a gunslinger he put onto me as well.

Then I managed to find Westbrook and he led me here to Austin and to a house I can give you the address of. I arrested him but he pulled a gun on me and so he's dead now as well. I searched the house and found a room full of things which I am sure belong to him. I'm sure you can straighten that out but in a suitcase I found those papers which I am sure you will find very interesting."

"Well, Timber I sure found the right man when I found you. Just glancing through these I can see they will be very useful. There are a couple of names here that eluded me last time too. I'll get the house looked into Timber you can leave all of that with me. It is good to see you again, now you keep up the good work."

"I sure will governor," Timber got up to leave.

"So where are you going now?"

"I don't rightly know."

"Well seeing as you are here. There is something you can look into for me. There is a gang of outlaws of which I am not sure how many, that have been very successful in stealing some rather valuable letters and forms that give the information of pretty much the legal system in the territory. It is questionable whether they even know they have them as they were taken along with a quantity of gold all of which was being transported by stagecoach a few days ago and we would rather like to have it all back."

Timber nodded, "That sounds like a job for me, do you have any information for me that might help me track them down?"

"Not personally but my assistant will fill you in on what we have," Fullerton rang a bell on his desk and the woman who had greeted Timber walked in the office, "Give Timber the information we have on the letters theft will you?"

The woman nodded and waited for Timber who turned to Fullerton, "It looks like we'll be meeting again."

"I sure hope so," Fullerton watched as Timber went out with his assistant.

Timber sat with her for a while as she gave him what information he had then Timber left. Getting outside he reckoned he had earned himself a bath, a good meal and a soft bed for the night before he went off working for the governor again.

THE END

Printed in Great Britain
by Amazon